"Alpha One Bravo, Alpha One Bravo," came back an angry voice. "This is Bumblebee. Get the hell off this frequency, you are not authorized to be on it. Out."

Sergeant Bingham felt a mix of emotions at the response: elation at finally raising someone and frustration at being told to get off the frequency. But he wasn't getting off. "Bumblebee, Alpha One Bravo. We are separated from our unit. We have been lost for more than twenty-four hours and need assistance. Over."

"Alpha One Bravo, I told you to get off this frequency," the angry voice came back. "Now get off it. You talk English good, Charlie, but we're on to your game. That squad got wasted. Now get off the air."

Also by David Sherman
Published by Ivy Books:

CHARLIE DON'T LIVE HERE ANYMORE
THERE I WAS: THE WAR STORIES OF CORPORAL
    HENRY J. MORRIS, USMC

THE
SQUAD

David Sherman

IVY BOOKS • NEW YORK

Ivy Books
Published by Ballantine Books
Copyright © 1990 by David Sherman

Grateful acknowledgement is made to R.C. Suciu for permission
to reprint his poem appearing on pages 112-113 Copyright © by
R.C. Suciu

Library of Congress Catalog Card Number: 90-93295

ISBN 0-8041-0727-0

Manufactured in the United States of America

First Edition: January 1991

To

The U.S. Marines and other Allied forces who won the
Tet Offensive on the battlefield

Author's Note

While this book is a novel, a work of fiction, there are scenes that are loosely based on factual incidents. In those instances I have either omitted or altered unit designations or changed the locality. For example, in chapter twelve there is an account of part of the Hills fights that took place in April and May of 1967. In this scene I have "Charlie Company" assaulting "Hill 881." In historic fact, there were two hills involved: Hill 881 South and Hill 881 North. There was no "Charlie Company" involved in the taking of either hill. Hill 881N was captured by the Second Battalion, Third Marines, and Hill 881S by the Third Battalion, Third Marines. In all cases, the changes are made not to slight the Marines and units involved, but to avoid any unintentional identification between my fictional characters and their actions and any real people involved.

PART I

PROLOGUE

The After-Action Report

It was extraordinary, what those men did. That they could do it and some of them survive is a final proof, if one is still needed after all this time, of how superior the American fighting man was over there. But somehow the press didn't pick it up, not even after I let three different print journalists and one network TV reporter have copies of the after-action reports—on the sly of course—to be quoted as a confidential source. After Tet, after the battle for Hue City, when the remnants of the North Vietnamese force that failed to take and hold the ancient imperial capital were being pursued to their sanctuary across the border, the survivors were found. I, a captain at the time, was assigned to investigate what had happened and to report on it. What I learned was incredible, but the evidence was incontrovertible. The story of these men deserves to be told; they deserve to have it known. Since the news media chose not to tell their story I have now decided to.

A few years later, in a bar in D.C., I ran into one of the print journalists, who had by that time been long renowned as a big byline international reporter. At the time I was working in the Pentagon as a major in the Plans and Policy Directorate of the Joint Chiefs J-5; he was a bureau chief.

We had both been recently divorced and were nominally out on the prowl that night, which is how we both happened to be in the same bar. There are thousands of single women in the nation's capital—working for the government and looking for husbands—and one-night stands will often substitute as promissory notes. The pickings can be very easy for men on the prowl. But neither of us particularly had our hearts in it that night. Prowling seemed a somehow degrading way to get laid. This journalist and I had met each other here, there, and everywhere in Vietnam's I Corps, and in Saigon. And, over the intervening years, in Ankara, Paris, Osaka, and other international spots, so we had an established relationship, though to call it a friendship would be to exaggerate. At any rate, we came to the mutual conclusion that we preferred each other's company that night to trying to pick up some senatorial secretary, so we sat and drank and talked together until closing time.

When the hour was late enough that the desperately-seeking women still left alone were on the verge of another night with the anguish of a lonely bed and we were no longer feeling pain, I put the question to him. I asked him outright why he and the others had so totally ignored the story I gave them on a quiet night long ago in Hue. A quiet night a month or two after many other very unquiet nights.

He shifted his attention from the staring-eyed dollies who were flashing their availability with every bit of body language at their command, to look at me with this cocked-head and -eyebrow expression that asked what was wrong that I didn't understand why the news media couldn't possibly pick up on that story.

"You still don't understand," he said, the same kind of expression in his voice that was on his face. "We couldn't report that story. The American people wouldn't have believed it."

Then it was my turn to look at him in incomprehension. "Why wouldn't they believe it?" I naïvely asked.

"Because the American people believed we lost the war at Tet." His tone of voice had changed from wonderment to pedantry, but his face remained the same.

I stared at him in disbelief. "But Tet was a major victory for us," I said. "If we'd followed up on it properly the war would have been over in another year, two at the most, and we would have won it."

His face lost its expression and returned to the half-drunk going on glazed-drunk it had held before I asked my question and he nodded. "Right. The Tet Offensive was a major victory for us militarily. That's the key word: 'militarily.' " He shook his head at this slightly-retarded youngster he was talking to. "Politically it was a disastrous loss."

I sighed a deep sigh at the futility of frustration. "I've never understood that," I said. "Charlie caught us with our pants half down all over the country and we stomped his ass anyway. The Vietcong were banking on a popular uprising to carry them over the top and it never materialized. If anything, the Tet Offensive solidified the people behind Saigon. All across South Vietnam, outnumbered American units fought off Vietcong battalions and regiments and the VC left more of their own dead on the battlefield than there were American defenders in the first place. And the same went for the NVA where they got into the fighting. Hell, the damn VC were never a real factor in the war after Tet, and if we hadn't allowed the Russians and the Red Chinese to pump so much support into Hanoi, the North Vietnamese wouldn't have been able to keep the war going much longer, either. Please explain to me, Mister Big Byline International Journalist, how it was this major military victory turned into a major political defeat before our very eyes?"

He hesitated, thinking about whether or not he wanted to answer, then hunched himself closer and said, "It's like this," and went on to give me the most understandable explanation I've ever heard for the most incredible journalistic screwup in the history of the world. He told me how we lost the war at the battles that were cumulatively our greatest military triumphs. And he did it without accepting or even acknowledging the slightest iota of culpability.

I sighed again when he finished, hoping the same thing wouldn't happen again, but afraid and certain it would. But there was nothing I could do about it, not then, not as an active duty officer. But it weighed on my mind, what those men had done and why their story was never made public. In the fullness of time I retired from active duty and decided to take matters into my own hands. I decided to write their story.

But first I had to track down the five surviving members of the squad. It turned out only three of them are still alive today; one died in an automobile accident a couple of years ago and another disappeared with his family, boat, and crew while sailing in the Caribbean—there were unsubstantiated rumors of drug trafficking at the time. I tracked down the remaining three and spent weeks interviewing them, in addition to the time I spent reviewing all of the official records and my own notes from the time. Each of the three was at first reluctant to talk about it, but I managed, with more patience than I ever exhibited as a Marine officer, to draw them out. It's been more than twenty years, but their stories, independently told today, did not vary at all from what they told me then. After several months' work I was finally ready to write down their story—but where to begin? I first tried to start it the night their odyssey began but quickly discovered that left too much out; it told nothing about the men. Finally, I decided to begin it at the beginning.

Respectfully submitted,
R. W. Thoreau, Lt. Col., USMC (ret)

CHAPTER ONE

Land the Landing Force

March 8, 1965

At a few minutes after 9:00 in the morning, Corporal Gary Parsons stepped off an amphibious landing craft into the surf of Red Beach Two in Da Nang harbor. He was the first man of the first American ground combat unit to set foot in Vietnam. None of the Marines of the Third Battalion, Ninth Marines, Ninth Marine Expeditionary Brigade's first assault wave had a clear idea of what to expect when they landed, but they hoped they were ready for anything they met. They weren't ready for what met them. Schoolgirls who were dressed in their finest clothing and were carrying garlands of flowers, a band, the mayor, reporters, and photographers waited for them. There was a brief greeting ceremony between the commanding general of Vietnam's I Corps Tactical Zone and the Da Nang mayor on one side, and the American commanders on the other. Then the Marines moved through the lines of flower-bearing schoolgirls, university students, newsmen, and photographers to waiting trucks which drove them south to assume defensive positions around the Da Nang airstrip.

The war had begun.

CHAPTER TWO

The Right Thing, the Honorable Thing

March 8, 1965

"Well, well, what do you know," Percy Detwiler said and turned the page of his newspaper. "We finally did it."

"What did we do," Jack Hamilton asked without looking up from the textbook he was studying, "win a football game?" He half lay on a sofa in the freshmen lounge.

George Bingham crumpled a sheet of paper and threw it at Jack. "Idiot, this is basketball season." He sat on an overstuffed chair next to Percy's.

"Besides, the football team did win a game last season," Percy said. "Remember? It was the season opener."

"And lost the rest," George added.

"Anyway, I wouldn't be reading about our football team in the front section of the paper," Percy said, looking over at Jack. "As you'd know if you'd bother to look up from your book, you nincompoop. That's the thing with Jack," he said to anybody else in earshot, whether they wanted to listen to him or not, "he listens when he wants to, hears what he wants to, sees what he wants to. Old Jack Hamilton never bothers with anything anybody else thinks is important. Even when it's the most important news of the decade."

"All right," Jack said, looking up from the textbook, which he didn't close, "I give up. What did we finally do?" He knew that when Percy got started on being mysterious, the only way he could get back to his studies was to humor him for a few minutes. There was a momentary break in the conversation that was filled with the voices yelling on the TV in the corner and the subdued shouts of the other eighteen- and nineteen-year-olds in the room.

"Well, it wasn't actually us," Percy said. He was enjoying Jack's discomfort and annoyance and wanted to drag it out. "I mean, not the three of us sitting here in good old Houston Hall, or even the Red and the Blue that did it."

"Go to hell, Percy," Jack said and returned to his text. He had a paper due and needed to finish studying for it; he didn't have time to play Percy's silly games.

The speed and agility Percy displayed in putting his newspaper down, rising from his seat and dashing to Jack's sofa made George wish again the other man would join him on the track and field team.

"What are you reading here, Jackie old boy, that's so interesting you can't let Percy tell you what we did?" Percy said whipping the text from Jack's hands and slamming it closed to look at the front cover. "*Studies in Mesopotamian Cuneiform Writings*," he hooted and danced away from Jack's grasping hands. "No wonder! Jack, I know you want to be an archeologist like your dear papa, but once in a while you really should come back to the present and look around yourself. After all, I mean to say, it's what's happening today that's going to affect what will happen tomorrow." He hesitated, not wanting to be too harsh before adding, "Of course, I do understand that what happened yesterday will have an impact on what you're going to be doing tomorrow." Then he realized that what he had just said strengthened his original argument and grinned. "And what we just did is something that happened yesterday and will influence the tomorrows of a lot of people, maybe even including yours."

"All right, Percy, we'll do it your way," Jack said, exasperated. He let out a breath while he sat up straighter and held out a hand for the return of his textbook. Percy was at his wordiest and had to have his say. "What was it we finally did, even though it wasn't actually the three of us or the Red and the Blue?"

Percy cocked his head and moved the book in his upheld hand a few inches farther from Jack.

Jack rolled his eyes toward the ceiling. "And who was it who did it?" he added.

"Now that I've got your attention," Percy said, handing back the textbook, "I can let you know that—" He noticed that only the TV was making noise in the background and looked around the lounge to see many of the other freshmen had turned and were watching him. "—the United States government, that is, our government, which is us, finally sent in the Marines yesterday." He beamed, enjoying the attention he was getting from the other students.

"What?" After a brief moment the questions starting coming rapidly at Percy. "Sent in the Marines?" "Where?" "Why were they sent?" "Where are they?" "Is there fighting?" And many more questions that were drowned out.

Percy stuck out his chest and looked smug. Obviously, none of the others had read the afternoon *Bulletin* yet. Those who were reading newspapers were reading either the morning *Inquirer* or the early edition of *The New York Times*. "I'm sure you've all heard of a country called Vietnam," he said. "It's somewhere over in Indochina. You must have read about it in your current events courses back in high school. The communists have been trying to take it over. We just sent in the Marines to stop them."

There was a moment of stunned silence while the other young men in the freshmen lounge tried to remember which of the obscure Asian, Latin American, and African countries they had studied in high school current events was this Vietnam. Then the eyes of one of them opened wide and he exclaimed, "It's somewhere near Indonesia."

"No it's not in Indochina," someone said, "it's next-door to Malaya."

"Hey," another said, "it's near the Philippines."

"The Philippines is an island, dummy," someone else shot back, "it doesn't have neighbors."

"Enough," Percy said. "You're all in the right general part of the world but, sadly, you're all wrong. It's right here." He held up his newspaper to display a map. "On the South China Sea, south of Red China, next to Lae-ose and Camp-oh-dee-ah," he said, struggling with the unfamiliar names of equally unfamiliar countries.

MARINE UNIT LANDS AT VIET JET BASE,
SIGNALS STIFFER LINE.

The headline didn't blare its message. It was above the fold on the front page, but was only two columns wide.

George sat back, stunned. He had been following the events in South Vietnam ever since President Kennedy had increased the number of U.S. advisors back when he had been a sophomore in high school. It had looked to him like America would go to war in that country to stop the communists from taking over, especially after President Diem was assassinated. But America hadn't gone in, and the situation looked like it would go on indefinitely. Suddenly, the Marines were sent in just when it looked like South Vietnam might fall. The Marines.

George's father had enlisted in the Marines in 1943 and fought the Japanese in the Pacific. He was promoted to sergeant after the Okinawa campaigns. A cousin had been a Marine during the Korean War and was a corporal in the landing at Inchon. After Congress passed the Gulf of Tonkin Resolution, George wanted to join the Marines instead of entering college, but both his father and cousin talked him into starting college in the fall as planned. That way, they told him, he could go in to the Marine Corps as an officer which, they agreed, was far better than being an enlisted man. And now the Marines had gone to war in South Vietnam without him. He had to think about this. President Kennedy had said, "Ask not what your country can do for you, ask what you can do for your country." What should George do? Finish college and let the war go on without him, possibly end without him? Or should he suspend his studies for a few years and fight his country's battle?

The rest of the spring term went by in a blur of schoolwork. There were midterms to study for, papers to write, and finals to cram for. And there were the endless discussions about what on earth the United States was doing in a country about which most of the students had only the vaguest knowledge. Some students, trying to sound impressive in their knowledge of foreign affairs, touted the domino theory as a sensible theory. Others, trying to demonstrate erudition, quoted the 1954 Geneva Accords and talked about the national elections that were never held. One of the former looked up the accords and replied that they only called for some ambiguous kind of national elections and, anyway, nobody signed them. Besides, this wasn't a civil war, it was a war against communist domination. The latter argued that the National Liberation Front was strictly a legitimate nationalist reunification movement and had nothing to do with communism. And so what if the accords weren't signed? There was verbal agreement.

Neither side convinced the other.

George Bingham didn't actively participate in the discussions. He just listened to them, read the newspaper accounts of what was happening in South Vietnam, and thought about what he should do. He was in his room in the Quad doing his last-minute cramming for the last of his finals when he heard on the radio that the Army had sent the 173d Airborne Brigade to Vietnam. That was when he decided he couldn't wait any longer. That afternoon, immediately after handing in that last exam booklet, he went to the registrar's office in Logan Hall and cancelled his enrollment for the fall term. Then he went to the Marine Corps recruiting office on North Broad Street and told the recruiting sergeant, "I want to enlist."

The recruiting sergeant just grinned at him. "That's the nicest thing anybody's said to me all day."

After a boot camp that was tougher, though less brutal, than he had expected, Pfc. Bingham felt he had truly earned the right to go to war as a Marine. But the Marine Corps frustrated his enthusiasm after infantry training by assigning him to the helicopter facility at New River, North Carolina, where he trained as a helicopter gunner for a year. Then Lance Corporal Bingham was transferred to Camp Pendleton to serve with a rifle company in the Sixth Marines. In 1967, with his four-year enlistment half over, he began to despair of ever getting to war. The Army's grand strategy of a war of attrition, though it seemed to run counter to the Marine Corps philosophy of how to win the war, seemed to be working. The Americans and their allies were winning all of the battles and the Vietnamese people's support appeared to be swinging in the direction of the Saigon government. Then it happened. In August he received orders to Vietnam and was promoted to corporal a few days before boarding the Pan Am DC-7 that flew him to Da Nang.

CHAPTER THREE

It's Like Walking into the Middle of a Movie

Sergeant Melville and the seven men in his squad crouched in the shallow ravine with another understrength squad and waited for the supply bird to land. They sprinted to the top of the hill while the bird was in its final approach. The helicopter came in low and fast. It settled long enough for two men to jump off and for the crew chief and gunner to shove a pallet of ammunition, and another of C rations and water, out the rear hatch to Melville and his men. The chopper was on the ground for less than fifteen seconds before becoming airborne again.

The Marines from the ravine ignored the new arrivals for a moment while the squad leaders directed their men in picking up the cases of ammo and food and water, then Melville turned to the new men and said, "Each of you, grab a case of Cs and a water can and let's get the hell out of here."

The younger of the new men looked at the older, a corporal by the name of Bingham, to see if he should obey this man's orders. The man giving the orders didn't have any rank insignia and the new man didn't know if he should obey him. The corporal didn't look back at him, just slung his rifle, hoisted a case of C rations on his shoulder, and picked up a five gallon water can. The first man shrugged and did the same. Then he hurried to catch up with the men scurrying down the shallow ravine. An explosion behind him made him drop the food and water and hit the deck. He looked back and blanched when he saw a puff of dust and debris rising from where he had just stood on the hilltop.

"Move it, newby, he missed you," Sergeant Melville called back to him. "Newby," the new guy. He hoped it wouldn't stick.

Suddenly Corporal Bingham was at his side helping him pick up the supplies again. "That's why he told us to get the hell out of there," Bingham said. "Charlie's got a mortar that zings the

LZs. Let's catch up with the others." He turned and went down the ravine as quickly as he could without losing his balance. The younger man swallowed and rushed after him.

Fifty meters down the small ravine a smaller gully cut into it from the side. The Marines climbed it to the cover of trees. A short distance into the trees they stacked the supplies in an area cleared of underbrush and spread out, back to their perimeter positions. Bingham followed Melville, who he only knew as the man who told him what to do on the hilltop, and the other man followed Bingham because he didn't know what else to do. They caught up with Melville when he stopped to talk with another Marine sitting on the lip of a fighting hole. A PRC-20 radio sat next to him.

The man with the radio looked at the two new men. "These them?" he asked Melville. He didn't wait for an answer. "You found them, you can keep them. Unless the skipper says he wants them in someone else's platoon."

Melville nodded. "I don't like getting two newbies, Aaron," he said, "but I need the men." He turned and asked, "Either of you on a second tour?"

They shook their heads.

"I'm Sergeant Melville, call me Herm out here. This here's"— he yanked a thumb at the other man—"Aaron, he's our platoon commander. Out of the field you call him Lieutenant Copeland. In the boonies you don't call no one by rank, got it? Now who are you?"

"I'm George Bingham," Bingham said and smiled crookedly, he understood why they didn't use ranks in the boonies. "In garrison they call me corporal."

"PFC Davis reporting," the other said. He was nervous and hadn't understood what was being said about not using rank designations.

"Get with the program, Davis," Melville said.

"Dick."

Copeland said to Bingham, "Goddam, we could call you Choo-choo, you've got a name that sounds like a train porter. You see the Top before you came out here?"

Bingham nodded. "He swapped us our SRBs for rifles and 782 gear, piled us on that bird, and here we are."

"How long you been in-country?"

"I landed at Da Nang day before yesterday."

Copeland looked at Davis.

"I came in on the same flight with him," Davis said, flustered.

"Neither of you been here before, right?" Melville asked. They nodded their heads. "Shit. You said that already." He shook his head. "Either of you got grunt experience?"

"I was with the Sixth Marines at Pendleton," Bingham answered.

"Shit," Melville said again. "Well, if you're a corporal you must have been at least a fire-team leader," he said to Bingham.

"They gave me my second stripe the same day they gave me my orders," Bingham said after admitting he had been a fire-team leader as a lance corporal.

"You don't have any other corporals," Copeland said to Melville. "Make him a fire-team leader. If you keep carrying the blooker yourself you can make three three-men fire teams with Longfellow and Rivera as your other team leaders. Longfellow's up for promotion anyway. He can break Davis in. Get them squared away. I'll tell Ives about it when he gets back in."

"Right," Melville said, and added, "Come with me," to Bingham and Davis. He led them through the trees back to where the ammo, food, and water had been dumped. Most of what had been brought from the chopper was gone, already distributed.

One disheveled Marine stood next to the few remaining supplies. He looked up when Melville approached. "You sure there wasn't a mailbag here?" he asked.

"You got it," Melville said without looking at the man or slowing his pace. "The post office comes through despite snow, sleet, or the gloom of night. Nobody said anything about war."

"But we always get a sack of mail when the supply bird comes in."

"Not this time."

"Shit. I been expecting a letter from my girlfriend. She ain't writ to me in a month."

They left the disheveled Marine to worry by himself about why a mailbag wasn't delivered and why his girlfriend hadn't written to him in a month. Soon after that they reached a line of shallow holes, little more than excavated depressions in the side of the hill.

"Here we are," Melville said.

"Right," Bingham said, wondering where "here" was.

"Hank, Dago, up," Melville called in a voice that was low but carried. He sat on the lip of one of the holes. Two short, battle-worn Marines joined them. One was husky and Latin dusky, the other even shorter, with sun-baked brown skin. Together they said, "Yo."

"Got a couple newbies," Melville told them. "I'm reorganizing the squad into three fire teams and you two get to be the second and third fire-team leaders." He paused to fish a bent cigarette out of a crumpled pack and straightened it before lighting it with an engraved Zippo.

Lance corporals Henry Longfellow and Diego Rivera eyed the new men suspiciously. "Who gets first fire team?" Longfellow asked.

"George Bingham here does," Melville said and pointed at him. "He's got the stripes." He looked at the two as though daring either of them to challenge him on the arrangement. They both looked like they weren't about to accept a stranger as the new number-two man in the squad but neither said anything. Longfellow hawked off to the side. "Hank, you get Dick Davis," Melville continued, "and keep Emerson. Dago, Harte and Morse are yours. I'm giving Copley and West to George. That's it." The others got up to leave and Melville said, "George, sit here with me for a few minutes and I'll fill you in."

Bingham sat near Melville and waited. And looked around. This was forest like he'd never seen before. Trees grew tall and slender, not branching until high above the ground. Vines hung from them and wrapped around their trunks. No grass grew on the ground; the dirt was red where it was bare. Brightly colored, broad-leaved bushes crowded each other where sunlight managed to break through the overhead cover.

When Melville didn't say anything immediately, Bingham asked who Ives was.

Ives was the platoon sergeant. He was out with the platoon's other squad on a recon patrol. First platoon—George's new platoon—was company reserve so it got the extra patrols and the extra jobs like humping the supplies from the choppers.

Bingham wanted to know if there was another platoon downhill from them.

Melville twisted his mouth in a humorless sort of smile. He continued to look down the hill. "No. The skipper thinks there's nobody downhill from us, that's why we're company reserve." Bingham asked and was told the "skipper" was Captain Bernstein. Captain Bernstein was okay as company commanders went, he just had some odd ideas about how to set a defensive position. Like the current situation, with the recon patrol somewhere to the west supposedly providing all the security that side of the hill needed.

"I hope the man knows what he's doing."

Melville shrugged again, still looking downhill, and said they hadn't lost any men yet because of anything the skipper did. He was quiet for a while longer, then started talking without waiting for any more questions. "George, I sure as shit hope there were some people in your platoon at Pendleton who were over here, because what they taught you in ITR about fighting a war don't teach you a goddam thing about how to survive over here or keeping your buddies or your men alive. This war's the real thing and it ain't nothing like John Wayne movies or the Mickey Mouse they teach at Geiger and San Onofre." Camp Geiger in North Carolina and Camp San Onofre in California were homes of the month-long infantry training centers all enlisted Marines went to immediately following boot camp.

Bingham nodded. He said a third of the men in his platoon at Camp Pendleton had been grunts in Vietnam, had the Combat Action Ribbon, the Vietnam Service Medal, the Vietnamese Campaign Medal. Some of them had more medals than that. They knew the other men in the platoon were going to go to the place some of them called "Vee Cee Land," so they tried hard to teach them everything they knew about how to stay alive there.

"Did they shoot at you—with real bullets? Did they set booby traps, real booby traps, for you to walk into and lose a leg?"

"No." •

"Then they didn't teach you everything they know." He looked at his new corporal for the first time since making his personnel assignments. "You got the stripes, so that makes you second in command in this squad. I got some good men in this squad. Men who've been shot at and missed, shot at and hit. They've been through some kind of hell. If anything happens to me, you're in charge." He looked away again, back down the hill and his voice trailed off, bitterly. "Because you got the stripes." Then he added out loud, "You watch me. You watch me like you've never watched anyone in your life. You learn from me and when you're in charge maybe you won't get anyone wasted because you did something dumb. In the meantime, don't go pulling any John Wayne shit, don't do anything unless I tell you to. That way maybe you'll live long enough to learn." What he didn't tell his newest and only NCO was that he, himself, was rotating back to the World in less than two months, he didn't want Bingham to think he'd be taking over the squad so soon. He stood up. "Come on, I'll introduce you to your men."

Pfc. John Copley was a twenty-year-old black Marine of less than average height. His round face had the kind of beard that still didn't need to be shaved off every day despite the Marine

Corps making him shave every day for more than two and a half years. He didn't shave while out on operations and his face now had what most men would consider a three-day stubble. Pfc. Ben West was taller than average and his skin was burnt so dark by the tropical sun he would have looked Puerto Rican if it hadn't been for his straight, narrow nose, and his blue eyes. He was eighteen and had been in the Marines for less than a year. They were from opposite coasts of the country, Copley from Washington State, and West from Maine. Both wore tiger-stripe camouflage utility uniforms and canvas high-top jungle boots, Copley's much more worn than West's. In those respects they seemed very different from each other, but there were similarities that made them look alike. Both had the gaunt look of men who have seen too much war in too short a time with no chance to assimilate that vision of hell into a worldview that could be dealt with—too much that simply had to be blanked out of consciousness. Both had the constantly shifting eyes of men who needed to see everything at all times in order to stay alive. And each had the same thing written in black marking pen on the back of his shirt: "Yea, though I walk through the Valley of the Shadow of Death, I will fear no evil, 'cause I'm the meanest motherfucker in the Valley."

They looked briefly at Bingham before continuing their vigilant watch. They weren't impressed by his rank; their eyes seemed to tell him if they didn't like his orders in the field, they'd do things their own way. They had survived too long by taking care of each other to die depending on some inexperienced stranger's judgment. He'd have to prove himself to them, he understood that. But he also knew he'd have to let them know soon that he wasn't going to take any crap; that they had to do what he said when he said it.

"This is yours for as long as we're here," Melville said about the shallow hole in the ground Copley lounged near and West stood in. "Or until I move you. I'll let you know when Ives gets back." And he was gone, back to his own position which he would have to man alone until he rearranged his squad's fighting positions.

Bingham tried to make small talk but the other two wanted to know only if he had been in combat before. After that, they didn't want to talk to him; they thought they'd each be doing the fighting of one and a half men. There wasn't much point in getting to know a man who probably wouldn't be with them all that long, wouldn't be with them long because he'd probably do something dumb and get himself killed.

So Bingham tried to draw them out by talking about where the company was and what it was doing there.

"How long have you been on this operation?"

"They say" its been two weeks on that particular operation. But that was only because its name had been changed two weeks before. The battalion had been out in the field for a month so far.

"Who are we fighting? I mean what size unit?"

"They say" there are two battalions of main force VC in the area, but the platoon had only hit a couple of fire fights and some snipers. It was the booby traps one had to look out for, not the gooks.

"Have there been many casualties?"

"They say" they are light. The squad had lost four men, one dead to a booby trap, two others wounded; one with a punji stake through his foot, one hit by a sniper. One other got dysentery. The dead man and the sniper's victim were both corporals. They said that to let him know that junior NCOs had short life expectancies.

"Are we putting a hurting on Charlie?"

"They say . . . "

Everything he asked the answer was "They say." "They" weren't the men Bingham was talking to. "They" weren't the squad leaders or the company's officers. "They" were the brass sitting in air-conditioned Quonset huts back at Phu Bai and Dong Ha. "They" were the intelligence people drinking drinks with real ice with the brass. "They" were the people "in the rear with the beer," not the grunts doing the fighting.

"All right," Bingham finally said, "that's what 'they' say. What do you say?" His tone of voice indicated that he expected to hear their opinions.

"I say we ain't doing dickshit out here," West said. "We can't find the little sons a bitches."

"If we could find them," Copley said, "we'd put their little yellow asses so deep in the hurt locker they'd never find their way back out."

"But all we can find are their goddam booby traps."

"Except when they want to find us." Copley stared into the trees downhill for a long moment, then added bitterly, "One of the two times they found us, all they found was us, Alpha Company. After we chased them away we found so goddam much fucking blood we must of killed a couple hundred of them. There's only five hundred men in a gook battalion." He turned to Bingham. "This company lost twenty-two men that day, and not all of them dead. I say when Charlie stands and fights us, we kick his motherfucking ass." He looked away again. "But the little yellow cocksuckers don't stand and fight."

Staff Sergeant Ives and the squad he was with came in an hour before sunset. It was long enough before sundown for Ives to report to Copeland and Bernstein. They had followed the route they were supposed to, and Ives described what the terrain and vegetation were like along that route and said that they hadn't found any sign of the elusive battalions they were hunting. Long enough for the men with him to eat a quick meal of C rations and have a last smoke before the sun set and the smoking lamp was out. Long enough for Ives to meet Bingham.

"Who were you with back in the World?" Ives wanted to know.

Bingham told him what company and battalion of the Sixth Marines and who his platoon sergeant, company gunnery sergeant, first sergeant, and company commander had been.

"Gunny Dicks. Built like a beer barrel? Forearms like most men's thighs, with an eagle-globe-and-anchor tattooed on his shoulder?" Ives asked. "Good man," he said, when Bingham agreed with the description. "We were in the same company at Kay Bay, came over here with Three Four back in sixty-five. He served a full tour while I went back to the World." He slapped his left thigh. "Still got pins in the bone from where they put it back together like a jigsaw puzzle." He didn't say how the bone had turned into a jigsaw puzzle. "Gunny Dicks. He was platoon sergeant of first platoon, and I was platoon sergeant of third platoon. If I hadn't gotten hit, I'd probably be a gunny now, too." His look bored into Bingham. "He teach you anything?"

Bingham nodded. "Every time anybody got orders the Gunny made sure that man got extra training. He said if we did everything he told us we'd double our chances of coming back in one piece." He didn't say the rest of the time Gunny Dicks was a gold-plated prick whose favorite activity for the troops was making them prepare for junk-on-the-bunk inspections.

It was Ives's turn to nod. "That man don't bullshit you. Real hard-ass hard-charger. Won a Bronze Star and two 'dumb medals' in Korea." "Dumb Medal" was what combat veterans sometimes called the Purple Heart: you got it when you did something dumb and put yourself in the way of a bullet.

"He picked up a Silver Star here."

"I'm not surprised. You do everything like he told you to, you'll be okay. He knows his shit. Do it like he said and you and me gon-

na get along fine. You're going to be a good one, I can tell. Gunny
Dicks saw to that." Abruptly he changed the subject. "These dinks
out here"—he swept his arm, indicating the surrounding forest—
"aren't like the Red Chinese we fought in Korea. They're ballsy,
but they can't shoot for shit. We kick ass on them every time we
catch them."

"I hear we don't catch them very often," Bingham said, automatically using the first person pronoun rather than the second. If
he was assigned to this platoon in this company, he had to start
thinking "we" and "us" and not "you."

Ives nodded again. "That's why we stay out here a month, two
months at a time. That's how long it takes to catch Charlie's ass
and put a hurting on him. Now get back to Melville. He'll give
you ammo, food, and water for your fire team. We move out at
dawn. He'll fill you in."

"You know as much about it as I do," Melville said when
Bingham asked him for the scoop about moving out at dawn.
"For all I know we'll be here for another week. Take this shit."
He gave Bingham ammunition for his fire team—ten sixty-round
bandoliers of rifle rounds and fifteen grenades; ten fragmentation,
three white phosphorus, and two smoke. "Copley and West already
filled their canteens and took a case of Cs. Fill yours, they've got
your chow."

Bingham filled his canteens from the five-gallon water can near
Melville and returned to his hole. Copley was in it. The squad's
positions had been rearranged so the squad leader didn't have to
spend the night alone, and West was a few yards away in a hole
with a Marine Bingham didn't remember seeing before. Four boxes of C rations sat with their tops down on the ground behind
the hole.

"We emptied the case upside down and mixed them up and
drew," Copley told him.

C rations came in cases of twelve boxes; each box held a different meal. The entree was printed on the top of the box and some
were more desirable than others. The only way to be certain of
an equitable distribution of the better meals was to turn the boxes
upside down and mix them up, then everybody picked blindly.
Bingham wasn't surprised that after Copley and West had made
their choices, the leftovers included Scrambled Eggs and Ham,
and Ham and Limas—the most hated meal in the military cuisine—and didn't include any of the better meals, like Beans and
Franks or Turkey Loaf.

Bingham checked West to make sure he and the man he was

with had their watch rotation set, then made his own arrangements with Copley. Two hours awake, two hours sleeping. Copley got to sleep first. It became dark and he sat leaning against the front of the hole peering into the night, wondering what was going to happen. He was a fire-team leader who would have to gain the respect of his men. The other two fire-team leaders in the squad seemed to resent him. His squad leader didn't want to trust him yet. The platoon sergeant seemed too ready to depend on him right away. And he had been in-country for less than forty-eight hours. Two days before, he had been half a world away in California. His biological clock would need days to adjust to the different time zone. He knew his system needed to make its adjustments from the subtropical warmth of Southern California to the stifling heat and humidity a thousand miles north of the equator. He laughed silently. Just getting through the days without having to do anything for the next week was going to be hard enough. How the hell was he supposed to win his men's confidence, gain his squad leader's trust, and not prove to his platoon sergeant that he couldn't be relied on, all at the same time? Chickencoop hadn't told him about this part of war.

The night passed uneventfully.

CHAPTER FOUR
Just a Walk in the Woods

For a while after the sun came up, Bingham didn't know whether Melville was right or not about them maybe staying where they were for another week, but he did know Ives had been wrong about the company moving out at dawn. For the first half-hour after dawn, muted sounds drifted through the trees of Alpha Company's hill: deep coughs as men with too little sleep cleared their throats of the night's phlegm, soft hacking as the day's first cigarettes hit tired lungs, spattering water and low grunts as men emptied bladders and bowels, light scraping of metal against metal as the Marines cut C ration cans open to eat their morning chow.

Bingham went ten yards downhill and scooped a small hole in the dirt to squat over. His stool was loose and came fast. "Shit," he thought, "I've got diarrhea on top of everything else. How do I get out of this Mickey Mouse outfit?" Not that he really thought Alpha Company was Mickey Mouse—had petty-minded commanders. It was just a way of phrasing how out-of-kilter he felt on this first full day with his new unit. His body was rebelling from too many changes too fast. It wasn't only the time zone that had changed. A riot of colors had assailed his sight ever since he stepped out of the airplane's door. The smells of the Orient had assaulted his nose even before he reached the door; the fish aroma that pervaded the coastal areas, the darker odor of rotting vegetation, alien dust floating in the air, the pervasive sweet stench of human waste— both decaying civilian feces and the burning crap from military outhouses—and yet another smell, one he couldn't identify, that was unique to Vietnam. If any birds or insects made noise around him while he was squatting over his hole, he didn't notice.

When his bowels stopped running, he used the small roll of toilet paper that came with the C rations to clean himself as well as he could, covered the cathole and returned to his fighting hole.

Melville was waiting for him there. "Where the fuck were you?" the squad leader asked with a hard edge in his voice.

"Taking a shit."

"You want to get killed?"

Bingham wondered what that question was about. "I got the shits and I had to go, just like everybody else."

"Right, you have the shits. What did you think you were going to do if Charlie tried to zing you with a B-40 rocket, plug your asshole with it?" Melville's lips moved but his jaw didn't; it was clenched.

"What do you mean?" Bingham's eyes hardened, matching the sergeant's.

Melville held up a rifle. "I believe this is yours?"

Bingham looked at the weapon and felt his heart lurch. The ten-hour time difference between here and the West Coast and the change in climate were so abrupt his mind was foggy. He had forgotten one of the most basic rules of an infantryman: Always keep your rifle with you because you never know when you'll need it. "Oh, shit," he said out loud. "I forgot." He reached for the weapon. The hardness left his eyes and his hand quivered.

"You're married to this fucker, Marine," Melville said harshly, slamming the rifle into Bingham's hands so hard he crushed it to his chest and staggered him backward a step. "Don't you ever again take even one step without it in your hands. Understand?"

Bingham nodded numbly. "I only make mistakes once." His eyes were wide and his hands held the rifle so tightly his knuckles whitened. In his imagination an entire squad of black-pajamaed, heavily camouflaged Vietcong snuck up on him while he had his trousers down around his knees and his rifle back at his fighting hole.

"Once is all it takes," the sergeant said. His eyes burned into Bingham. He wanted to take him out behind the barracks and kick his ass for leaving his rifle behind. But there was no barracks to take him behind, and on an operation was no place to fight with his men. Instead he said, "Don't make any more mistakes. Mistakes get people killed. I don't know you yet, so I don't care if you get killed, but your mistakes might get someone else killed and that would sure as shit piss me off." He spun about and went to check the rest of his squad.

Bingham looked around hoping no one had seen the incident with Melville and his rifle, but knowing they must have. He was right—they had. A few yards away Copley and West sat together grinning at him. He glared at them and they turned back to face the forest, their shoulders shaking with silent laughter.

* * *

The night before, division headquarters had received new intelligence on where the hunted Vietcong battalions might be and ordered First Battalion headquarters to keep its companies in place until the intelligence could be fully analyzed. Battalion headquarters got the new information an hour after dawn and took some time to draw it on acetate overlays on its tactical maps. Then new orders for the day's movement had to be written and coded for secure radio transmission to the company commanders. Then the company commanders had to meet with their platoon commanders and platoon sergeants to tell them what was happening. By the time the platoon commanders and platoon sergeants met with their squad leaders, it was late enough that they finished their instructions with, "Have your men chow down first. We're moving out in half an hour." So the "we're moving out at dawn" Ives had told Bingham turned into moving out at noon.

"Police your trash, people," Melville reminded his men. "Remember, anything we leave behind is something Charlie can use against us. Pick it up, pick it all up." There was mild grumbling among the troops, but everyone picked up every bit of his trash.

"Lemme show you how it's done, new honcho," West said, a supercilious smile curled his lips. "What you do is you cut the bottoms off your C rat cans so you can flatten them." He demonstrated what he was saying. "Then you put all the flat cans from all three meals we ate here in one C rat box, and all the little scraps of paper and everything goes in that same box. Then you rip up the other C rat boxes you got left over and stuff them in that same C rat box. Unless you got some brass, that is. Then you keep one box and put that brass and any grenade pins you got left in that box. That way you carry everything you got left in less space than it took in the first place. Understand?" He looked up, grinning at Bingham. His grin faded fast.

"You mean like this?" Bingham held a C ration box open for West's inspection. Flattened cans and other trash were stuffed into it. The box was only half full.

"Yeah, like that," West said nodding. He looked at his new fire-team leader quizzically.

Bingham closed the box and shoved it into the bottom of his pack. "I'm new here," he said, and looked at West hard. "That doesn't mean I don't know anything. I had this good buddy back at Pendleton, called him Chickencoop. He was down in Quang Ngai Province with the First Marines last year. He tried to teach me everything he knew about fighting this war. Just because I forgot to take my weapon when I took a shit this morning doesn't mean I forgot everything Chickencoop and a bunch of other Marines taught me. I'll tell you when I don't know something. Do you understand?" His steady gaze burned into the other man.

West swallowed and nodded. "Yeah, Honcho. I got you."

In the background Copley snickered softly. West shot a glare at him.

"Second platoon's got the point," Melville's voice came to them. "Third platoon's got rear point, we're in the middle. Hank keeps contact with second platoon; Dago, you watch your ass. I'll be in the middle with Bingham. Stand by to move."

Bingham looked at the other two fire-team leaders to see what they were doing; he followed their example getting his men in line for the march, West in front of him and Copley following, and making sure each of them knew which side of their route to watch. Melville stepped in line between him and West. Suddenly Bingham noticed his mouth and throat were dry and he couldn't swallow. He pumped his jaw up and down, trying to work up some saliva. None would come.

"Chew some gum when you go out the first time," Chickencoop's voice came to his mind across many weeks and thousands of miles. "You're going to be scared because you don't know what the fuck's going on and your mouth and throat will dry up. You can't have your mouth and throat dry if you're a fire-team leader because you have to talk to your men." He remembered the corner of Chickencoop's mouth twisting in a mockery of a smile. "The second time you go out you'll be scared shitless because then you'll know what the fuck's happening." Chickencoop visibly relaxed. "Then after a while, you won't give a good goddam anymore. Just don't stop caring so much you do something stupid and get your dumb chuck ass killed. Remember, when we both get out of this mean green machine you're supposed to check in with me in Chicago on your way back east. I'm gonna take you out to the best places in the Windy City and we're going to get blind drunk together."

Bingham smiled at the memory, and the tension building in his neck muscles relaxed. He reached into his shirt pocket for the pack of gum he put there, unwrapped a stick and folded it into his mouth. The wrapper went into his hip pocket.

One hundred seventy-four Marines had gone into the field as Alpha Company. After one month and thirty-two casualties who hadn't been returned, plus fifteen replacements, Alpha Company

numbered 157 effectives to move out on that day's noon. The first
man in the company moved off the hill at about the same minute
Melville told his squad to stand by. When the first man had gone
five yards the second man followed him. Then the rest of the
company at five-yard intervals. The point man moved at a slow
speed, checking at every step for the will-o'-the-wisp glimmer
low above the ground that might signal a trip wire across his path,
searching for any disturbance in the ground or leaves ahead of his
feet that might indicate a booby trap. Bingham stood chewing his
gum for twenty minutes before Melville nodded to Longfellow and
signaled him to send Emerson after the squad they would follow.
Then Melville nodded to Bingham and it was his turn to take the
step that would lead him off the hill into the unknown.

The hillside was steep. Not too steep for a few men to climb
without grabbing handholds, but steep enough so that by the time
enough men had gone down it, tramping the decaying leaves
on its side to a slick mess and churning the mud beneath the
leaves, it was too slippery to walk without handholds. Fifteen
yards ahead Davis fell with a clanging of gear and slid downhill
into Longfellow's legs. Longfellow was just turning to look back
to see what caused the noise when Davis crashed into his legs
and knocked him down. Together they sledded down the hill
a few more yards, until Longfellow was able to grab a small
tree trunk and stop himself. He kicked out and hooked Davis
in the armpit, stopping his descent. Longfellow cautiously pulled
himself to his feet, digging the sides of his boots into the mud
of the hillside for stability, and quickly inspected his rifle to
make sure its muzzle was clear of mud and debris. He looked
at Davis.

"Where's your weapon, Grace," he demanded.

Davis looked around himself, surprised. His rifle wasn't in his
hands and he didn't know where it had gone to. He didn't say anything, just looked confused and wished he was somewhere else.

"Here it is," Bingham said. He scuttled to where he had seen
Davis's rifle slide down the slope. He went half sideways with the
sides of his boots slamming into the muck underfoot to keep from
losing his footing. A year earlier he had learned how to negotiate
worse hillsides than this one on the slopes of Old Smoky at a
time when the southern California rains had been so bad there was
danger of mudslides and feet often sunk into the mud to more than
mid-calf. Davis's rifle was jammed against a tree trunk. Bingham
looked it over while Longfellow helped Davis back to his feet,
then handed it back to him. "You better clean this before we get

into a fire fight. There's mud in the muzzle and the chamber's probably fouled, too."

Davis nodded dumbly and wondered if the company would stop before they got into a fire fight so he could clean it.

"When we get to the bottom, break it down and put your cleaning rod through it," Longfellow said. "And don't forget to check out the magazine, make sure there's no shit in it so you won't have a jam. Now stay on your goddam feet." He spat his disgust—he didn't want to have to teach a boot how to be a combat Marine in the middle of an operation.

Davis almost fell again while pondering the problem of cleaning his rifle on the move. He caught his balance and kept going, thinking about how nothing like this happened to John Wayne in any of the war movies he ever saw.

Melville clapped a hand on Bingham's shoulder and nodded approval without looking at him.

The afternoon wore on with the column advancing in starts and stops at a speed of about two kilometers an hour. Bingham's senses peaked and stayed at their peak. He expected gunfire to break out at his side at every second. He knew, or thought he knew, it was the point that was in jeopardy, sometimes the end of the column, usually not the middle where he was. But he couldn't shake the sensation of being a target. The only thing he felt he really knew was there were some little yellow people out there somewhere who wanted to kill him—little yellow people he had never met or even seen. When the Pan Am charter that flew him in a great circle across the Pacific let him off at Da Nang he saw what looked like hundreds of Vietnamese civilians on the base—cleaning girls, barbers, laundry people, grounds maintenance men—the plethora of people rich America hired in poor foreign countries to tend her military installations. There were soldiers, too: a battalion of ARVNs, the regular South Vietnamese Army; a company of Regional Forces; and a platoon of Popular Forces, the militia recruited to defend their home villages and dressed in mixes of uniform parts and civilian dress. At Dong Ha, where he turned in his seabag and was issued a rifle and the rest of his field gear during the few hours before being flown on the supply helicopter to the company in the field, he saw more Vietnamese civilians and soldiers. Everyone he asked assured him they were okay, "They're our gooks, that means they're good gooks." How do you know for sure, he asked. "They aren't shooting at us," he was told.

And everywhere, the smells.

Now he was out in the boonies, the bush. The home of the bad guys, the gooks who would shoot at him. Intellectually he knew the point was in the greatest danger. Intellectually he also knew the VC sometimes let the point go through and opened fire on those following. Intellectually he knew he was in little immediate danger in the middle of the company-long column unless a firefight started up ahead and he had to rush forward to join it. In his guts he knew a little yellow man had him in his rifle sights and at any instant he might not finish the step he was taking forward.

The smells were the same in the bush, but somehow different. It smelled as if someone had taken a shit on a pile of rotting fruit after which something came along and died on it, George thought at some point. So his senses peaked and stayed peaked. For a while.

It was the adrenal glands pumping out their juices that made the senses peak. Fear turned them on and their product provided extra strength, speed, endurance, and agility to fight or to flee. But when there was neither fight nor flight, eventually the body tired of producing adrenaline. A crash followed—there was a sudden and noticeable reduction in energy. All Bingham felt when his adrenal glands finally stopped pumping enough to keep his senses peaked was a deep and pervasive lassitude. His adrenaline level remained high. It had to. His body was still operating on Pacific Standard Time—although during the previous three and a half days it might have adjusted to Hawaiian Time. Whichever, the difference in time zones from what he was used to, to where he actually was, turned his body clock's time upside-down. Whatever, without the pumping adrenaline, he wouldn't have been able to keep going.

Alpha Company was in jungle. Single-canopy jungle, not double- or triple-canopy. The single canopy provided shade dappled with sunlight, unlike the eternal twilight in a triple-canopy jungle. This broken cover allowed observers in helicopters and fixed-wing aircraft flying above the spreading treetops to see spots of ground through occasional breaks in the tree cover, and to follow the courses of rivers and larger streams. Other than that, the greenery, seen from above, gave the impression of a gently rolling landscape—sort of like grassy savannah land with an odd tree poking its top up every here and there. But that gentle roll was only an illusion caused by the trees in the low places growing higher than their fellows on the higher ground. Underneath the spreading treetops were steep hills and jagged crags of rock. From above, the land looked clean and uncluttered, but the sunlight coming through allowed plants to grow ariot. The ground was covered, matted, with a tangle of brush, vines, and saplings. So much so that a couple of hundred yards off the company's nighttime hilltop the point man had to stop looking for booby traps and start using a machete to chop his way through the undercover.

It was safe to stop looking for booby traps. The Vietcong seldom put them out off the trails. They could hope to wound or kill someone walking on a trail—but off it, where could a booby trap be put to catch someone? So the Marines avoided the trails and moved slowly through the brush while the VC used the trails and went quickly. The VC could use the trails safely—after all, they planted the booby traps, they knew where they were and could avoid them. Hacking with the machete was hard work, and the Marines had to rotate frequently on the point to avoid exhaustion. The ground leveled, but the brush was thicker than it had been in the hills. Gradually the interval between men closed to less than five yards, and the column shrunk to far less than its original half-mile length.

It was only an hour or so after moving off the hilltop before Bingham's mind sort of numbed over and his body trudged along on automatic pilot. If he had been more aware he would have known it wouldn't be long before he paid a price. But at twenty-one, he was young enough to still believe he was able to take any physical punishment, and his body acted like it. He could take it. His shoulders automatically shifted forward or back, to one side or the other, maintaining his balance on the frequently uneven footing. Without thinking of what his feet were doing, he dug the edges of his boots for purchase into hillsides and avoided falling. A well-conditioned body used to cross-country marching doesn't need an aware mind to do that. He didn't even notice the smells of the Orient anymore.

Neither, at first, did he notice the sounds of a firefight coming from the front of the column. He didn't notice until after he walked into Sergeant Melville's back. Melville, like everyone else in the squad except Bingham, had dropped to one knee at the first shot. Even Davis was awake enough to notice when Longfellow knelt, and he followed suit. Maybe he was more scared or anxious than the older Bingham and his adrenal glands kept exuding their hormone longer.

Melville was holding his PRC-6 radio to his head, listening for word of what was happening or orders on what to do. The sergeant rolled and spun, dropping the radio and bringing his rifle to the ready. He saw who had bumped into him in time to stop his finger from pulling the trigger. "Shit. Giddown," he swore, returned to his kneeling position, and picked his radio back up.

Bingham started, as soon as he realized what had happened to him. He was both angry and annoyed at himself. The continuing gunfire from ahead caught his attention and the adrenaline started pumping again. He tried to ignore Copley's soft snickering behind him. "What's happening?" he asked Melville.

The squad leader shook his head and grimaced. He didn't have time for anything that sounded like a dumb question. "Busting caps. Hell, I don't know. Probably just a sniper." His ear stayed against the radio's receiver. The shooting ahead slowed to an occasional shot, then picked up again. Bingham could hear at least three different kinds of rifles being fired in addition to the booming of an M-79 grenade launcher, but he didn't know what they were other than the Marines' M-14s. He swallowed and chewed harder on his gum.

Suddenly Melville murmured a few words into the radio and turned to Bingham with a sour look on his face. "Aaron called squad leaders up," he said. "That means you're in charge here. Just keep everybody in place until you hear from me." Then he was on his feet, trotting forward past the line of men disappearing into the forest.

"Shit," Bingham swore under his breath, "he took the radio with him." He wanted to listen to the radio so maybe he could find out what was happening. He looked around. Everyone he could see in the squad was watching him. "Watch your flanks, people," he snapped in a low voice, "watch your flanks." They slowly turned their heads and looked into the trees at the sides of their line of march, some of them muttering about how the fuck were they supposed to see anything to their sides, the brush was so thick? Bingham ignored the mutters; even if the brush was too thick to see into, someone close enough inside it would make some sign of his presence—he thought. He returned his attention to the firefight ahead of him. It sounded to him like several hundred rounds had been fired at the head of the column. An M-60 machine gun added its cacaphony to the noise of the firefight.

Melville was back in a very few minutes with Longfellow following close behind. "Dago up," he said when he reached Bingham, waving to the third fire-team leader. He huddled close with the three fire-team leaders. "Nobody knows what's up ahead except it's more than a sniper. The platoon's pulling a hundred meters to the side and going forward to flank it. The skipper doesn't think it's a bunker complex, so maybe it won't be bad." He spat to the side. "We'll go as far as the CP and drop our packs there. Let's go." He stood and hurried to the head of the squad so he'd know when the rest of the platoon moved out.

The fire-team leaders passed the little information they had to their men and waited. Bingham found his gum could no longer make his saliva flow. When it was time, they surged forward as far as the company command unit and dropped their packs on the run. Here they were only a hundred yards from the firing and could make out some shouted commands. None of the voices sounded panicked and there weren't any cries of "Corpsman up." The gunfire sounded to Bingham more like the measured firing on a rifle range than what he imagined a firefight would sound like. It sounded to him it had settled into random shooting meant more to keep heads down than to hit targets. Except for an occasional return shot, the only firing he heard now was from the Marines at the head of the column.

First platoon cut to the left, away from the rest of the company and, for the first time that afternoon, had to break its own way through the jungle undergrowth. Bingham heard crashing of bodies in the brush ahead of him, sprinkled with muffled curses. There were thuds as hurrying feet got tangled in stay-awhile vines and bodies fell to the ground. Bingham's feet were caught up and he stumbled badly, but didn't fall. He forgot to watch his rear and just hurried to keep up with West, glad the ground they were running over was more level than the hills they had earlier clambered over. After what seemed like far too little time, but had to be longer than it seemed, the platoon stopped. The gunfire was now to their right and slightly to the front.

Melville listened to his radio and said a couple of words into it. He went along the line of the squad telling his men, "Got a rock pile up ahead." They waited for a few minutes, then advanced again and came to a jumbled rock cliff with vines and creepers hanging from its face. Weeds and saplings sprouted where they could find purchase. A jagged outcropping of mountain-making rock rose more than twenty feet above the ground, with trees growing on its top. It wasn't marked on Copeland's map. The acrid tang of cordite drifted on a gust of air along the cliff face.

A few yards to the left someone had found a way to the clifftop and the Marines cautiously climbed it, helping each other so they could climb as quietly as possible. They weren't exposed on the cliff face; the forest grew too close to it for them to be exposed. But they knew Charlie had to have men on top of it. Melville had gone up at the head of the squad and left Longfellow behind to make sure they all made it up. Longfellow used few gestures and fewer words to direct the way.

"Sling your rifle. Up there, see him? Go." He slapped Bingham's shoulder and turned to wave Copley to the foot of the cliff.

Bingham looked where Longfellow pointed. A few feet up and slightly to the left, a Marine he didn't recognize stood on a small ledge and held his rifle down for him to grasp. Bingham pulled a pair of heavy cloth work gloves from his hip pocket and put them on. Cuts and rope burns suffered on his hands while climbing the hills of Southern California had taught him the value of gloves in the field. He looked down and stepped high onto a chunky rock. Standing on it he reached up for the offered rifle. The Marine above pulled and he stepped to a higher foothold, then another and he joined the stranger on the small ledge. The man nodded and pointed up and right, then indicated the next foothold on the route and gave him a light boost. Bingham reached up with his hands and a foot and pulled himself up. A second Marine reached down extending a rifle to help him up farther. When he reached that ledge the Marine boosted him over the top of the rock. The cracks of the firefight came more from the right side now; the Marines' M-14s and machine gun were slightly to the rear. He hardly had time to move away from the lip of the cliff before Copley joined him.

Melville was there putting his men in an assault line. "We figure Charlie's on the side slope," he explained, "but he's got to have security topside. Second squad's reserve." Two squads would advance across the top of the outcropping on line and the platoon's other squad would stay back to help wherever the line might need it.

This is it, Bingham thought, this is what I enlisted for, busting caps and killing gooks. He swallowed, saliva was flowing again. He dimly realized that two and a half years earlier he would have been frightened but even more excited about the prospect of combat. Now he was older, more experienced and knowledgeable, and was just as excited as he would have been earlier but more frightened. When he was nineteen, he had been invincible. At twenty-one he knew he was mortal. But he was a Marine and he had a job to do, this was what he had been training for, for over two years. More than fearful of getting killed or maimed, he hoped that he did well, didn't make any mistakes that would get another Marine injured, didn't freeze when the first bullets came his way.

Melville rushed from one end of his squad to the other telling his men, "Watch me, I'll signal when to move out. Watch your dress and stagger it. Don't fire until you have a target." He took his own place in the line, looked in both directions to see his men following his instructions to line up in a staggered row, and turned to raise a thumb to Lieutenant Copeland.

Copeland nodded at the all-ready sign—he had already gotten it from the third squad leader. He spoke briefly into the handset of his radio then raised his arm above his head and dropped it forward. The two squad leaders waved their men forward and twenty Marines stepped out in a staggered line. Copeland and Ives followed with a radioman. Second squad trailed in their wake. Gunfire from a few rifles in front of them grew louder and masked the noises the Marines made on the broken rocks they walked across. The foliage they advanced through was so thick they almost missed the sentry the Vietcong had placed on top of the rocks to cover that flank.

The boom of an M-14 a few feet to his left made Bingham drop to the ground.

"Got one," West shouted, and put a second bullet into the body that slumped into the ground hollow the VC lay in.

Copeland ordered his radioman to tell the company to cease fire and yelled to his men, "Let's go! Move, move, move."

Suddenly excited shouts from the Vietcong were added to the the sounds of the Marines crashing through the brush, and the cracking of the VC rifles became more rapid. The Marines at the head of the company column had stopped their fire, and the VC were shifting their attention to the Marines flanking their position.

"Move, move, move," Copeland shouted.

Ives's yells echoed him, "Move it, move-it, moveit!"

"Go, go, go-go, gogo," the squad leaders screamed.

The Marines ran, panting as they crashed through the brush. Bullets cracked through the air around the advancing Marines. Broken twigs and torn leaves rained down on them. One Marine fired his rifle, then another, then another and then nearly all of them were shooting. And they started yelling.

A startled yellow face suddenly appeared in front of Bingham and he felt the blood drain from his face, and his throat and anus constrict. He pointed his rifle and pulled the trigger before he had time to think about what he was doing, before he saw the VC swinging his own rifle at him. The small man collapsed backward, and Bingham continued running past him. Then the only sounds were the Marines' voices and the booming of their rifles.

"Cease fire, cease fire," Copeland and Ives yelled. The squad leaders picked up the chant. "Get down, everybody down in place," Copeland yelled, and his order was repeated by Ives and the squad leaders.

Bingham dropped to the ground, panting. He wiped the sweat from his brow so his eyes could search the surrounding brush for more enemy soldiers. His rifle's muzzle pointed everywhere his eyes looked. He saw only the forest.

Silence fell over the jungle.

"Casualty count," Copeland called after a moment.

"Team leaders report," the squad leaders shouted.

Bingham didn't hear the voices on a conscious level, but he had been in the infantry long enough to automatically respond to the order. "West," he shouted.

"Yo," West said back.

"You all right?" Bingham heard other fire-team leaders checking their men.

"Would I say 'yo' if I was dead?" West said.

"Copley."

"I'm okay, Honcho."

"First team okay," Bingham reported. He did it all automatically while continuing to look for more enemy.

"Anybody see anyone else?" Copeland asked.

The squad leaders repeated the question to their fire-team leaders who, in turn, asked their men. No one saw any living people except other Marines.

Behind him, Bingham heard Ives and Melville talking but their voices were too low for him to hear them clearly. He was concentrating too hard on looking to his front and getting his pounding heart and lungs under control to try to eavesdrop.

"Bingham up," Melville shouted. Bingham crawled over to his squad leader. "Over here," the sergeant said and led him back the way he came. "I was watching you, man. You know during that assault you only fired one round. Did you know that?"

Bingham shook his head, he was slightly dazed from his first combat.

"Well, you put that one round right where it did the most good. Look." Melville stopped and pointed to the ground.

Bingham looked. A large doll lay flung on its back. He started at the incongruous sight, then looked again. It wasn't a large doll, it was a small man. A red-rimmed black hole above the small man's right eye oozed blood. The right eye was tightly closed, the left was rolled upward as though trying to examine its forehead. The man's jaw hung slack.

"One shot, one kill," Melville said. "I think maybe you're going to be all right." He slapped Bingham on the back.

The slap doubled the suddenly limp Bingham over and he dropped to his knees heaving. The realization that he had killed a man shuddered through his body and he threw up. Copley and West exchanged knowing glances. Melville waited patiently. He thought it was a completely normal reaction.

Five Main Force Vietcong were killed in front of Alpha Company's advance that afternoon. One, so badly wounded the corpsman wasn't sure he'd live was captured. That one told the interrogators his squad had been left behind to slow down the Marines, to cover the withdrawal of his battalion. His information must have been accurate because in the next three days, the Marines made no further contact with the enemy. The battalion was pulled out of the field for a rest and a different battalion was sent into the same area with orders to move westward. It was a continuation of the same operation.

CHAPTER FIVE

Throwaway People

Someone once made the observation that the life of the combat infantryman consists of long periods of absolute boredom punctuated by brief moments of absolute terror. George Bingham didn't meet the brief moments of absolute terror during his first week in the war; the one firefight he was in on his second day with Alpha Company was too brief. Though he had been frightened during the fight, he had been too mentally tired to experience the absolute terror—too jet-lagged that day to be truly aware of the danger. However, during the next month he did become intimately acquainted with absolute boredom.

When a company of Marines was stuck on a fire base out in the middle of nowhere with nothing to do but sit perimeter security and run patrols with no enemy contact, life got pretty boring in a hurry. The only diversions were mail call—but not everybody got mail every day, and how many times could the same letter be reread?—and every once in a while a supply chopper might bring in a few cans of warm beer per man. Then there was card playing—mostly hearts and pinochle, sometimes acey-deucey or blackjack—and rereading the same limited supply of paperbacks over and over again. It was dull.

That month was also when George Bingham happened to have his first brief moments of absolute terror. Twice.

Bingham didn't know how to play pinochle and he was tired of hearts. Acey-deucey was a losers' game, he said, and he had lost ten dollars at blackjack without once winning dealer, so he threw in his hand and found a spot of bare dirt to lay down on without any trash or pebbles cluttering it, thinking maybe he'd cop a few Zs before the sun set and he had to start his watch. He hadn't gotten any mail in a few days and didn't feel like rereading again the last letters he'd gotten from his father or kid sister, and nobody had any paperback novels he hadn't read yet that they weren't reading themselves. So copping a few Zs was about the only thing left to do. A man who's been on a combat operation for a while can lie down and catnap anytime he gets the chance. A man who's bored out of his skull running security patrols and pulling perimeter duty can't. Bingham stretched out as comfortably as he could and pulled his soft cover over his eyes. He wished he could sleep, but the harder he wished the more wide awake he became. He had even gotten over the jet lag and was used to the smells, so he didn't even have them as diversions anymore.

A quarter of the Marines not out on security patrols lounged in or on top of bunkers just inside the banked rows of concertina wire that circled the fire base. They were lazily watching the trees beyond the cleared area outside the wire. They didn't expect to see anything except an occasional wild or semi-domesticated animal peeking out of the trees or a returning patrol trudging its way back in. The rest of the Marines sat singly or in small groups or lay back alone to snooze. There was kibitzing at card games and some small conversations here and there. Everyone spoke softly other than an odd triumphant cry from a winning card player. Darting insects buzzed and once in a while a forest animal would cry out. It was a quiet, lazy summer afternoon. November in the tropics.

Bingham wiggled his back and hips, hoping to make his little patch of bare ground more comfortable; maybe if it turned soft he could doze. His helmet and flak jacket were in the bunker his fire team shared with Rivera's, but he had his rifle propped on his right thigh where he could find it in a hurry if he needed it. In the distance he heard a dim *whump*. The soft quiet on the hilltop suddenly disappeared into hard silence for a few seconds until someone screamed, "Incoming."

During Bingham's first few days in-country, Sergeant Melville had told him in a very serious manner how to react to various stimuli. The shouted warning "incoming" was one of them; Bingham remembered Chickencoop had told him the same thing. Melville had reiterated many of his injunctions to Bingham when Alpha Company retired to the fire base, and both West and Copley had told him what to do in many of the same circumstances, adding many gory details. Hank Longfellow told him about incoming fire and gleefully added, "But you're too much of a newby to remember all that shit, so you'll probably get your ass wasted the first time." Longfellow always made it clear he didn't have much use for men who had served more time in the Marine Corps than he had without having served a combat tour. Especially when those men were placed in positions senior to him.

It took a few seconds for Bingham to realize the significance of the shouts and the meaning of the mad scrambling he heard. He raised his head and tipped the bill of his soft cover away from his eyes to see men bolting into bunkers. He sat erect and swiveled his head, no one was in sight except for one or two last men diving into their bunkers. "Oh, shit," he said, finally remembering what "incoming" meant, and jumped to his feet. Halfway to the bunker he remembered his rifle and spun back to get it. The first mortar round hit in the far side of the fire base just as he bent over to pick up his weapon. He saw it explode. The small puff of dust and debris it kicked up looked huge to him, and the noise seemed to be the loudest thing he had ever heard. Bingham flattened himself on the ground and tried to melt into the earth. Two more mortar rounds crashed into the far side of the fire base, then there was momentary silence. In the background he heard the *whump* of more mortar rounds being fired and knew he had only a few seconds to reach the safety of a bunker before the rounds hit inside the perimeter. Bingham jerked around to face his bunker, which looked light-years away, jerked up to a position like that of a sprinter in the blocks, and ran faster than he had ever run before. He was off his feet, sailing through the air, several yards before he reached the bunker's entrance. The next mortar round hit just as he tumbled headfirst into the bunker. It exploded near where he had lain clutching his rifle.

"Nice, Honcho," West said. "You training for the Olympic long jump?"

Copley giggled. "No way, pano," he said. "Didn't you see that was a half gainer? New honcho's going out for the Olympic diving team."

Rivera looked at him impassively. Harte and Morse just hunkered down and ignored the corporal who didn't have enough sense to come in out of the mortar shower when everybody else did.

"Think Hank saw that?" Copley asked.

"You better believe it," West said. They both knew what Longfellow had said.

"Think he'll say something?"

"You ever know him not to say something?"

They giggled. More mortar rounds hit inside the wire.

Bingham swallowed a few times, sagging against the sandbag wall of the bunker. When his breathing slowed he leaned toward the bunker entrance and looked out. A shallow crater dimpled the ground a few yards from where he had tried to doze. His imagination took over and he could feel every one of the places where a mortar fragment might have hit; he saw himself laying broken on the ground, his life's blood oozing, seeping, flowing, spurting onto the bare earth, being sucked into the dry ground, giving it life while he lost his own. Another mortar round crashed into the fire base. Bingham flinched away from the entrance and sat stiffly against the sandbags, the blood drained from his face and his eyes rolled up. He gagged. A vivid imagination is not always a good thing to have. Oh, shit, Chickencoop, he thought, I gotta remember better what you told me.

"Shee-it, lookie him," West said, giggling again. "That's just like you looked the first time you took incoming."

"Bullshit, man. I ain't never been nowhere near that white," Copley said.

The taller-than-average white man and the shorter-than-average black man from opposite ends of a continent wrapped their arms around themselves, rolled their heads together and shook with laughter.

Bingham started trembling with thoughts of what might have been. The trembling became violent and he rolled on the deck with it. But he didn't throw up; he'd enough of getting sick when he saw his first dead Vietcong. The barrage stopped after eighteen rounds hit inside the perimeter. He didn't have time to continue thinking about the might-have-beens.

"First platoon, saddle up," Ives's voice rang over the area. "Helmets, flak jackets, weapons, and ammo. We're going to get those sons a bitches." "Going to get," he said, not, "Going to try to get." There was hardly a man in the platoon who didn't know Ives was being overly optimistic, that the VC would probably be long gone by the time they reached what by now had to be a deserted mortar site.

But there was scrambling and the thudding of equipment as the Marines pulled on the gear they were taking.

"Squad leaders report," Ives shouted toward the men milling in front of him, aligning themselves into a semblance of military order.

"First squad, all present and accounted for."

"Second squad, everybody's here."

"Third squad, present and accounted for."

"Column of ones, second squad, first squad, third," Ives ordered. "Move it out on the double."

The three ragged rows of Marines peeled of into one line and quickly shuffled through a break in the perimeter wire. Lieutenant Copeland and his radioman inserted themselves between second and first squads, Ives and a corpsman, Doc Eggleston, joined the line following first squad. Outside the gate the point man slowed to a walk so he could watch for booby traps.

"Step it out on the point," Copeland shouted. "Charlie hasn't put anything out here today."

"Right," the point man muttered, "but what about last night or the night before or any other time." But he quickened his pace to a slow trot, still trying to look for booby traps.

The first hundred yards or so was easy going, it was across ground that had been cleared so the Vietcong couldn't get too close to the fire base without being seen. Once the clear ground was past the point man had to bull his way through dense forest undergrowth, but that wasn't too bad either because it was down-hill. Then they had to climb through the jungle junk up the hill the mortar had fired from, and that was hard going. Something more than half a kilometer as the crow flies into the jungle, nearly twice that far as men have to walk, Copeland signaled the point to slow down. A fresh man was put on the front of the platoon's column. A little farther and Copeland called a halt. Somewhere nearby was where the mortar had fired from; somewhere nearby there might be enemy soldiers. From that point on they used hand signals, silent communications. The Marines followed the hand-gesture orders and quietly spread out from their column into a line across the route they had followed. They eased their way forward, eyes straining to see any movement, any shape that didn't belong in the forest, their ears alert for any sounds, listening for any noise not made by themselves or by the forest animals.

Bingham was still jittery but not as frightened as he had been during the shelling of the fire base. He had been in a firefight before and wasn't terrified by that prospect—he thought he knew what it was like. Besides, he wanted to believe what the old salts said about the mortar team: the Vietcong were probably long gone.

They were. The platoon searched the area for more than an hour without finding anything, not even after a squad from one of the other platoons, a squad that had been on a security patrol with a machine-gun team when the mortaring took place, joined in the search. They found a small clearing where the mortar had probably been set up, but there was no sign to confirm it. Copeland got on his radio, reported their lack of success and was given orders to come home. First platoon, reinforced by a squad and a machine-gun team, set out on a different route to return to the fire base. The order of march was first squad, third squad, second squad, the other squad. Lieutenant Copeland was again behind the lead squad and Staff Sergeant Ives was once more in front of the rear squad. The machine-gun team was in the middle.

The rule of the infantry patrol was to never return by the same route taken on the way out— If a patrol was seen on the way out, it could be ambushed along that route, on the way back in. Of course, combat troops were usually too smart to go back the same way they went out, so ambushes set on outward routes seldom caught anyone on the way back in. And, as it so happened, first platoon had been seen going out. A lot of things have been said about the Vietcong over the years, some true, some not so true. One of the things said was that they could always catch Americans whenever they wanted to, which certainly seemed to be true enough. Charlie knew the Marines were good combat troops and probably wouldn't go back the same way they went out, so he had looked around for the platoon's likely return route and set up on it. He guessed close enough to right that it didn't make much difference.

Second team had the point, Longfellow had volunteered for it. He was one of the salts who knew Charlie was long gone and he wanted his newby, Davis, to get some experience as point man. Besides, giving the point to someone who had only been in-country less than a month gave the men who had been there longer a break. Let the newby bust *his* ass breaking trail.

The platoon was down near the bottom between the two hills when it happened. The Vietcong assigned to set the ambush off saw only one man entering his killing zone, but he could tell by the angle of the Marine's march that there wouldn't be more than one man in his killing zone at any one time anyway, so he pulled the cord that pulled the pin out of the grenade anchored at head height in a tree along the Marines' probable route.

Bingham was just noticing the quiet in the jungle. The forest stillness was disturbed only by the muted noises and muffled voices of the Marines as they made their way down the hill. Then the quiet was shattered by an explosion.

The grenade went off and the VC who pulled on the cord saw the Marine in its killing zone fall. When the grenade exploded all forty-five VC in the ambush opened up with everything they had— mostly old French MAS-49 rifles and Russian SKS carbines, though two had the Hanoi-manufactured versions of the French MAT-49 submachine gun and one carried a Chinese-made Type 56 automatic rifle, the Chicom variation on the AK-47.

Bingham saw the leafy blast from the grenade and immediately screamed over the noise, "Hit the deck, get down!" He didn't hear Copeland and Melville shout the same thing, he was too busy diving for cover himself. He did hear screaming from ahead, from near where the grenade went off, and cries for a corpsman behind him in the column. He also heard the roaring of a beast, a beast about to bound, claws extended, teeth bared, onto his back, to bite, to rend, to maim, to kill. To send him home in a plastic bag, for a closed coffin to be displayed at his funeral. His eyes dilated and he hyperventilated through clenched teeth. He looked around wildly, trying to find the beast—he had to find it and kill it before it reached him, if it could be killed. But first he had to figure out what direction it was in. The beast he heard was gunfire from the ambush.

"On the right, they're on the right," Copeland shouted. His cries were dimly heard by Bingham and he turned in that direction, eyes piercing the forest, searching for the beast, firing as fast as he could, hoping to hit the beast.

His rifle stopped firing when the first magazine emptied and Melville's shouts of, "Right flank," finally broke through to him. He finally heard the individual shots from the VC instead of the roaring of the beast.

"Copley, West, fire right, fire right," he yelled.

The return fire from the Marines grew and quickly overpowered the Vietcong. Then only the Marines were firing.

"By squads, move forward," Copeland ordered. "First squad, forward twenty meters, move. Second squad, cease fire. Third squad, lay down a base of fire. Keep those other people in reserve."

"You heard the man, people," Melville said to his squad. "On the double." Most of first squad surged forward twenty meters through the jungle tangle. They dropped at his order and lay down a base of fire for the other two squads that were now coming forward.

By now Bingham was calm. He coolly directed Copley and West in their fire and methodically pumped bullets himself into the greenery at his front, his earlier terror now forgotten.

The platoon leapfrogged again, to a shallow gully where the VC had lain in ambush. The gully was shallow, about three feet deep, with steep sides thickly covered with vines and weeds. The side the Marines approached from had bare areas hacked in the weeds for the VC to lay in. Copeland ran the platoon beyond the gully, then set them in defensive positions around it, one fire team uphill on the gully and another downhill, one searching the gully itself and the rest of the platoon on its far side. Then he called for a squad leaders' report. Second squad had two men down on the trail, being patched up by Doc Eggleston, but the lieutenant already knew that.

"I don't have Davis," Longfellow reported to Melville. "He got hit by that grenade."

It took a few seconds for Bingham to realize what Longfellow had told Melville; the image of the beast was still too fresh in his mind. Then his stomach turned in panic that he might have somehow missed one of his own men going down. "Copley, you there?" He was. "West?"

"My dick's still swinging, Honcho."

The fire team searching the gully found a small pool of blood staining its side and a line of blood drops leading uphill. There was no way to tell whether the signs were from the same man or if they indicated two casualties.

"Pull back," Copeland ordered. "Regroup where we were." The squad leaders organized their men and returned to where they were when the ambush opened up on them.

"Hey, Doc," Melville shouted as they neared their previous position, "you check out my newby yet?"

Eggleston waited until the sergeant was in sight before answering. "Look for yourself," he said and turned away, his face twisted in a grimace.

"Oh, shit," Melville groaned when he saw Davis. He dropped to his knees and doubled over, trying not to throw up. Longfellow came up behind him and gagged.

"Jesus," Copeland murmured when he got close enough to see. "Wrap him in his poncho and let's di-di."

The grenade used to set off the ambush was a World War II–vintage Russian F-1. Like all cast-iron pineapple-type grenades, it had an unreliable burst pattern. Part of the body of this grenade facing Davis had pulverized into tiny fragments that peppered the right side of Davis's face and neck with tiny punctures. One larger chunk had scythed through the air intact and hit his head just under his tipped-back helmet. That chunk had taken out a large piece of his skull. Davis lay facedown with the pulpy gray mass of his brain bulging out of the hole in his head.

As gently as he could with trembling hands, Melville pushed Davis's brain back into his head, then he, Longfellow, and Emerson rolled the body onto its poncho. While they were doing that, Rivera cut down and trimmed a small tree. They inserted the tree through the closed poncho for a carrying handle, and first platoon set out again. Third squad had point. The two casualties from second squad were walking wounded.

The rest of the way back to the fire base, Bingham thought about the firefight. He thought about the beast that had tried to kill him. He thought about two men wounded and one dead. He thought about two marks of blood in the gully. He thought about how the VC had won that fight. He thought about Davis, nineteen years old forever. He wondered if he would wind up being twenty-one forever.

Copeland had radioed ahead for a medivac, and a helicopter was already in sight approaching the fire base by the time the platoon reached it. There was just enough time to transfer Davis from his poncho to a waiting body bag before the bird set down. The body was unceremoniously thrown aboard while the two walking wounded climbed aboard on their own power. Those two would be back in a few days. Davis was on his way home, home to a six-foot hole in the ground after not quite a month playing the big game called war.

CHAPTER SIX

Rumors, Miracles, Hope, Despair, and More Warm Bodies

There were whispers drifting about. The whispers were heard in the highest circles of the Allied Command in Saigon. They were heard in the lowest levels of the infantry companies. And they were heard in most levels in between. The whispers weren't necessarily believed in the highest levels, and most of the levels in between didn't care one way or the other. But the whispers were of vital concern to the men in the infantry companies.

The Marine Corps tried to keep the infantry battalions in the Third Marine Amphibious Force (III MAF) up to full combat strength under any circumstances, rumors or no. The attempts the Marine Corps made during the late months of 1967 to keep its battalions in Vietnam up to full combat strength served to convince many Marine grunts that the whispers were true.

"No scuttlebutt, man, I'm telling you this is the straight scoop," the privates and PFCs and lance corporals told each other. "Charlie's getting ready for something big. He wants to put an ass-kicking on us, put us so deep in the hurt locker we'll di-di-mau the fuck back to the World most ricky-tick and never come back here." Translated that meant, "The truth of the matter, and this is not a rumor, is the Vietcong are planning to make a determined attack against us and score so convincing a victory that we'll concede defeat and quit the war." Some of the corporals and sergeants and lieutenants and captains told each other similar things, though less dramatically. And, the higher in the ranks it went, the less colorful the language.

So while Alpha Company sat on its hill, guarding its perimeter and running countless security patrols and ambushes, several of the CH-46 Sea Knight helicopters that came in with supplies and mail also deposited additional troops to swell the company's roster to something closer to the numbers called for in the Marine infantry's Table of Organization. The first helicopter after the ambush to bring in troops came in on the second day after the ambush; it also brought back the two men from second squad who had been wounded in the ambush.

"Hey, man, you hear what happened to that newby got hit in the head?" the returned men asked.

"What newby, you mean Davis?" the men in first squad asked.

"Yeah, that's the one, Davis. The newby."

"What do you mean, what happened to him?" they demanded. "He got his fucking head blowed away, that's what happened."

"You mean you really didn't hear?"

"What is there to hear? I was there when it happened, he was wasted, he got his fucking head blowed away. I told you that's what happened," they said with a snarl.

"No, man, I mean after. Did you hear what happened to him after he got his head blowed away?"

The men of first squad looked at each other and wondered what kind of game the two returnees were playing. "They shipped his wasted ass back to the World and stuck it in a hole in the ground, that's what happened," they said to the two men from second squad.

The two men from second squad laughed. "They didn't hear what happened to that newby," they told each other.

"All right, we'll bite," one of the men of first squad said, "what the fuck happened to him? And this better be good." They thought they were being jerked around and were getting pissed off about it.

"They stuck his ass in a body bag . . . "

"No shit, Sherlock, we put his ass in that body bag right here." Their anger was growing and a few of them started clenching their fists.

"And then they flew him and us to Dong Ha," the two men from second squad continued as though they hadn't been interrupted. "Bodies was coming into Dong Ha from all over the fucking place, so they stacked the body bags alongside the airstrip to wait to be flown out of there."

"So tell me something new, fuckface."

"That fucking newby woke up."

"Bullshit!" Sergeant Melville screamed and grabbed the man from second squad who said that by his lapels and pulled him close. "You're fucking with me, dipshit. I put Davis's brains back in his skull where they fell out. No way you wake up from that."

The man from second squad paled and tried to pull back from

the sergeant. "That's no bullshit, it happened."

"He started yelling," the other man from second squad said, "but there wasn't nobody near to hear him."

"Straight scoop," said the man still trying to break free from the enraged sergeant.

"A C-47 came down to take the body bags," said the other one, "and the fuckers loading the bags into the plane almost dropped the one that newby was in when they picked it up and he kicked and yelled."

Melville eased his grip, and the man in his grasp jumped back out of reach. "That's no shit," he said, his color starting to come back. "That ain't no shit. We got it from a chief corpsman and he even let us see the newby for a minute."

"Man, he looked like he should of been dead," said the other man, "but he wasn't. I tell you he woke up."

Melville's breath came in snorts. When he calmed enough to speak clearly he told them, "I'm going to check this out. If you two asswipes are shitting me, *you're* going back to the World in body bags. I guaran-fucking-tee you that."

Captain Bernstein was the company commander of Alpha Company. One of his many duties, and the one he considered the most onerous, was writing letters to the families of his men who were killed, telling the families how their sons died bravely in the line of duty and assuring them their sons lives were not lost in vain—telling those parents, wives, sisters, and brothers their lost men had been well liked and were missed by their fellow Marines. These letters were supposed to be written at the earliest opportunity, but Captain Bernstein stalled on writing the letter to Dick Davis's parents, waiting to see if he would have to write more than one letter. He wasn't hoping he would have more KIAs in his company, it was just that he found writing two letters at once was less than twice as difficult as writing one letter now and another one later. Some company commanders assigned junior lieutenants to write the letters to families and merely signed them. Captain Bernstein was too honorable to do that; he was in charge, writing the letters was his responsibility and he would do it whether he wanted to or not. But Alpha Company hadn't had any more casualties since that ambush, and he couldn't delay writing the letter to Pfc. Dick Davis's parents any longer, so he took pen in hand and started to compose it.

Captain Bernstein was very startled when Sergeant Melville burst into his command bunker without being announced. The company gunnery sergeant was running after Melville, grabbing at him, booming in his best parade-ground voice for Melville to stop and go through proper channels if he wanted to see the skipper or he, the gunny, was going to personally see to it that Melville lost every one of his stripes. Melville ignored the gunny.

"Skipper, what's this shit I hear Davis woke up?"

Captain Bernstein blinked. He had never personally met Davis and wouldn't know him if he ran into him, but that damnable letter was heavy on his mind and he was willing to grasp at straws. "What'd you say? Let him go, Gunny."

"I said I just heard Davis ain't dead," Melville said, pulling his arm from the gunny's grip. "He woke up when they were putting him on a C-47 to fly him out of Dong Ha."

Captain Bernstein blinked again and shook his head to clear his ears. He didn't think he could have heard right. "Back up, Sergeant. Tell me from the top what happened."

So Melville told him about the two men from second squad and what they had just told him about Davis.

When Melville's story was finished Bernstein snapped to the company gunnery sergeant, "I want the Big Six on the horn right now so I can get to the bottom of this. If Davis is alive I should have been told about it." The "Big Six" was battalion headquarters. He didn't believe the story, but it was another excuse to delay writing that damned letter for a few more minutes. "If those men are pulling some sort of stunt, their asses are mine."

The company gunnery sergeant grinned and went to tell the radioman to raise battalion. He didn't grin because he believed the story and was glad to hear Davis wasn't dead. He grinned because he didn't believe the story and was looking forward to serving the asses of those two men from second squad to the skipper. To the gunny, these new men coming into his Marine Corps didn't have the right attitude, they wouldn't last a month in the spit-and-polish corps he had served in so well since the end of the Korean War. He wanted to publicly hang somebody as an example to the others.

It took half a day to do it, but a search was made through the proper channels and official word was finally sent back to Alpha Company. Davis was alive and expected to make it. The surgeons who had seen him were amazed that a man with so severe a head wound could possibly survive. The men of Alpha Company had mixed reactions to the news about Davis. Some of them didn't care one way or another, either because Davis had been a newby who they didn't know, or because they subscribed to the nihilistic philosophy that was succinctly summarized in the statement, "It don't mean nothing." The few men who had come to know Davis were glad for his sake. Some frightened men gained courage from the knowledge that it was possible that even the most abominable wounds didn't necessarily mean death. A few others, more perverse than the rest, imagined themselves waking up in a body bag and not being found in time. These men wanted to ask their buddies to make absolutely sure they were dead before they got put into body bags. "Put a bullet in my fucking head, or slit my goddam throat," was what they wanted to tell their buddies, but not many of them said anything.

The battalion S-1—the personnel officer—gave Captain Bernstein a half hearted apology for not notifying him earlier that Davis hadn't died from his wound. In the course of making his apology he managed, without saying so, to suggest that someone else had screwed up by not letting him, the S-1, know in the first place. Captain Bernstein was very glad that Davis was still alive. He was glad only partly because he was happy for Davis and for his family. Mostly he was glad because he didn't have to write that goddam letter.

The reinforcements that came along with the drifting rumors served to bolster the feeling that something big was in the air. Three of the new men went to first platoon's first squad, one to replace Davis and two to fill the other four vacancies in the squad's roster. They were Pfcs. Win Homer, a soft-spoken black Marine from Alabama and Chas Russell from the lake country of Minnesota. Both of them had been in the Corps for more than a year. The third man was Private Bill Rush, a Mohawk Indian from upstate New York who had been a Marine for little more than six months. Naturally, they called Rush "Chief." Marines always called Indians "Chief."

Sergeant Melville looked at his new men, then at his short-timer's calender, and then he looked at the rest of the men in his squad. He had to reorganize the squad now that it was twelve men instead of ten. He also was getting short—less than a month from rotating back to the World. So he went through the roster of the entire platoon, at the fire-team leaders in particular, to see who might be appointed squad leader to replace him if a new sergeant wasn't brought in when he left. It seemed more likely to him that Bingham would be the new squad leader than any of the platoon's other fire-team leaders—there were only three other corporals in the platoon and none of them knew his squad's men as well as Bingham did. Melville wanted to reorganize the squad with an eye to the future, so the transition would go as smoothly as possible. Not that it would likely matter. There would probably be more new men in the squad by the time he left it, and probably some of the men in it now would no longer be here. Bingham, or whoever the next squad leader turned out to be, would want to reorganize it differently. Sergeant Melville always tried to make contingencies to allow for probabilities, but usually based his plans on the assumption they wouldn't pan out. He reorganized his squad the way he wanted it to be for the present.

"Harte, you've fired one of these suckers before, haven't you?" he asked, holding out the M-79 grenade launcher.

Harte nodded. "Yeah. They made me put five rounds through one in ITR."

"Close enough. Trade weapons with me. You're my blooker-man now." Having the luxury of a grenadier in his squad also meant that Melville could give the squad's radio to someone else to carry when he didn't feel like humping it himself. Harte understood he'd have to hump the extra weight of the radio and looked distinctly unhappy about handing his rifle and magazines over to the sergeant and taking the shotgunlike M-79 from him. "Hey, it ain't so bad," Melville told him. "You get a .45 and a K-bar, too." Getting the K-bar, the legendary fighting knife that every Marine wanted, helped Harte make the transition. But not much.

"How about you, Bingham. You think you got your shit together enough to break in a newby?"

Bingham rolled his eyes toward his squad leader. "I'm not sure I've got my shit together enough to take care of myself, much less break in a newby."

"Good, I knew I could count on you. Keep Copley and West and I'll give you Rush."

Bingham groaned inwardly. He knew the battalion would soon go out on another operation and didn't want to have to babysit a new man. But he also knew he really didn't have any choice in the matter.

"Hank, you're such a goddam Johnny Reb I just got to give you a homeboy. Keep Emerson and take Homer."

"Which one's Homer?"

"The 'Bama boy." Melville nodded at Homer.

Longfellow looked. "Ah, shit, Herm. What you wanna do that to me for."

Melville grinned. "No choice. I give you Russell, he's such a damn Yankee he probably won't be able to understand your accent. Homer's from across the state line from you. Alabama and

Mississippi talk pretty much the same language, don't they? He'll be able to understand what you're saying when you mush-mouth at him."

Homer could understand all right. He could tell a rednecked bigot when he saw one. Melville didn't seem to be that way, and Homer wondered why the sergeant was assigning him to someone who hated blacks.

"Dago, that leaves Morse and Russell for you."

Rivera grunted. As long as Russell could follow orders and not collapse from heat exhaustion, Rivera didn't care how green he was.

Two days later helicopters came in to take Alpha Company on an assault near the demilitarized zone. Bingham remembered the beast that roared, fought within himself, and didn't quail outwardly.

CHAPTER SEVEN
Hi Ho, Hi Ho, It's Off To Town We Go

Something was brewing in the fall of sixty-seven, but nobody knew for sure what it was. Intelligence reports clearly showed that traffic was up on the Ho Chi Minh Trail and more intelligence reports were coming in from all over about heavy Vietcong activity and North Vietnamese movement throughout South Vietnam. Allied infantry battalions all over the country were spending more and more time on search and destroy, and search and clear operations. But the battalions weren't finding the massed enemy the intelligence reports said had to be out there. Many battalions found the same level of resistance they had encountered previously, some found more, and some found less. Over all, it averaged to pretty much what the Allies had encountered during the earlier seasons of that year.

Alpha Company's battalion was one that found next to no enemy activity—or evidence of any. They trudged the damnable jungle hills for two weeks without getting into a single firefight or losing any men to booby traps. It would have been a long dull walk in the sun if it hadn't been for the jungle canopy. As it was, it was just a long dull walk in the sweat.

First squad had the point again, and Melville put first fire team up front.

"Chief, keep your eyes peeled," Bingham told Rush. He had made himself the second man in the column with Copley behind him, and West maintaining contact with the machine-gun team to his rear. Melville and Harte came next, followed by the rest of the squad. Second platoon was somewhere over to the right with the company command group and mortar section, and third platoon was still farther to the right.

"I sleep with my spirit eyes open, Honcho," Rush replied and stepped out on the almost invisible game trail the platoon was following. Rush had grown up in New York's Adirondacks and from early childhood had spent as much time as he could either alone in the mountain forests, stalking and observing animals, or with his grandfather, who had gone to live in the forest when he retired from his cow tending job on a dairy farm. His grandfather had taught him all the forest lore he could absorb, and young Bill Rush was a very willing student. After puberty he had been able to hire himself out as a nature guide and, during the deer, bear, and bow seasons, as a hunting guide to make his pocket money. Seasons. That was a problem—he hadn't had work all year around. His age was another problem. Too many city dwellers who came into the mountains to hunt didn't want to believe that a teenage boy was a good enough woodsman to lead them to the best salt licks, water holes, and nesting areas—and not get them lost in the process. If he was going to make a living he had to go to work for someone else. So he had enlisted in the Marine Corps. It was a way of getting steady work without having to go to a farm or a town. He asked for and got infantry, figuring it would be closest to being a woodsman. The Marines would have put him in the infantry anyway, either that or communications if they could have come up with another Mohawk to team him with.

The tangled tropical jungles of Vietnam's northern I Corps were alien to him at first, but he applied his temperate forest woodsmanship to that alien forest, and in a matter of days was comfortable, if not fully at home, moving about in it. After a week Melville wanted him on the point as often as possible. Not because he was a newby, and therefore expendable, but because he was the best man in the squad—maybe in the platoon or even the entire company—at finding a way through the jungle underbrush and spotting booby traps before they were sprung. For his part, Rush liked being point man. Being point man implied he was trusted; he wouldn't let himself believe it was because he was expendable. He also felt more in control of his own destiny up front than he did back in the column.

The game trail Rush picked to follow was barely a thinning of the brush. It had seen little recent use and was rapidly being reclaimed by the jungle. Rush suspected most of the animals that normally used it had fled the sparsely settled area because of recent increased human activity. To him, increased human activity meant Main Force Vietcong units or North Vietnamese soldiers were in the area. This game trail would be safe to walk on, though. If any enemy had discovered it, they would have been using it themselves and the jungle wouldn't be reclaiming it.

Rush knew that game trails didn't just sprout randomly. Every one went from one specific place to another specific place. But neither were they planned. If an animal was in its favorite sleeping area, then wanted to go to the nearest or best waterhole, it picked the path of least resistance. If from the waterhole it wanted to go to a salt lick or a good feeding place, it again followed the path of least resistance. Many animals, mostly males, had territories and marked their boundaries regularly. They followed the path of least resistance around the boundary. When a path of least resistance was followed often enough it became a game trail and was more easily followed by other animals—and men. A territory eventually became crisscrossed with trails, and people often followed the game trails, turning them into footpaths. Over the centuries, some game trails could grow into superhighways.

So when the game trail he was following abruptly turned left, Rush stopped. The jungle was denser in that direction and was reclaiming the trail more rapidly after it made that turn. Why, Rush wondered, would the animals turn here, away from the path of least resistance? Something they wanted to avoid must be up ahead, he thought. He left the game trail and, more cautiously, followed the path of least resistance. Twenty-five meters farther he found what it was the animals were avoiding. He eased himself down to one knee and waited for Bingham to come up.

"Whatcha got?" Bingham asked in a low voice.

"Ville," Rush answered just as low.

They knelt, peering through breaks in the brush a few meters from the edge of a clearing. Ahead of them, most of the underbrush had been removed and only the tallest trees and some coconut palms were left standing. The nearest hootch canted at an angle less than four meters from the edge of the jungle brush. Bingham made a quick count and estimated that fifteen or sixteen bamboo-and-palm-frond hootches sat in the dappled shade under the trees. A flock of tiny, screaming children swarmed in play among the hootches and here and there women and old people squatted doing small work. The closest was an old woman sitting on her haunches, working over a wok set in front of the nearest hootch. Her back was to the Marines and she was engaged in shrill, sing-song conversation with several other adults scattered around the other hootches. Insects buzzed and chirruped in the background.

"Keep an eye on them," Bingham said in that low voice combat troops develop, a soft voice that is louder and clearer than a whisper, but that doesn't carry as far. He edged back into the forest. He sent Copley forward with his automatic rifle to keep watch with Rush. Farther back he found Melville waiting for information on why they had stopped.

"There's a ville forward, maybe fifteen or so hootches," he reported. "There's a bunch of baby-sans, some mama-sans and a few old papa-sans in it. I didn't see any young men."

Before Melville could reach for the radio Harte handed it to him. "Alpha One Six wants to know what the hangup is," Harte said. The call sign meant Alpha Company, First Platoon Commander. "Six" designated the commander's radio.

Melville took the radio and murmured into it. He followed the "I speak, you speak" rhythm of radio communications to report the unexpected hamlet they had found. "Aaron's on his way," he said after signing off.

The lieutenant joined them a few minutes later. His topographical map of the area was in his hand. "Either we're way off the map or this ville's new," he said. "Either way, there's nothing on it indicating permanent habitation. Let's take a look at what we got." He didn't sound concerned about the hamlet not being on his map; a lot of important structures and landmarks weren't noted on the maps the Americans used.

The lieutenant, the sergeant, the corporal, and the lieutenant's radioman joined Rush and Copley as close to the edge of the hamlet clearing as they thought they could get without being seen.

"What're they doing?" Copeland asked in a low voice as he knelt next to Rush.

Rush shrugged. "Kids are playing, folks're doing what they're doing. Nothing," he said.

"Anybody see you?"

"Nobody even looked this way."

While the others were watching the hamlet, Bingham looked up. As clear as the area looked after the jungle brush, he expected it to be open to the sky, but it wasn't. The interwoven branches of the spreading treetops formed an almost continuous cover over the hamlet. It would be almost impossible to spot from the air. He wondered how old Copeland's map was, and how much older its data was. The hamlet had the look of a new settlement about it, except for the one canting hootch, though he couldn't tell the exact age of any of the hootches. The only sounds were the continuing buzzing and chirruping of insects in the background, the voices of the old people, and the playful cries of the children.

Copeland and his radioman pulled back from the clearing so his soft voice speaking into his radio, reporting their find to company headquarters, wouldn't break the quiet. After a short discussion he called for Ives and the other two squad leaders to come up. Then they returned to silently watch the hamlet again until the others joined them to look over the scene. When he thought they had seen enough he pulled the platoon sergeant and all three squad leaders back into the forest and huddled for a conference. Bingham maintained his watch over the hamlet but edged close enough to hear the quiet voices in the huddle.

"The skipper gave his okay to check it out," Copeland said. "Ives, I want you to take third squad around and set up a blocking position on the far side of this ville. This is where I think we are, this is where I want you to establish the blocking position." He tapped his map twice with a fingernail.

Ives looked at the one inch to one kilometer map and realized if he tried to follow exactly Copeland's instructions he and third squad might get lost. He nodded and pointed through the hamlet. "About fifteen meters inside the brush on the other side, right over there," he said.

Copeland looked where his platoon sergeant was pointing. "You got it."

"Give me two zero. I'll call 'the kick is blocked' on the radio when we're in place."

"Got it." He looked at the other squad leaders and continued. "First and second squads will get in line right here, first on the right, second on the left. When third squad is in place we'll sweep through. Gather all the people into one place and search all the hootches. There's got to be a path leading into this ville from this side. Anybody see one?" They shook their heads. "All right, we'll find it while we're getting on line. Second squad, you put a fire team on that trail to cover our asses once we make our move. After we've secured this place the skipper and second platoon will join us, and the Kit Carson scout will interrogate the people." He paused to think through the plan again; it sounded as good the second time through. He then asked, "Any questions?"

No one asked "why." "Why" wasn't an allowable question. The only questions that could be asked were to clarify the orders. The orders were clear; they even understood why second platoon wouldn't join them until after they secured the hamlet. There were no questions.

"Then let's do this thing."

The huddle broke and Melville came to Bingham while the others disappeared back into the forest. "You hear any of that?" the sergeant asked.

"All of it."

"Good. Pull your team back into the bush, then move over thirty meters. You've got our right flank." Melville rose to get the rest of his squad.

"Herm?" Bingham stopped him.

"Yeah?"

"Nobody looked this way."

Melville followed Bingham's look at the people under the clearing trees. "So? They don't know we're here."

"That's not what I mean." Bingham hesitated before continuing. "I don't mean nobody glanced in this direction. I mean they didn't even turn their heads in this general direction. Everywhere but this way. It's like they're deliberately avoiding looking this way. And the baby-sans are playing farther away from us now."

Melville considered the implications of that, that the villagers knew they were there, then said, "Maybe they're just minding their own business and hoping we'll go away." He turned to leave and added, "I'll tell Aaron."

It took nearly all of the twenty minutes Ives had said he'd need to get his blocking squad into position for the rest of the platoon to get in line to sweep the hamlet. There was a path leading into the clearing from the near side and a fire team lay in ambush on it. The last few of the twenty minutes waiting after Copeland got the radio message, "The kick is blocked," seemed to take a couple of hours.

Then Copeland shouted an order and twenty Marines rose to their feet and stepped into the open. Like silent green forest giants, they advanced on the people in the hamlet.

The children continued to run about playing and the adults ignored the western giants advancing on them until a Marine reached the squatting woman closest to him. The Marine reached down with one hand and gently lifted her by the arm, then all movement and talk stopped. "Come on, mama-san," he said as friendly as he could, "we're going to powwow nice and easy."

The old woman's face showed no emotion when she looked up at the Marine. He wasn't sure her face could show emotion; it looked to him like a mask carved from mahogany by a practiced but unskilled hand. The other people in the hamlet stood and silently faced the approaching Marines until they were swept along by the moving line of green warriors. There were twenty adults gathered in what was now a circle of Marines. Women of all ages and old men. There were no men of military age. Eleven children from a baby suckling at its mother's breast to a girl in her early teens completed the group.

"I wonder where everybody else is," Copeland asked, looking around at the fifteen huts. "That many hootches, there must be sixty, a hundred people living here." He used body language to tell the villagers to sit on the ground. One fire team was assigned to watch them while the rest of the Marines searched the one-room hootches. The lieutenant informed the company commander they had the hamlet secured and were commencing their search. He repeated the map coordinates on the radio and was told the command group and second platoon would be there in about a half hour.

The hamlet, cleared of most ground brush and saplings, gave an appearance of age. So did the soundly built hootches, but the construction turned out to be mostly new and the furnishings more spartan than would be expected of an established hamlet.

"Search? What the fuck we supposed to search, Honcho?" Copley complained when he and Bingham entered the first hut.

"Everything," Bingham answered. "How the fuck am I supposed to know? You're the one who's searched people's hootches before. You tell me what we're supposed to search."

"Shit. I ain't never seen no place people lived this empty before."

Bingham examined the lone room of the house by the dim light that came through the doorway behind them. The ceiling was barely high enough for Bingham to stand erect. A woven mat lay rolled up against the far wall. In one corner sat a two-foot-high covered urn. A small table with religious objects and two faded, framed photographs on it stood next to the door. There was a small, open chest against one side wall. A conical straw hat hung from the center rafter. The room was otherwise barren. The room's bare dirt floor was packed, but hadn't been in use long enough to become rock-hard.

"Unroll that mat, I guess," Bingham said. "I'll look in the chest." Copley grunted and knocked the mat over. Bingham tentatively poked through the chest. The chest was galvanized metal sheet with leather straps and hinges; it was obviously hand-made. In it were two sets of white clothes in the style the Americans called pajamas and one pair of black pajama pants. The walls of the chest were thin, there were no hidden compartments in it.

"Nothing in here," Copley said, rolling the mat back up. He propped it against the wall where he had found it. "We got to search them, we don't got to fuck them over," he added when he saw Bingham watch him return the mat to its place. He went to the urn and lifted its cover. "Rice." He unsheathed his knife and probed into the rice.

"Check it all the way to the bottom," Bingham said. Copley shrugged and shoved his knife and hand as far into the urn as they'd go, almost to the bottom. He didn't feel anything. One of the photos on the shrine table was old and faded, cracking in places. It showed two young people, a man and a woman, in what must have been ceremonial dress. Bingham guessed it was a wedding picture, it had the same air about it as his own parents' formal wedding portrait. The other photograph wasn't as old. It showed a young man, not the one in the other photo, in an army uniform, standing at attention, and holding a bolt-action rifle at a stiff port arms. Colored slips of paper with Nom, the old Vietnamese writing that looked like Chinese ideographs, on them surrounded a crude print of a Buddha. There were a few other small objects on the table; they meant nothing to the American. The table did not have a false bottom.

While Bingham examined the contents of the table and checked its bottom, Copley removed the conical hat from the peg it hung from and felt along the rafter. There was nothing hidden on it. They left that hootch and went on to the next one. It was just as devoid of possessions and contraband.

"They hate us," Rush said when he and West finished searching their last hootch and were standing in front of it looking at the small knot of people gathered nearby.

"How can you tell?" West asked, squinting at the women and old men who watched them. The children were hiding behind the adults.

"Look at them, look at their eyes. Like that old man in the gray shirt." He pointed with his chin toward a gnarled old man wearing rolled-up black shorts and a white shirt that age had turned gray. A goiter swelled the old man's neck. "Back where I come from, the white people have a saying, 'if looks could kill.' Well, if that old man's looks could kill, we'd all be dead."

West peered at the old man. "You sure?" he asked. "He ain't giving us no look, he's just squatting there waiting for us to di-di and hoping we don't fuck him over too bad."

"The eyes are the windows to the soul, Ben. I look in his eyes and I see hate in his soul."

West shook his head and looked away from the old man. "Chief, I don't know how you think you see anything in that papa-san's eyes. His face looks like someone took a chipped chisel to a chunk of rotten sandstone. He don't got no expression."

"It's there."

They were interrupted by the arrival of second platoon with the company command group. Captain Bernstein and the lieutenant leading second platoon conferred briefly with Copeland, then second platoon broke into squads and went back into the forest to set a defensive perimeter around the hamlet.

The Kit Carson scout was a former Vietcong who had switched to the government side. He immediately separated himself from the command group and addressed the villagers. One old man replied, and the Kit Carson scout squatted in front of him, their knees almost touching. The Kit Carson pulled a pack of Salems from his shirt pocket and offered one to the old man, then lit both cigarettes with an engraved Zippo lighter. They held their cigarettes pinched between forefinger and thumb so their palms cupped their chins when they took a drag. They smoked quietly for a moment, then the Kit Carson said something that set the old man off on a long monologue that was incomprehensible to the Americans. He gestured wildly, frequently pointing off to the southwest and clutching his hands like he was firing an automatic weapon. The Kit Carson nodded, talked, and gestured in reply.

When the old man finished his tale, the scout jumped to his feet and made a hurried inspection of several hootches. Then he returned to the people, held out his hand and said, "*Can couc.*" He wanted to see their government ID cards. They all passed them over. He examined the cards, copied down the names in a dog-eared notebook, and returned the IDs. Then he reported to the captain.

"He say they come here from to southwest. He say boo-coo fight there. Vee Cee come, numba ten, take food, take young men, burn down hous'a, kill people, rape women. He say ARVN come, take food, take young men, burn down hous'a, kill people, rape women. He say America come, destroy food, take young men, burn down hous'a, kill people." He grinned before continuing, "He say America Ma-deen numba one. America Ma-deen not rape women."

Bernstein smiled weakly at the left-handed compliment. He knew in Vietnam anything left-handed was an insult. The left hand was used to clean the anus after defecation; it was the contaminated hand. He had noticed a collective shudder go through the women and old people squatting scrunched closer together when the scout mentioned the VC. "Where did they come from?" he asked.

The Kit Carson shrugged. "Maybe A Shau, maybe somewhere else."

"How long have they been here?"

"Maybe one month, maybe two. They stop here because not see fight here."

"Where are their young men?"

"Vee Cee take, make Vee Cee. ARVN take, make ARVN." Modern press gangs at work. Both sides took men from the same villages as draftees in their war so men who grew up playing together and, as adults, farmed together, sometimes found themselves killing each other.

"Have they seen any Vee Cee here?"

The scout shook his head vigorously. "He say they not stay here there be Vee Cee here."

Bernstein stared at the villagers for a moment, then looked around at the fifteen hootches. "Where are the rest of them?"

"They not got farm. Other people in forest, find food."

The captain thought for a moment before asking his final question. "Do you believe him."

The Kit Carson looked at the villagers. A soft sigh escaped from him. "I think," he said slowly, "he tell truth. I think they want us di-di, they want America di-di, want Vee Cee di-di. I think they want be leave alone so they can farm and live good life. I think that be truth." He nodded at his last sentence.

Bernstein stared hard at his Kit Carson scout for a moment, trying for the twentieth time to decide if he could trust this little man who had recently been fighting on the other side. Finally he decided. "All right, Alpha Company, let's move it out," he called. "Second platoon straight ahead, first platoon, you come with the command group. Saddle up and let's do this thing."

There was minimal grumbling as the men of the two platoons assembled themselves into marching order and moved back into the forest. Their diversion had been brief and it was over. Second squad had the point for the command group; first squad brought up the rear.

CHAPTER EIGHT
People Come and People Go

Alpha Company's discovery of the new, previously unknown, hamlet was the high point of the operation. It wasn't much of a high point, and a decision was made on the highest levels of command to pick the battalion up and deposit it someplace else. Someplace where higher command hoped the hunting would be better. So the companies of the battalion trudged through the forest to an open area—a hilltop that was open thanks to a flight of B-52s that had dropped tens of tons worth of thousand-pound bombs on and around when intelligence reported several VC battalions and a high level VC command post on it. Marine recon teams that searched the hilltop and its environs afterward failed to find evidence of the purported VC battalions, or any other enemy. If nothing else had been accomplished by the bombing, at least the Marines had an instant helicopter landing zone in the jungle out of it.

They got to the new area of operations and a helicopter came in later in the day with some supplies. It also had good news for one member of first squad, bad news for another, and a disappointment for a third man.

"Herm up," Ives passed the word. "Hank front and center."

Melville's heart beat a little faster at the order. His time was so short, he was beginning to taste hamburgers and see California girls in his sleep. He knew he was going to be pulled out of the field any day and put on a Freedom Bird back to the World, a one-way flight home.

Longfellow knew how short Melville was and every time the squad leader was called to the platoon CP he wondered if he'd ever see him again. Longfellow looked at Melville quizzically, wondering why he had been called front and center. If Melville was leaving, they weren't going to make him squad leader—Bingham had more rank; he'd get it.

Ives was stirring a packet of cocoa mix, some sugar, and instant creamer into a canteen-cup of hot water when the two men arrived at the platoon CP. Copeland was rooting through his pack. The platoon's radioman sat nearby with a knowing smile on his face and a stranger sat a few feet behind him. A blank sheet of paper lay on Copeland's crossed leg.

"I've been saving this for a special occasion," Copeland said, not looking up, still rummaging through his pack.

Ives looked at the two while continuing to stir his cocoa. "Hank's been a fire-team leader for what, two months now?" he asked.

Melville nodded. "Yeah, something like that."

"You satisfied with his performance?"

Longfellow looked baffled.

Melville looked at him. He was beginning to realize why they had been called to the CP. "I guess so," he said. Now he knew it wasn't yet time for him to go home, and he was disappointed at that, but he grinned anyway. "At least he ain't got nobody wasted for no reason."

Ives nodded wisely. "Thought you'd say something like that. Aaron's got something for him."

"Here it is," the lieutenant said, he finished his rummaging and pulled an unopened bottle of Canadian Club from his pack. "Sorry we can't do this up right, Hank. We'll have a proper ceremony when we get out of the field." He turned over the sheet of paper on his thigh and started reading. "To all who shall see these presents, greeting: Know ye that reposing special trust and confidence in the fidelity and abilities of Henry W. Longfellow 2013242/0311, I do appoint him a corporal in the United States Marine Corps to rank as such from . . . " He read the promotion warrant all the way through while Ives, Melville, and the radioman grinned at the newly promoted corporal. After reading the battalion commander's signature at the bottom he handed the warrant over with his left hand and offered his right to be shaken. "Congratulations, Corporal."

Slightly dazed and with his jaw working, Longfellow accepted the sheet of paper and shook the hand. "Thank you, sir," he stammered.

Copeland cracked open the bottle. "Even though we're in the field, I think this deserves a drink. Get out your canteen cup."

"Just because we're in the field, don't think we're skipping all of the ceremony," Ives said. "There's one part that isn't going to wait." He turned away and called softly, "First platoon, all NCOs up."

Bingham joined the small CP group. So did Sergeant Butterfield and Corporal Gershwin, the other two squad leaders, and the corporals from their squads. Second and third squads each had two corporals. "What's up, Honcho?" they asked.

"Hank just got his second stripe," Ives said, grinning. "I'm first." He stood next to Longfellow and pounded him twice in the left biceps with his fist. "Herm's got next shot," he said and stepped aside.

"Not too hard, people," Copeland said. "He may need his arms again before we're through with this operation."

"You got it, Aaron, not too hard," they said. "No problem, Aaron. He'll be able to feed himself again in a few days."

They went through the informal ritual of "pinning on the stripes." Every enlisted man in the Marine Corps, of equal or greater rank, had the right to slug a newly promoted man on the shoulder one time for each stripe the rank held. Some considered pinning on the stripes to be an obligation rather than a right.

Longfellow grinned and tried not to flinch from the blows. "Don't tell anybody from the other platoons," he said. The rite of pinning on the stripes expired an undefined but finite number of days following the promotion; anyone who didn't get him by then wouldn't be allowed to.

"My turn." The stranger rose from where he sat behind the radioman when the others finished and walked to Longfellow to pin on his stripes.

"Who the fuck are you?" Longfellow objected. The Marines didn't wear rank insignia in the field and he had no idea if this man was a private, an officer or something in between. If the stranger was an NCO he had the right, but not unless Longfellow knew who he was.

"He can do it, Hank," Ives said and nodded to the stranger, who hit Longfellow's shoulder twice with only a token amount of force.

"This is Corporal Chuck Peale," Copeland introduced the stranger to his NCOs. "He's a newby with us, but he's been here before. He just got here from Schwab. Before that he spent a couple months in JP getting fixed up from some—what was it, shrapnel?"—he looked at Peale for confirmation—"he picked up somewhere in Quang Nam Province."

The others looked at Peale for a moment, digesting this information. This newby had gone to a hospital in Japan after being wounded on an operation in central I Corps and then to the Marine installation called Camp Schwab on Okinawa before joining them.

Butterfield was the first to speak. "Who were you with before?" he asked.

"Three One," Peale answered. He knew what they were all wondering—why hadn't he returned to the Third Battalion, First Marines if that was the unit he was with before returning in-country? He didn't wait for them to ask it. "I wanted to go back to Three One but at Da Nang they told me I was going where men were needed most, and Three One didn't need men as badly as this battalion does."

That seemed to satisfy them, for the moment at least, but they didn't want anyone in their platoon who wasn't wanted by his previous unit. A man who wasn't wanted by the men he had been with could be too dangerous to the men he joined.

They asked other questions, easier ones. "How much time you got in grade?" "Were you a fire-team leader when you got hit?" "How much longer on your tour?" Later would come the personal, non-professional questions like, "Where are you from?" and "How old are you?" and "You got a steady girl back in the World?"

Mostly, they were glad to have him aboard—experienced men were always welcome—but his arrival was bad news for one man in the platoon.

"Three of this platoon's fire teams are led by lance corporals," Copeland said. "Chuck's got the rank, that means he bumps one of them. I had the Top check it out. Sorry, Herm, I know Dago's done a good job, but he's the junior lance-corporal fire-team leader in the platoon. Give Chuck his fire team."

"Ah, shit, Aaron," Melville said. "That isn't fair. Dago's a numba-one fire-team leader. He deserves to keep it." Calling Rivera number one meant he was a very good fire-team leader.

"I know it's not fair," Copeland said. "But Chuck's got the rank so someone's going to get bumped. I've got three good lance corporals doing good jobs as acting corporals and one of them has to get bumped. Dago's junior to the other two, and besides, if one squad has more corporals than the other two it should be first squad. Chuck gets Dago's fire team and that's that." He looked at the sergeant for a moment then added, "Anyway, you're leaving soon. Unless another sergeant joins us then, one of the corporals in this platoon will take over your squad. Dago can get a fire team back then."

Peale felt uncomfortable. There was a special comradery among combat troops that didn't exist anywhere else. It was difficult for a stranger to be accepted into the fellowship; he remained an unknown—an outsider—until he proved himself under fire. A fire team, the most basic infantry unit, was an even tighter group. Sometimes the men in a fire team became closer than brothers; sometimes they almost became appendages of one another. A fire-team leader could be the big brother of his men, the one who took care of them. A new man coming in and kicking big brother out of his position could have big trouble because of that. Men could die because a stranger supplanted that big brother.

Rivera didn't like losing his fire team. "How come, Herm? Didn't I do a good job? What the fuck am I getting busted for? When did I fuck up?" His eyes narrowed and his nostrils flared.

"You didn't fuck up, Dago," Melville said patiently. "The only thing is, Chuck's got the goddam rank. I can't put him in one of the other teams, and I can't put him under you. He's got to be a fire-team leader." The patience in his voice was feigned; he resented having to be the one to explain to a man who was doing a good job why he was losing that job.

"Why not put him in second or third squad?"

"Because if one squad has three corporals and the other two have two, it's got to be first squad, that's why."

Rivera jerked his head from side to side as though searching for an escape route. "But the other squads had two corporals when we only had one."

Melville shook his head. "I don't make the rules," he said, "I only do what they tell me to. Listen, you want the blooker? I'll make you blookerman, how's that sound?"

"No I don't want the goddam blooker," Rivera snapped. He didn't want to have to carry the squad's radio, and he knew there was no way he could remain a fire-team leader. "Put me in Hank's fire team, I can deal with that."

"You got it." It was a solution. Not the best solution, and he'd have to keep an eye on Rivera for a while to make sure he didn't resent the situation so much he'd get someone hurt, but it was a solution. "I'm going to di-di out of here most ricky-tick," he said, trying to mollify Rivera. "When I do, Bingham's probably going to be made squad leader. You'll get a fire team again then."

Rivera looked at him solemnly. "Yeah? What happens if they bring in a new sergeant instead of giving it to Bingham? What happens if they bring in a new corporal when you leave? I don't get a fire team then, do I. Man, I'm being fucked out of my second stripe."

All Melville could say was, "Don't worry about that shit, it won't happen that way." Rivera hadn't been a lance corporal long enough to be up for promotion, even though there were corporals in the platoon who had been in the Corps for less time than he had. For some reason that Melville had never heard, Rivera hadn't been promoted to PFC until he had been in for a year and a half, and it had taken him nearly two years longer for him to reach lance corporal. Promotions had come very slowly for the Latin—slower than was normal for the peace-time infantry Melville had enlisted into nearly four years earlier.

So it was settled, but nobody in the squad was happy with it.

The next week brought more of the same uneventful patrolling, except no one found any unknown hamlets. The operation was turning into a real bust and the battalion commander was getting upset. Other battalions were making contact and scoring victories against the enemy, but not his. Hell, he didn't even have any men wounded by booby traps. This was no way for him to punch his ticket on the way to a hoped-for promotion to full colonel. He started agitating for his battalion to be lifted to a third area, to one where other units had recent contact with the VC. He was told to stay where he was, intelligence assured the division's commanding general there were North Vietnamese around there somewhere. It was his battalion's job to find them.

When Melville's time came it came abruptly, minutes after Alpha Company had stopped to settle into its night defensive position.

"Herm up," Ives said. "Tell him to bring Bingham."

The word was passed from man to man to man along the perimeter until it reached first squad. Melville groaned and kneaded his stiff back with one hand. "Come on, let's go see what the honcho wants." He'd had false alarms before and didn't want to get his hopes up that he was leaving.

They reached the platoon CP and hunkered down in front of Copeland and Ives. "Wha'zup?" Melville asked.

"Saddle up, Herm, you're moving out," Copeland told him.

Melville grimaced. "Shit. We pulled ambush last night, let somebody else do it. I'm too goddam short for this kind of shit." He spat into the mulch covering the hillside.

"You're right, Herm, you are too short for that kind of shit,"

Copeland said and smiled. "Someone else is pulling ambush tonight. There's a supply bird coming in in a few minutes. You're going out on it."

"Goddam fucking ambush," Melville swore. "I only got less than two weeks before I catch that old Freedom Bird and head back to the fucking World and you say I got to—" He stopped and a wide grin split his bearded face. "You say I'm going out on that supply bird, Aaron?"

"That's what I said, Herm." Copeland was still smiling. "You think Bingham here can handle your job now that you're gone?"

Melville spat again. "Shee-it, man. My man Bingham's numba fucking one gyrene honcho."

"You had best get saddled up," Ives growled, "because I want your scuzzy ass off my hill in five minutes." His tone was harsh, but his eyes were smiling—smiling as much as they could considering where he was.

Melville worked his jaw from side to side, trying to mold his face into a civilian expression. "And I won't never darken your doorstep no more," he finally said, and a fresh grin split his face. He left to get his pack and was back well before the supply helicopter, a grasshopper-shaped UH-34, touched down. He helped unload it, then threw his pack in and boarded it. He hung out the door waving at the men he was leaving behind until the helicopter banked away and he couldn't see the hill anymore.

It had taken George Bingham more than two years to reach the war he had enlisted to fight. After two months in the combat zone, he was a squad leader and found eleven men's lives depending on his leadership.

First things first, though, he thought. "Aaron," he said. "It okay with you if I give Rivera a fire team again?"

"Were you satisfied with the job he did for Herm before Chuck arrived?"

"Yes."

"Do it."

Rivera's reaction surprised Bingham. "Big deal," he said. "It's only until another corporal shows up."

"I'll talk to Aaron, see if he can do anything about getting you your second stripe. You won't get bumped again if you get it."

"Don't bother. Somebody got a hard-on for this Chicano. I ain't getting no promotion to corporal."

That night, first squad pulled an ambush patrol. It was time for Bingham to take charge.

CHAPTER NINE
Same Man, Same Place, New Job

Everybody in the squad respected Bingham—except Peale, who knew little more than his name and his face, and he didn't count because he was a newby anyway—so it wasn't as difficult as it might have been for him to take charge. It was easier than it had been taking over a fire team when he'd first joined the squad. Now everybody, except Peale, knew he could be counted on when the shooting started. He hadn't gotten anybody killed yet. And it helped that for his first week as squad leader Alpha Company didn't run into any kind of real combat, just the occasional sniper and the ever-present risk of booby traps. Bingham didn't ever have to tell anybody to do something that might get him killed during that first week. But it was really the first ambush patrol that established him as the squad leader.

Bingham had Longfellow, Peale, and Rivera join him at the platoon CP for the ambush briefing. Copeland was busy on the radio but kept half an ear on the briefing.

"This is where we're at," Ives said. "Second platoon's over there fifty meters, and third's a hundred in that direction. Company CP's with second." He held his map spread open on the ground with his left hand, and his right held a ballpoint pen with its point retracted. With each direction, he pointed out the map location with the pen and then gestured, pointing with it, showing Bingham and his fire-team leaders where everybody was both on the map and in the forest. Where they were was on a tree-covered, triangular hilltop. Each of the three platoons held one straight side and one corner of the hill. Mostly they circled the crown some twenty meters down from the top. "Here's where we think Charlie is." Ives tapped another point on the map half a grid square away and pointed through the trees past the defensive line formed by the other two squads of first platoon. "Recon reported several speed trails running through this area." He brushed the blunt point of the pen over an area of the map and swept his arm beyond the hill. "One of them goes not far below this hill." He traced a line on the map. A speed trail was a large, well-tended trail along which men and supplies could be moved rapidly.

"Now, Mister Charles knows we're in this area, and he might want to send some people around to try and fuck us over," Ives continued, this time with the rationale for the night's ambush. "If he's sending snipers in, or a larger unit for an assault, we think they'll probably use these speed trails. So I want you to go out there to this nearest speed trail and put anybody using it into the hurt locker." He looked the four men in the eye, then returned his attention to the map. "Right about here—" He touched the map with the point of his pen, then pointed into the trees. "—about three hundred meters in that direction, the speed trail makes a sharp turn. You're going to set up there, where you can cover the trail in both directions."

He looked at them again. Longfellow stared into the jungle, as if he were Clark Kent, with X-ray eyes that could see through the intervening trees and brush to the speed trail and examine it, picking out the best approach route and ambush location. Peale tried to make his face expressionless, but the nervousness showed through his still hospital-pale skin. Rivera was stoic, his eyes following Ives's pen, and looking where it pointed. Bingham, chewing on his lip, brow furrowed, was obviously working hard at absorbing every bit of information he could. He looked as if he wanted to say something, so Ives started talking again; he'd let Bingham know when it was time to ask his questions.

"I want you to go out in fifteen minutes. That'll give you three-quarters of an hour's worth of daylight to get to your objective and set in. No packs. Cartridge belts, rifles, ponchos, ammo, and grenades. I'll give you some star clusters. Take a prick-twenty." The star clusters were hand-fired illumination flares and the ponchos were to carry any casualties back to the hill, though that was understood rather than said. "No chow—eat fast before you leave. Your call sign is 'Whippoorwill,' we're 'Birdhouse One.' Make a sitrep every half hour." He glanced at them all again, then settled his eyes on Bingham. "Any questions?"

"You say Charlie's a half klick over here"—Bingham pointed on the map—"and our ambush site is three hundred meters from here."

"Right."

"That puts us closer to where Charlie is than to where the company is." Bingham looked at Ives. "If we get in deep shit, Charlie's closer to us than you are."

"If anybody too big for you to handle comes along, let him go," Ives said patiently. "Don't pick any fights you can't win." He paused, aware that Copeland was no longer talking on the radio; he wanted what he said next to be exactly what the lieutenant would want to hear and for it to be the right thing to say. "Use your radio; report all activity on that trail, whether you intercept it or let it by. Understand?" He waited until Bingham nodded. "Anyway," he continued, wanting to calm the fears of the men he was sending out, "that speed trail you'll be on doesn't go to where we think Charlie's base camp is. It runs closer to us than it does to him. If you get into trouble and need help, we can get to you first."

Bingham looked back at Ives for several seconds; he was also aware of Copeland sitting back, listening. "If we make contact do we move?" he asked.

"Negative." He shook his head. "You stay in place until I tell you to come back in after dawn. That jungle out there is pretty dense. You hit some snipers diddy-bopping along the trail, Charlie's not going to know back in his base where your fire's coming from. Shit, Charlie might not even hear it." He shook his head again. He knew it was a lie the Vietcong might not hear the gunfire, and he knew Bingham knew it as well. But the jungle foliage's muffling effect would mask the location, they both knew. "If you need help, we'll get it to you. Remember, there's a whole company sitting on this hill."

"Uh-huh," Bingham said. Sure there's a whole company on this hill, he thought. But there's no way they can get to us in time if we need them.

Ives glanced at his watch. "You've got thirteen minutes. Any more questions?" There were none. "Team leaders, get your people chowed down and saddled up. Bingham, I'll give you everything you need."

Longfellow, Peale, and Rivera rose to their feet and shuffled back to the squad. Bingham stayed with Ives to accept the star clusters and radio. He looked hard at the other man and briefly at the lieutenant. He knew this ambush held more potential danger than any other mission he'd been on so far, and if things went wrong, it could easily get his squad wiped out. He wished Melville was still there and running the ambush, or at least there to advise him. He thought about it and knew how Melville would have reacted to these orders and what he would have told him. "Sandbagging job," the sergeant would say. "You go out there, and if somebody comes by you can take, you take him. Somebody comes along you can't take, you let him go by. Get on the horn and report it. Stay down, keep your ass covered, and come back in in the morning, that's all. No sweat." But Bingham didn't know what Melville would have thought about it.

He stuffed the five star clusters Ives gave him into his pockets and slung the radio over one shoulder by its packboard straps. "Whippoorwill and Birdhouse One," he said. "Sitrep every half hour."

"Starting when you get into position."

"Right." Without another word, Bingham turned back to his squad.

Cold C rations bolted so quickly there was hardly time to taste them sat heavy in their stomachs when the twelve men of first squad, traveling light, but heavily armed, descended the hill to the jumbled geology of the land below. Rush held the point; Peale's fire team brought up the rear. Bingham felt uncomfortable in his position between the lead and middle fire teams, the squad leader's position. Harte followed him by a few paces, grumbling under his breath about the twenty-pound weight of the radio on his back, then became as silent as the others.

Time was short and the hillside should be safe, so Rush didn't lead the squad on a route that would provide cover for stealthy movement, he simply chose one that would be fast and quiet. At the foot of the hill he looked back at Bingham and was gestured onward. He continued on a quick, quiet route until he came across a well-beaten path four feet wide and stopped. Bingham joined him. Together they looked both ways along the trail. In one direction it continued straight until it disappeared into the dimness of the late afternoon jungle. In the other, the direction they were going to follow, it bent a hundred meters away. Bingham looked at the bend and thought it was less than three hundred meters from Alpha Company's hill.

"Let's cross and parallel it," Bingham said close to Rush's ear.

Rush nodded and hurried to the forest cover on the trail's other side. Bingham waited until he was in the trees, then sent Copley across. He stayed where he was, sending each man to the other side as soon as the previous man disappeared into the trees and brush. When all the others were on the other side he stepped onto the trail and rearranged the foliage his men had gone through to hide the signs of their passage. Then he slipped into the trees in a different spot, careful not to disturb the brush he passed through.

The squad was in a line waiting for him. He took his place and signaled Rush to lead on. The going was slower here; they needed more than simply quiet movement now. The enemy could pass by on the trail at any time, and the Marines couldn't afford to be spotted.

When Rush came to the bend in the speed trail, he stopped and waited for the squad leader to join him. Seventy-five meters farther was another turn in the trail, a sharper bend than the first one. Bingham nodded at Rush and pointed out their direction with another nod. Rush nodded back and continued only a few meters from the trail.

The second bend was almost ninety degrees; it was their ambush site. Working as quickly as he could, using only touches and gestures, Bingham positioned his men. Peale's fire team, the only one with four men in it, went back along the trail leg the squad had followed in while the remaining two fire teams were along the other. Rush and Copley were at the end of the line, the first men the VC would pass if or when they came along. Bingham and Harte were at the apex of the bend where they could easily watch in both directions.

Harte eased the packboard off his back and set it so the radio was in easy reach. Bingham took the handset, clicked the speak lever twice to alert the CP to expect a message, then said into it, "Birdhouse One, Birdhouse One. Whippoorwill in place, over."

"Roger, Whippoorwill. Birdhouse One out," came the instant reply. Now all they had to do was wait.

And then it was night. While they were settling in, the cries of forest birds became a cacophony as the day birds settled on their roosts for the night and woke the night birds who screamed back. Somewhere in the distance a dog barked, then fell silent as the light over the ambush site faded from perennial twilight to full black in a matter of minutes.

"Everyone awake for the first hour," Bingham told each pair of men as he positioned them and checked their lines of sight. "Then a fifty percent watch until 0430. Everybody awake again then. Understand?" Everybody said they understood. The two-man positions were close enough to each other that a man in one could stretch out and touch a man in the next, but far enough apart that there was not too much danger of making noise in doing so. Bingham strung a cord from one end of the L-shaped ambush line to the other. A jerk on the cord was the signal if anyone came along the trail.

An hour after sunset Bingham said into Harte's ear, "Cop some

Zs if you want to, I'm going to stay awake for a while." He felt more than he heard Harte's murmured reply, and Harte lay down. Bingham sat upright with his legs crossed. For his own part, Bingham was afraid to fall asleep. He looked through the brush bordering the speed trail and was afraid because he couldn't make out where it was. He knew he was less than ten feet away from the four-foot-wide path the Vietcong were almost certain to come along during the night, but there was no way he could tell by looking that he was even facing in the direction of the trail. So many stars sparkled far above the trees that the sky looked more gray than it did speckled black, but under the trees men were blind from lack of light.

Bingham stared gape-eyed at the blackness in which nothing was distinguishable and thought about his responsibilities. The responsibility for the ambush and for the lives of every man in the squad were his. If, when, someone walked into the ambush, it was his responsibility to decide whether that someone was to be taken or was too big to fight—someone to let by. The night was so deep he had to tell by sound, not sight, how many enemy there were, and decide whether or not to fire. He knew by the time enough of them came past for him to discern if there were few enough, they'd be too far through the killing zone for him to open up and expect to get them all. Yet if there were few enough, he had to give the order that would trigger the ambush, that would kill those enemy soldiers before they could harm other Marines.

The knowledge of his responsibilities was the most frightening of all the things he was afraid of, and the cause of all his other fears. At the prescribed half-hour intervals he double-clicked the speak lever on the side of his radio's handset and murmured, "Birdhouse One, Whippoorwill. Situation as before, over," and listened to the "Whippoorwill, Birdhouse One. Roger out," that was the instant reply.

Eventually, long beyond the two hours after which he should have woken Harte to take a turn on the watch, fatigue overcame his fear and Bingham woke his grenadier so he could sleep himself. "Wake me in an hour and a half," he said when Harte sat up, and he handed over his wristwatch with its luminous dial. He made a last radio report before giving the handset to Harte. Then he lay down and put his helmeted head on his forearm and closed his eyes. Slowly, he drifted into a light sleep, one that would ease his fatigue but not drain it from his body.

Harte put the watch on the inside of his wrist and peered closely at its face so he'd know when to wake his squad leader. The hour and a half started off with no problems, but the longer it stretched the more tiring it became. There were no tugs on the cord, and he couldn't see anything except the slowly creeping hands on the watch face. He managed to make it to his first radio check before becoming nearly mind-numbingly bored. By the time he made his second radio check, he was looking at the watch nearly every minute. During the last half hour he was looking at it constantly and could almost swear its hands were sweeping backward. But the hour and a half was finally over and he reached over to lightly touch Bingham's shoulder.

Bingham was fully awake instantly. He listened for a few seconds before moving, then sat up and put his mouth near where he thought Harte's ear was. "I'm going to check the line," he said. "Make the radio check while I'm gone." Melville only checked his ambush line when there was a new man in the squad. Once he knew how everybody in his squad acted overnight he never took the risk of leaving his own position; the risk of making noise that could give away their position, the risk of getting shot by one of his own men—a man too edgy and trigger-happy from fear of the unknown or from too much combat.

He started on the long leg of the ambush line. Homer was awake, sitting and looking toward the speed trail. West lay sleeping lightly at his side and awoke to the presence of a third man in the position. They didn't exchange many words and the few they did didn't travel more than a few feet. Peale was sleeping on his stomach alongside Russell. Russell sat leaning back against a tree, his chin on his chest.

Bingham froze and listened to the silence of the night, wondering who had seen them getting into the ambush, how anybody could have gotten to them to kill a man without being heard by anyone else. He swallowed and swore silently, shaken about losing a man like this, especially on his first night as squad leader. He put his hand on Peale's shoulder. As soon as he felt him stirring, he shifted his hand to the other man's mouth, signaling him to silence. Peale didn't know what the problem could be, but knew there was danger. If there had been any light to see by, Bingham would have seen Peale's face pale again. Certain they were both alert now, Bingham put his hands on Russell's shoulders, to lay him down and check his wounds.

Russell snored when he was moved. Bingham snapped back to kneel upright. "What the fuck?" he said louder than he intended to. He shifted forward again and used light touches to examine Russell's throat, chest, back. The new man wasn't dead, like he'd

thought; he was asleep. Emotions rolled over him, first relief at
discovering he hadn't lost a man, then anger at finding a position
with no one awake. "Whose watch is it?" he asked Peale, though
he knew the answer.

"Russell's. Why?"

"I'm going to kill his ass. The fucker's sleeping." Bingham
slapped a hand over Russell's mouth to keep him from crying
out and grabbed the front of his shirt with the other. He shook
him hard and when the man in his grasp started struggling he
jammed his face close and grated through his teeth, "Wake up,
fuckface, and stay awake."

Russell struggled to push Bingham's hand away from his mouth.
When he could speak he said, "I wasn't sleeping, you were too
quiet sneaking up on me."

"Bullshit," Bingham snapped. "Your ass is mine, boy. Fucking
dickhead. You had best be awake the next time I come around
here." He turned back to Peale. "And it's your ass, too, I come
here again and both of you are sleeping. We could all get killed."

He was struggling to control himself, to stop his trembling
before it became violent, as he returned to his position. He sat
there for a few minutes, breathing deeply and trying to relax before
continuing to check his positions.

Bingham hadn't made much noise waking Russell, but it had
carried as far as Harte. The grenadier hadn't known what it was
and first prepared himself for an enemy attack from that flank.
Then he heard enough to guess what was happening. And once he
made that guess, he wasn't bored anymore, he wasn't even sure he
could go back to sleep when Bingham took over the watch. Harte
waited until Bingham was breathing more easily before asking
what had happened. Bingham's confirmation made Harte think
about the danger the new man had put them in. If someone had
come from that side the squad would have been surprised and too
many of them could have wound up as casualties. I'm going to
get that cocksucker, he swore to himself.

When he felt calm enough, Bingham checked the positions on
the long leg. One man was awake, one sleeping in each position.
No one had seen or heard anything during the night. Although
Rush and Morse, who were both awake, pointed faces with invisible quizzical expressions at him, wondering what it was they'd
heard moments before at the other end of their line.

It wasn't until after 2 A.M. that there was any sign of enemy
action, and that was the sound of somebody else's firefight.
Bingham listened to the distant sounds of battle for a moment,

trying to figure out where it was. But the jungle had a muffling effect, it muted and dispersed the sounds so he could place it only generally, somewhere to his right, maybe right front—if it wasn't in an altogether different direction. Forget about how far away; sometimes it sounded a mile off when it was close, while some few sounds pierced the forest so clearly they sounded like less than a hundred meters distant when they were actually much farther. He held his radio's handset to his ear and waited. What he wanted to do was check his line again, wake everybody up. But he knew all that would do was ease his own nervousness and cause his men unnecessary anxiety. They were probably tense enough on their own, listening to this firefight that was someplace else.

Then his radio crackled to life. "Whippoorwill, Whippoorwill, this is Birdhouse One, Birdhouse One. Over."

"Birdhouse One, Whippoorwill. Go," he said into the mouthpiece.

"Whippoorwill, Birdhouse. Bad guy probers have been repulsed from this location. They may be headed in your direction, stand by for them. Do you understand? Over."

Bingham swallowed. "Birdhouse, Whippoorwill. Roger. You."

"Give a sitrep if you see them, Whippoorwill. Birdhouse out." And the radio returned to its soft static.

Bingham tapped Harte's shoulder and whispered close to him, "Everybody up. Charlie might be coming." His throat was dry and talking was difficult. He fished a stick of chewing gum out of his shirt pocket, unwrapped it, and stuck it into his mouth. He gave it a couple of chews before leaning to his other side and touching Emerson. He repeated the message he gave to Harte and added, "Pass it and pass the word back." Passing the word down and back wasn't the most efficient way of letting everybody know what was happening, but it worked. Whatever instruction was being given was passed from man to man along the line. When the last man received it, he gave it back to the man he got it from, and so forth back down the line. When the word got back to the man who originated it, he'd know how faithfully it had gone down the line. If it never got back to him, he'd know it hadn't reached the end of the line.

Harte told West and Homer without waiting to be told, he had been around long enough to know the routine. In two minutes the entire squad was alert to the possible approach of Vietcong. Most of them lay prone. A few not certain they could stay awake if they lay down assumed kneeling or sitting firing positions. They waited. It was a long wait.

Long enough for Russell to decide it was a false alarm and lay his head down on his forearm. His breathing became regular and heavy in a few minutes. Peale heard it and clamped a hand on the back of his neck. "Wake up, shit-for-brains," Peale snarled into his ear. Russell started, and mumbled something about not being asleep. "You go to sleep when I tell you to," Peale said, "and then you do it by the numbers. Understand?"

Before Russell could answer Peale tensed. Russell noticed the difference in the way his fire-team leader held him and didn't say anything back. Then he heard what Peale had heard: the patter of feet coming along the trail toward them.

Peale groped for the cord, momentarily forgotten when he was distracted by Russell's sleeping, and gave it a hard jerk. The jerk was repeated man by man until it reached Rush at the other end of the line. Suddenly everybody was more alert than before.

Bingham listened. His nerve endings tingled and he trembled all over. He could hear the sounds of several people coming from his right. He wished he could see, could know how many men were approaching. Then he'd know what to do. His eyes strained into the blackness where he knew the trail was. More sounds reached his ears, voices. He was incredulous, the Vietcong were chatting as they quick-walked along the trail; they had no suspicions that Marines might be nearby. Then there was something that amazed him even more. So confident were the VC of their safety along this speed trail they were using a hooded flashlight to guide their way. A narrow slit of light bobbed along the trail toward the Marines. Bingham looked carefully and saw the gleam of a second flashlight farther back. In between he saw the bobbing coals of lit cigarettes. He made a rough estimate of the distance between the two lights and decided if they marked the front and the back of the group of men approaching, there were few enough for his ambush to take. His heart speeded up and his breathing became rapid and shallow. He made sure two star clusters were ready by his right hand and waited with his rifle in his shoulder.

The lead VC entered the ambush's killing zone. Seen in the slight illumination from his flashlight, it was clear he carried a rifle dangling losely in his other hand. Bingham waited motionlessly, hoping none of his men would be spotted by the passing black-clad soldiers, hoping none of his men would trigger the ambush before he was ready, watching and listening beyond the second flashlight for more men coming. The second hooded light passed where he knew Peale waited with Russell, he knew the first light hadn't yet reached Rush.

"Fire!" he screamed and pulled his trigger, pointing his muzzle near one of the bobbing coals. The coal arched away into the air. The rifle bucked in his shoulder and he shifted the aim of his muzzle. He pulled the trigger, the rifle bucked, and he shifted aim—pulled the trigger, buck, shift, pull. To both sides other rifles blasted out at the night, while next to him Harte fired his .45—he was too close to use his grenade launcher. Fire spouting from the muzzles of the Marines' weapons strobe-lit the night. The flashlights flew from hands that dropped them or were knocked away. The voices on the trail panicked, screamed, shouted confusion.

There were a few answering shots, followed by the pounding of running feet. The Marines rained bullets down the trail after the fleeing Vietcong, heard screams cut off, heard the crashing of bodies into the forest at the sides of the trail—or onto the trail.

"Cease fire, cease fire!" Bingham shouted when he couldn't hear any more sounds from the trail. The Marines stopped shooting and he listened. The night was stone silent. Except for the rasping of his own breath, Bingham might have been as deaf as he was blind.

"Cover me," Bingham called to his men, "I'm going to check the trail." His trembling continued, though it was less intense. He picked up the two star clusters laying near his hand, rose to his feet, and stepped to the trail's edge with his rifle held in the crook of his left arm. He tucked one flare into his front trouser pocket, looked in the darkness for a spot at which to aim the other, picked blindly along where he thought the trail was, and slammed the heel of his right hand against the bottom of the tube in his left. The flare shot up with a bang, glanced off a tree branch and tumbled through the foliage until it sputtered to life. The strings of its tiny parachute caught in twigs and it swung wildly back and forth, side to side, casting a garish green light onto the trail below.

Four bodies lay on the trail, two in front of the ambush, two farther along. Their torsos were twisted in death, their limbs splayed, their faces frozen in shock. Their trousers were wet and moisture spread on the ground from their crotches where their bladders emptied and their anal sphincters let go in their dying spasms. Rifles lay near both bodies. Bingham scooped up the weapons and shoved them at a pair of hands reaching from inside the trees.

"Chuck, watch where they came from, there might be more on their way," Bingham ordered. "Dago, check out these two bodies, search them for documents. Chief, come with me to check out those other two. Hank, cover us." He trotted a few yards down the trail where he was joined by Rush and stopped him for a few seconds. The light from the star cluster dangling in the trees wouldn't last much longer. He grabbed the one in his front pocket, pointed it almost parallel to the trail and slammed its bottom against his thigh. The tube banged and the flare shot out of it with a whoosh to hit the trail a few meters beyond the bodies and skitter until it snagged against something on the trail's edge. It sputtered to life.

Bingham and Rush pounded down the trail nearly shoulder to shoulder. The first body they reached had died instantly when a bullet tore through the back of its head and left a gaping hole where its nose had been. Rush frisked it while Bingham picked up its rifle and watched farther along. The fourth body was partly inside the brush along the trail, he had tried to crawl to safety before dying; more likely someone had tried to drag him away as there was no weapon next to this body.

The flare was burning out. "Let's get the fuck out of here," Bingham said when Rush was through searching both bodies. They ran back to the rest of the squad. Rush peeled off back into his position and Bingham rushed to the corner where Harte waited for him, radio handset held out.

"Birdhouse One is on the horn," Harte said. "I told him what happened, he wants you to call back with a full report."

"Right," Bingham replied and grabbed the handset. Then the word "report" clicked in his mind. "Oh, shit," he swore and his trembling increased. In the excitement he'd forgotten one of the squad leader's basic jobs following an action—he hadn't checked his own people for casualties. "Team leaders report," he called out low but loud enough for his words to reach all three.

"First team all present and accounted for," Longfellow replied immediately. He was probably waiting for that, Bingham thought. I wonder what he's going to say later and how long he'll keep saying it.

"Second team, A-okay," Peale answered.

"Third team fine," Rivera.

Then he called Birdhouse One to give his report.

"That's affirmative," he said when asked how positive he was they'd had four kills, "I have four bad guy bodies." He swore silently when given his last instruction, but said out loud into the radio, "Roger, wilco." Birdhouse One signed off.

"We wait here until dawn, but we got to bring in those goddam bodies," he told his fire-team leaders when they joined him on his command. "Dago, your team goes to get the far ones. Hank, cover them." When all four bodies were assembled in front of the ambush site he had one fire team watch in each direction while the other wrapped the corpses in four ponchos and rolled them into the trees on the other side of the trail. Then they waited for the twilight that would announce that day had dawned.

Bingham was still trembling slightly when morning came and he pulled his ambush. Nobody seemed to notice but Longfellow and Peale nodded their approval at him; he was a leader they would follow. A couple of the others also acknowledged him in some slight way. The trembling was over by the time they reached the hill.

"Out-fucking-standing," Lieutenant Copeland said when they reported in with the four bodies.

CHAPTER TEN

After-Action Report, Before-Action Report

Rumors flew in those days. Charlie was getting ready for something big, something that would win the war for him. What did anybody think of the rumors? Well, it depended on who was asked.

Some, but not many, of the generals and colonels in Saigon who were responsible for running the war would admit there were intelligence reports that indicated something big was in the offing. Something real big. But most of them would simply point to their charts and graphs that clearly demonstrated Charlie was losing men so fast he didn't have enough warm bodies left to try something big. They'd say that at the current attrition rate, it was only a matter of time before Charlie and his NVA buddies were rendered ineffective as fighting units.

The colonels and lieutenant colonels commanding the regiments and battalions doing the fighting would probably lick their chops at the prospect of Charlie trying something so dumb as a major push where he'd meet their people in open combat. Those officers knew their troops always beat Charlie to a bloody pulp whenever Charlie was dumb enough to stand and fight on even terms. They'd say there were indications Charlie would, but they didn't think it was possible for him to do it. But I hope he does, they'd say.

The Marine generals and colonels responsible for running their part of the war from Da Nang had to be circumspect about what they said. They were involved in a long-standing, quiet war with the Army generals and colonels in Saigon, a philosophical war about how the shooting war should be fought. The Marines were losing that quiet battle. The Army had overall command of strategy in the shooting war and there were those high ranking, very high ranking, Army generals in Saigon who didn't like the Marines, didn't want them there, didn't have any confidence in their leadership or fighting ability and, frankly, wished they'd go away. But it was the only shooting war in town, and the Marines didn't want to go away.

But what about the troops doing the fighting? They were too busy swallowing, working their jaws, chewing gum to moisten their dry throats to answer rumors. They didn't want to believe those rumors because the rumors meant more of them would get killed or mutilated—a lot more. They knew that "they," in the collective would win, of course, but they also knew too well that individually they stood a greater chance of not making it home if Charlie did make the big push the rumors called for.

Why did the rumors persist? Simple—they were true. And the Marine commanders in I Corps wanted to do something about them. They knew Charlie and his big brothers in the NVA were massing somewhere in western Quang Tri or Thua Thien provinces, and near the DMZ. They tried to find them. And they responded in battalion strength to reports of enemy activity in the areas they knew the enemy had to be massing.

"Charlie's out there someplace in battalion strength," Staff Sergeant Ives told first platoon's squad and fire-team leaders in a briefing the evening before the battalion was to pull out on another operation. The junior men sat or knelt in the dirt in front of him in a bunched semicircle just outside the bunker that was the platoon CP. "We've got all kinds of intelligence reports that say so." He grimaced and shook his head before saying, "We've got everything except reports from Marine recon saying exactly where he is. So it's our job to find, fix, and fuck him. Reveille is at 0530, morning chow at 0600. The first wave of birds is taking off at 0700. Every rifleman carries six full magazines, four bandoliers, two days worth of Cs; automatic riflemen hump an extra magazine and bandolier. Grenadiers get thirty rounds HE, ten willy peter. A dozen frags and three willy peters per fire team and the squad leaders carry three smokes. Any questions?" He looked not quite expectantly at his junior NCOs.

"How long we gonna be out there?" Gershwin asked.

Ives looked like he couldn't quite believe he was being asked that question again. "For as long as it takes us to find, fix, and fuck Charlie." His patient voice was tinged with something that wasn't patience. "Any other questions?" His expression said there better not be. There was one, though.

"What about replacements," Butterfield asked. All the squads were short a few men, and second squad was more short-handed than the other two.

Ives shrugged. "Maybe we'll get them along the way," he said. "Maybe they'll be waiting for us after this operation. You know how it works." How it worked was that hardly any of the troops had much idea of what was going on, even though it was their lives that were most directly affected by it. "Any more questions?" There weren't. "All right, squad leaders, it's yours." He swung his arm at three piles of munitions, the bullets and grenades for the three squads. "Don't forget to set your watch rotations for tonight, we're still responsible for our part of the perimeter." Ives rose to his feet and ducked into the CP bunker. He needed privacy to calm himself so he could get some sleep before the next day's operation, and to psych himself up to face its dangers.

Wordlessly, the squad leaders each moved to one of the piles and equally distributed their contents to their fire-team leaders. The team leaders carried the bandoliers of bullets and the tubes containing hand grenades to their fire teams. The squad leaders picked up their own ammunition and grenades and their grenadiers' rounds and headed toward their own positions. They barely acknowledged each other when they parted company for the night.

"Reveille at 0530," Bingham told Harte when he gave him his 40mm grenades. He stretched himself out on the bare ground and thought for a while about the injustice of making them stand perimeter duty the night before taking off on another operation instead of letting everybody get a good night's sleep. The next thing he knew Harte was waking him. It was night and his turn to watch.

Naturally, the first wave of helicopters didn't arrive until 0800, an hour after it had been scheduled to leave. Alpha and Bravo companies were ferried to an area a kilometer south of the jungled, hilly area where the NVA battalion was suspected of being. Their job was to sweep northward, either crushing the NVA battalion or driving it to where Delta Company waited north of the area. Charlie Company was battalion reserve.

CHAPTER ELEVEN
Old Home Day

A few days into the operation—an operation that seemed to be an endless, meaningless walk in the noonday sun—Alpha Company stopped and set a perimeter around a hilltop. Not long after that a string of helicopters landed and off-loaded supplies and people.

"Squad leaders up," the company's platoon sergeants cried from their respective platoon command posts moments after the helicopters left.

Bingham rose to his feet. "Hank, take over," he called. The short Marine waved a hand at his squad leader and looked to see where the other members of the squad were. Bingham nodded his satisfaction at Longfellow's automatic actions and headed toward where Ives waited. Sergeant Butterfield was already squatting at Ives's side when Bingham reached him, the platoon sergeant was sitting, knees up, feet spread. Gershwin arrived seconds later. Six men in clean utilities knelt in the dirt behind Ives.

"I want each of you to take two cases of Cs for your squads," Ives said without preamble, "and we even got four cans of fresh water for the platoon to divvy up. You each get two cans of seven sixty-deuce and a case of grenades. You'll get your mail soon's I get a chance to sort it out." He hawked onto the ground between his feet and flipped some dirt onto it with the toe of his boot.

Gershwin took advantage of Ives's pause to ask, "What do we need the ammo for? We ain't used none to replace." Gershwin was right. Only a few rounds had been fired during the three days Alpha Company had spent humping in the boonies, and all at noises, none at seen targets.

"When we need it, you'll be glad we got it now instead of not getting it at all." Ives's eyes fixed on Gershwin's and his voice was steady. Gershwin looked away first, and Ives continued. "Now I got some bad news and and I got some good news. The bad news is," he looked the squad leaders in the eyes, "we're humping out of here in ten minutes and you got some boots to integrate into your squads by then." He jerked a thumb at the six strangers kneeling behind him. Gershwin and Butterfield looked expressionlessly at the new men. But Bingham smiled past Ives's shoulder.

"Bingham, all three squads have two corporals and we got a new one here, so I'm giving him to first squad, that's you. His name's—" He referred to a slip of paper in his hand. "—Corporal Cooper. You also get the tall one. Hey, mighty mite," he called past his shoulder, "what's your name?"

"Private Trumbull, John," a nervous-looking teenager answered. Bingham wondered how tall he actually was. Kneeling, Trumbull towered over the other five new men.

"Right. Trumbull. Russell needs someone in that squad he don't have to look down at." At six foot three, Russell was the tallest man in Bingham's squad.

Bingham nodded at Trumbull, then looked back to the black man who was grinning at him. "Yo, Chickencoop," he called softly, "good to see you, man."

"You got it, bro," Corporal Jim Cooper said and held up a fist in the modified black power salute he called a green power salute—he claimed it was the only proper salute for a Marine to use.

Ives glanced quickly at Bingham but didn't say anything, then he assigned the other four men to Butterfield and Gershwin. "That's it. We move in eight minutes. Get 'em saddled up." He rose to his feet and took a step in the direction of the company CP.

"Wait a minute, Ives," Gershwin said, "you said you had some good news."

Ives turned half back. "The good news is you're finally up to TO." TO. Add six men and the platoon was up to full strength. Butterfield and Gershwin shook their heads; some good news this was, getting up to TO in the field.

Trumbull was tall. In his combat boots and helmet he stood more than six and a half feet. Young though he was, he wasn't accustomed to being ignored, so he stood, trying to look confident and capable while uncertainly shifting his weight.

"The Mean Green Machine sent you back here, huh," Bingham asked when he and Cooper released each other from the bear hug they threw while the others walked back to their squads.

"Yeah. You know how it is," Cooper said, still grinning. "A man don't get the job done right the first time, this Bad Green Machine keeps making him do it again until he gets it right. 'Sides,

I didn't get my quota before. Gotta get my quota before they let me go back to the World for real."

Bingham laughed and shook his head. This was the Chickencoop he had served with at Camp Pendleton in California. Cooper had frequently joked about how he would wind up serving a second combat tour. "You chuck dudes get thirteen months duty over there, but us bros got us a special deal, a quota. When we kill our quota of little yellow people they send us back to the Land of the Big PX. No time limit." But he was a short-timer in the Corps with less than a year left until the end of his enlistment. He already had a short timer's calendar drawn on the back of his camouflage helmet cover. The reunion was brief.

"Man, we got us an operation here. Let's go get you that quota most ricky-tick so you can haul ass back to the World for good," Bingham joked back. "Got to get you assigned, meet the squad. Come on, pano." Bingham slapped Cooper on the shoulder and started to lead him to where the rest of the squad waited. Two steps later he turned back to Trumbull, who was still standing where he had been left, shifting his weight from foot to foot. "You, too, baby-san, let's go."

"Baby-san," Cooper chuckled. "You got that right, bro. They letting them into boot camp younger every month." He chuckled and seemed relaxed, but the closer he came to the treeline where the squad waited, the more wary he grew and the more closely he eyed the terrain.

The tall Marine with the baby's face followed briskly behind. His expression made him look like someone's kid brother about to take his first ride on the Loop of Death roller coaster in some gigantic amusement park.

Having Cooper with him was especially meaningful for Bingham. From their past service together he knew Cooper as a good Marine who knew the field and had little fear for himself. The fact that he was now on his second tour and was experienced made him a valuable addition to the squad. He should fit in easily with the other men. And now Bingham had a friend in that strange, foreign country.

Bingham had his squad realigned by the time the company started to move out. Trumbull was assigned to Chuck Peale's fire team and Russell moved to Longfellow's. Part of the realignment had been difficult. Bingham briefly explained it to Cooper.

"You're taking the place of a man who's a good fire-team leader, but he's a lance corporal with no time in grade," he said. "He got bumped when Peale joined this squad. He got a team back

when I became squad leader, now he gets bumped again." He
shook his head. "Poor fucker thinks somebody's got a hair up
his ass about him." They joined Rivera and Morse. Bingham took
Rivera aside.

"Dago," Bingham said, "I hate to do this to you, man."

Rivera looked at the new man who came back with Bingham
from the squad leader's meeting and turned away. He knew what
was coming.

"We got a new corporal in the squad. I have to give him a fire
team. The other two teams have corporals. I have to give him
yours." He waited for Rivera to say something. Rivera didn't,
he kept looking away. "You want the blooker?"

"No, I don't want no fucking blooker." Rivera's dark eyes
stared blankly at the forest.

"If you want I can put you back in Hank's fire team, you won't
have to be with a man you don't know."

Rivera didn't say anything for a while and Bingham waited
patiently. "I'll stay where I'm at, trade rifles with Morse." Morse
carried the automatic rifle, Rivera would take it.

"You're sure?"

"Yeah."

"All right."

Dago Rivera didn't say anything, but Cooper could easily see
the junior man was angry about being relieved as a fire-team
leader, again to another stranger. Bingham looked at Cooper and
silently wished him luck. He tried to tell him with a look not to
hesitate to call for help if he had any trouble with the man he was
bumping, then he left to check his other fire teams.

"Don't sweat it, man," Cooper tried to assure Rivera. "I've
been here before. I got my shit together."

Rivera didn't reply, he just continued to stare sightlessly at the
trees.

A hundred meters to their west, a squad peeled off the barren
hilltop and moved down into the jungle. Squad by squad, the rest
of the company followed. All signals were given by soft-voiced
radio messages and hand signals. Off the hilltop was Charlie's
home. The Marines trod gently there, alert for booby traps and
ambushes. In the forest, more than on the top of the hill, was
where unseen danger lurked, and no one wanted to be the first
man to die.

The company followed an angling, well-established game trail
halfway down the hill. This trail, unlike some that Rush had found
and followed, was easy for anyone to find and follow. It was the

kind of trail booby traps were set on to kill or maim the unwary—
the kind of trail where it was less dangerous to walk through the
virgin brush where no one would know where to plant a booby
trap. So a hundred meters along, the point man stepped off the
trail and broke a path through the forest's underbrush. The going
was relatively easy in this section of the forest. The brush wasn't
as thick as it was in some other places in the jungle; the heavy
double canopy overhead prevented much sunlight from reaching
the ground, so the undergrowth was stunted.

A Marine rifle company in the forest. Two hundred men, armed
and dangerous. At four-meter intervals they formed a line close to
three-quarters of a kilometer going through the forest. Too much
distance for the rear of the column to react fast if the point made
contact with an enemy. Not long after leaving the trail Captain
Bernstein held up the lead platoon and sent first platoon a hundred meters to its left. Then third platoon went parallel a hundred
meters to second platoon's right. Two hundred men forming a
rectangle two hundred meters wide, and a little deeper. The company command unit was between the second and third platoons,
the mortars were with the command group. A danger existed of
Marines getting caught in a crossfire from their own company if
they ran into enemy soldiers in the wrong location, but the entire
company could react more quickly from this formation than from
a column if any part of it ran into trouble.

Peale's fire team led first platoon. Rush had the point. Longfellow's team linked with the rest of the platoon following them.
Bingham kept Cooper in the middle of the squad so he could be
close to his old friend, and to give him a chance to readjust to
the bush without having too much immediate responsibility. He
had seen the small byplay between Rivera and Cooper and knew
the proud Mexican-American resented being replaced again by a
man he didn't know. Bingham also wanted to keep an eye on that
situation to be sure nothing happened.

The hills Alpha Company climbed over grew higher and steeper. Fewer trees could cling to the slopes, more sunlight streamed
down, and the undergrowth grew thicker. The way was slower
and the point would have to be changed frequently to give the leading men respite. Many trees had fallen from the monsoon winds
and bombings of war, causing slight detours. The company formation fragmented and the distances between the platoons widened or narrowed as the terrain demanded. Some of the tree trunks
had to be climbed over. Some of the fallen trees caused bigger
problems.

"What's the problem up there?" Bingham asked, pushing himself past Trumbull and Homer to where Peale stood a foot or two higher on the hillside than Rush.

"That is," Peale said. He looked up, to his right and to his left.

Bingham followed his gaze. "Goddam," he swore softly. A tangled wall of fallen tree trunks, twice the height of a man, stretched as far as he could see in both directions through the broken forest. Most of the trunks were oriented in a general uphill-downhill direction but some were at sharp angles away from that and a few could be seen to be perpendicular to the slope. A massive air strike on the hilltop above them had leveled all the vegetation on it and tumbled this line of trees down its side.

"Probably booby-trapped," Peale said.

"That's why I just stopped when I got here," Rush said. "No way I want this badass mother blowing up in my face or falling on me."

"Check it out topside, see how far uphill it goes," Bingham said. "I'll tell the chief honcho about it." Peale nodded at Rush and jerked his head up the hill. Rush dropped his pack and stepped past his fire-team leader. Peale followed him. This part of the hill was steep. Both men had to grab bushes and tree branches to pull themselves up in some places.

Bingham unslung the radio, held it to his head, and depressed the speak button on its side. "Alpha One Actual," he said into the mouthpiece, "this is Alpha One One. One Actual, One One, over."

"One One, this is Alpha One. Over," the fuzzy response came almost immediately, but it wasn't the lieutenant.

"One, One One. Give me the Actual. Over."

"One One, One. Wait one." The platoon's radioman, who carried the much heavier and more powerful PRC-25 radio on his backpack, would tell the lieutenant Bingham wanted to talk directly to him.

Goddam, why do I have to be in first squad, first platoon, Bingham thought. A man could lose track of all those 'ones' on the radio.

Cooper arrived at Bingham's side. His jaw dropped slightly at the sight of the wall of jumbled tree trunks. "Oo-ee," he whistled, "I've never seen one of these before."

"Looks like a logging camp gone wild," Homer said. "I worked one a couple of summers ago. Hard-ass work. Sometimes the log trails look like this when they're getting ready to haul the lumber out."

"Bullshit, Homer." Bingham said back, "only summer job you ever had was in the cotton fields."

"No way, man." Homer slowly shook his head while continuing to look at the wall of trees. " 'Bama cotton fields are in the country, not in the city like they are in Mississ-hip and like that. Don't got no cotton fields in Birmingham. Ask Longfellow, he'll tell you."

"Don't have to ask Longfellow. He's the one who said the only summer job for deep south splibs is the cotton fields." Longfellow had started that story about rural splibs, the Marine word for "nigger." He was from rural Mississippi and thought all blacks were like his rural neighbors. Many of them considered cotton picking to be a good job. It may have been stoop labor, but it often was better than most of the other options. He enjoyed baiting the three black men in the squad, especially the six-foot-tall Homer. They usually didn't rise to the bait, but instead matched him insult for insult.

Homer enjoyed the cotton-picker taunts, they gave rein to his imagination and he encouraged Bingham to join in. He spat to the side and scuffed dirt over the spot. "Chuck dude's from Mississ-hip. Don't know diddle-shit 'bout Alabama. In Alabama some splibs even got jobs better than cleaning shithouses. Back in Mississ-hip Longfellow wanted to get a good job. That's why he enlisted in this man's Marine Corps. Recruiting sergeant told him he could get work cleaning shithouses in the Crotch." Chuck was Marine slang for "honkie." There was a brotherhood in the use of the slang terms and little sting in them.

Bingham glanced at Cooper. Longfellow was a good combat Marine and a good fire-team leader, but he was as rednecked a racist as Bingham had met in the Corps. He wondered how his old friend would take the garbage Longfellow would throw at him. He didn't have to wonder for long. Cooper's dark face split in a wide grin.

"Lawdy, Mistah Bingham, suh," he said. "Massah Longfeller sound lak one badassed massah know how to keep us darkies in our places. Ah gots to meet this massah, suh. Ah wants ta show him us No'thun blacks ain't lak them Mississ-hip darkies he be used to. Ah goan eat his ass fo a 'tween-meal snack and use his backbone fo a toothpick." He paused for a second and his face grew more serious. "Massah Longfeller do hab a backbone, doan he, suh?"

Bingham laughed briefly. He hoped Cooper was joking about

eating Longfellow's ass. "Yeah, Chickencoop, he's got a back-bone. It's not a long one, but he's got one."

All humor left Cooper's expression and voice. "What color is it?"

"Depends on where you are." Bingham became as serious as Cooper. "If I was you, I wouldn't want to run into him in a dark alley—it's pure redneck there. But in the boonies it's Marine green and he doesn't give a damn what your color is out of the field. In the boonies you won't find a better man to have at your back."

Cooper looked at Homer for confirmation. The other black man nodded. "In a base camp he's one dipshit motherfucker," Homer said, "but Bingham's right about the boonies. Out here the only two skin colors he sees are yellow and green. You're as green as I am, man, and I'm as green as he is."

Bingham didn't hear the rest because his radio chose that moment to squawk at him.

"That's an affirmative, Actual," he answered to Copeland's question about their way being blocked, "we have one bodacious obstacle here. I request the Actual come forward. Over." He listened for a moment then said, "One Actual, One One, roger." Copeland signed off. To the Marines waiting to hear what was happening he said, "We wait."

A crashing and stumbling uphill made them spin with their rifles pointed toward the noise, all except Trumbull who was too new and too startled and too nervous to know what to do.

"Second team recon coming down," Peale's voice called to them from the direction of the noise. Bingham, Cooper, and Homer visibly relaxed. Seconds later Peale and Rush scrambled into view, digging the sides of their boots into the dirt and grabbing at branches to slow their descent. The two dropped panting to the ground when they reached Bingham. "Motherfucker goes all the way to the top," Peale gasped. "We ran into a recon from second platoon scoping out how far it went downhill."

Bingham swore under his breath. Aloud he said, "I want two men to go and see how far down it goes. If they haven't reached the end in a hundred meters, come back." He was about to make his selection when Cooper stepped forward.

"I'll go," Cooper said. "Send me and Dago."

"No way, Chickencoop," Bingham said. "You just got back here, man. You need to reacclimate yourself before you do any-thing like that."

"Bullshit, I can do it." Cooper grinned. "Me and Dago, we'll be a team Charlie can't beat."

Bingham glanced at Rivera. The other man was looking more or less downhill along the tree wall, seemingly oblivious to the talk going on between Bingham and Cooper. Cooper looked expectantly at Bingham, and the squad leader could almost hear his old friend begging him to send him with Rivera on the recon. He thought about it; it made a certain sense. Sending the two on a recon together might improve Rivera's opinion of the man who replaced him as fire-team leader.

"All right," he finally, reluctantly, said. "Chickencoop and Dago, check it out."

Cooper grinned and without hesitation said, "Let's go," to Rivera and started down the hill without looking to see if he was being followed. Rivera's eyes bored into Cooper's back for a moment. He glanced quickly to see Bingham watching him, rolled his shoulders in a slight shrug, and followed the man he didn't know.

Lieutenant Copeland arrived a moment later and whistled at the barricade. "How far does it go?" he asked.

"All the way to the top," Bingham answered. "Peale and Rush checked it out and ran into a team from second platoon reconning it. Cooper and Rivera are checking it out below."

Copeland nodded. While they waited, Copeland held his radio's handset to his ear and listened to the traffic on the company net. Third platoon and the command section were on the other side of the hill and hadn't run into this obstacle. Because the hill was in the way he could only hear second platoon on the radio and had to guess at what the command group was saying.

Cooper and Rivera were gone fifteen minutes before pulling themselves back into view. "It goes farther than we went," Cooper gasped. Sweat ran down his face and neck, soaking his entire shirt. He looked back the way he had come. "Someone else came by, though. I found traces of several men passing, starting about thirty meters down. Looked like at least a squad. Maybe a platoon."

"How recently?" Copeland asked.

Cooper shook his head. "Couldn't tell for sure. Maybe yesterday, maybe this morning."

Rivera stood aside listening passively. His expression had lost the hardness it had directed at Cooper.

"How'd it look to you?" Copeland asked Rivera.

The stocky Latin shook his head. "Man's got better eyes than I do. I looked at the same things he did and didn't see as much as him." He looked blankly at the stranger grinning at him before continuing. "I saw enough to know Charlie was there."

"That's what eleven months of chasing Charlie teaches you, pano," Cooper said. "It's like I said, man. I been here before and I got my shit together."

"Maybe," Rivera said. The man who took his place as fire-team leader was still unproven as far as he was concerned, but Cooper's sighting of the traces of enemy movement down below raised him in Rivera's eyes.

Copeland heard Captain Bernstein's voice asking for him on the radio and he replied immediately. After he told of finding the traces of Vietcong movement downhill the company commander told him to hold tight for a minute. There was brief static on the radio, then Bernstein was back and ordered first platoon to follow the tree wall to the bottom of the hill and around it to the other side. Second platoon would follow first down the hill. The mortars, the command unit, and third platoon would go around on the unobstructed side of the hill.

"I found the traces, let me take the point," Cooper said.

"You don't have to," Copeland told him, "this is your first day with us and you're a fire-team leader."

"Don't mean nothing. I've got good eyes. I can pick up the trail where Dago and I turned back, follow it for a while."

Bingham's gaze hardened at Cooper when he said "don't mean nothing." It was an expression the grunts used to help them accept the death or crippling of friends, the chance of being killed or wounded themselves. It was a fatalistic phrase that sometimes meant the man saying it was ready to take foolish chances—or no longer cared whether he lived or died.

Cooper saw the look and grinned at his squad leader and friend. "Don't sweat it, Honcho," he said. "I gotta get my quota. No way I'm taking any chances that'll fuck me up before then."

"If you want the point, Cooper, you've got it," Copeland said, taking the question out of Bingham's hands. "Go." He wanted to see how sharp his new NCO was and didn't have Bingham's qualms about putting a friend in a dangerous position.

"Dago behind me, then Morse," Cooper said. "Emerson brings up the rear." He headed back down the hill. Copeland nodded approval; his newest NCO already knew his men's names.

It was almost like climbing down a chimney. On one side was the thick living forest, on the other the eerie wall of fallen tree trunks. Overhead the trees blocked out the sky except where the falling trunks had broken off branches. The earth underfoot was wet, growing slick after the passage of several men. The Marines dug the sides of their boots into the soft dirt to gain purchase and grabbed bushes and saplings to keep from slipping and falling. Everyone cast anxious glances at the fallen trees, afraid they might collapse on them, hoping they wouldn't.

Forty meters down, Cooper looked back toward Bingham and pointed at the ground. When Bingham reached the place where Cooper had pointed he looked. There was a fragmentary print in the soft earth, one inch wide and six long, of a worn tire tread— the mark of the ubiquitous Ho Chi Minh sandal worn by most Vietnamese civilians and Vietcong, at least those who didn't go barefoot. Bingham looked farther and saw a few more footprints. Some of them led to the wall, the others went along it. It was obvious someone had come this way and gone around the wall to the downhill side, the same route the Marines were taking.

Ten meters farther downhill Cooper paused and squatted to examine a thin vine laying across the ground in front of him. Careful not to disturb the vine, he traced it from the middle to one end where it disappeared under a pile of humus two feet off the trail. Gently, he probed the humus with the point of his bayonet. He felt something hard.

"Booby trap?" Rivera whispered to him.

"I do believe so. Pull everybody back while I disarm it." Using light touches, Cooper brushed the leaves and mud away. Underneath them was a number ten can filled with gravel. A C ration can sat in the middle of the gravel and the top of an American hand grenade poked out of the C ration can. The handle of the detonator had been removed from the grenade and the pin was pulled most of the way out. A slight tug on the vine would pull the pin the rest of the way out and arm the grenade. Seconds later it would explode, sending the gravel flying in all directions like a nondirectional claymore mine. Gingerly, Cooper pushed the pin back in the hole and bent its ends back to secure it. Then he cut the vine from the grenade and followed it to its other end. Another homemade mine was tied to that end. Anyone giving the vine a tug would be blasted from both sides. Once the second mine was secured he cut the vine free from it and threw it away.

"All secure," he called softly up the hill. A moment later Bingham and Lieutenant Copeland scrabbled down to him. Almost without words he showed them the two mines and described how they had been set. "Want to remove them, Lieutenant?" he finished.

"No, we better not. Sometimes they put a bouncing betty or some sort of pressure release device under a booby trap to catch anyone sharp enough to spot the trap. I'll arrange for them to be blown in place by second platoon after we're all out of the way." Copeland signaled for Cooper to continue down the trail and stayed by the booby traps until his own place in the column caught up with him. While he waited, he talked to Two Actual on the radio and told him about the booby traps. Two Actual agreed to blow the mines after his platoon passed them.

Cooper stepped slowly down the tree-tunnel on the watch for more booby traps, but didn't spot any. He soon reached the bottom of the hill. The wall of fallen trees was higher there and more spread out. He had to climb thirty meters up the next hill before he was able to turn around the end of the trees. When he reached the bottom again he stopped and looked back to Bingham for directions. The squad leader told him to go into the brush and circle the hill ten meters up from the bottom.

CHAPTER TWELVE

The Hoblie-Goblies Will Get You If You Don't Watch Out

The hills here weren't round or oval; they were long and narrow with a generally east-west orientation. Looked at on a north-south axis from a sufficient altitude or looked at on the right kind of map, they could be imagined to be a badly beaten washboard going up your line of sight. Turn the viewpoint ninety degrees and the hills formed a series of broken ridges and valleys leading from the South China Sea to the mountains of Laos. Some of the hills had gentle slopes that would be easy to walk, if it weren't for the dense jungle brush. Some of the hills were sheer-sided, climbable only with ropes, pitons, and caribiners. Some of them topped off a short distance from one end and maintained that altitude until they declined near the other end. Others split off, branched into two or more ridges. Still other hills rose to spiky peaks and yet others were topped with multiple, rounded crowns.

First platoon was navigating one flank of a hill from east to west when it was stopped by the fallen tree wall. The Marines descended to a narrow valley between it and its southern neighbor to circumnavigate that wall. The climb back up was a northwest arc turning north by the time they reached the company CP unit. They had gone around one of three round hilltops that sat on this ridge. A broad, easy, kilometer-wide saddle stretched from where Alpha Company was to the next rounded crown. But that saddle and the next height showed only on the maps the officers and some of the NCOs carried; the forest hid them from naked eyes and would reveal them only to walking feet.

"We're more than an hour behind schedule already," Captain Bernstein told his platoon commanders. "We're past that wall and know where we are relative to each other, so let's move it out and maintain our positions. We've got ground to cover before we reach our night position. Do it."

So Alpha Company set off across the saddle, once more in a line of platoons—this time, second platoon was on the left and first was between it and the command group. The same bombing raid that had created the tree wall they went around had knocked down trees in the saddle, torn gaping rents in the canopy overhead. The sunlight pouring down through the holes in the ceiling gave life to a newly sprouting riot of jungle floor vegetation; shattered, fallen tree trunks and tangled undergrowth made the easy saddle harder to navigate than any other terrain they had crossed in the days they'd been out.

Copeland looked into the jumbled saddle and swore. "Shit. Bingham, you got the point," he said. "Put Chief up front. If there's a way through that garbage he'll find it."

First squad was in the same route order it had been in when the wall was found. The going was slow, the tangle was too new for animals to have established new trails through it. Some fallen tree trunks were small enough to step over, some could be easily climbed over. Other trees had to be gone around. It took half an hour to cover the first half kilometer toward the next hilltop. It would have taken much longer if Rush had bothered to look for booby traps instead of just trying to find a way through. He figured either Charlie hadn't had time to booby-trap the area yet or, more likely, he couldn't figure out any good places to set them. Bingham flip-flopped his squad for the second half kilometer, Longfellow's fire team up front, Peale's bringing up the rear. He kept Cooper in the middle with him.

At the foot of the next rise Cooper said, "Better put me up front, Honcho. People're gonna get pissed if I don't take a turn." His breathing was heavy and he had to blink sweat out of his eyes. He was hitting his water hard and he knew it. Hopefully, they'd get resupplied before nightfall.

Bingham saw that the hump was tiring Cooper, but he agreed. He could see this hill hadn't been bombed and would be easier going than the saddle had been. And the thinner brush made this a less likely place for Charlie to set an ambush. That helped his decision. "Put Morse up front," he said. "It's been so long since we've run into any shit we could probably put a blind old woman on point and not have to sweat it."

Cooper stared hard at his friend and thought about that blind old woman. It bothered him, he had been around long enough to know that when you get complacent is when you're most likely to run into something that bites—and that is absolutely the wrong time to run into a biter. "I'll tell him to be careful," he said.

One thing about the war most Americans on the home front never really understood was that whenever the Americans and the Vietcong fought a pitched battle, the Americans won. Hands down, almost every time. That's why the Vietcong went to great lengths to avoid pitched battles. They'd snipe and run, they'd throw in a few mortar rounds or rockets and run, they'd ambush and run. Any time they had a choice, they'd hit hard and fast and run. Di-di-mau the fuck out of there, as our foot troops put it. Any time they didn't have that choice they'd simply try to run. Everybody agreed the Vietcong were especially adept at the art of ambush and run—the quintessential form of guerrilla combat.

When the B-52s bombed that hill the Vietcong guessed it wouldn't be long before some Americans came through on foot. They sent two one-hundred-man companies to the hill under the command of a senior captain. The senior captain examined the terrain and made his best educated guesses about what the most likely routes of approach would be for the Americans who were sure to come. He then had his men prepare elaborate, well-camouflaged positions from which to strike in their ambush. He had them prepare enough positions to hold a battalion of five hundred men. That was because he didn't know from what direction the Americans would come and he wanted to have good defensive positions regardless of where he had to fight. Then the Vietcong booby-trapped each position—though they didn't bother to booby-trap any of the approaches—and waited for the Americans to come. VC scouts spotted Alpha Company long before it reached the ambush site on the second crown of the ridge and reported back to their captain. He issued one of several sets of previously prepared orders and his men disarmed the booby traps in the positions from which they would hit the Americans, so they wouldn't accidently set them off and kill themselves. Other platoons were dispatched to follow the Marines into the ambush site. Then they waited for their victims to arrive in the killing zone.

Second platoon's point entered the killing zone of the ambush. On its left were fifty men in camouflaged positions with two machine guns. Third platoon entered the killing zone and there were fifty men and two machine guns in camouflaged positions on their right, each ambush line extended farther in both directions than the smaller platoon it was hitting. Twenty-five men with two more machine guns were dug in ahead of the Marines to prevent them from breaking through in that direction. Behind Alpha Company, seventy-five more VC with four machine guns cat-footed to positions to cut the Marines off from retreat. They waited with directional mines for the Americans to come back to them.

The two flanks of the ambush were wrapped downhill from the crest of the ridge so when they fired, their bullets would go up and over the hilltop—they could both fire without danger of hitting each other. Alpha Company was also about two hundred men, bigger, stronger men. Men armed with better weapons, carrying more ammunition, they had organic mortars with them; and they had artillery and maybe air support at their command. But the Marines were standing upright and the Vietcong were hidden beneath the surface of the ground. And the VC knew it would take time for the American artillery and air support to come into play and that their mortars couldn't be used inside the forest. The trailing troop commander reported the Marines were totally in the U-shaped ambush and both sides of it opened fire with rifles and automatic rifles.

The world erupted with noise and Bingham dropped to the ground. "Get down!" he shouted to his squad, "Get down!" Confused voices added their shouts to the bursts of automatic rifle fire and staccato hammering of the enemy machine guns and the Marines' rifles started returning the Vietcong fire. Bingham strained his ears, trying to make out anything coherent in the cacophony. He heard the voices of Copeland and Ives rising in excitement, but they weren't shouting at him. "First squad, team leaders report," he called and soon heard Longfellow, Peale, and Cooper answer that they had no casualties. At the same time his mind sorted out the sounds of the firefight and he realized the company was being hit from both flanks but not the front or the rear. He looked to the sides and saw that the rise of the earth on his right shadowed first platoon from the gunfire from that side. The ground curved down to the left and they were protected from that direction as long as they stayed down. It was a simple matter for them to survive where they were, just stay down. All they had to do now was wait for orders.

The rates of fire seemed to even out, and then the Marines' firepower quickly overcame the initial VC advantage. But neither side seemed to be able to gain true superiority over the other. But the VC could pull back if they wanted to; the Marine platoons in the killing zones were pinned down.

In the company CP, the forward air controller traveling with Alpha Company called for a flight of attack bombers to aid them. It was promised and would arrive in fifteen minutes—if it wasn't diverted somewhere else first. The lieutenants commanding second and third platoons weren't confused for long and gave Captain Bernstein concise reports on their situations. Captain Bernstein puzzled over the reports for a few seconds. He was well aware of parallel ambushes, ambushes set with the attackers on both sides of their victims. But usually the attackers held high ground on the sides of their victims, not the other way around, although in this situation it was a tactic that could work well for a time. And they sometimes had a blocking position ahead and sometimes inserted a blocking force in the rear. Alpha Company was in a difficult position, but its commanding officer didn't spend much time worrying about it. He was a decisive man and made his decision quickly.

"Get One Actual on the horn," he told his radioman. "Four, send your section chief with half the mortarmen to reinforce One," he said to the weapons platoon commander, who was lying on the ground a few feet away from him, "keep the rest of them here to secure the CP." He didn't wait for an answer, he knew, and he knew the weapons platoon commander also knew, the mortars were useless under these trees. He took the offered handset from his radioman and said into it, "One Actual, Six Actual. Leave one squad and one gun in place as reserve and pull the other two back to where you can lay down enfilade fire on the little people who have Two pinned down. Mortars will reinforce you. Understand?"

"Roger that, Six Actual," Copeland replied. "Will do. Over."

"Do it. Six Actual, out." Alpha Company's maneuvering started. Bernstein turned to the FAC and asked casually, "When the fast movers get here, we're under double canopy. How do you plan on telling them where we are and where the bad guys are?"

The forward air controller looked at him blankly; he was a fighter pilot, new to the forward air controller business, and hadn't thought about the lack of visual contact between the company and its air support. "I'll work it out," he said, but he didn't know how he was going to do it.

Ives called first platoon's squad leaders up and briefed them quickly. "Second and third squads and mortars," Copeland said without preamble when the squad leaders and mortar section leader joined the platoon CP, "we're pulling back a hundred meters, then swing around and flank the bad guys who have second platoon pinned down. First squad, assemble right here with me." He looked hard at Bingham and said, "If they need us I want to be climbing their asses before Aaron even says 'out' on the radio, understand?" Bingham nodded. Copeland looked at the other two squad leaders and the mortar section leader. "Questions?" he asked.

They were mum. Even Gershwin didn't have any questions.

"Let's go," Copeland said, and signaled Butterfield to move out. Ives stayed in reserve with first squad.

Bingham scurried back to where his men waited and told his fire-team leaders what was up. "Follow me," he finished, and ran in a low crouch, with Harte at his heels, to where Ives waited with one of the machine-gun teams attached to the platoon.

The idea was for first platoon to back up a little more than a hundred yards, then cut right and get in a position to rain fire down the long axis of the ambushers' line—a basic infantry tactic. But flanking maneuvers don't always work right away, not when the defenders have set up their defense to encourage flank attacks.

They hadn't gone the whole distance when the forest to their front erupted with blasts in their faces. The first five Marines in line were thrown backward by the mines the VC set off. The rest of them dropped in place; only the ones closest to the explosions opened fire at their unseen enemy and the men farther back in the column couldn't shoot without the risk of hitting their own people.

"Second squad, swing left," Copeland yelled. "Get on line and lay down some fire so we can get these wounded out of here. Move it. Mortars, swing right."

"Let's go, people," Gershwin shouted and dashed at an angle to his left. His squad followed him. "First team here," he said and pointed when they had gone far enough to fire without hitting third squad. The men dropped and opened fire at the faceless foliage. "Second team," he shouted a few meters farther, and those men dove to cover and started firing. Then he dropped himself and signaled his third team to set in on his other side.

The ten mortarmen did the same on the other side. The return fire from first platoon built up enough to keep the Viet Cong from taking full advantage of their surprise, but the VC fire was heavy enough that no one could move forward to aid the casualties.

"Tell my Five to get his ass up here on the double," Copeland told his radioman. "Five" was radio talk for the number two man in a unit, in this case Ives.

The radioman spoke into his handset, listened, said, "Out," turned to Copeland and said, "On their way."

What might have been only seconds later, but was probably closer to a minute, Ives and Bingham dropped down next to Copeland.

"Second squad's pinned down directly in front of us and they've got casualties down ahead of them. Third squad's on line left, mortars right," Copeland told the two men. He didn't look at them; his eyes darted around the forest from where the hidden enemy was fighting, trying to locate them. To Bingham he said, "Get your people up there with Two, lay down heavy enough fire that those wounded can be pulled back. Go." Then he switched his attention to Ives to tell him what to do with the machine gun.

Bingham didn't hear what Copeland told Ives, he was scuttling back the ten yards to where his squad waited, everyone laying prone with rifles ready to fire. "We're going up to lay down covering fire so some wounded can be pulled back," he told them. "Let's go."

They rose to low crouches and followed him at a fast trot past Copeland and his radioman. Ives was already gone to place the machine gun. Second squad wasn't on-line; the men who weren't hit were in two bunches, one slightly ahead and to the side of the other. A corpsman was with them. Both bunches were behind dense bushes. No fire was coming directly at them; the Vietcong's attention seemed to be concentrated on the units to their sides. First squad dropped as soon as they came in sight of second.

"We can't move," Butterfield shouted when he saw Bingham. "They open up whenever they see us look around these goddam bushes."

Bingham twisted around in his prone position. Longfellow's first fire team was directly behind him. He pointed at the short corporal and then pointed emphatically to the left. He pumped his fist up and down. "Fifteen meters," he shouted.

"Let's go," Longfellow snapped to his men. They bolted to their feet and dashed to the left side. VC fire tore through the air around them, but no one was hit. They quickly covered the distance and dropped into position to open up on the unseen enemy.

Bingham pointed at Peale and to the right, then pumped his fist up and down again. He didn't bother shouting how far to go. Peale and his men dashed through new fire on that side.

Cooper's fire team and Harte were all that were left with him. "We're going to get between second squad's two positions and put out everything we've got," he shouted at them. He looked back to the front, braced himself against the ground, and jumped up to a low, running crouch. Midway between the two large bushes second squad was hiding behind he dropped down and started blasting the forest in front of him. He heard the other men open up on his sides and was relieved—he hadn't looked back to see if they were following.

The fire from a whole squad was heavy enough to encourage one of the men in second squad to crab-scuttle to the nearest wounded man. He reached him and was able to drag him back to concealment behind the bush. The other men in second squad saw this, and two of them rushed to the casualties. The rest of the squad edged to the sides of the bushes and added their covering fire to first squad's.

Bingham stopped firing and, with a hand motion, told Harte to hold his fire. He lay flat on the ground and raised his head as high as his neck would go, turning from side to side, listening. All he could hear was the fire from the Marines and the crying and moaning of the wounded and the curses and shouts of the men moving the wounded. Whoever had set off the explosives wasn't firing at them now.

"Slow fire, everyone," he shouted to his squad when the last of the wounded were retrieved, "ten seconds between rounds." A heavy enough rate of fire to keep heads down on the other side, light enough that they wouldn't run out of ammunition in a hurry. He kept listening for any sound that would allow him to tell his men where to fire to kill an enemy. The VC kept their discipline.

"Cease fire, cease fire," Copeland shouted. He, too, had been listening for the enemy. The squad leaders echoed him. Even the wounded stopped their moaning for a few seconds. The Marines listened in the sudden silence in their part of the jungle. Someone running up behind them was all they heard. It was another corpsman.

"Where are they?" Someone pointed to the two men who were behind one bush; the other three were being treated behind the other bush by the corpsman who was on the scene already. He started his examination. "Holy shit," he swore. One man had a chunk of muscle torn out of his right arm; he had already wrapped his compress bandage around it and was cradling his arm and trying not to cry from the pain. The other was unconscious and blood dripped from multiple lacerations on his face; his helmet lay next to his head with a deep dent in it. Of the other three, one man lay with vacant eyes staring at the treetops; he was dead. Another lay curled, with his arms wrapped around his exposed intestines. The left arm of the last man was hanging from a scrap of flesh. Someone had tied a tourniquet around it a couple of inches above the wound. The corpsman gave these last two men shots of morphine before treating their wounds. The wounds of the man with the lacerated face looked more spectacular than they were—his treatment could wait.

Satisfied that his wounded were being cared for and not hearing anything from the front, Copeland said into his radio, "Alpha One, on your feet. Keep it on-line and let's move forward. Be careful, somebody might still be out there."

The squad leaders spoke softly and used hand gestures to get their men up and moving. Every man in the line kept his eyes moving and the muzzle of his weapon moving with his eyes. The Vietcong waited for their signal to open up again on the advancing Americans.

Rush was in the middle of the line and was the first one to see anything. He pulled the trigger of his rifle twice in rapid succession. The first bullet traveled less than ten feet before smashing through the face of a VC who wasn't as well concealed as he thought he was. The second bullet wasn't needed. "We're on top of them," Rush shouted and hit the deck. He landed within arm's reach of the man he had just killed. The rest of the Marines started blasting away and dove for cover as soon as they heard Rush's first shot. It was a few seconds before the VC leaders realized what was happening and gave their orders to shoot back; the Marines had initial fire superiority.

Bingham wriggled into the ground but didn't fire. He didn't want to give away his position. He listened to the others. They started firing rapidly, but slowed down when they realized they didn't know what they were shooting at. Then the Vietcong opened up and bullets seemed to be flying at them from all directions at once. Bingham saw a muzzle flash in a bush six feet from where he lay. He pointed his rifle at the middle of the bush, low to the ground, and *bang, bang, bang,* fired three rounds into it. The bush shuddered and he didn't see the muzzle flash again. He guessed the interval of the ambushers at four or five meters and picked another nearby clump of brush as a likely hiding place for an enemy soldier. The bullets he fired into it skimmed a mere few inches above the ground, aimed low to hit a prone body. A scream from the brush told him he had guessed right and the smile he smiled was a death's mask. He fired a few more rounds into the brush to make sure whoever he hit was dead, then looked around for other likely targets. Bingham felt no fear in this firefight, even though some part of his mind knew they were probably outnumbered and might get wiped out. It happened that way sometimes; the more dangerous a situation was, the less a man in it cared—he knew trying to hide didn't matter, he was probably dead anyway, so he might as well take as many with him as he could.

"Fire low," Bingham shouted, "they're on the ground under the bushes. Keep your shots low so you can hit them."

The return fire from the Vietcong was noticeably less than it had been moments before. The Marines' fire was having an effect on the hidden enemy. There were no more shots coming from his front, so Bingham rolled to his left. The forest in front of Cooper's fire team seemed quiet also. "Hold your fire," he told them. "Wait until you're sure somebody's there again." Then he rolled right. An automatic rifle was zapping bullets through the brush just above the heads of Longfellow's men, keeping them pinned and unable to do more than point their rifles and pull the triggers. He searched the forest in front of them and saw leaves buzzing in a bush in time with the banging from the automatic. He picked a spot in the bush behind the buzzing leaves and fired the rest of the rounds in his magazine into it. The automatic rifle stopped.

"Don't fire unless you see or hear someone," he shouted while he reloaded, then scuttled to the other end of his squad. Peale had already ordered his men to cease fire. A few shots were still coming from the remnants of second squad. That was all, that and the continued firefights on both flanks of the main body of the company.

"Squad leaders report," Copeland shouted.

"First squad okay," Bingham shouted back. He had seen that none of his men were hurt when he checked them. The rest of the platoon had no new casualties. Rush's sharp eyes and immediate reaction had saved the Marines.

"Stand by and listen," Copeland ordered. Their part of the forest was deadly silent. "Bingham, send a fire team forward to check for bodies," the lieutenant ordered after a minute. "Everybody else, look sharp."

"Hank, swing out in front of Chickencoop and sweep across our front. Remember to watch for booby traps."

"You better believe it, Honcho," Longfellow said. "You heard the man, people, let's go. Careful, there's boo-coo gone gooners out there and maybe some not so gone." He led West, Copley, and Emerson in front of Cooper's fire team and lined them up to sweep through the bushes in front of the platoon to find the bodies of the dead VC. As long as they were careful about checking the bodies they should have been all right. But there were another sixty Vietcong soldiers in this blocking force.

All ambushes are basic in their formations and there are certain standard responses that are effective against them. Both sides in a war that makes extensive use of ambushes are familiar with all forms of ambush and the appropriate reactions. Some reactions are equally effective against other kinds of enemy formations. Just like the Marines pulled back a platoon to roll up the flank of one ambush line, so did the VC send a platoon to roll up the flank of that Marine platoon.

"John, check bodies, Ben cover him," Longfellow ordered. "I'll cover Ralph checking bodies. Let's go." They stepped toward the first bodies and a hail of hand grenades fell among them. West and Copley saw the grenades sailing past them in time to spin from them and duck under cover. Longfellow and Emerson were slower. They screamed as shrapnel tore into their bodies.

"On the left," Copley shouted, "they're coming from the left front," and opened fire in the direction the grenades had come from.

"Chickencoop, turn them around," Bingham screamed. "Chuck, get your people over here."

He flattened himself on the ground next to Russell and fired into the jungle to the left of the platoon. Screams, yelling, and chants came from that direction, along with the heaviest fusillade of rifle fire first platoon had faced that day. And more grenades.

The advancing Vietcong pointed their muzzles down to avoid shooting over the Marines and hitting their own men on their far side; most of the rounds slammed ineffectively into the dirt long before reaching their intended targets. Many of their Chinese grenades were duds. Then they broke into sight. Their voices rose in howls and they charged the prone Marines who were pumping bullets at them as fast as they could. Some of them carried automatic AK-47 rifles with flame stuttering from their muzzles; others carried longer, semi-automatic rifles. A few had long, spiky bayonets jutting forward from under their barrels.

Bullets slammed into the ground in front of Bingham, kicking twigs and dirt up into his face. He jerked away and pointed his rifle up to blast at a VC who was almost on top of him. The small man staggered under the impact of the hits, then fell forward. Bingham rolled from him, but the bayonet on the dead man's rifle slashed his left arm. The VC ran past the Marines and the Americans twisted around to fire at their backs, then the mortar men on that side opened on the VC as they were starting to turn back to hit first squad again. Bingham aimed at another VC lunging toward him with bayoneted rifle extended full length and nothing happened. He froze for an instant with panic welling somewhere inside him as he realized his weapon was empty. Then a jolt of adrenaline kicked through his body and he sprang back and upward to his knees, avoiding the flashing bayonet, and swung the butt of his rifle around in an arc that slammed the little man in the ribs and threw him to the ground. In one motion he reversed his grip on his rifle and hammered its butt plate into the head of the VC who was curled up, clutching his side and gasping for air. Flesh split and bone shattered, blood sprayed into the air and onto Bingham. He didn't notice how heavily he was breathing as he knocked the empty magazine out of his rifle and slammed a new one in, then jammed his bayonet over its flash suppressor.

The two groups of men closed in hand-to-hand combat. The Americans were huge next to their foes, close to six feet tall and not much less than two hundred pounds each. The VC were hardly more than five feet tall and weighed little more than a hundred pounds. The advantage the little people had was numbers, but they had lost too many men before choosing to grapple. The twenty Americans left standing could have beaten them even if Ives hadn't arrived with Gershwin's squad. The VC bolted for safety when the reinforcements arrived to help out. Bingham grabbed one of the little men running past him and was throttling him when an unimaginable force hit the side of his helmet and knocked him to the ground. Before losing all consciousness he heard a rushing sound that could have been blood coursing through veins in his ears—or could have been jet aircraft arriving to break up the last of the ambush.

CHAPTER THIRTEEN

The Basics of Warfare Are Bullets and Bandages, Beans and Beer. Not Necessarily in That Order.

"Hold still there, Marine, don't move."

Bingham moved anyway. He turned his head and opened his eyes to see who was talking to him and where he was and a jolt of pain that made him wish he hadn't moved shot through his head. He saw a metal partition with a tiny window in it and a shadow behind it.

"Shit! Don't you ever listen, Marine? I told you not to move, goddam it." The voice came from behind the metal partition. "Now I got to put your head back in place and take this goddam picture again." A man wearing white trousers and a white lab coat stepped from behind the partition.

"Where am I?" Bingham asked through the pain. His voice was so low and rusty he wasn't sure it was his. The lack of response from the man in the white coat made him think the minor, squeaky voice hadn't been heard so he gathered his strength and tried again. "Where the fuck am I?" His voice was stronger this time, but he groaned from the throbbing in his head the effort caused. He could tell from the coldness under his back that he was laying on a metal table; it felt like he was naked. Other than the metal partition, the whitewashed room seemed to be bare.

"Hold your head just like that," the man in the lab coat said. His hands moving Bingham's head were far gentler than his voice. He went back behind the partition. "I got a good one of the profile, now I need a straight-on. X ray," he added almost as an afterthought. Now Bingham looked straight up and recognized the device hanging above his face. He relaxed; he was in a safe place now. The down-pointing cone whirred briefly and the technician came out of his hiding place. "Man, you must have run into a steam roller or some such shit out there," he said. "Or Uncle Ho's palace guards or something like that. It took three HUS-1s to haul all your scuzzy asses in."

Two more corpsmen entered the X-ray room and the three lifted Bingham onto a gurney and placed a sheet over him. That's when he knew he was naked, his boots and helmet and the pieces of the uniform cut off his body were already on the gurney. A lump on his left arm told him it was bandaged; he guessed it was probably the same dressing applied in the field. "And I could tell none of you goddam grunts took any showers lately, neither," the X-ray tech continued as the others rolled Bingham away. "Not only did you guys get blood all over my nice clean X-ray room, you got to stink it up with your smelly bods, too." His voice faded into a distant drone that mingled with other hospital noises until it was lost in the background.

Suddenly the gurney pushed through a slamming double door and he found himself in a room filled with other wounded men, some laying on gurneys like him, some on litters, others sitting on chairs or the floor. Most of them were still wearing parts of the same filthy uniforms they were wearing when they got hit. He could tell that the room had been cleaned recently by the strong aroma of disinfectant in the air, but it looked like its walls and floor had never been scrubbed. Mud was tracked all over the floor and blood spilled on it. The walls were covered with daubs of mud and smears of blood.

"Yo, Bingham," a weak voice said.

He propped himself up on his good arm, made the mistake of shaking his head to try to clear it, and fell back gasping with dizziness and pain.

"Lay quiet, Marine," a woman's voice said and a hand held him down by his good shoulder. "We don't want you moving around until we know how your head is."

Bingham opened his eyes and saw a soft face surrounded by a halo of black hair topped with a white cap looking down at him. He tried to smile.

"It's okay," the nurse looked at something he couldn't see and read, "Corporal Bingham. You just relax and the doctor will see you as soon as he examines your X rays. Do you hurt anywhere?"

"Only when I move," he said and tried to smile again.

"See?" she said. "That's why we don't want you moving. It hurts. Just lay quietly for a few minutes." The nurse started to turn to someone else and paused to add, "Your wounds don't seem to be all that bad, you'll be all right in no time." She smiled down at him. "You'll see." She looked reflective for a moment and added in a flat voice, "I'm glad I don't have to see whoever it was you boys were fighting with," and moved on to someone else.

"Yo, Bingham," the weak voice said again. "Hold still, pano, I can make it over to you." He heard a strange clomping and the sound of feet scuffing along the floor to his right and then Cooper was looming over him, leaning on crutches. A smile only partly disguised the concern on his face. "Got your bell rung," Cooper said. "You been awake long enough to see your helmet yet?"

Bingham was careful not to shake his head, he said no.

Cooper reached for something at the foot of the gurney and brought his hand to where Bingham could see the helmet. Half of the left side of it looked as though it had been beaten with a nine-pound sledgehammer. The indentation wasn't deep, but it was large, and the camouflage cover was burnt off around the damaged area. "Big piece of something whapped you right upside the gourd," Cooper said.

Gingerly, Bingham reached up with his left arm, trying not to cause pain where he was cut, and felt the side of his head. It was tender, but he didn't feel any blood or scabbing.

"You got one bodacious bruise, but it didn't break the skin."

"What about the bone?"

"Nah, your skull isn't broke, it's too damn thick. They just took the X rays to prove it to the doctor." Cooper smiled weakly.

"What happened to you?"

"Piece of shrapnel in the thigh. I'll be okay in a few days." The words were nonchalant, but the expression in his eyes was haunted.

Bingham grinned wanly and said, "You ain't never going to get your quota this way, pano."

"Straight scoop," Cooper laughed. "That's why I have to be okay in a few days, get back out there and score some points on that quota." Then he turned serious. "We got fucked up pretty bad out there, about twenty people got medevaced."

Bingham interrupted him, "In the platoon?"

"No, in the whole company. There were more in the company who weren't hurt bad enough to be pulled out."

Bingham pursed his lips to whistle then thought better of it. "What happened after I got beaned?"

"A couple Phantoms came by, dropped a load of shit on Charlie's ass and he bugged out of there. Then the skipper told them to drop everything they had left on the top of that hill to give us a head start on clearing a landing zone for the medevacs. It took almost an hour before enough trees and brush were cleared for the choppers to come down and pick us up. Shit," he grinned, "there I was bleeding from the goddam leg and they called me walking wounded, made me hump stretcher cases up that mo-dicking hill."

"Anybody besides us in the squad get hit?"

Cooper nodded. "Longfellow got a lot of shit in the leg, it looked like he might lose it. Emerson's all fucked up, I don't believe he'll be back. That quiet brother, what's his name, the one from Alabama, Homer? He got grazed but they didn't evac him."

"Nobody wasted?" Cooper shook his head and Bingham sighed deeply, relieved. "What about the rest of the platoon?"

"Second squad had a man wasted and another one doesn't look like he's going to make it. Four others got hit, one right near the end of the fight. Three of them will probably be back. I don't know about third squad, I don't know anybody from there, so if some of them are here, I don't know it."

"What'd we do to them?"

"I'm not sure. The last I heard we counted twenty, twenty-five bodies and a shitload of blood trails. They may have found more after we were medevaced."

A corpsman in a blood-stained white coat came through a dou-ble door on the other side of the room and called, "Cooper. Which one of you is Corporal Cooper?"

"Yo," Cooper replied and to Bingham, "Catch you later, pano."

Bingham waved at his back and waited to hear the official results of his X rays. There was no fracture in his skull, but they needed to keep him for a few days' observation because of the concussion. They also wanted to administer anti-coagulants to clear up the bruising on the side of his head. "You can go back to your company as soon as we're sure your arm won't get infected," they told him. The medical personnel always phrased it positively—can, instead of have to, because they didn't want anyone to think he was returning into greater danger than he had come from. It wasn't necessary, though. The grunts knew how much danger they were in and went willingly anyway— they were Marines and it was their job. As one of them said years later:

> In Vietnam
> I bit through
> two pipe stems
> and one helmet
> strap, but Marines

are never afraid . . .
. . . terrified perhaps,
afraid, never!

Bingham got to see Longfellow before he was flown to Japan for further treatment prior to being returned to the United States. He found him in an amputee ward. Neither was very good at small talk so they got to Longfellow's condition pretty quickly.

"How's your leg doing?" Bingham asked, looking at the huge lump under the sheet.

"How the fuck I know? Doctor tells me it's gotta come off, I told him go fuck himself. He says there's no way it'll ever heal, I told him I know a reverend back in the World grew this dude's leg back after a railroad train cut it off. He said even if it doesn't get gangrene and kill me, there's no way I'll ever walk on it again; says there's too much bone missing." Longfellow stopped talking and beads of sweat popped out on his forehead as he strained, trying to move his toes. He couldn't feel them and Bingham didn't see any movement under the sheet. "Don't know, but if it heals, I'm sure as shit going to walk on it again." He looked up at his squad leader. "Man, this fucker don't get well it's gonna put a serious crimp on my ass kicking and pussy whomping."

Bingham laughed and clapped Longfellow on the shoulder. "Well then, you had best get that leg working again, wouldn't want to put a crimp in your ass kicking—or your pussy whomping." He cocked an eye and added, "I bet there's plenty of round-eye pussy that'll go for a man who can't run away, though."

"Sure 'nuff," Longfellow laughed back. "Gonna get me some." He jammed a fist into the air, then turned more serious. "Down home I was one serious ass kicker. Any time some good old boys was having a set and wanted to make sure they won, they got me on their side. I kicked some ass hard."

"I believe you did," Bingham said, "and you will again." But he didn't believe it, not the part about fighting. Longfellow was tough and acted tougher. The act could have saved him from a lot of harassment because of his small stature, but his toughness couldn't have given him a big enough edge in a knock-down drag-out with big men.

Bingham didn't visit long. Soon he promised to relay to the rest of the squad that they were all invited to visit Longfellow in Mississippi when they returned to the World, even the black Marines. They exchanged a few last, inane remarks and he left in search of Emerson but didn't find him.

He didn't get to see much of Cooper, either, until they returned to the company almost two weeks later. The operation had ended during their absence and Alpha Company was back on a fire base running security patrols and ambushes. A week later there was a company formation for awards presentation.

The battalion commander came to the awards presentation. He wouldn't normally come himself; he preferred to allow the company officers to present things such as promotions up to three-stripe sergeant, Purple Hearts, Navy and Marine Corps Medals, Navy Commendation Medals and Navy Achievement Medals. Actually, he didn't much care for awards and promotion ceremonies that weren't for officers. He came to this one, though, because his boss, the regimental commander, came. And the only reason the regimental commander was there was the division's assistant commanding general came to award a Silver Star to someone in third platoon for something he had done during the second week Alpha Company was in-country.

The assistant division commander was a salty old brigadier general who belatedly understood the only reasons he made one-star rank were the Medal of Honor and Navy Cross he won in World War II and the second Navy Cross he earned in Korea. He knew the only way he was ever going to get his second star was via graveyard promotion, so he treated his duty in Vietnam as a farewell tour and pretty much did what he damn well pleased. He had already started the paperwork that would have him retired from active service shortly after his return home.

The general showed up to present this Silver Star wearing fluff-dried utilities (not starched and sharply pressed like the other generals and field grade officers wore) and his boots weren't spit-shined either. "Any idiot who'll go to where a real live enemy is shooting real live bullets and not take precautions is an asshole who deserves to get blown away by the first sniper who sees him," is how he explained his uniform. The troops loved him for that. He didn't carry a well-oiled, ceremonial .45 in a spit-shined holster on his hip, he had a well-used .357 magnum. It was loaded. He intended to be able to defend himself if he had to. Somehow, wearing his Medal of Honor around his neck and the Navy Cross with its silver star indicating a second award over his left shirt pocket didn't spoil the effect of being a grunt's general.

He didn't bother to use the public address system that had been set up for his benefit, a PA system the other officers who'd already spoken had used. He read the Silver Star citation in a voice that could have carried clearly over a parade ground large enough to hold an entire regiment. Then, after pinning the medal on its recipient's shirt, said *sotto voce*, "Son, after reading that citation, if it was up to me you would've got one of these," and tapped his thumb against the medal on his own chest.

Since he was there anyway, the general then pinned Purple Hearts on the shirts of the fifteen men in the company who had been wounded and returned to duty in the past month, including Bingham and Cooper. After that he said a few words to the company, saluted it and followed the battalion and regimental commanders back onto the helicopter and took off for his next farewell appearance. He was making the best farewell tour he knew how. The troops would remember him well, even if the other generals and colonels would be glad to see him retired.

Then Captain Bernstein took over. "To all who shall see these presents, greeting." There were promotion warrants to hand out. Copley and West got their BB guns—lance corporal. Bingham was promoted to sergeant. Longfellow, naturally, missed the ceremony. After that it was party time.

"Shee-it, bro, what is this happy horseshit," Cooper groused at Bingham after the ritual pinning on of the stripes. None of the other sergeants had hit Bingham on his still mending left arm—as it was, his good arm now hurt more than the wounded one. Cooper complained, but he smiled while he did. "I've got TI on you in the Crotch and time in grade and here you go and get your third stripe before I do. Don't that beat all." He shook his head. "Ain't no justice in the world." TI meant "Time in," a very important concept to enlisted Marines. It determined who was senior and got to pull rank.

"No justice, shit." Bingham grinned back. "I got promoted first because I'm more badass than you are." They joked about it, but they both knew the truth. Bingham got promoted first not through pure merit, though he did deserve the promotion, but because of simple luck. He just happened to be in a position to become a squad leader when there was an opening and Cooper hadn't been in such a position.

Cooks were busy broiling steaks and baking potatoes at a half-dozen barbecues made from fifty-five-gallon drums cut in half lengthwise. Ten more drums cut in half the other way were spotted around the company area. These drums were filled with water—water for lack of ice—and loaded with canned soda and beer. The beer was unlimited for the men who received medals or promotions, everyone else was limited to two for the evening because they had to return to perimeter security and pull ambush for the night. Bingham and Cooper each managed to get two steaks and two potatoes. They raided a water drum of beer and filled a haversack with the slightly cooled brew and headed for a part of the perimeter where there was no one else nearby. They found a bunker that didn't have anyone in it. It was their first real chance to catch each other up on what had happened since Bingham left Pendleton for Vietnam. And to reminisce.

"Remember that place in L.A., that burlesque theater we went to?" Cooper asked when he finished his first beer and was almost through with his second steak.

"You mean the one with Honey Bunns, Miss Fifty-Nine?" Bingham laughed at the memory.

"Yeah, that's the one."

Bingham remembered it, all right. The burlesque theater was only a few blocks from the Greyhound bus station. Nearly every place the Marines from Camp Pendleton went to when they pulled liberty in Los Angeles was near the bus station. Unless they headed for Hollywood. It was a grand old house that had hosted the performances of Blaze Starr and Sally Rand in their primes. More recently Candy Barr had graced its stage with a raunchier strip routine. But it wasn't just a strip joint, it was a real burlesque theater. Earlier generations had laughed to the antics of George Burns and Jack Benny on that stage. The comics it footlined today were unknowns who had been unknowns since they entered the business and would remain unknowns for the few remaining years until their retirements. That's why they were footlined instead of headlined. The women were the headliners now and families no longer came to be entertained there.

One week the headliner was Honey Bunns, Miss Fifty-Nine. Bingham saw the ad in the L.A. *Times* and whistled. "Oo-ee, Chickencoop, lookie this." He held out the paper and his eyes focused on some never-never land. He was used to the 36–24–36 figures displayed in Playboy and couldn't imagine a fifty-nine-inch bust.

Cooper took the paper and studied the ad for a few seconds. "No, man, you got it all wrong. That's not her bra size, it's her age."

"No way, Chickencoop. Look at what it says there, it says fifty-nine-inch bosom, not fifty-nine years old."

"So it's a misprint. Newspapers do that sometimes, you know, print something wrong."

"But this is an ad. They never get the ads wrong, the people who pay for the ads'll stop putting them in, they get the ads wrong. Let's go up to sin city and see this thing."

"Man," Cooper cocked his head, "you want to go watch some old lady older than my grandma take her clothes off, you got some kind of problem." He put the back of his hand against Bingham's forehead. "Tell Doctor Chickencoop where it hurts."

But two days later, when they boarded the Los Angeles bus in San Clemente, Cooper was as excited about seeing Honey Bunns, Miss Fifty-Nine, as Bingham was.

Most of the lights in the theater were dim long before the curtain went up, the lights were kept dim to save on the cost of electricity. The lobby was dim, so its former grandeur was hinted at but not seen to be faded. The proscenium was dim, and the threadbareness of the carpets and the old stains on the brocade wallpaper weren't visible. The curtained side aisles were dim almost to blackness and only the musty smell gave notice they were no longer aisles of glory. Only the central seating area was well lit. And that was so customers could easily see their way to their seats—and the management expected no one would object too strenuously to the tattered seat covers.

Several uniformed ushers waited in the proscenium to escort theater-goers down the two aisles between the central seating area and the side areas. But the seats weren't reserved, and if a customer didn't like where the usher sat him, he could point out where he did want to sit and the usher would shrug and lead him there. The seating capacity on the main level was more than five hundred. The wing boxes and balcony could hold several hundred more. A live "orchestra" of piano, drums, one sax, and three horns—all late middle-aged—wandered in and out of its pit preparing for its part in the evening's festivities. Two other theater employees, middle-aged men in drab suits, prowled up and down the aisles hawking magazines and novelties, including something they did not call Spanish fly but to which they vaguely attributed the same properties.

Bingham and Cooper prowled the rear of the theater for a few moments, looking into the rapidly filling orchestra seating to pick where they wanted to sit.

"Over there," Bingham slapped Cooper's arm with the hand he wasn't pointing. The seats he picked were in a row that was filled to the midway point from the left side. Three rows of seats directly in front of where he wanted to go were empty and so were two rows behind it.

Cooper looked and nodded. "You got point," he said.

"Shit, I always got point," Bingham said back. Grunts were constantly translating daily situations into infantry tactics. He started toward the seats he had picked.

"That's because you're a damn boot. When you get some salt on you you won't have to be point anymore." He looked thoughtful for a second and added, "If you can find someone more boot than you."

An usher carrying a flashlight that he didn't bother to turn on stepped in front of them and said, "Follow me, please." He didn't stop at the row Bingham had picked.

"Whoa, we want to sit here," Cooper said.

The usher turned back, shrugged with his eyebrows, allowed them to sit in the row they wanted, and returned to his station.

They sidled into the row and hunched down in their seats, trying to maintain their dignity, trying not to giggle, and not quite succeeding. They repeatedly poked each other in the ribs and whispered in squeaky voices that neither understood, but the lack of understanding of the words did nothing to lessen the humor they heard in each others voices. After a few moments they calmed down and rubbernecked. In the shadows on the sides and back of the orchestra they saw drab-looking, middle-aged and older men sitting quietly, patiently waiting for the remaining house lights to dim and the curtain to rise. Young, short-haired men crowded the orchestra pit and the stage, hooting and hollering for the show to start. The rest of the lit area was filling with more young, short-haired men. A few were in uniform, mostly Navy.

"I used to have a sailor suit," Cooper whispered, "when I was five years old."

"Me, too," Bingham whispered back. "I'd feel silly wearing one now." Again, they failed in their attempt not to giggle.

When they calmed down they looked at the audience again and played a game of picking out which of the short-haired young men were Marines, which were in the Army or were un-uniformed Navy. They didn't even think of Air Force.

The musicians settled down in their pit to flex their fingers, roll riffs, run through scales. When they were all ready one of them soft-spoke a countdown and they started. Then the house lights dimmed and a spotlight flashed on the closed curtain. The light wavered briefly before settling on the center of the curtain.

The MC pushed the curtain open and stepped through. "Good evening, ladies and gentlemen," he crooned into his hand-held microphone. "There are ladies out there, aren't there?" he asked and leaned forward with one hand shading his eyes. "I know there's no men who aren't gentlemen in the audience and"—he waved at the curtain behind himself—"I *know* there's ladies in there." The audience laughed and hooted to bring on the girls. He cracked one-liners for a few minutes while his audience grew louder and cheerfully booed him. At last he introduced the first act and the curtain opened and the spotlight focused on a bleached blond in a sequined blue dress who was striking a pose in the middle of the stage. The orchestra went into a *boomp-de-boomp* and the blue-dressed blond strutted around the stage, teasing the audience and slowly peeling off her clothes until she was left in pasties and g-string for a final, too brief couple of moments before the spotlight blinked off and the orchestra hit its final crescendo.

The spotlight lit again and found the MC at the side of the stage where he told a few more lame jokes before introducing one of the comics. That's the way the show went. The MC and comics made jokes that could be truly appreciated by no one post-pubescent and the strippers absent-mindedly strutted their stuff, bumped and ground around the stage almost in time with the orchestra, and slowly peeled their clothes off until they were left with only pasties and g-string (neither of which were ever removed). The audience ate it up. They didn't care how stale the jokes were, they were delivered live on a real stage on which Red Skelton had once performed. And they didn't care how lethargically and impersonally the women strutted and stripped. Most of the men in the audience were eighteen, nineteen, and twenty years old, and few of them had been this close to a nearly naked woman very many times. Seeing real, live women take off most of their clothes made this an exciting evening. For most of the middle-aged and older men in the audience, this was as close as they got to a nearly naked woman anymore—unless she was as middle-aged or old as they were—and they told themselves they needed to see someone young and attractive take off most of her clothes. Even if they couldn't touch her or do any of the other things they wished they could still do to nubile women.

Finally the MC reappeared at the front middle of the stage for the first time since the opening. "Ladies and gentlemen," he boomed. "Ladies? Are you there, ladies?" shading his eyes again, then turned to leer at the curtain. "Ah, yes, ladies," and smacked his lips. Then back to the audience, "Direct from the Court of St. James and the Champs Élysées, here she is for your enjoyment and edification, the woman with the most perfectly formed fifty-nine-inch bust in the en*tire* world, *Miss Honey Bunns!*"

The spotlight's glare glittered off the sequins covering the scarlet gown worn by the hefty blond woman who had dark roots that no one in the audience noticed. There was nothing desultory about her act. She preened when she strutted, she looked into the darkness hiding the audience as though she was staring into the eyes of each man in it. Her bumps had force and her grinds were the most meaningful bits of eroticism nearly every man there had seen. There were fewer catcalls and more deep-throated howls as the young men felt the primordial call of Honey Bunns's gyrating hips. Too much makeup had been applied to her face to be able to do anything but make that face a mask, much less hide the age visible there, but hardly anyone looked closely enough at her face to be aware of it. She boomed, she squatted, she writhed. She made three hundred penises tumescent.

A perfectly formed bust, the man said? When freed from their bra their globular masses hung nearly to her waist. A slab of fat covered her abdomen and, if she had been a little heavier, would have sagged to hide her pubes. More fat pushed her buttocks a few inches farther out than her back. Nobody cared. Honey Bunns put on an *act!* and that act was all that mattered. If any of the young men in the audience saw her without the makeup and in street clothes, he would have to admit she looked like his mother on a bad day. The middle-aged and older men would have noticed a depressing resemblance to their wives, those of them who still had wives. But their mothers and wives didn't put on acts like this.

Once upon a time Mary Ellen Magonigle, which was Honey Bunns's real name, told a reporter, "Even if I wasn't too old and fat to be a go-go dancer, I'd still strip because stripping is easier work. Besides, as headliner, I make more money. It's my job to entertain those boys and, by god, I'm going to do just that." So she put on an act that made her audience think not of heavy set earth-goddesses but rather of Aphrodite. And they forget their mothers and wives.

When she strutted her last strut, bumped her last bump, ground her last grind, and the lights went out, her audience was alternately limp and more excited than most of them could imagine. Everyone smiled leaving the theater.

"I want some of that," Bingham said when they reached the street.

"You can have it," Cooper said. "If there's any left over after I'm through."

"Bullshit, Chickencoop. I don't want the comedians, not even before you're through with them."

"Fuck you."

"No thanks, I'd rather fuck the girls."

They laughed through the rest of the evening and all the way back to Camp Pendleton.

By the time they finished remembering Miss Honey Bunns, the sun was setting and half the beer they had taken was gone. That was all the talking they did about the World. They both had too long to serve in the combat zone to want to think right then about what they had left behind and what they wanted to return to. Instead they talked about where they were and why.

"What the fuck are you doing back here, Chickencoop. Seriously, don't give me any shit about a quota, there ain't no such thing. I thought it was policy no one gets orders for a second tour until everybody's been here." Bingham's voice was somber when he asked the question.

Cooper opened another beer with his bayonet and stared into the night for a long time before answering. He finally said in a voice as somber as Bingham's, "They didn't send me. I volunteered to come back."

"Why?" The word cracked like a bullet. Almost no one in combat or who has been there can understand why someone would willingly return after having been released from it.

There was another long pause before Cooper answered again. "Because I had a job to do here and I left before it was finished."

"Bullshit! You did your job, let someone else have a turn, let someone else put his ass on the line."

Cooper started talking again before Bingham finished, "Remember Braunner and Jackson? They joined the company maybe a month before you shipped out. They were in Combined Action Platoons."

"So?"

"So when I was here the first time I was on some County Fair operations, protecting the people during their rice harvesting and giving them medical attention. I got to meet some of the people." He pulled his knees up and wrapped his arms around them. "Do you know who they are, these Vietnamese they tell us we're fighting for?"

"Who?" Bingham's voice was disinterested, like he expected to hear something he wouldn't want to believe.

"They're farmers, they're small-time farmers who only want to be left alone to grow their rice and make their babies and practice their religion."

"What's that got to do with Braunner and Jackson?"

"Hang loose, you'll find out. Anyway, there's people out there," he nodded at the night outside the perimeter wire, "who want to take that away from them. People who want to turn South Vietnam into something like North Vietnam or Russia. These other people aren't going to let the South Vietnamese farmers grow their rice for themselves, they're going to make them grow it and then take it away from them. They're communists, maybe they'll take their religion away from them. I don't know, maybe they'll let them keep on making their babies."

"You saying the guys in Saigon are the real good guys?"

Cooper's silhouette hunched in the darkness. "No. They're totalitarians, too." He paused for a few seconds, grinning in the darkness, wondering if Bingham was going to say anything about him using four-bit words like "totalitarian." When Bingham didn't, he continued, "I'm not sure any totalitarian is any better than any other, communist or not. But the ones in Saigon can have an election and get voted out, get some people in there who'll care about the people. These people don't have a great life now and all they've known for thirty years is war. The war makes life tougher for them. I think if the communists win it's going to get worse for these people."

"If the communists win?" Bingham said, startled by the idea. "How the hell can they win? No matter what they do to us, we're kicking their ass. Look, a couple of weeks ago we walked into an ambush and they put a hurting on us. They hurt us bad, man. You know they did, you were there and you got hit samee-same me. But when it was over we found more of them dead than they wounded of us, and we don't know how many more of them we wasted that they carried away. Fuck a bunch of 'if they win.' It's not going to happen. No way." He shook his head emphatically. "Let somebody else take a turn getting shot at, that's all."

"Pano, I got a hard truth for you, something maybe you can't understand. You're a chuck dude and that's why you don't understand. Me, I'm a splib. You know what it's like being a splib back in the World? It sucks, man. Back in the World splibs are shit."

"I know there's prejudice back in the World."

Bingham couldn't see Cooper's head shake. "Maybe, but you don't know what it's really like. If you're black, everybody's trying to get over on you, everyone thinks you're stupid. That's kind of like what's happening to the farmers over here, everybody's trying to get over on them. The Saigon honchos are ripping them off, the district chiefs are ripping them off, and the communists are ripping them off. Everybody's ripping them off except us and sometimes instead of ripping them off we kill them." Bingham started to say something but Cooper wouldn't let him. "Shut up and listen, just don't say nothing until I'm through. So what I think is if we straighten things out here, get this country so nobody's putting something over on the farmers, white America will look and see how they did something good for one group of people who aren't white and realize they're doing something bad to Americans who aren't white. And maybe that'll change things for blacks back in the World."

When it sounded like Cooper was through Bingham asked, "What if white America doesn't think that way?"

"Then there's going to be one hell of a lot of brothers who know how to use weapons and fight a war," Cooper said with more angry passion than Bingham had ever before heard in his friend's voice.

They were tensely silent for a long moment, then Bingham asked, "What's that got to do with Braunner and Jackson, they're white?" and the tension broke.

Cooper laughed so hard he almost fell off the bunker. Bingham had to grab his arm and pull him back upright, then pound his back to bring him under control. Cooper's laughter was fading into giggles when a voice boomed out of the night, "Shitcan the grab-assing up there. Charlie's got ears, too, you know." That set Cooper off again.

Bingham wrapped his arms around him and wrestled him to the ground, tying to smother the laughing against his shoulder and chest. "Shut up, Chickencoop, shut the fuck up," he said through teeth clenched against his own laughter. "That sounded like the gunny, pano. You don't shut up the gunny's going to come up here and kick both our asses."

Cooper curled himself tightly in Bingham's arms and his chest heaved with the effort of not laughing. "Gunny can't kick our asses," he managed to gasp between laughs. "The gunny only thinks he's real badass, but there's two of us and I know we're badass." It was hard for him to talk without laughing, but he finally got himself under control. "So what the fuck's the gunny gonna do, send us to Vietnam?" Another peel of laughter burst from him and Bingham squeezed tighter until the laughing stopped and the heaving started again. After a while the heaving subsided and he shook himself free and sat up.

"Have another brew, bro," Bingham said and opened two more with his bayonet. His body needed to laugh but he knew if he did, it would only start Cooper again. After a while they both calmed enough to talk quietly again.

"You weren't paying attention to me," Cooper said. "Braunner and Jackson were in a CAP. That's how we're going to win this war. CAPs protect the good little people in the villes from the bad little people out in the boonies and they keep the district chiefs from ripping them off too much. Sooner or later the little people in the villes are going to figure out that if they work together nobody's going to be able to fuck them over and when that happens this country's going to be all right." His voice became serious again. "That's how the example of what white America can do for non-white people is going to happen. As soon as I've been here long enough I'm going to volunteer for CAP duty."

Bingham mulled for a moment then said, "Chickencoop, you're fucking dinky-dau, you know that? You know what a goddam CAP is? A CAP is a few Marines all by their lonesome out in a ville someplace where Charlie can come in and bust caps on them all over the fucking place. A CAP doesn't have enough firepower to defend itself when Charlie comes in with more than a platoon. Sure, most of the time Charlie's too busy someplace else, trying to keep some grunt battalion from wasting his young ass to fuck with a CAP, so most grunts think CAP is candy duty." He paused for emphasis, then continued, "But if they ever do fuck with a CAP, it's dead meat."

Cooper shook his head vigorously enough for Bingham to see it in the dark. "Don't work that way, pano. A CAP has a PF platoon with it. . . . "

"Fuck a bunch of Popular Forces," Bingham snorted. "Those worthless little shits are like the goddam reservists back in the World, they're nothing but draft dodgers who sign up so they don't have to go and fight. Those little fuckers are around when shit hits, they'll either bug out or turn on you. No way they're going to stand and fight next to a Marine. You know that, you've patrolled with them. Shit, you told me what worthless little fuckers they were back at Pendleton."

Cooper shook his head again, but more gently this time and Bingham didn't see it. "Maybe regular PF units are like that," he said softly, "but not in the CAPs. The CAP PFs are trained by the Marines and the Marines lead them. What Braunner and Jackson said was half the little people in their CAPs were so good they made them honorary Marines."

"Sea story."

"No sea story. Both of them extended their tours over here to stay in their CAPs and they both said they were going to volunteer to come back if they could get in another CAP. They believed in it and that's good enough for me. As soon as I'm here long enough I'm going to volunteer for CAP duty. I want to help these little people get their freedom. That way when I go home I can be free."

"You're fucking dinky-dau."

They were silent for a while, each with his own thoughts. Cooper thought of how much good he could do in a Combined Action Platoon, of how much more important that would be to the war effort than being a fire-team leader, or even a squad leader, in a grunt battalion. Bingham thought about how much safer he was buried in the midst of the thousand Marines of an infantry battalion than he would be in a CAP with only a rifle squad, or maybe even only a half-dozen Marines along with a platoon of Popular Forces who he couldn't trust.

Then Cooper started talking again. "Something I'm happy to see this time."

"What's that?"

"What kind of rifle you carrying?"

Bingham cocked an eye at the shadow in the darkness that was Cooper. "An M-14, samee-same you. What kind of stupid question is that?"

"You know what I carried when I was here before?"

Bingham shrugged. "M-16 I think."

"Right. I never told you how I got hit before, did I?"

"No."

"It was on Hill 881."

Every man in Charlie Company knew the bad little people were out there. Only this time the bad little people weren't Vietcong guerrillas, they were North Vietnamese Army regulars. Tough little bastards who had a reputation for having no regard for their own lives and were not only willing to die in killing enemy soldiers, but were said to prefer death in battle to life in peace. The men of Charlie Company were U.S. Marines and knew they were the best fighters in the world. But they never expected to fight fanatics who would throw their own lives away to give their comrades an edge. Fanatics are tough to fight because they'll do things no sane man will do. The NVA scared the Marines of Charlie Company. It wasn't a fear of losing the battle, they knew no goddam little gooks could kick ass on a Marine battalion. It was an individual fear of death. Fanatics would keep fighting after anyone else would break contact. Fanatics eventually all got killed off, of course. But before they did they killed other people who should have survived the battle.

Lance Corporal Jim Cooper waited with the rest of his platoon in the pre-dawn darkness for the artillery to stop its bombardment of the hill. So many rounds were landing on the target their explosions made it look like the sun was rising behind it, though it was west of where the Marines waited. They had already tried to take the hill, but the NVA were too deeply entrenched, and the Marines had pulled back to let the big guns and attack aircraft soften it up some more.

Cooper ran his hand over his new rifle again—the M-16 the Army had used for the past three years but that the Marines were just now getting—and again wished he had a proper cleaning kit and a chamber brush. And proper instructions on how to clean and maintain the M-16. The damn thing had jammed on him three times in the past two days. Twice he was able to clear the jam by jerking the bolt to the rear; that kicked out the jammed round. The third time he'd had to remove the magazine, lock the bolt back and pry the cartridge out with his bayonet. Hell of a thing to have to do when people were shooting at you. At least it hadn't happened when that crazy gook came charging at him with his bayonet sticking out in front of his rifle. He'd been able to blow that one away with a six-round burst. Good thing he'd been able to shoot because he didn't have his own bayonet fixed, unlike that poor son-of-a-bitch he'd heard about in second platoon who gave someone an upper butt stroke. The damn plastic the stock was made from wasn't strong enough for that and shattered. The next one who came along killed him because he couldn't fire his weapon with its broken shoulder stock. Thinking that, Cooper pulled his bayonet from its scabbard and slid it over the flash suppressor on the muzzle of his rifle and seated it on its lug. He wished he still had his M-14. It was a bigger, heavier, harder-to-maneuver weapon, but he had carried one for two years before getting the M-16 and had only had one jam in that time. And that two years carrying the M-14 included ten months in combat.

Nervously he cleared his weapon and tried to stick his pinky in the chamber. It wouldn't fit, but he twisted his fingertip on the face of the chamber anyway. Maybe that would help. Maybe. Damn, he wished he had a chamber brush. But they didn't issue cleaning kits with the M-16 and nobody had a chance to buy a civilian-issue cleaning kit when they got these new rifles. All Cooper had was the cleaning rod he hadn't turned in when he exchanged his M-14 for an M-16. He'd like to get whoever it was that had said these things never fouled and never jammed and put him out in the boonies for a couple of weeks and then have him make an assault with one. Then let's hear him say how the M-16 never fouled and never jammed.

"Saddle up." The word came down the line of Marines. It wasn't necessary, everybody already had their gear on. They all tensed and got ready to move out as soon as they got the order. That word came a few minutes later. "On me," the squad leaders told their men. "Watch your dress and stagger it. Let's go." And the line of forty Marines in the platoon rose to its collective feet and moved out along with the company's other platoons. Elsewhere Alpha and Delta Companies also rose and advanced toward the hill. Bravo Company was in battalion reserve.

The sun came up behind the advancing Marines and the artillery barrage lifted. The silence that settled over the hills above the Khe Sanh plateau was momentarily stunning. Then, from the east, came the roar of several flights of F-4 Phantom jets, heavily laden with bombs to be dropped on the hill's top and forward slope, leading the Marines and giving them close cover until the last possible moment. The thunder of the jets flashing low overhead shook the earth, their bombs rumbled it like earthquakes. The Marines climbed the hill holding their fire until they were shot at or saw someone to shoot. Different elements of the three companies engaged the enemy at different times.

A machine-gun burst splattered the dirt a few yards to Cooper's right. "Hit the deck!" his squad leader screamed and the squad dropped down and started firing toward where they thought the machine gun was. Most of them fired at different places; none of them knew where the gun was until it opened up on them again. "Cease fire," the squad leader shouted. When they did he told them to fire where he hit and he popped a white phosphorus round from the M-79 grenade launcher he carried at the place he had seen the machine gun's muzzle flash. The willy peter spewed its rosy flower of destruction and the squad poured its massed firepower on that spot. The machine-gun crew ducked under cover. "First team, up ten," the squad leader shouted, and the first fire team advanced ten yards under the covering fire of the rest of the squad. By fire teams they maneuvered toward the machine-gun nest that was only firing at them sporadically, until one man got close enough to lob a fragmentation grenade into it. The gun became silent and the squad advanced as a whole once more. Two men walked past the machine gun on opposite sides of the nest. Both stopped long enough to pump a bullet into each of the three men lying already dead in it.

When the battalion's assault companies were so close to the top of the hill that the Phantoms couldn't continue to drop their bombs without endangering them, the jets let the rest of their ordnance loose on the hill's back slope and returned to their base. Then the rest of the Northerners came up out of the deep tunnels they had hidden in and opened up on the Marines.

Cooper and his squad were totally pinned down. So was the rest of its platoon and a good chunk of the rest of the company. The elements of Charlie Company that weren't pinned couldn't advance much farther because the part pinned down would leave it with an exposed flank. That meant that the entire battalion assault was slowed down and in danger of being stopped altogether. So the battalion commander called for more artillery and the 155s at the Rockpile restarted bombarding Hill 881 with their heavy-duty guns. When the rounds started hitting less than fifty meters away from him, Cooper didn't understand how the NVA could stand it, much less survive and continue with enough fire to keep the squad pinned down. But they did for a while.

Eventually the artillery rounds tearing up the hilltop stilled enough of the NVA fire that the Marines were able to pick up their advance again and they made the crest of the hill. The artillery had to stop then; there was no way it could fire into the battle without causing massive American casualties. The top of the hill was only wide enough for one company to take, the other two companies swept over its flanks and held tight. The NVA came back out of their deep tunnels now that the artillery had stopped and resumed fighting the Marine infantry. They closed to hand-to-hand range and were driven back by hand grenades. The Marines opened up with their rifles, shooting their fleeing foes in the back and the remaining NVA dropped into their bunkers and other fighting positions and poured out enough fire to once more halt the Marine advance. This time the assault line was fragmented.

That's when Cooper's rifle jammed for the fourth time. This jam was different from the others—the other times the round hadn't gone all the way into the chamber. This time it had and it had fired, but when the bolt flew back it left the empty cartridge lodged in the chamber. The bolt tried to ram another round into the chamber and, of course, failed. All it managed to do was drive the empty cartridge in tighter. Cooper removed the magazine and tried to engage the cartridge by forcing the bolt home so it could be ejected. It didn't work; he had to fieldstrip his rifle and assemble the three sections of his cleaning rod, then ram it down the barrel to knock the cartridge out. He was plunging the cleaning rod down the barrel when an NVA platoon swept around to flank his squad and wipe it out. All he had to fight with was his rifle's receiver-barrel group with its fixed bayonet and his assembled cleaning rod.

So that's what he fought with. He looked like some bizarre distortion of a warrior in a Steve Reeves movie, wielding his bayoneted receiver-barrel group like a spear and his cleaning rod like a rapier. It worked. Cooper was average height by American standards, but a giant next to the diminutive Vietnamese. He laid five of them low before one was able to get inside his reach and slash him open across the ribs. But that NVA only managed to wound the cornered giant and paid for his efforts with his life.

Then the battle was over and Hill 881 was in U.S. Marine hands. Cooper was one of several hundred men from the two battalions that took the hill complex who had to be evacuated because of wounds. He had little more than two months remaining on his Vietnam tour, and it would take nearly that long before he could return to full duty, so they sent him all the way back to the World instead of to a hospital in Japan.

AFTER-ACTION REPORT:

Weapons

From the Analytic Notes of R.W. Thoreau, Lt. Col., USMC (ret.)

What happened? Why did he have so much trouble with his rifle? Was Cpl. Jim Cooper some sort of oddball undisciplined Marine who wasn't bright enough to keep his weapon clean enough that it wouldn't malfunction? Or was there another reason for his problems?

Historically, this is what happened. Prior to World War II, the German army started looking for a replacement for the rifle it had used since the late nineteenth century. They ultimately developed the Sturmgewehr MP43, which was a compact, select-fire assault rifle. The MP43 saw extensive use on the eastern front and greatly impressed the Russians with its effectiveness. So the Russians went into their own weapons R&D and came out with the Kalashnikov AK-47, a lightweight, compact, select-fire assault weapon that fired an over-powered .22-caliber bullet.

The United States Army also noted the success of the Sturmgewehr and, following World War II, commissioned the Operations Research Organization to conduct studies on how and where firefights were fought in combat.

ORO's conclusions were threefold. Conclusion one: The overwhelming majority of firefights take place at ranges of less than three hundred meters. Conclusion two: The typical soldier, if he sees an enemy soldier at all, does not aim his weapon—he points it in the general direction of the enemy and fires away blindly, if he pulls the trigger at all—and it was conclusively demonstrated that a startling number of combat troops never did actually fire in the heat of combat. Conclusion three: It is the volume of fire, rather than its accuracy, that slows and stops the enemy's assault, or keeps his head down to allow a counterassault to be successful.

United States Army policymakers studied these reports and pondered the conclusions in conjunction with the German experience with the Sturmgewehr and the Russian development of the AK-47. Then they measured the weapons carried by American troops against those studies and the conclusions and started developing a new weapon. The weapon they came up with was the M-14.

The M-14 was a lightweight, compact, select-fire version of the M-1 Garand that had seen action through World War II and the Korean War. The M-14 was a highly accurate rifle capable of killing a man at more than a thousand yards. It weighed about a pound less than its predecessor, was loaded with a twenty-round box magazine instead of an eight-round clip, had a flash suppressor that reduced recoil and muzzle flash, and fired the NATO standard 7.62mm round.

The accuracy of the M-14 was nice, but unnecessary in light of ORO's first conclusion. Its twenty-round magazine was a distinct improvement over the M-1's eight-round clip and was blessed by conclusion three. That it could be modified to full automatic fire was beneficial—except that it was actually too lightweight relative to its powerful ammunition for an average soldier to properly control on automatic fire. Its weight and the weight of its ammunition, even though it and its ammunition weighed less than the M-1 and its ammunition, limited the number of rounds the individual infantryman could easily carry, somewhat nullifying its value in accordance with conclusion three.

The policymakers pondered these two positives and two negatives along with many other factors and decided they weren't satisfied with the M-14 as the standard-issue rifle. What they wanted was a rifle that was accurate to three hundred meters. They wanted a fully automatic rifle that could be controlled by the typical infantryman. And they wanted it and its ammunition to weigh little enough that the individual rifleman could carry lots and lots of ammunition into combat so he could lay down massive fire. What they wanted was a born-in-America version of the AK-47.

What they got to replace the M-14 was the Armalite M-16.

The M-16 was accurate to three hundred meters. It had a flash suppressor that reduced recoil and muzzle flash. It was loaded with a twenty-round magazine. It was adjustable to full automatic fire. It had a straight-line stock that sent the recoil back rather than up, allowing the average infantryman to control it on automatic fire. It weighed a couple of pounds less than the M-14. The M-16 used lightweight 5.56mm (.223-caliber) ammunition.

The Army brass was happy. Instead of being overburdened by carrying three or four or five hundred rounds for a rifle that preferred to fire one bullet at a time and needed to be aimed in order to hit its target, the individual rifleman could now be overburdened by carrying six or seven or eight hundred rounds for a rifle that would keep firing as long as he held the trigger down and had about an equal chance of hitting its target whether it was aimed or not.

The Army armed itself with the M-16 as fast as it could. The United States Marine Corps was given no choice but to follow suit, though it had to wait until the Army had all its M-16s before getting any of its own. The Air Force held out longer—but the Air Force does most of its fighting from airplanes, so what kind of rifles its ground-bound airmen carry doesn't really matter all that much.

The Marines weren't totally happy with the M-16 right from the beginning. They had taught and used aimed fire ever since the Continental Marines saw action as marksmen firing from the rigging of ships of the line during the Revolutionary War. The Marines saw the war in Vietnam as one for the hearts and minds of the people. They wanted to fight the war on the coastal lowlands where the population was. The coastal lowlands were covered with rice paddies and sugar cane fields—areas with long lines of sight. "You can see a man all the way across the rice paddies," many of the Marines said, "and if you can see him all the way across the paddies you can kill him all the way across the paddies." They could with the M-14, anyway. But not with the M-16. But the biggest problem the Marines had with the M-16 was one claim made by the manufacturer. According to the manufacturer, the M-16 didn't need to be cleaned. So confident were they of this claim, they not only didn't provide a cleaning kit for it, they didn't provide a butt-stock well to store one. A lot of Marines believed that claim and didn't bother to clean their weapons as well as they should have—with the cleaning kits they didn't have anyway.

So it was that many Marines discovered the hard way that the M-16 as initially issued to them was a delicate weapon. Any grit or fouling in the barrel could throw the bullet off its path—or stop it in the barrel. The cartridges were prone to jam in a fouled chamber. Any acquired grit on the rounds could cause jamming. And someone had made the decision to produce the issue ammunition for the M-16 with a cheaper gunpowder than the gunpowder used in its testing. That cheaper powder tended to foul the chamber very rapidly.

Life can be very tough and brief if your rifle jams in a firefight and you have to fieldstrip it to clear the jam. The Army had never acknowledged jamming problems with their prize baby. When it became public that Marines were getting killed because their M-16s jammed in combat, the Army brass said that the M-16 had been designed to be foolproof, but no one had thought to make it Marine-proof.

So in a way it was Cooper's own fault his rifle kept jamming and he got wounded because of it. After all, he was the one who neglected to give it the careful and constant cleaning it needed. Then again, he was not the one who had claimed it didn't need constant and careful cleaning, who didn't provide a cleaning kit for it, and who filled the rounds with powder that fouled the chamber and caused it to jam so easily.

After enough Marines couldn't clear their jammed rifles fast enough during firefights to keep from getting killed, the Marines withdrew the M-16s from the combat zone and reissued the M-14 until the basic problems with the new rifle were worked out. The M-16s had their chambers chromed and a cleaner gunpowder was used in making the bullets.

Mattel Toys made a toy rifle that looked just like the M-16.

CHAPTER FOURTEEN
Meanwhile, Back at the Ranch

A lone street lamp glowed feebly in the drizzle, casting its dim light across the alley's mouth. Big Gun and the Derringer Kid huddled patiently under the slight cover offered by the fire escape. Someone would come by, someone always did. They had all night to wait. When someone came by they would leave the alleyway with money in their pockets and that someone would remain, crumpled and bleeding, on the wet sidewalk.

"When's he coming, Big? How much longer we got to wait," the Derringer Kid jittered while he whispered. The Kid always called Big Gun just plain Big. As long as the other Scarlet Vipers called him Kid without adding the Derringer to it, he shortened their names. When he used the shortened nicknames was the only time he didn't use more words than necessary.

Fred Remington's shadow shrugged slowly. The big youth wished the Kid would shut up and wait as patiently as he did. The Kid might make some noise that would scare their prey off before he got close enough for them to pounce.

The Derringer Kid jittered some more and shifted his weight rapidly from the ball of one foot to the other and back again. His slender fingers twisted around the zip gun he carried. The minutes dragged slowly for the Kid and his eyes kept darting into deeper shadows he and Big Gun had searched before settling down to wait. He always jittered and found it hard to be quiet but here, on the Spotted Jaguars' turf, he was more jittery than usual. The Spotted Jaguars were tough. They were the only gang always willing to stand up to the Scarlet Vipers.

More time passed. The steady drizzle became a steady rain, then lightened back to a drizzle and almost stopped. But still no one came. Suddenly Big Gun's relaxed shadow tensed and his head slowly swiveled.

"Is he coming now, Big? Is that what you looking for?"

The Derringer Kid's voice seemed too loud and harsh to Big Gun Remington. He shot out a huge hand to silence his small partner, then made a silent pirouette and sank deeper into the shadow under the fire escape. His eyes bored into the blackness deeper in the alley. The Kid's eyes widened and he turned to peer behind himself. A rusted tin can's muted clank was followed immediately by a barely heard shushing. The Derringer Kid felt rather than saw Remington extend his arm. A snub-nosed thirty-two poked its tiny nose out of Remington's big hand. The Scarlet Vipers's leader rated it the best weapon in their armory. More soft sounds came from the alley, closer this time than the tin can's clank; the squish of a soaked tennis shoe, the whish of wet corduroy, a too-long-held breath released. Remington's left hand found the Derringer Kid's right arm and lifted it to point its zip gun at the noises. The Kid swallowed and waited for Big Gun to make the next move. He was almost blinded by the muzzle flash near his eyes when Remington fired. Reflexively, the Kid fired his zip gun, sending his lone twenty-two short flying into the depths. Shouts answered the shots and Remington fired twice more and heard someone scream in pain before he grabbed his partner's arm, almost yanking him off his feet in his dash out of the alley. At its mouth he turned away from the lone streetlamp and ran for the shadows at the nearest corner. At the corner he fired another round back at the alley to discourage close pursuit before turning onto the cross street. Nobody came to windows to shout at the shooters and nobody called the cops. The incident wouldn't receive any coverage in the morning papers, probably not even in the tabloids, but word would be out on the street soon enough. Then Remington would find out who he shot and whether the Spotted Jaguars knew who did it. If they didn't, he'd see to it they found out. Big Gun never shot anyone on the sly. The survivors always knew if it was the leader of the Scarlet Vipers. That knowledge was supposed to scare them.

Five minutes later the two stopped running. They had crossed the invisible boundary between Scarlet Viper and Spotted Jaguar turf. Big Gun was in charge here and the Derringer Kid was his aide-de-camp. They swaggered along the street through the on-again, off-again drizzle until Remington slapped the smaller boy's shoulder. "Go home now, Kid. I'll see you tomorrow."

"Later, Big. See you tomorrow." The Derringer Kid stood for a moment, watching his leader walk into the soft night rain, then headed the two more blocks to the three-room tenement apartment he lived in with his mother and five brothers and sisters.

Before the Derringer Kid reached his home, Remington ducked into an airway between two rows of brownstones and went to his knees to tap on a basement window. After a moment the window popped open and a sleepy voice said, "Freddy, what are you doing here? My parents . . . "

"Fuck your parents, girl. Your man is cold and wet and just killed someone and I need me some loving." He dropped in through the window and latched it behind himself.

A nightlight gave faint illumination to a small room with stained and peeling wallpaper. A three-quarter bed was pushed against one wall. A small chest of drawers, a vanity with a kitchen chair and a canted end table at the head of the bed completed the room's furnishings. A small girl of sixteen appeared almost as a shadow before the bed. Her bare feet were planted heel and toe together on a throw rug and her arms were wrapped around her shoulders as protection against the night's damp chill; the baby-doll nightie she wore was too light to give her warmth. Her wide eyes reflected the nightlight's glow.

"Come here, girl. Your man needs loving." Remington's arms spread, beckoning her to him. Reluctantly, the girl stepped off the rug onto the bare concrete floor and let the big youth embrace her. Moisture from his rain-wet clothes quickly seeped through the thin material of her baby-doll and she shivered in his embrace.

"You miss your man, girl." He nuzzled her hair. "You shaking, you want me so much."

She nodded against his chest. Big Gun was no one to be denied anything. Those who did suffered for their stupidity. She held herself motionless under the cold hands roughly wandering over her back, even when one inserted itself inside her panties and squeezed a cheek. Only when the cold fingers probed between her thighs did she resist, but only for a second. Two minutes later she was naked on her bed. Remington's big body weighed her down, his pelvis grinding against hers. The damp shirt he still wore prevented his body from warming her, made the skin of her breasts and belly feel clammy.

A back-arching spasm announced his climax. When it was over, he sighed deeply and rolled off her. One arm wrapped around her shoulders holding her tightly to him and his other hand kneaded her small breasts. He kissed the side of her mouth. "That was good, girl. Your man needed his loving tonight." He kissed the side of her mouth again and lurched to a sitting position. "You know I hate to fuck and run, girl, but when the Spotted Jaguars come looking for your man he's got to be ready for them." His hand groped on the floor for his discarded underwear and jeans. Without another word he pulled his clothes back on, stepped to the window, unlatched it, and climbed to the pavement. He left the window ajar before continuing home.

In the basement bedroom, the girl lay unmoving on the bed. A tear that she couldn't let fall glistened in the corner of her eye. Her period was two weeks late and she didn't know how to tell Big Gun, he'd probably get mad at her for being pregnant.

The Spotted Jaguars didn't come looking for Big Gun Remington that day nor did they come the next, even though they knew he had to be the one who fired the shot that crippled one of their own. The thirty-two that crippled the club's sergeant-at-arms told them it must have been Remington, but they wanted to be absolutely certain before taking on the leader of the Scarlet Vipers. And they needed time to form a plan to get their revenge, a plan that wouldn't get too many of them hurt when they took on the big man. They were going to ask someone who would know for sure Remington had done the deed.

Late in the evening of the second full day after the shooting, the Derringer Kid was walking alone less than a block from his home, well inside the bounds of Viper territory, when a shadow lunged from an airway mouth and threw a burlap bag over his head. A second shadow looped a rope around his arms, pinning them to his sides. The two shadows hauled the Kid out of sight. It wasn't until the next afternoon that the other Scarlet Vipers realized no one had seen the Derringer Kid for a couple of days, decided he was missing and started to look for him. Ten hours of looking later they found him in a place that had already been searched twice before. A crudely lettered note was stapled to the corpse's chest with a hat pin. The note said Big Gun Remington would have full opportunity to rue the wounding of the Spotted Jaguars' sergeant-at-arms. He was going to be the last of the Scarlet Vipers to die in the gang war he had started.

Remington led his followers in laughing off the threat, but they stopped traveling alone and made sure they were always armed. The laughter was hollow and it wasn't always possible for two or more Vipers to be together and watchful. In little more than twenty-four hours three more of them were dead: one was found in the girls' lavatory at school; one died in his own bed; the third was discovered in a trash receptacle on the border between the Viper and Jaguar turfs. No one had seen any Spotted Jaguars in Scarlet Viper controlled areas.

Big Gun led his gang on a sweep through the enemy's territory, but no Spotted Jaguars were found on the streets or in any of their hangouts and none of them were at home. The enemy had gone to ground. One by one over the next couple of weeks, more Vipers died. This many gang killings did get the attention of the press and TV, but nothing seemed to slow it down. Not even massively increased police patrols had any effect on the attrition. The Jaguars chose their times and places to be seen. When they did choose to show themselves to a Viper, he didn't survive to tell his brothers who had done it to him. Two and a half weeks after the killing started the Scarlet Vipers were down to half their original membership and secluded themselves in an abandoned tenement they were busy fortifying.

"Yo, Gimp's at the back door," Redman said.

Big Gun nodded his permission to admit the visitor. Redman removed the police lock and undid both dead bolts. Gimp crutched in half dragging his useless right leg. A childhood accident had crushed his hip and left him crippled. While they never let him truly join them, the Scarlet Vipers gave Gimp a sort of associate membership. They let him hang around and gave him protection. It was an easy boon for them to grant because no one molested him anyway. And Gimp was able to do some limited spying they couldn't do themselves. The warring gangs also found him useful as a messenger.

Gimp was trembling with fear and his voice shook as he came straight to the point. "Jags say they giving a truce, end this war. All you got do is give 'em Big Gun." He didn't look at Remington.

The brief hush following the announcement erupted into babble as the surviving gang members tried to deny any willingness to comply, threatened their enemy with extinction. Remington's voice grew loud to silence them. A pact was vowed to the death. There would be no turning over of their leader.

Later, when the others thought Big Gun was sleeping, they discussed the Spotted Jaguar ultimatum. Despite Remington's earlier insistence that they would be betrayed if they agreed to the offer, they were afraid: if they continued this one-sided fight, they would all die. If they acquiesced, they might live. The "might" was more potent to them than the certainty. Before dawn they would all leave the house and leave it unlocked behind them. Then they'd send Gimp as an emissary to let the Spotted Jaguars know where they could find Big Gun Remington alone.

The Scarlet Vipers' leader wasn't in the house when the Jags came to kill him. He hadn't been sleeping, he had been awake and listening for any talk such as he heard. He had waited for a few minutes after the others left before making his own departure.

The Scarlet Vipers and Spotted Jaguars never saw him again, except for one of them. Big Gun Remington didn't vanish ignominiously into the night. On his way out of town he made a side trip and found the leader of the Spotted Jaguars. The gang leader was possible to find because his knowledge of the Vipers deserting their leader at their hiding place convinced him of his own safety. Remington left a note stapled to the corpse's chest with the same hat pin that had been used on the Derringer Kid. The note read:

"Big Gun joining the mareens. going to wor kill lots of yellow people. when he come back you watch you ass cause he do the same to YOU."

It was raining the night Remington left.

Why shouldn't he join the Marines? The Marines' recruiting posters were full of slogans like, "The Marine Corps Builds Men." And everybody knew they were the toughest, meanest ass kickers around. They knew how to kill people and make it stick. Remington knew being in the Marines would keep him away from his enemies long enough for them to forget him. Then he'd come back and bathe the streets with their blood. Besides, he was a strapping big boy, and the Marines had just committed to a war and they needed strapping big boys.

Boot camp was tougher than anything Remington had imagined. The DIs were hard-eyed, steel-nerved men who called down on every challenge and could outdo every one of their charges at everything and always let the maggots know it. Maggots. They weren't Marines, not even recruits. They were maggots and the DIs never let them forget it. Boot camp was tough. Tough enough to break a hard-eyed tough guy. But Fred Remington, like most hard-eyed tough guys in boot camp, decided early on he wouldn't let the DIs break him. He'd show them he was tougher than they were. He tried so hard they made him a squad leader. On the rifle range he qualified as an expert, scoring the highest in his platoon and second highest in his recruit company. At graduation he was one of five men in his sixty-eight man platoon promoted to PFC. Fred Remington, Big Gun, had showed those DIs they couldn't break him. But they had. The DIs made him into one of their own kind. It rained the day he graduated from boot camp.

Fred "Big Gun" Remington, hard-eyed tough guy, leader of a badass street gang, punk killer, didn't exist anymore. In his place stood Pfc. Fred Remington, USMC. Hard-eyed, steel-nerved. A dangerous man, a disciplined killer. Bold, daring, a weapon waiting impatiently to be fired, fired with deadly accuracy. But the Marines didn't fire this weapon. Not yet. They kept it on hold for two years. Then they sent it to Vietnam, assigned it to Alpha Company, and gave it to Sergeant George Bingham.

PART II

CHAPTER FIFTEEN

Remington the Rain God

It was raining. It had been raining for days, days that had turned into weeks—weeks of unending rain. It rained in torrents, it rained in sheets, it rained cats and dogs. Once in a while it just drizzled. Sometimes it stormed the biggest, baddest thunder-bummers any man in Alpha Company had ever seen. The only constant was that it rained. That and the way it felt to the men of Alpha Company. They hadn't seen the sun in more than a week—then only for a half hour—and they felt like they'd have to get to heaven in order to ever again see the sun. The rain seemed eternal. Clear skies and dry air were things entering the realm of myth, things dimly remembered in so distant a past no one was sure they had ever been real. Hygrometers said the relative humidity was in the high nineties, but the men knew that was only because hygrometers weren't capable of reading relative humidities in the low one hundreds. Any fool could see they were underwater.

All fabrics, papers, and leather goods not already mildewed were in imminent danger of becoming so. Every bit of metal not constantly wiped dry and repeatedly oiled turned to rust and corroded away.

The rain was the northwest monsoon, that never-ending annual rainfall that gives life to two-thirds of the world's population. The monsoon is a rain that kills and floods and renders uninhabitable by man any land not diked and channeled and canalled to receive its waters, shunt those waters aside. It is the world's mightiest rainstorm, a monster killer that brings life to the most densely inhabited part of the world.

It was that part of the world where neither wheat nor corn is the staff of life; that part of the world where so simple a meal in the Western cuisine as meat and potatoes is a near-unheard-of luxury. The monsoon left in its wake flooded quiltwork fields, sometimes terraced on steep hill- and mountainsides. Those quiltwork fields are called rice paddies and their rice feeds two-thirds of the world's population, provides ninety percent of the diet of the majority of humanity, gives life to the survivors after the monsoon rains and storms and floods have destroyed and killed.

To Western man, unused to rains that continue for weeks or months without end, monsoons are mind-numbing events, rains that kill the spirit and drive men mad. Things happen to men when it rains all the time. The monsoon drives Western man mad—it increases the population of Eastern man.

"Squad leaders up." The word came to the bunker where Bingham and Harte, Copley and West were trying to bail out, trying to keep the rains from flooding them out. It was a losing battle and they knew it, though anyone who admitted it out loud was going to be roundly and soundly berated by the others, made to bail out alone and exiled from the overhead cover that kept the rain from beating down on his head when he failed to empty the water from the bunker's floor. Bingham didn't reorganize his squad into three short-handed fire teams after losing Longfellow and Emerson. Ives told him they were getting replacements soon, so he attached Copley and West to himself and, along with Harte, they served as a fire team.

"Why not," Bingham muttered when the word came down. "No way I can get any wetter than I already am." He threw his poncho over himself and crushed his boonie hat tight on his head. He carried his rifle muzzle down under the poncho to keep rainwater from filling its barrel. Dressed like this, most of the rain would run off him. He'd only have to worry about the water that ran inside the neck hole of the poncho, the rain blown up under his poncho by the wind, the puddle splashes that filled his boots and soaked his trouser legs. He ducked into the open and slogged to the platoon's command bunker. Gusts of wind buffeted him as he climbed the hill. He was wrong—he did get wetter.

"Take it off and hang it up," Ives said when Bingham poked his head into the CP. It was built on slightly higher ground than the perimeter bunkers and flooded more slowly. Ives didn't want any more water brought in than necessary. It also had wooden pallets that had recently served as platforms for cases of ammunition, C rations, and other supplies, serving as a floor above the red mud. When enough pallets were available all of the bunkers would have wooden floors. But the troops weren't dummies, they all knew that as soon as their bunkers had wooden floors the company would pull out and go to someplace where the bunkers didn't have wooden floors. Bingham pulled off his rainwear and hung it on a nail inside the hanging tarp that served as a door. Gershwin was already there. Butterfield arrived a moment later. Ives repeated his litany, "Take it off and hang it up."

The CP bunker was fifteen by eight feet by six feet high, a little longer and wider but no higher than the bunkers that were assigned two to a squad. Only short men could stand upright in it, unhampered. Two bunks were stacked along each end of it. Three kerosene lamps on a narrow table along the wall opposite the entryway provided sufficient, though flickering, light and their heat took the edge off the wet air's chill. A lance corporal sat on a camp stool tinkering with a PRC-25 radio near one end of the table. Copeland sat on a folding chair at its middle drawing on a sheet of tracing paper paperclipped to a topological map. He frequently looked at another map and a paper next to it. Ives squatted, arms folded across his chest, on another camp stool facing the squad leaders.

They waited quietly. The only sounds in the bunker were the tinks and clinks made by the lance corporal trying to make his radio work and the squeaking of Copeland's grease pencil sliding on the tracing paper. The shifting winds outside brought the sounds of Ronny and the Ronettes on U.S. Armed Forces radio playing on a transistor radio in one direction and the Animals on Radio Free Cambodia from a different direction. If those two stations ever manage to play the same song at the same time this war'll end by mutual consent, Bingham thought. But only if Hanoi Hanna plays the same thing, too.

"Couple of things," Copeland broke the silence and turned to the squad leaders. He was finished with his drawing. "First thing is we have a three-day patrol starting at dawn. S-2 says Charlie's got a food cache out there and we've drawn the short straw for finding it. I've got the route drawn out; you'll each get a copy just in case." He didn't say in case what, but they knew what he meant: in case the platoon ran into something too big and got fragmented or nearly wiped out, all the squad leaders would have information on where they were going, where the artillery checkpoints were, and how to get back to the fire base. "We'll talk it over and get everything straight before you re-join your squads. The other is we've got some new men. Staff Sergeant Ives will take you to the company CP when we're through here and get you squared away with your new people. The whole company's back up to TO as of today." He looked at Butterfield. "You've got three new men and Jones is back, so you're only short one man and he should be back soon." He grinned. "Alpha's TO on paper. Between men in the hospital or on R and R it's ten percent short," and shook his head. "This platoon's lucky, now we're only short two men in the hospital and one in Bangkok." He pulled a small folding table into the space between himself and the squad leaders. "Come close and I'll tell you about the patrol. Then Ives will take you to the company CP."

After the briefing the squad leaders accepted their tracing paper overlays and folded them into the aluminum cigarette cases they all carried to hold small objects that needed protection from the wet. Without those little boxes, lightly oiled inside and out to protect them from corrosion, the tracing paper would turn into wet tissue in minutes. Copeland's own overlay, like Ives's, was on acetate and didn't need that protection. Then they put their ponchos and boonie hats back on and followed Ives through the rain to the company CP bunker.

"This is a switch," Gershwin said as they slogged through the rain above and the mud below, "getting newbies in base camp instead of in the field in the middle of a fucking operation."

"Yeah," Butterfield grunted, "we get one whole night to integrate them before going out. Big fucking deal."

The company CP bunker looked much the same inside as the platoon CP did except everything in it was bigger. A total of twelve bunks were stacked against the two end walls and the table opposite the main entrance was wider. A string of flickering light bulbs running the length of the ceiling provided brighter illumination than the hurricane lamps in the smaller bunker.

Fifteen men sat cross-legged, hip to haunch, on the board floor in front of the first sergeant who was finishing his welcome-aboard briefing. Alpha Company's top, First Sergeant Ratkowsky, always enjoyed giving his welcome speech to the new men. He worded his introduction to scare the new men into line with stories of how tough things were in the company's operating area. He usually succeeded. And his stories weren't always that far off. The other two rifle-platoon sergeants and the weapons-platoon sergeant, along with most of their squad leaders, stood around the room's sides. Fourteen of the new men sat erect on the boards, wearing clean, fairly new uniforms and the leather toes and heels of their jungle boots showed traces of spit-shine polishes. They looked like a bunch of nervous high school kids, their close brush haircuts making them look even younger than they were.

The fifteenth man wore clean utilities that were faded from too many washings with too much bleach and his boots didn't look like they had ever held the mirror finish of a spit-shine. He didn't sit nervously erect; he hulked and still seemed to sit higher than any of the other newbies. A barroom brawl–type scar slashed an angry pink across his dark cheek. His hand continually loosened and tightened on the pistol grip of his rifle and his index finger kept poking in and out of the trigger guard.

"Look at that fucking newby finger-fucking his trigger," Butterfield whispered to Bingham and Gershwin. "He's trying so hard to look badassed, I bet he shits hisself the first time some gook pops caps at him." The first sergeant didn't miss a beat in his prepared speech, just glared at the barely heard interruption. Butterfield swallowed and shut up and tried to look like he hadn't heard the one who was talking.

The first sergeant recapped. "Charlie's planning something, we know that, something big's coming." Odd how everybody kept saying that. "We don't know what or when, but every swinging dick in I Corps had best act on the assumption whatever it is is going to happen to him right now. If it happens and you're not ready for it, you're fucked. Worse than that is you're going to fuck the Marine next to you and that'll piss me off something fierce. Now look around this room." He paused to let the newbies rubberneck for a short moment, then continued, "Those men are your platoon sergeants and squad leaders. They're the ones who are going to keep your young asses alive. But they can only keep your young asses alive if you do exactly what they tell you to exactly when they tell you to do it. Now the gunny will assign you to your platoons."

Gunnery Sergeant Pike stood up. Gunny Pike was well on his way to having the kind of barrel body most junior enlisted men associated with senior NCOs. His black hair, burred, was turning gray despite the fact he was only thirty-six years old, his heavy eyebrows met in the middle. He didn't bother with any welcoming preamble, he simply identified the platoon sergeants to the new men and started rattling off names. He didn't mispronounce too many of them. The replacements joined the platoon sergeants they were assigned to and the platoon sergeants wrote their names down before handing them over to the squad leaders. Bingham got two men. One was a pasty-faced runt called Eakins. The hulking black man with the barroom scar was a corporal named Fred Remington.

They had some time before the dim illumination in the rain faded into the blankness that was night. Bingham gathered all of his men into his bunker so the new men could meet and be met. And new fire-team assignments made. With all fourteen men in it, the bunker was jammed, though they weren't packed any tighter than the company's fifteen newbies had been in the command bunker. The walls were closer and that made it feel tighter. None of the men who'd been in the squad grumbled at the crowding or at having to smell each other's smelly bodies. They radiated body warmth and the rainy chill was knocked out of the bunker, and they were used to each others smells, the smells seemed natural. Eakins, the pasty-faced runt, didn't seem to notice the smell—his eyes flitted about the bunker, looking like a claustrophobe searching for a way into the open. Remington hulked and looked at ease—nothing was going to faze this man.

Bingham named each of his men quickly. "Don't sweat not remembering them all now," he said when he finished the introductions, "you'll get them all straight soon enough. Now tell us who the fuck you are." He looked at Remington to go first.

Remington grinned the grin that had controlled his gang, threatened his gang's foes, helped gain him a reputation as a badass at Lejeune without ever having to stomp anybody to prove how tough he was. Well, hardly ever having to stomp anybody—not much more often than once a month or so. "I'm Fred Remington," he drawled, and gently placed an unbent cigarette between his lips. "They call me Big Gun, and that ain't only because of my size."

"Ooh, badass," Copley whispered to West and rolled his eyes.

"Big and bad," West whispered back.

"Big, bad, and black," Remington said, slowly swiveling his head to look at them. He snapped his Zippo open and ran it across his knuckles to light it.

They looked back, Copley wide-eyed, West with the tip of his tongue barely protruding from the middle of his lips.

"Ooh, you see the badass," Copley whispered, turning his wide eyes to West.

West bug-eyed and turned, almost touching his forehead to Copley's. "Ooh, bad. I bet he can bite bullets outta the air, scare the shit outta old Mister Charlie Cong."

"Ooh," Copley went again, his lower face twitching with an unborn smile.

"Can the grab-assing, people," Bingham snapped. He could tell Remington was a tough guy when he was hanging on the block back in the World, but he was in a different world now. West and Copley were capable of antagonizing the new man before he learned how things worked, and that might cause somebody to die needlessly. To Remington he said, "Where were you stationed before?"

Remington turned back to the front and didn't see Copley and West roll into each other to muffle their titters, but he knew they did it. A brother and a chuck like that, he wanted to spit on them, take the brother outside and kick the shit out of him. Instead he ignored them and continued smiling. The three-stripe dude up front was the first one he had to deal with, had to before he could control the brothers, make the chucks toe the line. "Jay-ville." He let the word roll out.

Bingham didn't grimace, didn't flinch, didn't roll his eyes, didn't do any of the things he felt like doing when his newbie gave Jacksonville, the liberty town for Camp Lejeune, as his duty station. That didn't stop any of the others in the squad, though. Someone barked a laugh, someone else coughed, a couple snorted. Elbows were poked into neighbors' ribs. Bingham shot a quick glare around the room and the noise abated.

"Who were you with at Lejeune?" Bingham asked, not playing the new man's game, but not calling his bluff, either.

"Two Two," Remington said. "And I was a brig chaser for a few months." His grin turned lopsided as he savored the irony of his having been a jail guard.

"Were you a fire-team leader with Two Two?"

"Squad leader." What the fuck, Remington thought, he ain't gonna check on it, he'll never know I wasn't.

"Tough, I'm the squad leader here. You're going to be a fire-team leader," Bingham said, and smiled a strained but friendly smile.

Remington's smile said it didn't matter. "I'll be a squad leader soon enough."

There were a few more questions. Big Gun Fred Remington was a rifle expert, pistol sharpshooter, had qualified with the M-60 machine gun and the M-79 grenade launcher. He knew radio communications, advanced first aid, how to fire a mortar—both 60 and 81mm. He wasn't afraid of anything that didn't kill him, and so far nothing had.

Bingham wondered how much of that was true. This man's going to need some watching, he told himself. Then he asked who Eakins was.

Pfc. Tom Eakins was a poor kid from Steeltown, USA—Pittsburgh. He'd been in for little more than a year and had spent a few months with a different battalion of the Sixth Marines than the one

Bingham and Cooper were with before getting his orders overseas in a replacement draft. He was a rifle sharpshooter; had oriented with but not qualified with any other company-level weapons.

"What'd you do in civilian life?"

"Went to high school." Tom Eakins was also shy, which left him uncommunicative with men he didn't know.

"Any hobbies?" Anything to draw him out, try to learn something about him.

"Did some hunting." What kind? "Varmint, mostly." Mostly? Anything else? A shrug, "Deer, bear. Whatever." What kind of weapons? "Twenty-two for varmints, 30.06 for bear and deer. Did some bow hunting for deer."

Rush had looked at Eakins when he said he was a hunter. Who was your guide, he wondered. Did you ever kill anything? Then he looked nowhere and didn't particularly listen, just relaxed and absorbed the radiated warmth from the bodies around him. Until Eakins said bow hunting. Then he had to ask. "Ever get anything?"

Eakins looked around for the questioner until he saw the dusky face with its eyes riveted on him. "Usually."

"How often's usually?"

Eakins eyes drifted up and to the side for a moment while he thought. "I think I didn't get a deer one season," he finally said. "It was the first time I went out."

"What kind of blind you use?"

"No blind. I tracked."

Rush stared at the pasty-faced runt for a moment longer, wondering how much of that he could believe. Then he turned to Bingham, "I want him to be in the same fire team with me."

Bingham sighed softly. Things were slightly out of hand here, there were too many antagonisms brewing. Every time he'd seen new men join the squad before they'd been met mostly with apathy and disinterest until they were known qualities. He decided to end this session.

"All right," he said firmly, "we're back up to TO. Chickencoop, keep Dago. You get Chief and the newby Chief said he wants to be with. Chuck, you got Ben as your AR-man, and you got Win and Baby-san. Remington," he wasn't about to call the new man Big Gun, not unless he proved he deserved it, "John Copley is your AR-man, listen to him, he's a good grunt and knows his shit. You also have Sam Morse and Chas Russell. Okay, get set for the night. We move out at dawn."

CHAPTER SIXTEEN
Soldiers in the Rain

They knew it was dawn because Lieutenant Copeland looked at his watch and said it was. The cloud cover was too thick and too deep for the sun to shine through, all that happened was over a period of time the blackness of night dimmed to a gray semi-light with no clear dividing line to say, "This is dawn." The early morning rain, when first platoon formed for its final inspection before leaving on its three-day patrol, was a light drizzle, little more than a heavy mist. Later, when the sun beat down on the tops of the clouds, warming up the air and stirring the clouds, the air's ability to hold moisture would be reduced and the rain would increase. But not yet. When Copeland's watch said it was dawn, the air near the ground was so cool the men wore long-sleeve undershirts or had towels draped around their necks or wore two shirts or huddled under their ponchos. And they shivered from the cold. Later, they'd feel that the heat and humidity were driving them mad—or at least killing them.

Lieutenant Copeland looked at the luminous dial on his watch, saw it was dawn, and turned to tell Ives to move the platoon out. He saw a Marine running toward them waving his arms and waited to hear his message. He listened, swore, nodded, and walked to Bingham, who was just starting first squad moving, to follow third squad through the opening in the concertina surrounding the fire base. "Harte's leaving today," he said. "Give someone else his blooker."

And just like that, another man was gone out of their lives forever. It was so sudden Harte didn't even have time to tell the moving men of first squad he'd write to them when he got back to the World, tell them what cold beer and soda were like, how good round-eyed girls looked and what it was like to fuck them. Oh, well, it probably would have been a lie anyway. Most men when

151

leaving promised to write when they got back to the World. Most of them didn't; they couldn't relate what they were doing at home to what they knew the buddies they left behind were doing.

There was a flurry of scrambling as Harte gave Copley his M-79, his belt with holstered .45, and his ammo bag; shook a few hands; and slapped a few palms. Then first platoon was out for a three-day walk in the rain, short four men; two in the hospital, one in Bangkok, and Harte packing to catch his Freedom Bird.

For the first hour they walked at a reasonable pace, slower than a brisk walk, faster than a searching-for-booby-traps prowl. They covered four kilometers through fairly open land in that first hour, about two and a half miles. Anyone who thought he was already soaked through at dawn found out different during that first hour. The early morning sun beat its rays down on the tops of the clouds. Enough light got through to let the Marines see almost a quarter mile and enough heat got in to burn off the night chill. The temperature rose twenty degrees in that hour. The more-than-one-hundred-percent humidity increased from a heavy mist to a steady, light rain. Clothing that was wet through and through became water-logged. Waterproof nylon-topped boots squelched water out through their drain holes with every step— and still remained full of feet, ankles, water. Web gear supposed to be water-resistant proved how weak its resistance was, especially around pack flaps. Not even the men wearing ponchos were immune to the rain—the rising temperature made them take off their rubberized rain gear to keep from overheating. They all got hot and sweated, and their sweat mingled with the rain in their clothes and their gear, coating their bodies. Now they were soaked through.

After that first hour, that first three kilometers when they became thoroughly soaked, Copeland ordered the point to slow down to watch more carefully for the enemy. They were beyond the range of normal security patrols for the fire base—Indian Country. Colorado Territory, someone had wanted to call this part of I Corps, like another area was called the Arizona Territory. Apaches—fierce, warlike—had lived in Arizona, making it deadly dangerous for its white inhabitants. The Cheyenne and Comanche Indians had lived in Colorado; fierce, warlike—deadly dangerous to white men. But the name didn't stick, so the men of first platoon didn't have a colorful label to use for the place they went through. They just called it Indian Country, home of the Vietcong, fierce, warlike. Deadly dangerous to Americans.

They waded through the rain for hours. The rain came down ceaselessly, pounding the earth, battering trees and shrubs, and numbing men. It created a background of noise that obliterated all sounds not close to listening ears or loud enough to be heard over the constant drumbeat of the rain. The ground had long since absorbed all the water it could hold, and the rain splashed on it, forming puddles that grew and grew until they could no longer stay in one place. Water flowed on the ground, dissolved the topsoil, and turned it to mud that grew deeper and thinner on its top until in places it formed a slurry. Leather-and-nylon–shod feet splashed into the flowing groundwater, sunk into the mud, and slithered through the slurry. Quickly, a thin coat of mud settled on and stuck to the boots, more mud stuck to the mud already on the boots. The mud added weight to the boots, made walking more difficult, and tired men more quickly than if it hadn't been raining. The passage of forty-four men cut a line through the mud, smoothed it where it hadn't been smooth before, making it slippery. As the marching hours wore on, some men slipped and fell on the slick mud.

Noon chow was a twenty-minute break where nobody wanted to sit in the mud but nobody wanted to stand. The need for rest won out over the aversion of sitting in mud.

It rained without letup all day.

But the Marines weren't too worried about running into Charlie, not until much later in the day. ARVN intelligence—"Isn't Arvin intelligence a logical contradiction," one Marine wag wanted to know—reports said the Vietcong in the area were doing the smart thing—staying in out of the rain unless they had something definite to do. The results of the first day's march seemed to verify, despite the misgivings of the would-be wit, the ARVN intelligence reports. First platoon had no contact, saw no sign of enemy activity by the time it stopped for the night, a half hour before sunset. The men took advantage of the remaining alleged daylight to warm up C rations and boil water for coffee over field stoves made from old C ration cans. In the barely distinguishable darkness of "night" they pitched two man shelters from ponchos, one used as a ground cloth to keep them out of the mud, the other as a low-lying overhead to keep at least some of the rain off them. Copeland called for a twenty-five percent watch that night, one man out of four awake and watching at all times. That way they could all get most of a whole night's sleep. He wanted to be on the move again before his watch said it was dawn.

Everybody was quiet, miserable, and tired from the rain and the long day's march, but content with not having run into Charlie or hitting any booby traps. Except, one man.

"Where the fuck's that badass Charlie?" Remington complained, with a louder voice than anyone was comfortable hearing in Indian Country. "Way we hear it back in Lejeune, Marines never get out of the wire without getting zipped by an ambush or snipers."

"Don't sweat it, new honcho," Copley said back to him from the next shelter, which he shared with Bingham. Morse, judged by Bingham to be steadier than Russell, shared Remington's position. "We'll run into Mister Charles soon enough and when we do you'll wish we'd waited longer." His grin was barely visible in the fading light of what would have been dusk if it hadn't been for the clouds.

"Shit, wish we waited," Remington snorted. "I joined the Moreen Corps to kick ass and take names, kill me some." He shook his head, a crooked smile twisted his lips. "Ain't killed nobody yet."

"Keep it down, people," Bingham interrupted them. "Voices travel. So far Charlie doesn't know we're here. Let's keep it that way." He was talking to both of them, but looking at Remington. He had set the newby corporal in the position next to his own to keep an eye on him. Eakins was with Rush on Bingham's other side for the same reason.

Remington spat into the rain, but didn't say anything more.

Soon men started drifting off into light, fitful sleep—sleep made fitful by the rain, by fatigue, by the nearness of danger; and light because of the everpresent danger. The night passed without incident.

They were all up well before the time Lieutenant Copeland looked at his watch and announced it was dawn. Bladders were emptied and small breakfasts eaten cold from C ration cans. Only the men who couldn't help themselves, the ones with diarrhea, dropped trousers to squat over shallow depressions dug in the slurry and soft mud—if they bothered to dig through the flowing groundwater at all. First squad had the point.

"Gimme point, Bingham," Remington said. "Point's most likely to get action, and I want some."

Bingham studied his new corporal for a long moment before answering. A platoon-size patrol in Indian Country was a dangerous situation; point was the most dangerous position of all. There were two kinds of men who were given point: men who were good at it—men who would spot ambushes before they were sprung and booby traps before they were tripped—and the men who weren't much good at all, the dispensable men who wouldn't be much missed when they got killed by not spotting the ambush or booby trap in time. Remington was brash and put on a real tough-guy act. But he hadn't yet come under fire, wasn't yet known as either good or dispensable. Bingham wanted to give Cooper the point, put Rush up front, the best man in the platoon for that job. There would have been no question about it if Remington hadn't asked.

"Your fire team is in the middle of the squad," Bingham said. "Chickencoop has point, Chief's the best point man in the platoon." He turned away to give the march order to his other fire-team leaders.

Remington stood staring into the darkness Bingham had just vacated. Chickencoop, he thought, Tom Turkey would be better.

Copeland looked at his watch, saw it was dawn, and said to Staff Sergeant Ives, "Move 'em out."

"First platoon, move out," Ives voice was pitched low. It was loud enough to reach every man in the platoon, but not loud enough to travel much farther.

Rush stepped off, followed close by Eakins. The newby claimed to be a tracker. Cooper wanted him to observe Rush, who he knew was a tracker. And he wanted to keep a close eye on his newby. Copley trailed Rivera. Bingham placed himself as near to Remington as he could.

Atmospheric conditions were the same as the day before. It was hot and the relative humidity was in the low one hundreds— they were still underwater. The unseen sun was past its zenith when Copeland finally called a halt for chow. Butterfield's second squad had the point when they set out again. When they stopped again, they set in a circular defensive perimeter, but the word was passed not to erect shelters, they were too close to their objective and wouldn't be staying long enough.

"Bingham up, bring Chickencoop," the word was passed.

"Chuck, take it," Bingham said when the word reached him. "Chickencoop, let's go." The two men set off for the spot of wet earth designated as the CP. They didn't see Remington follow-ing them, or lay down close enough to the CP to listen to them talk. Ives and the radioman had put up a poncho shelter so the squad leaders could be briefed without the maps, one of which was hand-drawn, getting wet.

"If I'm as good at land navigation as I think I am," Copeland said, "we're right here." He pointed at his map with the tip of his ballpoint pen. "The supply cache we're looking for is supposed to be right over here." He tapped another spot on the map an inch away.

Bingham looked at the map to orient himself and looked off in the direction of the suspected supply dump. A low, tree-covered hill lay in between.

"I'm going on a recon over there," Copeland continued. "It'll be me, Chickencoop, Chief. I want one more man. What do you think about that newby of yours, the one who claims he's a hunter, think he can cut it?"

Cooper answered before Bingham could speak. "I've been watching him for two days, he's got the moves. I do believe that man could snoop and poop up on a deer close enough to kill it with a knife."

"Okay, I'll take him, get a look at him myself." Then to Bingham, "How's your other newby?"

Bingham shrugged. "Too soon to know," he said. "Too soon to know about either of them. Gotta wait until someone busts some caps at us."

Copeland nodded; it was about the answer he expected. "Chickencoop, get Chief and your newby. We leave in zero five. Weapons, cartridge belts, rain hats. Go." The last word included Bingham.

Remington met Bingham when he got back to the squad. "Let me go on the recon."

Bingham stared at him, surprised. How did he know about the recon? "The chief honcho picked the people he wants. You're not one of them. Get back to your place." The two men stared at each other for a moment, glaring. When Remington finally jerked around to return to his position in the defensive circle, he did it in a manner that said he wasn't the one backing off. Bingham watched until Remington was settled. He knew his new man must have followed him and Cooper. Knew he'd have to keep a close watch on this man to prevent him from doing something that could get some good people killed.

"Don't be so goddam eager," he finally said in a voice that he wasn't sure traveled as far as Remington. He got no reaction.

The rain eased to a drizzle as the late afternoon lengthened toward night. Most of the men rigged shelters they could take down in a hurry despite the instructions not to. Ives let them. Ponchos tied to bushes or trees, draped over branches for men to huddle under, didn't do anything to keep them dry. The ponchos simply kept the rain from beating directly on their heads, pounding on their shoulders. Stopping the rain from its incessant drumming on their heads and shoulders was necessary to keep them from going crazy from the rain.

Copeland and his recon team returned at about the same time the eternal, day-long twilight under the clouds turned into night.

"Squad leaders up, fire-team leaders up," the word was passed around the circle. More than a third of the platoon, including the radioman, squeezed close around the strung poncho Copeland and Ives sat under. Copeland used a shielded red flashlight to illuminate his maps.

"Over here, a couple hundred meters beyond this hill," Copeland quickly sketched their position and the hill on a sheet of paper with a grease pencil, "is another hill." He drew in that hill's near side. "Right here," he made another mark, "is our objective." He held the sheet of paper up to make sure everybody saw it, then flipped it over and started drawing again—a close-up of the objective. "There's a sort of natural hollow in the side of the hill. At the back of that hollow is a cave mouth; I don't know if the cave is natural or man-made, and I don't think that's important. Right here, about thirty meters up and right of the cave mouth, is a machine gun. But that gun's no big deal, the place seems to be guarded by half a squad—four men, five tops. Unless there's more hiding inside the cave. Even if there are, that's no big threat, we can keep them bottled up with the blookers and LAWs. What is important is it seems the ground in front is heavily booby-trapped." He paused and looked at the shadows of his NCOs, bits of light shining on them from the glow from his shielded flashlight. "Chief says he can guide us through it. The newby, Eakins, says he thinks he can, too. If we can get within thirty meters of that hollow, we're home free." He paused again to look at the squad- and fire-team leaders, and to give them time to absorb the information. "Here's how we're going to do it. . . . " he concluded. "This is our rendezvous point if we get separated. Tell your people to drop their packs in place. Rifles, helmets, cartridge belts. Make sure they roll their ponchos up tight and secure them to their belts. Everything we won't need in a firefight stays here. Questions?"

"What do we need the ponchos for?" Gershwin asked.

"Casualties."

"Eakins looks good," Cooper told Bingham when the platoon was readying to move out on the last leg of its trip to the supply cache. "He moves as good as Chief. He must be telling us the straight scoop about tracking game."

"You trust him on the point?"

"Give him some practice, he'll do good. Then Chief won't have to be the one up front all the time."

Bingham grunted. Rush wasn't on the point all the time, only when his fire team was up front. Copeland rotated the three squads on the point regularly and he, Bingham, tried to rotate his fire teams as well. But Rush did have more than his fair share. We'll see, he thought.

The platoon moved out in the dark. They walked close together, each man holding on to the belt of the man in front of him, or touching his back to keep the line intact, so nobody would get lost. First squad was up front, Cooper's fire team leading, Rush on point. They reached the booby-trapped area in front of the hollow in the side of the hill without being detected. There was no dry foliage to rustle at their passing, no dry twigs to snap underfoot. The only noises they might make to give away their positions were the splashing of feet in the flowing groundwater, talking, and coughs and sneezes brought about by the cold and wet. The rain muffled any slight sounds they did make. And the Vietcong felt safe; they had no distant security out. It took the platoon more than an hour to travel the one kilometer to the cache.

CHAPTER SEVENTEEN

Traipsing Through the Toolies With You

Rush stopped where the already thin trees thinned out even more. Ahead of him, he could barely make out the mass of the hill they were headed for, fifty meters away. The column railroaded to a halt. "We're there," Rush whispered to Cooper. Cooper turned to Rivera, told him, and Rivera told Eakins, who told the man behind him. In the little more than a minute the word reached the end of the line. Men released the men to their fronts, held their rifles ready and faced to the side, one man right, the next left. Copeland reached the side of Bingham, Cooper, and Rush at about the same time the word reached the end of the column. He peered hard at the luminous hands of his watch. They had plenty of time.

"Are you ready?" Copeland asked in a low voice.

"Ready," Rush answered.

"Sure you can do it?"

"I do believe I can."

Eakins was suddenly directly behind them. "Let me help," he said.

Copeland looked at the others, or where he knew they were. "What do you think?" he asked. Sending two men to find a way would be better than sending one—if both men were good. Bingham, and especially Cooper, had had more time to observe the newby than he had. And it was mostly Rush whose life was on the line here.

"I think he can do it," Rush said. Bingham and Cooper murmured agreement.

"You know what to do with this," Copeland said. He reached inside his shirt, withdrew a roll of luminous tape. Rush nodded and lay on his belly. The lieutenant cut two pieces of tape and stuck them to the bottoms of Rush's boots after partly cleaning

159

spots to stick the tape to. He did the same with Eakins. Then he handed the roll to Rush. "Do it," he said.

Rush held the tape between his teeth and slung his rifle over his shoulders so it would be out of the way while he crawled. It would take time for him to unsling it and return fire if anyone shot at him while he was searching for booby traps, but he didn't think he had to worry about the VC on the hill until he was through their outer defenses. He turned to Eakins to signal him to do the same. He smiled when he saw Eakins already had. Rush pulled a folding knife from a pocket and locked its four-and-a-half-inch blade open. He inched forward, probing ahead with the knife. A foot to his side and slightly behind, Eakins did the same, using his bayonet. They were willing to take longer to go this fifty meters than the hour they took covering the previous thousand. A lot longer. Everyone else stayed in place. They would watch the progress of the luminous tape on the boot soles and follow fifteen meters behind.

Slowly, ever so slowly, the two men edged forward on their bellies. They probed into the waterlogged ground with the points of their knives, looking for any hardness in the soft earth. They reached ahead and to the sides, sweeping their bare hands through every inch of air as high and as far to the side as they could reach, feeling for vines, wires, cords, anything metallic. After three meters Rush stopped, Eakins stopped with him. He cut two strips from the tape roll, each about four inches long. He handed one to Eakins and poked a hole in the other with the point of his knife, then used a soft piece of wet twig to anchor the tape to the ground as far to his side as he could reach. On his other side Eakins did the same with his piece of tape; they marked a clear path for the others to follow. As long as everybody stayed between the strips of tape, they were safe. Rush and Eakins moved on. Twice more they stopped at three-meter intervals to mark their trail with the luminous tape. Then Eakins froze. Rush sensed the lack of movement at his side and also froze.

"Something," Eakins murmured when he felt Rush stop. His forehead was suddenly wetter than it had been; he knew it had to be nervous sweat.

Rush eased back so he was shoulder to shoulder with the other man. "Where?" he said into his ear.

"My right front, a wire. I'm touching it."

Moving gently to not jar Eakins's body, Rush lifted his body on top of him and crawled his hand along Eakins's outstretched arm. He stopped his hand movement when his reached Eakins's. "Don't move," he said, and hunched forward a few inches on his shoulders so his hand could move more freely to the sides of Eakins's. A loose wire hung in the air about six inches above the ground at an angle to their route. He brought his hand back.

"I'm going to lift myself off you," he said. "Move back and to the right to get out from under me, then crawl back. Tap my boot when you get behind me. Got it?"

"Got it."

"Go." Rush rose on his toes and left hand and leaned slightly to his left. He held that position while Eakins slithered out from underneath him. Then he put his right hand down near where he had felt the wire and held still until he felt the tap on his boot. He extended his left arm and pulled himself forward with his elbows. The trip wire was exactly where he thought it was, a few inches in front of his face. Using a touch softer than he would caressing a sleeping baby he didn't want to wake, he traced the wire with his fingers in one direction until he reached a sapling its end was tied to. He kept one hand in contact with the wire while he tore two strips from his tape roll and crossed them in an X. When the X was ready he used both hands to attach it to the wire next to the sapling, folding its top edges over the wire to adhere to the back of the X. He kept the back of his hand against the underside of the wire to follow it and used his right elbow and forearm to pull himself along. He wasn't certain what the object was he found at the wire's other end, but it was a lot bigger than a hand grenade. He put another X of luminous tape on that end and sidled away from the wire before twisting toward Eakins. Copeland was alongside the other point man.

"Trip wire with something big," he told the lieutenant. He had to swallow twice before his throat was moist enough to talk. "I marked both ends with an X. We can go around it."

"Mark your trail where you turn," Copeland said back. "Go."

The two set off again, curving wide around the marked booby trap. They went nearly another fifteen meters before finding a second one. Rush marked it the same way before they circled it. They only encountered one more booby trap before reaching the foot of the hill. They rose to crouches and waited for Copeland to reach them. The tape on the soles of their boots disappeared when they stood, which was the signal for the rest of the platoon to join them. While they waited, Rush cut a thin sapling and stripped it of leaves and twigs. The rain washed away any noise he made stripping the sapling.

Copeland arrived, put his hand on Rush's shoulder and squeezed, acknowledging a difficult job well done. "Go," he whispered into his ear.

Rush held the stripped sapling out at arms length and dangled it from his fingertips. He lowered it until it touched the ground, then raised it a couple of inches and set out slowly. If the twig hit a trip wire, hopefully it would warn him in time. He held his rifle by the small of the stock in his right hand, finger alongside the trigger guard. Copeland pushed slightly with the hand that was still on Rush's shoulder and they stepped forward. All along the platoon line, each Marine held his weapon with one hand while his other gripped the shoulder, shirt back, or belt of the man in front of him. They moved as quietly as possible, the light rain muffled the sounds they made.

Copeland stopped Rush when he thought they were far enough that all of first squad was beyond the entrance to the hollow containing the VC supply cave. "Wait," he said into Rush's ear, and went back along the column. He saw he was right and had Ives set second and third squads in position while he returned to Bingham.

"It's yours now," he said. "The signal will be willy peter from you in the machine-gun position."

"Right," Bingham said. They shook hands and Bingham went to the front of his squad.

"You feel up to this, Chief?" he asked.

Rush shrugged, invisible in the darkness. "Yeah," he said. It wasn't true, he wanted a break before going on. Even more, he wanted out of there altogether. But "yeah" is what he said. The only other man in the platoon he thought might be good enough to do the job right, to slip up on the machine-gun position, without giving them away, was too new for him yet to trust with his life. He turned to the face of the hill and started up. And the longer they waited the greater the chance of discovery.

Large, round bushes covered the hill. Not densely, but close enough to leave many trails where a careful man could walk without crashing through and making a racket. Rush kept his stick dangling in front of himself. Now he didn't only use it to look for trip wires, he used it to help find a way through the bushes. But the way was steep enough, the bushes thick enough, the path winding enough, and the ground wet enough that too many men in the squad were stumbling and slipping, making too much noise. Bingham halted them a third of the way to the gun position.

"Chickencoop, Chief, Eakins, and me will go on," he told his men. "The rest of you stay here until we blow the gun. As soon as you hear us open up, come to us. Chuck's in charge here. Got it?"

Peale and Remington said they did.

"Chief, trade weapons with John, make sure it's loaded with willy peter." After the weapons were exchanged he said "Let's go" to the three men who were going with him. Rush was still in the lead; the three men following him were able to keep their noise down.

Like when he led the platoon through the mine field, Rush was in no hurry. Here he wasn't as concerned about booby traps as he was that the men in the bunker might be alert. He climbed the hill to a point above the machine-gun bunker before turning left toward it. Then the four Marines were behind the VC position. Rush stopped and all four looked downhill. There it was, the rear of the bunker containing the machine gun—the Vietcong hadn't bothered to camouflage its rear as well as they had its front and sides. The Marines rested on the hillside for a moment, observing the bunker and listening for indications someone else might be nearby.

Rush nudged Bingham and pointed. The sergeant looked along Rush's arm. He thought he saw a blank-looking spot of blackness in the back of the clearly seen bunker; most likely, the entrance. Bingham tapped Rush's arm, tapped the M-79, and pointed downhill. Rush put the shotgun-shaped blooker in his shoulder and sighted along its barrel to aim at the bunker entrance.

The soft background sputtering of the light rain was suddenly drowned out by an explosion, and a streamer of red, pink, and white burning phosphorus arched out of the blackness that was the bunker entrance. Light flashed and glowed from in front of the bunker, flickering light was seen through the entrance, and smoke bellowed out of its openings. A few quick shots came from the bunker's front, and the few screams that started inside it stopped.

At the foot of the hill, at the entrance of the hollow, gunfire blasted out from the rifles and blookers of the two squads waiting for the white phosphorus signal.

Above the bunker, Bingham and the three men with him froze. The white phosphorus grenade hadn't been fired by Rush.

Bingham curled his right leg under his body, planted his left foot forward, clamped the buttstock of his rifle under his arm and pointed its muzzle toward the bunker. "Who the fuck's there?" he shouted. If he didn't get a good answer he would open fire.

"The Big Gun," came the answer, closer to them than Bingham had expected. A shadow suddenly loomed a few meters away.

Remington came the rest of the distance and dropped to his knees in front of his squad leader. His voice had a smile and a touch of sneer when he said, "Gone gooners."

Bingham stared hard at the darker shadow on the blackness that was the rainy night. His jaw was pumping up and down as he tried to control his anger. Abruptly, he dropped his rifle and pivoted forward, grabbing the bigger man by the front of his shirt and jerking him close. "You stupid shit!" he screamed in the other's face. "Are you trying to get killed, you dumb fuck?" He shook Remington in his anger, and his entire body trembled with fury. "A split second more and Chief could have killed you."

"Let go of my shirt," Remington said in a cold voice.

"I told everybody to stay below while we took the bunker," Bingham's voice wasn't quite a scream. He didn't hear the gunfire at the foot of the hill abating, or the shouted commands for those two squads to move into the hollow. "Shit-for-brains, why didn't you do what you were told? You want to get killed?"

"Let me go," Remington's voice dropped.

"What's happening here?" another voice called from the side. It was Peale. "First squad coming in."

Bingham's head shot in that direction. "Chuck?"

"Fucking newby, Remington, disappeared," Peale said, not yet close enough to see.

"Dipshit's over here," Bingham said and shoved Remington away.

Remington stood, towering over the other Marines who were crouching, sitting or kneeling to stay below the tops of the bushes. "That was a dumb-ass plan to take out that bunker," he said. "One man snooping and pooping had a better chance by his lonesome."

"Shut up, Remington," Bingham snapped.

"Throw a willy peter in the front, know you got it in there," Remington continued, ignoring Bingham. "Try to put one in the back from the blooker, maybe there's a tunnel goes crooked, the willy peter doesn't get inside, don't knock out the gun."

"Shut your fucking mouth, dipshit," Bingham said, his anger rising.

"Don't knock out the fucking gun right away, maybe it wastes some of our people down below. I got the fucking job done." He was through; he'd said all he had to say.

Bingham stood up, standing higher on the hillside so he stood above the other man. He pointed his arm at Remington and jabbed his finger for emphasis. He tried to control his shaking and the angry tremble in his voice. "I'm the squad leader. You do what the fuck I say, not what you feel like. It's my goddam job to keep your stupid ass in one piece. What you just did could have gotten you wasted. Don't you ever pull a shit trick like that again. I'll kick your ass around your ears if you do."

Brilliant lights appeared in the hollow, flares lit for the victorious Marines to see by to find and destroy the supplies. Voices called back and forth.

Remington had started to turn away; he slowly turned back when Bingham threatened him. "I don't believe you can," he said too low for anyone other than Bingham and one or two others to hear him.

"You do what the fuck I say, when I say it, how I say it," was the only thing Bingham could say. Unless he wanted to fight it out right then.

Remington walked away without responding.

There were four tons of rice in the cave, in hundred-pound bags kept dry by being stacked on wooden pallets and tightly covered with canvas tarps. Some of the bags were marked, "A Gift of the United States of America." The cave also sheltered medical supplies. Not only swabs and pills and bandages, but surgical and dental instruments, and everything that would be needed to supply a small, primitive operating room. Uniforms and civilian clothes were packed in watertight metal boxes. Hoes were there, and shovels and scythes and other farming equipment. And a hundred gallons of lamp oil.

"Get it all outside," Ives ordered. "Every last bag of food, every bandage, every tool. Everything goes. Metal in one pile, everything else in another."

But there weren't any weapons or ammunition.

"It's a damn shame," Copeland said to Ives when nearly everything had been removed from the cave. "It's a shame we can't just bring some village here and let them take all this stuff home."

"It'd just go back to Charlie if we did," Ives said dourly. "Where the fuck do you think those came from in the first place?" he asked, pointing at the rice bags with the American markings.

"Off the docks, straight into the black market." Copeland shook his head. "There's just too much aid we send over here that never gets to the people it was intended for."

"Maybe. Some of it gets sold to the Vee Cee by the villagers."

"Or Charlie just walks in and takes it without paying."

When everything from the cave was in the two piles Ives supervised pouring the lamp oil onto the stack with rice, clothes, bandages, and everything else that would burn. Thermite genades were placed on the other pile, chemical grenades that burnt with an intensity that would melt armor plate. The platoon withdrew, followed the path marked by the still-visible pieces of luminous tape, far enough for safety. Then Copeland quickly pulled the pins on the thermite grenades on the metal pile and backed off before they ignited. The grenades cast an evil looking, deep red glow that put out little light. They started melting the medical instruments and metal chests and hoes and shovel blades. He pulled the pins on two more thermite grenades and tossed them on top of the burnable pile. He stood there for a moment, watching the flames begin flickering to life on the food and clothing and other materials. Then he turned and trotted to join his men.

They didn't have the same need for silence and stealth now that they had on their way to the hollow with the cache-cave. If any Vietcong were in the area, they knew someone else was there. Either those VC were bugging out and didn't need to be worried or they were now looking for the Marines and speed was needed. First squad was in the middle of the platoon's line and Rush got a break from the point. Once they got through the mine field, the platoon followed a route a hundred meters to one side of the route they had taken before and reached the place where they'd left their packs in less than twenty minutes. They stopped long enough for the packs to be slung onto backs and set out again at not much slower than a forced march. Copeland wanted to put distance between the platoon and the destruction they'd wrought. Nobody argued, nobody disagreed, even though most of them were too tired to want to go that fast.

A couple of hours later they stopped to eat and rest before finishing their return to the fire base. Remington grabbed Copley by his arm and pulled him to where Homer was setting his pack down to lay on. He looped his free arm around Homer's shoulders and drew both men to Morse, who was eating in the dark from a C ration can. Remington had all of the squad's black men together, all but Chickencoop.

"I showed that jive-ass chuck dude back there," he said to the other blacks.

"Say what?" Copley demanded.

"Jive-ass chuck?" Morse asked. "What the fuck you talking about, dude?"

Homer didn't speak.

"The man, the squad leader. Wanting all the glory for himself, leaving us bros out of it. I showed his ass we better than him."

"Whoa, dude," Copley said. "Chickencoop ain't no chuck and neither is Chief."

"Shee-it, Chickencoop ain't no bro, he the man's pet tom turkey."

"Bullshit, man," Morse said. "You didn't take nothing away from Bingham. What you did was, you come too close to getting your ass wasted doing something dumb."

"I hear you talking about chucks and bros, dude," Copley said in measured tones. "One thing you got to understand you don't seem to know, you want to make it back to the World alive. Ain't no chucks and bros out here, dude. We only got two colors in the boonies; Marine and gook. Out here, Bingham's no chuck and I'm no bro. We both Marines. And that's all that matters. We keep each other alive. Charlie's the bad man, Charlie's the one gonna waste us if we don't all work together. Back in the World, maybe Bingham's a chuck and so're all the rest of the white dudes. Here, they're my brothers. I watch their asses and they watch mine."

"You watch their asses and they watch yours, huh," Remington said. "Sounds to me like you suck their asses and they kick yours."

"Fuck you, Remington," Copley said. To the others, "Let's go."

Morse picked up his pack. He and Homer followed Copley away from Remington.

First platoon moved out again an hour after dawn. The rain was coming down so hard when they got back to the fire base that visibility was limited to less than a hundred feet.

CHAPTER EIGHTEEN

Here We Go Round the Mulberry Bush

First squad returned to the three bunkers it was assigned to on the perimeter, and that return was accompanied by grumbling from the men who had manned those bunkers in their absence. Those men grumbled because they had to go out into the rain, back to bunkers that would seem smaller because they would have four or five men, more than there was room for, crammed into them. Bingham had to reassign his squad because of the personnel changes during the eighteen hours before this last patrol.

"Chickencoop," he said, "your team takes the right bunker." I should go in the middle with Remington, he thought, but I'm liable to waste the dumb shit's ass if I'm stuck in a bunker with him. Or he'll waste me. "Remington, left bunker. Win, go with Remington."

Homer looked blank-faced at Bingham for a moment. In its own way, getting stuck with Remington was almost as bad as going into that rednecked Longfellow's fire team when he'd first arrived. "What's the matter, Honcho," he said, "don't you like me anymore?" Since he said it too softly for anyone to hear, he felt safe adding, "if you ever did."

"Chuck, John and I will be with you in the middle."

Peale nodded an it-don't-make-me-no-never-mind nod. Copley and West grinned at each other. Together again for the first time since they got promoted.

"All right, take your shit from the bunkers they're in and put it in the bunkers you've got now." He turned to Remington and Eakins. "You two newbies get your shit from the company CP. Be back here in ten."

Remington grunted. He threw his pack into the designated bunker and headed toward the company CP. Eakins hurriedly dropped his pack into his bunker and ran after the big corporal.

Bingham sagged a little inside when he hauled his meager belongings into the middle bunker. The men who'd been in it during his platoon's absence had left it trashed, and it needed cleaning out. And after two nights out in the rain, he'd forgotten how small the bunkers were. "A claustrophobe would go absolutely bugfuck in here," he commented to no one in particular.

Trumbull, big baby-faced Trumbull, the tallest man in the squad, looked at Bingham and thought, Not only claustrophobes. He could not stand up straight inside the bunker, and the only way he could stretch out to full length was diagonally. He knew the other men in the bunker wouldn't allow him to do that.

Bingham found a more or less dry set of utilities to change into, stuck the rest of his things where he could find them without too much trouble, shrugged his poncho over his shoulders, and ducked out of the bunker. He saw Eakins a few steps away from his bunker and assumed Remington was already back from getting his gear from the company CP. He headed toward the platoon CP. After the stunt Remington had pulled at the cache hillside, Bingham didn't want him in his squad. He hoped Copeland and Ives would agree with him.

"Say, top honchos," he said, stepping through the tarp flap covering the entrance to the bunker. "Here's your favorite train porter."

"Come on in, George," Ives said, laughing.

"Glad you came by," Copeland said. "We were going to send for you anyway." He was smiling.

"They're glad," snorted the radioman. "Shit, I'm glad. I was the one woulda had to go out in the rain to get you."

Bingham smiled also. They were in a good mood; this was going to be easy. He carefully stripped off his poncho and hung it on one of the nails inside the entrance. Ives, barefoot on the wooden floor, was stripped to his skivvies and was shaving. Then Bingham saw the fourth man in the bunker his smile froze.

"Come on in, George," Remington drawled, smiling crookedly.

Copeland was grinning. He said, "Your newby here was just telling us how he blind-sided that bunker while you covered him," and gestured at Remington. Remington's smile changed subtly, into something that was almost a smirk.

"Sounds like you got yourself a real badass this time," Ives added. His razor made scratching sounds on his neck.

Bingham stared at Remington, who curled his lip slightly in response. "He tell you how he almost got his ass wasted?" he said to Copeland.

"Say what?" Ives cocked an eyebrow at him while scraping the thinning suds on his jaw.

"I wasn't covering him; I didn't know he was there," Bingham said coldly. "Chief was about to put a 40mm willy peter through that bunker's rear entrance when the newby's grenade went off."

Ives turned his face toward Remington and raised both eyebrows, the kind of expression used by a parent who had just been told a favorite child did something less than perfect. "Is that true, Fred?" he asked the other man, hoping the answer would be no.

Remington twisted his shoulders in a shrug, the kind of shrug a favorite child uses when caught being slightly naughty.

"The whole squad would make too much noise going up that hill," Bingham said firmly, the voice of a teacher trying to impress on parent and child the seriousness of an error. "I took Chickencoop, Chief, and the other newby to take that bunker and told Chuck to keep everyone at the bottom until I called them up."

Copeland lounged back, his eyes darting from one to another to the other of the men. He decided this was a matter for his NCOs to settle among themselves. Ives was a good judge of men, he could probably straighten it out with no action taken.

"Did George tell you to stay put?" Ives asked, waving his safety razor like a baton. He wanted an answer he could accept as real, one that wouldn't force him to take action against Remington, one that he could use to mollify Bingham.

Remington shrugged again and the corners of his lips turned up a little more, the smile of a child lying and knowing his lie was obvious but unprovable. "I didn't hear him say that."

The corner of Ives's mouth twitched. If he hadn't wanted a tough black dude to develop into a squad leader so badly, he probably wouldn't have accepted that answer. He said, "Well, listen up better next time. We don't want any dead heros around here. They can't help us fight tomorrow." He drew his razor in long strokes down the side of his face.

"Bullshit," Bingham almost shouted. "He's fucking lying, he knew he was supposed to stay behind."

Remington looked wide-eyed at Bingham, innocent. "How was I supposed to know? You was talking to Chuck, you didn't say nothing to me about staying."

"I told both of you and you both answered."

"I didn't hear you say nothing."

"Then why'd you say you understood?"

Remington held his arms out to the sides, his bewildered expression claiming he was accused of something he hadn't done. "Last

I heard, we were going up to take that bunker. I went to take the bunker. What'd I do wrong?"

"Nobody told you to go to that bunker the way you did," Bingham snapped. "Nobody knew you were there. When nobody knows where you are you can get your dumb ass wasted."

Ives swirled his razor in a canteen cup of water. "No one got hurt," he said calmly, and paused to wipe a towel over his face. "The job got done and that's what's important."

"But this fuckface disobeyed orders."

"That's enough," Copeland said without rising from his lounging position. "Ives is right, nobody got hurt." He knew what his platoon sergeant was doing; he didn't totally agree with him, but he had to back him on it and get this situation defused.

Bingham glared at the lieutenant, breathing hard. "I don't want that man in my squad."

If the announcement shocked anybody, they didn't show it. Copeland looked at Bingham blandly, knowing he was on the spot, determined not to get stuck on it. Ives put his razor away as though nobody had spoken, certain the lieutenant would back him. Remington's smile exposed his teeth; he knew he was putting Bingham where he wanted him.

"I said I don't want him in my squad."

"I heard you, George," Copeland said slowly. "The man's been with us what, three days, four? Give him a little time. He's smart, he'll learn." Maybe, he added to himself.

Bingham stared at the lieutenant, a leaden feeling in his stomach. He glanced at Ives. The platoon sergeant was studiously ignoring him, and he knew Copeland was backing him. Ives could let the lieutenant deal with this problem just now. Then he turned to look full at Remington. This man had been a badass hanging on the block back in the World. He didn't understand this was a different world, that being that kind of hanging-on-the-block badass here could get him and other people killed. But he'd learn. And when he did he'd make one bodacious squad leader.

"He fucking well better learn most ricky-tick," Bingham snapped, still looking at Remington. He grabbed his poncho off the nail, almost tearing it as he ducked out of the CP bunker. He was halfway back to his squad's sector of the perimeter before he realized he hadn't put his poncho on. By then he was already soaked through.

Bingham didn't bother to strip out of his wet uniform when he got back to his bunker; he didn't have a dry one to change into. He

lay on his poncho with his arm flung over his eyes, in so obvious a
leave-me-alone-I'm-thinking posture no one said anything to him.
They all glanced his way and went about their business—playing
a game of hearts.

He was angry. Remington was going to screw up and get somebody killed, he knew it. But Copeland and Ives didn't seem to
understand that; they seemed like they didn't want to.

Bingham lay on his back, his unfocused eyes pointing at the
roof of the bunker. He flopped his arm out, hand palm up, and
said, "Someone give me a cigarette."

The others stopped their card playing for a short moment and
stared at him. Why did he want a cigarette? They just got back
from a patrol, they weren't about to go back out again. Not yet.
West finally shrugged. He reached into the bottom of his pack
and pulled out the miniature pack of Viceroys he kept in the hope
he'd find someone dumb enough to want to trade something good
for them. He tore the pack open and gave Bingham one of the
cigarettes. Bingham took the cigarette and held it between his lips.
The other four men watched him, waiting to see if he had the balls
to ask them for a light. When he continued staring blindly, silently
at the roof, they went back to their game.

After a few moments Bingham started patting his pockets for
matches. He found a crumpled matchbook and, one-handed, bent
a random match over to strike. He lit the Viceroy and took three
drags before noticing the taste. He took the cigarette from his
mouth and stared at it for a few seconds. "Who gave me this
piece of shit?" he asked out loud.

The others flickered their eyes at each other, pausing briefly
on West, didn't answer, and kept playing their game. After a few
more drags Bingham stubbed out the cigarette and stuck it in his
right hip pocket—he'd fieldstrip it later, outside the bunker.

For the next few weeks Alpha Company sat on its fire base and
ran patrols, none of them as big as the raid on the cache. Bingham
and Remington talked only as necessary to do their jobs, the rest of
the time they seemed to ignore each other. But each kept a cautious
watch on the other. Ives also watched both of them. He didn't like
two of his NCOs not talking to each other, especially when one
was a squad leader and the other was one of his fire-team leaders.
It would have been bad enough if they'd been in different squads,
but in the same one . . . well.

One day, after the constant rain started to break up so there
were whole hours when it didn't rain and the sun came out every

now and again, Ives took Remington aside.

"You don't like Sergeant Bingham, do you?" he asked.

Remington cocked an eyebrow and one corner of his mouth echoed that eyebrow's curve, but he didn't speak.

"I don't know what it is between you two," Ives said, looking into Remington's eyes, searching for an answer, a clue to how to bring the two men together. "But it shouldn't be there. He's a good Marine, a good squad leader. He's got experience, he knows his shit."

Remington maintained his expression and didn't say anything.

"You should talk to him, get to know him, how he thinks. Listen to what he says. He can teach you a lot, how to stay alive out there." He nodded in a random direction away from the fire base. He waited for what Remington didn't say, then went on. "I hope you're not thinking any kind of race shit. Yeah, he's white. But the only colors he sees are Marine green and gook." Ives tipped his head and raised his eyebrows. "How many colors you see out here?"

The curled half of Remington's lips separated and he said, "Green and yellow." And black, he thought. Green jungle, black bros, yellow everybody else—the enemy.

Ives stared a few seconds longer, then nodded, hoping he'd gotten a point across. "Bingham's a good Marine. Get to know him."

"Right on," Remington said, his mouth curling to a full grin.

Ives nodded again. "Do it," he said, and turned back to the CP bunker.

Then it got to be mid-January and one of the war's few set pieces was about to take center stage.

CHAPTER NINETEEN

Modern Warfare Is a Brutal Form of Hunting

"Straight scoop, man. I heard the Top talking about it. We're invading over the Zee."

"Bullshit. Clean your ears out with C ration shitpaper, dude. Straight scoop is we're going to Laos."

"No way, man. Top said over the Zee. You got some bad scuttlebut. Hanoi's over the Zee, that's where we're going."

"You believe everything you hear the Top say?"

"Shit, no, you think I'm crazy?"

"Fuck, yes. You're the most dinky-dau dude in this platoon."

"No, he ain't," a third man interrupted. "Both of you are, the way you always want point." The first two speakers were Eakins and Rush. The third was Trumbull. He grinned down at the others. Calling them crazy for always wanting the point sometimes seemed to be the biggest thrill he got out of talking with the other men in the squad.

"Fuck you, Baby-san."

"You shut your pimple face until you're old enough to shave, Baby-san."

Eakins and Rush went back to arguing about whether they were going to invade North Vietnam by going over the DMZ or they were going to invade Laos to cut off the Ho Chi Minh Trail. Trumbull kept trying to interrupt them and tease them about always wanting the point. Eakins and Rush ignored him.

Trumbull started getting frustrated. He hated being ignored. No man who stood over six and a half feet tall in his helmet and boots should be ignored, even if he was only seventeen. Hell, they didn't even know he was only seventeen. He had lied when he enlisted; according to his records, he was officially eighteen. That didn't matter to the other Marines. He looked like an overgrown sixteen-year-old and the eighteen- and nineteen-year-old Marines treated him like he was sixteen.

"Can't fuck me," Trumbull said, "you ain't man enough." He stuck his lower lip out in a pout, then added, "I am so old enough to shave."

At the moment Eakins and Rush weren't concerned about what Trumbull thought or how he felt. They were relieving the late afternoon tedium by arguing a point neither of them cared all that much about. Going over the DMZ or crossing into Laos was the same to them. Either way, they'd be deeper in Indian Country than anyone except the generals and a few lifers wanted to go, certainly deeper than either of them wanted to go.

"Going into Laos, dude. That's the Ho Chi Minh Trail. We go there we cut Charlie's supply lines, he don't get shit from home. He's going deep in the hurt locker most ricky-tick."

"Fuck a bunch of Ho Chi Minh Trails. Cross the Zee. Go burn down Charlie's hootch, fuck his old lady, man. He won't need the Ho Chi Minh Trail and he goes deeper into the hurt locker even more ricky-tick."

Voices calling out in the background told Rush and Eakins that Captain Bernstein had ended his meeting with the platoon commanders and platoon sergeants and the lieutenants and staff sergeants were calling the squad leaders together. They didn't let the background voices disturb their argument.

"We cross the Zee, I bet we run through all kinds of shit before we get anywhere close to Hanoi. You know how far north Hanoi is, man? You trying to tell me you want to go through all that shit between here and Hanoi? I hear they've got something like twenty-seven tank divisions and an air force almost as big as ours protecting that big ville."

"Hell, yes, I'd rather go across the Zee. You've been near the border, man, you seen them mountains in Laos. You think you're half mountain goat or something? You got to be half mountain goat to climb those mountains. And maybe even then you can't fight when you're climbing them and then you're fucked."

Trumbull didn't hear the voices in the background that signaled the end of the platoon leaders' meeting and the beginning of the squad leaders' meetings. He was too upset about being ignored. Rush was a half foot shorter than him and Eakins was even shorter, only a pipsqueak short round. No way it was right for these two men to ignore a big man like him. "One of these days I'm going to forget to look where I sit and I'm going to squash one of you so thin I can curl your edges and throw you like a Frisbee," he said, trying to sound and look as tough as he was tall.

"We cross the Zee, dude, all we're going to find until we reach China is a bunch of goddam North Vietnamese gooks and they all hate us. Then, shit, next is China and all two billion of them hate us, too."

"Only thing we're going to find in Laos is the whole goddam NVA army and they're going to do their god-fucking-damnest to put little old me in the deepest pile of shit god ever shat."

"Team leaders up," came the call of the squad leaders. Their meetings were over and they were about to pass the word down to their men. Cooper, Peale, Remington, and Copley surrounded Bingham. Soon Rush and Eakins would know whether they were going across the DMZ or into Laos. They went to join the other members of their fire teams to await the word.

Trumbull didn't care if word was finally coming down to him. He was too pissed off about having been ignored and was trying too hard not to cry. Nobody would ignore him if he cried, and no way he wanted that kind of attention.

"First team up," Cooper called.

"Second team, on me," Peale ordered.

"Third team, get your asses over here," Remington demanded.

The lieutenants, sergeants, and corporals knew where they were going next. Now the junior men were going to find out.

"Here's the DMZ—" Cooper squatted and drew a line in the red dirt. "—and here's the border with Laos." He drew another line. "There's a big-assed combat base called Khe Sanh right here." He made a dot near where the two lines met. "A battalion from the Twenty-sixth Marines is there." Rivera ducked at mention of the Twenty-sixth Marines. He had enlisted in nineteen sixty-four, more than a year before the reactivization of the Twenty-sixth Marine Regiment and wasn't used to a Marine unit having so high a unit number. "The word is Charlie is building up to hit that base. Charlie's putting boo-coo supply runs through that area. We're moving out at dawn tomorrow on a search and destroy to find those supply runs."

Rush examined Cooper's simple map. The dot was closer to the line representing the Laotian border than the one for the DMZ. He elbowed Eakins in the ribs. "Look at that. What'd I say, dude, we're going into Laos, cut the Ho Chi fucking Minh Trail."

"I'll give you the Cs and ammo for the operation before sundown," Cooper continued. "Chow down and get your shit together now, there won't be time in the morning. We've got a twenty-five percent watch tonight. I'll take the last watch. Any questions?"

The only questions had to do with why. "Why" questions weren't ones that could be asked out loud.

In the short time remaining before sunset the squad leaders brought three cases of C rations to their squads, made sure each rifleman had five full twenty-round magazines and six sixty-round bandoliers of ammunition for his rifle and not fewer than four hand grenades. The automatic riflemen all carried at least six full magazines and eight bandoliers; the grenadier had forty assorted rounds for the M-79. They called it armed for bear.

"Saddle up, saddle up, saddle up." The sergeants and corporals who were the squad leaders of Alpha Company sounded their cries. With a lot of quiet grumbling and mumbling the men rose to their feet, hitched packs onto backs still tired from other operations, adjusted cartridge belts, checked the action on weapons, slung rifles and grenade launchers over shoulders, and looked nowhere in particular. And waited for their next orders.

"Fall in, fall in, fall in. Line 'em up, line 'em up, line 'em up." The platoon sergeant's shouted orders reverberated across the openness of the landing zone and were echoed by the sergeants and corporals who were the squad leaders. There was more mumbling and grumbling as the men shuffled into platoon formations, extended left arms to adjust their spacing from side to side, looked right to align themselves. Then stood at a loose attention and waited some more. Helicopters droned in the middle distance.

Alpha Company's officers were easing themselves out of the company CP bunker. They stood in a tight cluster, eyeing the formation, talking among themselves. The company gunny stepped to the front of the company. He wore new camouflage utilities, the leather toes and heels of his canvas-sided jungle boots were buff-polished, and his web gear was clean and unworn. When he addressed the men, his voice was loud enough no helicopter would dare try to drown him out.

"You know what our mission is," he bellowed, "you've all been briefed." His head swiveled stiffly on his neck and his eyes seemed to bore into every man in the formation. "This is the best damn company in the entire Marine Corps. I expect every swinging dick in this company to act like it and fight like it. We will go out there and do some serious ass-kicking and name-taking." He glanced at the nearing helicopters and, just before they were close enough to attempt to drown him out, concluded, "Let's get out there and kill some Cong."

The helicopters, banana-shaped CH-46s with a main rotor at each end, landed in waves. First platoon's first squad, along with a machine gun team, boarded a helicopter in the second wave. When they were all loaded and airborne again, they flew in formation westward. Their destination was a clearing south of the Khe Sanh combat base, north of a broad valley called the A Shau.

Light from the early morning sun flickered down through the thin canopy making confusing patterns of light and shadow on the lower hillside. The Marines of Alpha Company strained their eyes trying to make sense of the speckled shadows on the trail downhill from their ambush site.

"Think they're coming?" Copley whispered. A willie peter round was in the chamber of his M-79 grenade launcher. An array of high explosive and willie peter rounds sat near his right hand, positioned for rapid reloading.

Bingham grunted softly, his eyes shifted about on the rapidly changing shadows on the barely seen trail below them. "You better believe it," he whispered back.

The Marines on the hillside waited tensely for someone to appear on the trail and the order to open fire. They had moved in shortly after dusk the night before and spent the night on fifty percent watch. They were close enough to the embattled combat base at Khe Sanh to hear the rolling thunder of bombs and artillery rounds and sporadic small arms fire when the NVA probed the defenders' lines. Deep reconnaissance had reported this trail was used regularly to resupply the North Vietnamese holding Khe Sanh under siege.

Bingham's eyes left the trail and checked his squad's line. The Marines had dug no holes for this ambush, but they had found every wrinkle in the ground to lower themselves into; every fallen tree trunk protected a man from view and gunfire from below. First squad was in good positions. He didn't have to go to the bottom and look back up to know his men couldn't be seen from the trail they overlooked.

Finally Bingham's attention turned to the PRC-20 backpack radio laying on the ground between him and Copley. He motioned to Copley to give him the handset. Bingham hung the handset from the inner tube band around his helmet so he could hear any transmissions while keeping both hands free and returned his eyes to the shifting shadow patterns below.

Bombing raids on the trail had felled some trees and flattened much of the undergrowth. A recent run with napalm had burned off what remained of the undergrowth. Sight lines from the top of the hill to the trail at its bottom were clear, only shadows cast by the remaining trees obstructed the view. Tension heightened in ripples along the company line when the enemy supply train came into sight. In the lead was a six-man squad carrying automatic weapons. The bearers followed. Some were bent low under the weight of large bundles strapped to A-frames on their backs, others carried poles across their shoulders with rhythmically swaying bundles dangling from each end. The lucky ones balanced bicycles they pushed along, bicycles laden with as much as two or three men could carry.

The supply train was headed straight toward the blocking position second platoon had set with one squad and the platoon's two machine guns. When the point squad was completely in the killing zone the blockers would fire, signaling the rest of the company to open up. Third platoon, at the other end of the ambush, would then swing a squad and machine gun to block the rear of the column—if the entire train was past them.

The Marines on the hillside sighted on targets, then shifted their aim to different targets as the men they picked moved past their positions. Bingham felt the Marines on his sides pressing themselves closer to the ground, closer to protective tree trunks. Adrenaline pumped into his bloodstream, every sound came more sharply to his ears, and the shadows on the trail seemed to disappear.

The lead squad moved beyond Bingham's field of vision, and he knew the ambush was about to be set off. He lined his sights on a young man pushing a high-piled bicycle. The peep sight on the M-14 seemed to magnify the beardless head resting on top of the front blade sight. Looks like a kid, Bingham thought; he should be in high school instead of pushing a bike-load of supplies for an army. But you never can tell with these gooks, he could be thirty for all I know. His jaw clenched from the tension of waiting for the first shots to be fired. They look young until one day they become old. Or dead.

Bingham watched the young North Vietnamese lean forward sharply, eyes unfocused on the ground, lending his weight to the bicycle's faint momentum. He saw cords pop in his neck and sweat bead his brow from the effort.

Bingham pulled the trigger just as the young man's head snapped up at the sound of shots at the head of the column. He pitched forward, and the bicycle, with his weight no longer holding it up, fell onto his corpse.

Bingham raised his cheek from the stock of his rifle and looked for another target. There weren't any left standing on the trail. A few porters were curling themselves into tight balls on the ground, others were scrabbling up the opposite hillside. Thousands of bullets tore through the air at them, kicking gouges in the dirt alongside them, blasting holes in their frail-looking bodies. Bingham sighted on the back of one climber and took up the trigger slack. But he couldn't pull the trigger. The man he was sighting on was unarmed, had been unarmed to begin with. This is murder, he told himself, and raised his sights to shoot at the ground in front of the crawler, tried to stop him, to make him surrender.

A few meters to his side, Remington shifted into a modified kneeling position, a variation on the one Marines used on the rifle range to fire at a twelve-inch-diameter bulls eye at three hundred yards. He deliberately aimed and as deliberately pulled the trigger, pumping bullet after bullet into still moving bodies until they became merely still. His eyes blazed.

"Cease fire, cease fire!" the lieutenants and platoon sergeants started shouting.

"Cease fire," the squad leaders, including Bingham, picked up the shout.

"Cease fire," the fire-team leaders repeated. Except for Remington. He still had a moving target in his sights.

"Turkey shoot," Remington said in a voice only he heard.

"Goddam it, Remington," Bingham shouted, "cease fire."

Remington pulled his trigger one more time. He smiled, watching a shivering fetal ball jerk, then slump as only a dead man can slump. He turned toward his squad leader, still smiling. "Cease fire," he said.

Bingham hadn't been sickened by the sight of a dead enemy soldier since the first time he saw a man he'd killed. When the bullets stopped their noise, and the keening and cries of the not-dead on the trail below reached him he thought about it for a few seconds. Except for the squad in the column's van and a few other soldiers dotted here and there along its length, these men hadn't been armed, they were porters. This wasn't a firefight, it was a massacre, a slaughter. Bingham rose to his knees while thinking this. Suddenly, he doubled over and threw up.

He heard a laugh and turned his head toward it. Remington was grinning at him. He knew the big man now thought he had something he could use to gain control of his squad leader.

Not long after that another company found signs of an NVA regiment that was heading north to reinforce the units attacking the Khe Sanh combat base. Alpha Company joined in the search.

CHAPTER TWENTY

Old Marines Never Die, They Just Go to Hell and Regroup

"Shit. Don't them little people never stand and fight?" Remington wiped the sweat from his forehead and poked the bayonet on his rifle into a bush. The lack of enemy contact since ambushing the supply train was frustrating him.

"Only when they can't di-di," Eakins murmured. "And you can bet they ain't hiding in that damn bush you're sticking there." He was also feeling the effect of two weeks of humping without apparent reason. The early morning heat was already sweltering and the hottest was yet to come. There were only occasional, slight movements of air under the jungle canopy.

"Stick any goddam bush I want to." Remington thrust the bayonet into a thick patch of grass. "Don't know where they got a hidey place." He stomped around the small area jabbing his bayonet into the vegetation.

"Can the grab-assing, people, we're moving out again." Bingham's voice was barely heard. His eyes looked at everyone in the fire team, but his words were directed at Remington. The big man glared at his squad leader for a few seconds before ramming the point of the bayonet into the side of a tree.

"Stand by, people. Honcho says we moving out." Remington spoke to his men, but his eyes were on Bingham.

Russell shrugged at the order, it was the same to him whether they sat where they were or kept walking. Either way, Charlie would find them when he wanted to.

"Move out," Bingham's voice drifted quietly to them seconds later.

Cooper looked at his squad leader, who nodded at him. He nodded at Rush to take the point. Bingham came next and a machine-gun team followed him.

The short Marine hardly seemed to move as his arm brushed

aside foliage for his body to glide through. His practiced hunter's eyes searched the ground, examined every twig laying on it, saw every leaf and hanging vine, alert for booby traps or any sign of lurking enemy.

The hills the platoon moved through were steeper than the previous days' marches, though the vegetation was similar. Dense brush clogged the ground between towering jungle trees in the narrow-bottomed gullies between the hills. The hilltops had fewer trees but were just as dense except for patches of man-high grass. From the air, the surface irregularities didn't show up—the high trees in the gullies rose to the hilltops giving the landscape the appearance of being level. Stay-awhile vines seemed to be everywhere, but at least there were few tree leeches. The many thin game trails were avoided except for the instant it took each man to cross them.

Rush's skill paid off. He took his time leading the platoon through the brush. Forty-five minutes of movement found them less than three hundred meters from where they had started. Then Rush slowed his pace. He couldn't see or hear anything, but something didn't feel right. It took him another half hour to move the next hundred meters. At a place where there was the sound of water running in a stream he stopped, held his hand palm out to his rear, and took a step backward.

Cooper froze. His head swiveled on his neck and he resisted the urge to hurry to Rush's side to ask what he saw.

Rush backed up so slowly he didn't seem to move until he was suddenly within arm's reach of Cooper. He turned his head sideways so he could speak to his fire-team leader while keeping his eyes to the front. "We're in deep shit, Honcho," he said. "Get the big honcho up here. I almost stepped on a dink."

A faint tremor raced through Cooper's body, and he started backing away as motionlessly as Rush had. Then Bingham was with them. When the rest of the column halted he kept moving so he wouldn't have to wait to find out why they had stopped. Remington glanced at him quickly and shrugged. Cooper's attention remained to Rush's front. He signaled Bingham to back up. When they had moved behind the machine-gun team he nodded for Rush to report.

"Charlie's up ahead," Rush said again in the same soft voice. "I spotted three of them and a trip wire."

"Did they see you?" Bingham asked, a moot question. If Charlie had seen him, he would have reacted. The sound of running water was loud enough he didn't bother to keep his voice as far down as he normally would with the enemy so close.

Rush patted the air with his hand to tell Bingham to speak more softly and shook his head.

"How many do you think there are?"

"Too goddam many."

Bingham eased into a tense crouch, almost expecting an NVA charge to come at him. They backed farther away from the NVA positions.

A slight rustling behind them made Bingham turn his head. It was Lieutenant Copeland coming to find out why the point had halted. His radioman was a few feet to his rear. Bingham told what he knew and Rush confirmed it. While Ives placed the platoon on a line facing where Rush thought the NVA ambushers were, Copeland took the handset from his radioman and relayed the information to Captain Bernstein. Then he waited patiently for further orders.

The Marines of first platoon quietly stepped toe-first through the brush until they had moved as far forward as Bingham and Cooper. Soundlessly, they settled to the ground and pointed their weapons at the greenery to their front. They expected a fight at any minute. Some of them wondered if they'd have any chance to see who they'd be shooting at; some of them wondered if they'd have any chance to shoot.

Copeland's radio murmured at his radioman who murmured back into the handset and handed it to the platoon commander. Copeland went through the you-speak, I-speak routine for a moment and handed the handset back. "Skipper wants us to do a recon," he said, "try to find out how many there are up ahead." His Adam's apple bobbed with a nervous swallow while his eyes tried to penetrate the forest to the front, as though he wished he could see enough from where he stood to avoid the recon. "Who wants to go with me?"

No one spoke for a few seconds, or looked at anyone. Then Rush shrugged. "I'm the best in the boonies and I know where three of them are. I'll go." He didn't look at the others.

"Chief's my eyes," Cooper said, "he goes, I go."

Copeland nodded. "Chief, take the point. Cooper, follow me. Move it."

Rush squatted, peering at the brush to his front, fixing in his mind the location of the three NVA and trip wire he had seen. When his orientation was completed he rose into an easy crouch and stepped off at an angle to the left of his original path.

The three men melted from Bingham's sight into the brush and he settled in to wait for their return—or for the gunfire that would tell him they weren't going to return.

Fifteen meters into the brush Rush lowered to hands and knees and crawled a little farther before going to his belly and slithering forward. Copeland and Cooper did the same behind him. A smell wafted to him on a vagrant air movement. It was the distinctive, rotten-fish aroma of *nuoc mam* sauce and it was close. He froze and his ears strained for anything his eyes couldn't see. Half a minute later he heard a noise a few feet to his right front. It was the sound of a man adjusting his position in the undergrowth. Rush waited to see if the noise would repeat. When it didn't he slithered back to where Copeland waited nervously.

"I found another one," he whispered with his mouth close to the lieutenant's ear. Copeland nodded and signed with a hand movement for him to lead them on a loop to a point farther to the left. This time Rush duck-walked twenty meters before going to his belly and slithering toward where the NVA line might be. A muffled cough directly to his left stopped him again. He waited motionlessly, hardly breathing, for a minute. He wiped the sweat from his eyes and, careful not to make any noise himself, he reached a hand to a broad leaf and slid it over an inch or so. He could see a khaki shirt six feet away. He eased the leaf back into place and slithered backward. He didn't stop when he reached Copeland, just jerked a thumb over his shoulder and kept going. Copeland followed.

Three more times Rush looped left, crawled right and found an enemy soldier. The fourth time he circled around to the rear of the man he had discovered. That man was the last one in line. He led the way back the way they had come and repeated the process three times to the right of their starting point before finding the last man on that side. Then they returned to where Bingham and the platoon radioman waited. The recon had taken over an hour. The North Vietnamese were spread on a line more than two hundred meters long. If they were maintaining an interval of two or three meters between men, which is what Rush had found, it meant there was more than a company waiting in ambush.

Copeland radioed the information to Captain Bernstein. Bernstein told Copeland to pull his platoon back fifty meters and move it to the extreme right of the NVA company. Then he had the other two platoons line up to first platoon's left. He called a platoon commanders' meeting to outline his plan. The lieutenants then met with their squad leaders and told them what they needed to know. Alpha Company would line up and make a frontal assault on the NVA ambush.

Bingham wanted a cigarette. He was certain the NVA could sense the Marines in front of them, and his muscles knotted while he waited for them to open fire before Alpha Company was completely in position. His squad held the company's right flank. Peale's fire team was to his left, in contact with second squad. Copley was between Peale and Bingham. Next to the right was Cooper and his team. Remington anchored the far right. Bingham hoped the attack would come soon. The longer it took for the entire company to get in position, the more restless and anxious the men of first platoon would become. Restless, anxious men are more likely to let their edge slip, more likely to make mistakes that could cost them their lives. Throats parched in the humid heat and someone getting careless taking a drink from a canteen might make too much noise, causing a restless, anxious North Vietnamese to fire, setting off the ambush before the Marines were all in position. But he didn't worry about how the enemy soldiers felt waiting in the ambush they had been in longer than Bingham's squad had been in the area. A light drizzle started while they waited for the command to advance.

Private First Class Do Tan waited patiently for the Americans to come into his rifle sights. The murmuring of the stream to his rear was calming to the tired soldier. He liked listening to the stream because it eased his tiredness and made him feel protected. He felt it would mask any sound he and his fellow freedom fighters might make, mask those sounds from the ears of any particularly alert American point man. So he waited patiently for the Americans who had to come to this place because they would eventually need to get water from the stream. When they came he would kill as many as came in front of his rifle. To his right and his left were Combatant Nien Bia and Combatant Thi Chau. Together, the three of them held secure the left flank of their company's ambush line. Like Do Tan, Nien Bia and Thi Chau were veterans of the fighting in the Central Highlands. In that area, he knew, the Americans had two kinds of soldiers. There were the ordinary soldiers and the air soldiers—the air cavalry and airborne units. The air soldiers were braver men who fought much more fiercely than did the ordinary soldiers. When the officers selected their battle sites or set ambushes against the American soldiers in the Central Highlands they took into consideration which of the American soldiers they would be fighting against. Always the officers would be sure to have good escape routes planned for use when they decided to break contact. If the soldiers they were to fight were the air soldiers, the escape routes were planned more carefully and there were more of them. This was because of the greater fighting ability of the air soldiers, their higher determination to close and win the fight.

Do Tan had not fought against the American Marines before and did not know how good they were as fighters, though there was another thing he did know; with the river to their rear rather than to their front, the escape routes were poor. A brave and determined enemy could pin the company against it and cause great damage before the survivors could break away. So Do Tan knew the American Marines could not be very brave fighters. He waited patiently for them to come into the ambush's killing zone.

Do Tan never questioned his officers' decisions or asked how they made their plans. Decision making and planning was the job of the officers; his was fighting. If Do Tan had known the factors in Captain Mai Van Sang's decision to set his ambush against this river he would not have waited so patiently. The company was supposed to follow a particular trail to the high ground and proceed along the crests until it was out of the area where the Marine battalion looked for it and the other companies in its battalion. Somehow, the scout leading the company either missed the fork where they were to turn to the high ground or he took the wrong fork. Instead of reaching the high ground, the company went deeper into the valley.

The company reached a river that was not on Mai Van Sang's maps and he rested his men while he studied his situation. Reconnaissance scouts sent toward the high ground and across the river reported back with bad news. A Marine company was searching the land nearby on the far side of the river. A second company was on the slopes above and slightly ahead of them. To their rear and uphill, coming in their direction, was a third company. There was no route they could take that did not harbor great dangers for the tired men of the company. Captain Sang decided to set his company in an ambush several meters in from the river. Hopefully the river's noise would prevent either side from hearing the other and the Marines approaching them would pass them by. His company was too weary to give the American Marines a good fight, and they had no clear routes of withdrawal. After nightfall the company could climb the hill and quit the battlefield, leaving the Americans wondering where and how their foe had once again vanished. Captain Mai Van Sang smiled at the thought of the Americans' confusion about his people's elusiveness.

These were the things Do Tan did not know, but because he did not know them, he was able to wait patiently and calmly. He ignored the soft rain that started while they waited.

The river masked the noise of the approaching Marines from the North Vietnamese defenders. They were far better fighters than Do Tan had imagined. His tiredness and the soothing sounds of the river acted to lull him and decrease his necessary sharpness, so he was quite surprised when the forest to his front erupted in gunfire and it took him nearly five seconds before he was able to point his weapon and squeeze its trigger in response.

After what felt like far too long a wait, Bingham's radio whispered in his ear, "All Alpha Ones, this is Alpha One. All Alpha Ones, this is Alpha One. Do you hear me, over?"

"Alpha One One, here," Bingham whispered into his radio.

"Alpha One Two, go," Butterfield said.

"Alpha One Three, on," came Gershwin's voice.

"The Company is on-line. We have passed the line of departure. Check your time. We move out in three zero seconds. Pass the word. A whistle will be the signal to open fire."

"Roger, Alpha One," the three squad leaders replied.

Bingham looked at the sweep hand on the face of his watch, eased to his feet and signaled the men to his sides to do the same. The density of the brush prevented him from seeing the entire squad, only Cooper's team on his right and the gun team on his left, but he knew all his men were on their feet preparing to advance on the NVA company. He clamped the stock of his M-14 between his elbow and side and listened to the radio voice counting down the seconds.

Concentrating on the radio voice and looking to his sides kept Bingham from thinking frightened thoughts about what was about to happen. Cooper had been through this too many times before. His mind was trained not to think before the shooting started and men died. Peale tried to think of anywhere or anything but the enemy hidden behind the brush he faced. He, too, had seen too much death and mutilation. Remington wanted to fidget but didn't. The streets had taught him how much more savory victory tasted when he held quiet right before the fight. Bingham had no idea what the machine-gun team leader thought.

"Five, four, three," the radio voice said, "two, one, go, move out now. Keep a steady pace, move quietly. Go, go, go."

Bingham stepped off and waved his hands at the men to his sides to move with him. He watched to his flanks more than to the front, making sure the members of his squad he could see were maintaining alignment with him, while listening for the whistle that would signal the beginning of the fight—or the incoming fire that was the NVA opening on them first. His throat constricted with the fear that fighting men know in the lull before the battle, the fear that must be conquered if a man is going to fight a killing fight and live.

Tweee tweee, the officers' whistles trilled. Bingham opened fire to his front and stepped up his pace until it was a trot. "Move it, first squad, move it," he shouted, "let's go. Move-move-move. Movemovemove!"

Somewhere to his right he heard Cooper's voice shouting, "Fuck a lucky duck, fucka luckyduck fuckaluckyduck fuckalucky-duckfucka . . . " until the words blurred into each other. For the first few seconds it seemed as though the Marines were on an unopposed live-fire exercise. Then the NVA returned fire so heavy the advance faltered and stopped with the men of Alpha Company dropping for cover.

The Marine platoons each had nine automatic rifles and three M-79 grenade launchers. Everyone else was armed with semi-automatic M-14s—except for the officers and platoon sergeants, who were armed with handguns. Most of the NVA they were attacking carried either automatic rifles or rocket-propelled grenade launchers. The Marines outnumbered the North Vietnamese but were facing heavier fire than they were bringing to bear.

Along the company's entire line the Marines were stopped. Most of them tried to hide behind tree trunks or in ground wrinkles or behind broad leaves they hoped had suddenly become bulletproof. Most of them returned fire. The rest lay dead, dying, or too badly wounded to try to hide and fight.

"Team leaders report," Bingham shouted. An order to push forward or pull back would come in minutes. He needed to know if he had casualties before it came. There was a short pause while the fire-team leaders checked their men.

"First team, all okay," Cooper called. His men were all right.

"Third team, all right, and we are blasting caps." Remington was anxious to move against the little yellow people.

"Second team, West is down," Peale answered from the far end of the squad.

Shit, Bingham said to himself, I don't want any more dead. "How bad is he?" he said aloud to Peale.

"I think he's dead. He's not moving."

The fire was heavy on both sides for the first fifteen seconds after the Marine advance was stopped, then abated when too many men had to reload at the same time.

"We got them down now," Remington roared, "let's go get their dink asses."

"Stay down, Fred," Bingham shouted, but it was too late. Remington was on his feet rushing the end of the NVA line. Homer, Russell, and Morse followed him.

"Goddam shit, fucker's dinky-dau," Cooper yelled. "First team, let's go." Rivera, Rush and Eakins leaped to their feet after their fire-team leader.

"Lead them with fire," Bingham called to Peale's fire team. "Copley, pop your rounds ten meters ahead of them. First squad, lay some suppressive fire out there. Who's got West's AR?"

"I got it, Honcho," Peale called back. The automatic rifle, four rifles, grenade launcher, and—maybe most important—the machine gun fired as rapidly as they could in front of the eight Marines charging the NVA line.

Remington's bull body crashed through the underbrush. With Russell and Morse making as much noise as he did, the three managed to make the fire team sound to the surprised NVA like at least a reinforced squad. The men on the end of the ambush line fired briefly at the oncoming Marines, then bolted.

"They're breaking," Remington roared, "let's kick ass." They were beginning to pass in front of Bingham's position.

"First squad, cease fire," he shouted, "don't hit our own people." Bingham listened to the gunfire for a few seconds, then said into the radio, "Alpha One, this is One One. We have friendlies crossing our front, do you hear? Over."

"Alpha One. Say again, One One. Where did the friendlies come from?"

"Alpha One, friendlies coming across your front. One One is rolling up the flank. Out. First squad, let's go." The last was to the remaining third of his squad. They ran after the rest of the squad but didn't fire for fear of hitting the men in front of them. Almost immediately Bingham stumbled over three khaki-clad bodies. Then he had to leap over a green uniformed one. "Mother-fucking shit," he muttered and ran faster.

The squawking radio bouncing from his shoulder finally caught his attention. "One One," he gasped into it.

"One One, this is One Actual," the radio shouted into his ear. "Halt where you are. Hold your place, do you understand? Over." Even the tinniness of the radio couldn't disguise the anger in Copeland's voice—an angrier voice than Bingham had ever heard him use before.

"One, One One. Aye-aye. Out." Bingham put on more speed and in a few more paces reached Remington, grabbed his shoulder and yanked him to the ground. "First squad, halt," he used his best parade ground voice. "Regroup on me." He jammed his face close to Remington's ear and grated, "Who the fuck you think you are, John-fucking-Wayne, goddammit? Nobody told you to move your team, shit-for-brains. We've got men down back there because of you."

Remington twisted in Bingham's grip and fire burned in his dark eyes. "Charlie had us pinned down. I broke his hold." Then he turned back and fired along the line of the ambush.

Bingham glared at him for a few seconds longer than started shouting orders. "First squad, line on me. Lay fire down. Don't shoot to your left, you'll hit our own people. Lay it out and make Charlie keep his head down. ARs, short bursts. Everyone else, space your shots." He wanted to call for his fire-team leaders to report their status, but didn't want to know how many of his men were down. Not yet, anyway.

The volume of fire being put out by the squad became heavier and the rounds were more evenly spaced. Similar commands were being issued all along Alpha Company's line. Return fire from the NVA was spotty as the northerners sought to withdraw. The NVA ambush had been turned around to where the ambushers were effectively caught in an L shaped ambush with Bingham's squad forming the short leg of the L. The return fire grew more sporadic and finally stopped.

"Cease fire, all units, cease fire," came the order over the radio. The gunfire peaked as nearly everyone in the company cranked off a last round, a final burst. The sudden silence in the forest was almost ear-shattering in contrast to the din of battle. Orders shouted by platoon leaders were echoed by squad leaders who checked their squads for casualties. Then two squads from each platoon advanced to the NVA positions to make body counts, gather documents, collect weapons and equipment, and acquire souvenirs. Bingham's first squad advanced in the direction from which it had come, to locate the dead and wounded NVA it had swept through. Bingham didn't ask his team leaders for reports. He still didn't want to know how many he had down. Or who.

Seven khaki-clad North Vietnamese soldiers lay in a ragged line along their path. Six of them were dead and the other was unconscious from a grazing head wound. Documents identified three of the dead as Do Tan, Nien Bia, and Thi Chau. Five AK-47s of Chinese and Bulgarian manufacture, a Swedish K, and an American M-79 grenade launcher were recovered along with a squad radio. Not far from the body of the NVA with the M-79, Trumbull found someone's body, someone from the machine-gun team. There wasn't much left of his head. A high explosive round from the captured M-79 had hit him in the face. The young PFC almost threw up.

At almost the same time Trumbull found the gunner's body, Peale came across Bingham. The sergeant was kneeling next to another body. He was crying softly. The body, with very little blood around a single black hole near the inner edge of its left shirt pocket, was Cooper's.

Peale stared at the tableau for a moment before kneeling next to Bingham and putting his hand on his squad leader's shoulder. "With that little blood, he must have been hit in the heart and killed instantly. He didn't suffer, Honcho." He didn't know what else to say.

Bingham stiffened. He rubbed the heel of his hand across his eyes and forehead, then stood. "I'm going to kill that son of a bitch," he said in a voice so low Peale almost didn't hear him.

"Who, Honcho? Who you going to kill? Charlie's all dead. Except for one prisoner. Are you going to kill the prisoner?" Peale rushed to keep up with Bingham.

"Remington. That big black bastard's the one who started this shit. He's the one that killed Chickencoop. I'm going to waste his ass."

Grabbing Bingham's arm, Peale yanked on it hard. "You can't do that, man. That's fucking murder."

"Murder. That's what that motherfucker did to Cooper." He wrenched his arm out of Peale's grasp and started looking for Remington. He found him sitting cross-legged, leaning against a tree next to a Vietnamese corpse. He was going through the dead man's pack. He ignored the puddle of blood his left boot lay in. Copley, Eakins, and Russell lounged nearby smoking and laughing.

"On your feet, dickhead."

Remington looked up at the words. Bingham held his rifle tightly, the muzzle pointing at Remington's chest. The big man slowly moved his right hand to the small of his rifle stock laying across his crossed legs. "What if I don't?"

"Then I'll kill you sitting down."

Remington's left hand moved as inconspicuously as his right hand had to the forestock. "Why you want to kill me, dude?"

"Cooper. My main man, my number-one best friend is fucking dead. You killed him. I knew you were going to get people killed. You got the wrong one wasted."

"I didn't waste no Marines, man. I only killed them little yellow fuckers." He shook his head, but never let his eyes stray from Bingham's.

"You decided on your own to flank Charlie. Chickencoop knew you couldn't do it alone, so he went to help you. He's dead because of it. Stand up so I can kill your dumb ass."

Remington didn't flicker his gaze to the side where he saw Homer approaching Bingham and signaling Morse to come in from the other direction. "We was pinned down, dude. Cooper would have been killed anyway, like West was."

Bingham threw his rifle into his shoulder and raised his sights to Remington's forehead. "On your feet, dickhead. I want to kill you standing up."

To Bingham's right rear Homer looked at Morse, tapped his own chest and pointed up, then pointed at Morse and gestured downward. Morse nodded. Homer held up three fingers and chopped the air three times. When his hand went down the third time he lunged forward and knocked Bingham's rifle up and out of his hands. In the same instant Morse bowled forward and tackled his squad leader around the knees. A single shot rang out, the bullet going harmlessly into the treetops. Homer tossed the rifle aside and dropped onto Bingham's back. With Morse, he pinned Bingham to the ground.

"No way my honcho's going to the brig for wasting no Marine," he whispered into Bingham's ear. "Even if the Marine is a dumbass who gets good men wasted for no good reason."

Bingham struggled briefly before laying still. The two black men holding him down were each bigger than he was and he knew Homer was right. Remington could pay some other time.

Still leaning against the tree, boot in a coagulating puddle of someone else's blood, Remington let the corners of his mouth turn up slightly. "Chuck dude got careless," he said to himself, "bros come to my help. Day coming when I be number-one honcho in this badass squad." He dipped his head in a nod at the pile of bodies with Bingham on the bottom. Homer's words hadn't reached him. He didn't realize it was Bingham, not him, the two black Marines had saved.

CHAPTER TWENTY-ONE
Rounding Out the Parts

A couple of days after Cooper's death and the killing of the NVA company by the river, the Marine commanders decided the immediate threat to Khe Sanh from that direction was over. Half of the companies involved in that search and destroy operation were ordered to continue sweeping the area to act as an early detection and blocking force in the event the NVA tried it again. The rest of them were withdrawn to small fire bases where they could readily contest territory the enemy might want to occupy, and be ready as reaction forces to reinforce any established combat bases the NVA might attack. As incredible as the warnings about a major offensive at Tet might have seemed, the Americans did want to be prepared. Just in case.

One facet of the preparations was sending in replacements. George Bingham's first squad got two new men: Pfc. Gilbert C. Stuart and Pvt. Matthew Pratt.

Stuart was a quiet man who talked about himself only reluctantly. That was fine with the other men in the squad and they left him alone—until they found out he was from San Diego.

"Say what?" Russell said, somewhere between a gasp and a shout.

"You shitting me," West said, goggle-eyed—he hadn't been killed, only knocked unconscious when a piece of shrapnel smashed into his helmet. Copley held a hand over his mouth and giggled behind it. He rolled toward West, who rolled back at him until the corners of their foreheads touched. They laughed quietly into each other's chests, their bodies shuddering with the effort of keeping their laughs quiet.

Trumbull's eyes lit up. Here was someone who'd done something so dumb no way this newbie could call him "Baby-san." "I'm gonna like you, Gil," he said.

"If you're really from San Diego, why the fuck did you enlist in the Crotch?" Rush asked. "Don't you know any better?"

Stuart shrugged weakly and looked embarrassed.

"You must a lived back in the hills and never went near boot camp," Russell said.

Stuart shook his head again. "Any of you go through Dago?"

Copley, Russell, and Pratt had gone through Boot Camp at MCRD San Diego.

"You know when you stand on the Little Grinder and look up on the hill at those houses?"

They all remembered the pastel housing development.

"That's where I lived."

Copley and West stopped laughing into each other and sat up straight, gaping. Russell stopped chewing his gum. Rush grimaced and slowly shook his head.

Trumbull's eyes lit even brighter. Really dumb. Finally, there was going to be someone below him in the pecking order.

Pratt beamed. He hadn't known Stuart before, but anyone who could see Boot Camp and still enlist was someone he wanted for a friend. He was someone who really wanted to be a Marine.

Why? Copley, West, Rush, and Russell wanted to know. If you could see it, what on earth made you enlist? Who put a gun to your head?

Stuart tried to explain. From the yard of his home in the pastel housing development he couldn't hear the drill instructors screaming at the recruits. He didn't hear the gut-wrenching gasps of recruits pushing themselves far beyond what they'd thought were the limits of their physical abilities. He couldn't feel the leg-burning agony of standing motionless for what seemed like hours. He didn't experience the mind-numbing effort of recruit discipline. He was a stranger to the fear the DIs instantly invoked in the recruits. "All I could see was the PT and the close order drill and the parades. And the Marines have the reputation of being the best, and I wanted to be the best. Besides," he finished in almost a whisper, hollow-eyed, hoping they wouldn't hear, "it looked like fun from where I was."

After he said it looked like fun, nobody in the squad was willing to talk to him for a few days—they didn't want to risk contracting whatever mental affliction it was he had.

Nobody except big, baby-faced Trumbull. Tried to order him around, is what Trumbull did, now that there was somebody below him in the pecking order.

After about the third time Trumbull tried to order him around, Stuart said very firmly, "Go fuck yourself, Baby-san."

Trumbull looked at him with basset eyes. Sure, Stuart was tall but, gee, he was still a couple of inches shorter and it wasn't right for a shorter man to not show respect to a big man like him. He tried to explain to Stuart how he was supposed to show him respect and do what he said because of seniority.

Stuart put his hand on the taller man's shoulder and somehow managed to look down at him. "Tell you what, Baby-san," he said gently. "I'll souvenir you a magnifying glass and a pair of tweezers if you promise to go away by yourself and jerk off."

Trumbull was so deeply offended by this affront to his masculinity that he refused to talk to anybody for three days.

Pratt also wanted to talk to Stuart. Stuart didn't much care for Pratt's bushy-tailed enthusiasm, but at least he was someone to talk to who wasn't being a total asshole about it.

Pratt was a voluble Texan who would talk to anyone who would stand still long enough for it—or anyone who didn't run away too fast for him to keep up with. While the squad had already learned everything they wanted to know about Stuart, they couldn't shut Pratt up. He told them more about himself than they could possibly want to know.

Matthew Pratt was proud, almost inordinately so, of being a United States Marine. He was proud of everything he had done during his seven and a half months in the Marine Corps. In Boot Camp he had stood strong when the drill instructors went about breaking down their charges physically and psychologically in order to rebuild them as Marines. It wasn't necessary for the DIs to break Pratt down physically because he had been a four-letter athlete in high school and was already in fine physical condition. Nor did they need to break him down psychologically because his athletic background had combined with his Catholic upbringing and education to teach him discipline and an unfailing obedience to authority. The Rifle Expert badge he won was the crowning glory of his Boot Camp and could only have been eclipsed by promotion to PFC at graduation, but he was only the sixth best man in his seventy-seven-man platoon and missed promotion by one. Throughout Infantry Training Regiment he acted as a squad leader and expected to be promoted at the end of ITR, but no promotions were given to his training company. He told his squadmates confidentially he expected to be promoted in the next round of promotions.

Matthew Pratt was proud of the admiration he received from his high school buddies and the adulation of his family and friends when he went home on boot leave. He was very proud of the experienced way he made love with the former captain of the cheerleading squad when she seduced him near the end of his leave—she never guessed she was his first, he told his new buddies. He wanted them to know he was a sexually experienced man. Another thing he was proud of from that boot leave was the way he put down and left speechless an anti-war protestor who verbally assaulted him for wearing the uniform. He hadn't even used any swear words in the patriotic speech he defeated the protestor with. He was proud of his comportment and learning, both in garrison and in the field while receiving further training and being procceesed at Camp Pendleton for shipment to Vietnam. Matthew Pratt was quietly proud of the professional way he handled himself on his first patrols. He made sure everyone knew his squad leader, Sergeant Bingham, said he did well for a green boot—a Marine with no experience.

But the thing Matthew Pratt was most proud of was the new name the Marine Corps gave him. Private Pratt was his name now and he loved being called by that name. His recruiting sergeant had told him a Marine's proper first name was his rank, and the DIs in boot camp had confirmed that. Of course, he expected to soon be renamed Private First Class Pratt, and some day Lance Corporal Pratt and then Corporal Pratt—secretly he dreamed of some day being renamed Sergeant Pratt, but that wasn't the sort of thing one talked about until one was a senior corporal.

To be sure, there were things he didn't tell them about himself. There was, for example, the matter of his name. Private Pratt had a wonderful and manly ring to it. Even Matthew Pratt was fine as names went, and he would have had no problem with it if people called him by that name. But that was not the case. Everyone, except his mother and father, shortened the Matthew to Matt, noticed the onomotopoetic relationship between the two halves of his name, invariably called him Matt Pratt and, just as invariably, condensed it to Mattpratt. Just like Rodney Dangerfield, no one has any respect for a man called Mattpratt. Neither does a man called Mattpratt have any self-respect nor any reason for pride. Private Pratt, however, could be as proud as he wanted to be.

Then there was the matter of his high school athletic career. His football, basketball, and baseball teams seldom played close games; they were usually blowouts one way or the other. The same coach ran all three teams and his philosophy was to let the scrubs play once the score was so lopsided the losing team could win only if the winning team quit. Mattpratt was the only one-hundred-and-ninety pounder on the wrestling team, so he got to play all the time. He didn't tell his new friends he had been a bench-warmer in his three team sports, only that he was a four-letter man.

And he didn't tell the whole truth about Mary Cassatt, the girl-friend of Mattpratt, Romeo. The boys and girls in Matthew Pratt's high school were very even in numbers. One day Mary Cassatt looked around, saw all the boys were taken by other girls and gritted her teeth before saying, "Mattpratt, let's go steady." He grinned a bashful grin and turned red because one of the girls finally wanted to go steady with him. The grin disappeared and the blush deepened when Mary added, almost as an afterthought, "But if you try to get fresh I'll knock your block off." All he told them was Mary Cassatt had asked him to go steady.

He never mentioned to anybody how on his first day with his recruit platoon one of the drill instructors saw the name, "Pratt, Matthew," on the platoon's roster and made the immediate connection. From then until graduation the DIs and most of the other recruits called him Mattpratt except when an officer or a civilian was within hearing. Several members of his recruit platoon were in the same training company with him in ITR and Mattpratt continued to be what he was called there. A clerk at Camp Pendleton saw the obvious and called him by that name when several other men were around. They all called him Mattpratt. There was no one in Alpha Company who knew anything of Private Pratt's background, and he never told anyone his civilian first name. But Corporal Remington saw his name on a letter from his sister one day at mail call and exclaimed, "Mattpratt! No wonder you trys harder, boy." Pratt gritted his teeth at the hated epithet, but the name stuck again.

It's tough, he felt, to be proud and deserving of respect when you want the world to call you "Private Pratt" but the entire world insists on calling you "Mattpratt."

It wasn't long before the others tired of hearing Mattpratt talk about himself and they tried to consign him to the same purdah in which Gilbert Stuart, who should have known better, dwelt.

So the cast was finally complete for the extraordinary play that was about to unfold. Sergeant George C. Bingham; Corporals Charles W. Peale and Frederick Remington; Lance Corporals

Diego Rivera, John S. Copley, and Benjamin West; Pfcs. William
Rush, John Trumbull, Samuel F. Morse, Charles M. Russell,
Thomas Eakins, Winslow Homer, and Gilbert C. Stuart; and
Private Matthew Pratt.

AFTER-ACTION REPORT:
Some Historical Facts and Speculation

From the Analytic Notes of R.W. Thoreau, Lt. Col., USMC (ret.)
The View from Hanoi

Vo Nuyghn Giap was the commander of the North Vietnamese Army, the military genius who had defeated the French at Dien Bien Phu years before. He knew the war was not going well for his side.

The war was not going well in the north. The Americans were dropping too many bombs from too many airplanes, some of which flew so high they could not be seen or heard from the ground. Those high flyers seemed invulnerable to the jets and anti-aircraft missiles forming a protective ring around Hanoi and Haiphong, unlike the Phantom and Thunderbird tactical bombers that flew low and could be intercepted by the jet fighters of the People's Army, or shot down by the missiles. Bridges were being destroyed as fast as they could be rebuilt, roads damaged faster than they could be repaired. Everywhere, munitions and military supplies were in short supply because of the bombing. Russia and China were both reluctant to give the People's Republic of Vietnam the modern weapons needed to shoot down the attacking planes and arm the men fighting in the south. Civilians were being wounded and killed by the daily attacks, their lives were disrupted, and food and medicines and other items for the people were in short supply. Morale was suffering. The Americans were not being hurt at home. Something had to be done to ease this pressure—something drastic.

In the south, the Americans were proving to be strong and brave soldiers armed with many fearsome weapons. The National Liberation Front suffered casualties at a rate faster than new fighters could be recruited and trained. While the ARVN was unable to increase its force because the desertion rate combined with casualties to equal the conscription rate, and it was often reluctant to fight, the Americans seemed to have an inexhaustible supply of giant soldiers it could send into battle from its huge homeland across the sea. The Americans were winning the war in the countryside by simple power of greater force. Indeed, the North Vietnamese Army was assuming a greater portion of the fight in the Central Highlands and the area the Americans called "I Corps"—the areas where the Americans had their best fighters, their airborne, cavalry, and Marines. The people were beginning to think of the Americans as invincible. The National Liberation Front was experiencing desertions at a rate to almost rival that of the ARVN because too many of the young guerrillas were weary of fighting men they were becoming to believe they could not defeat. Something had to be done to turn the tide of battle—something dramatic.

American intelligence about the Ho Chi Minh Trail was improving greatly, and they were constantly managing to interdict with bombs and artillery the supply trains moving south through neutral Laos and Cambodia—a neutrality the North Vietnamese conveniently ignored. Fewer than half of the weapons and medical supplies leaving the north arrived at their proper destinations in the south. An army suffering casualties as fast as new men could be brought into the fight, and lacking in weapons and medical supplies, could not defeat a growing army of giants who were armed with the world's most advanced weapons. Eventually the giants would wear down the men. American ships and cargo aircraft in the south were nearly invulnerable to attack. Something had to be done to increase the flow of supplies and damage American logistics—something radical.

These were the things General Giap knew. He was the man who trained and led the men who fought the French colonialists from the end of World War II until he finally crushed them at the battle of Dien Bien Phu. He was the man leading the freedom fighters who would overthrow the government of the American lackey Nguyen Van Thieu, the general who assumed the mantle of the presidency, the mantle that properly belonged to Ho Chi Minh. Vo Nuyghn Giap would find something drastic, something dramatic, something radical. He knew he must defeat the Americans as he had the French, or make them quit the war. But how?

Giap saw the Americans as politically naive. The American people did not understand the war they were involved in; they did not understand it was for more than the reunification of the nation of Vietnam. This was a war to determine whether the Southeast Asian peninsula would be dominated by Communism or Imperialism. Eventually this war could make that determination for the archipelagio nations ringing the eastern half of Asia and for the nations of South Asia. All the Americans understood in their homes across the ocean was the war was killing their sons and brothers and husbands in a land most of them had never heard of until their sons and brothers and husbands were sent there to fight. After a brief period of patriotism when the Americans thought no one should be able to fire torpedos at their ships, even if those ships were trespassing in waters claimed by another nation, other voices began to be heard loudly crying out against American involvement in someone else's civil war. Public sentiment in America was turning against the war in Vietnam. General Giap would use this naïveté and antiwar sentiment to defeat the Americans.

The American people knew their sons and brothers and husbands were fighting a technologically inferior people, a people they considered almost primitive. They knew their sons and brothers and husbands were being killed by these backward people who never stood to fight their more potent foe. Too few Americans understood the amount of damage their sons and brothers and husbands were inflicting on their weaker enemies. If there would be a pitched battle won by their small opponents, a battle that cost the Americans thousands of lives and a combat base, that might be enough of a blow to the American psyche to cause them to rise up and demand their government withdraw from Vietnam. Giap examined his tactical and strategic maps and his intelligence reports for a target. One location jumped out at him.

In the northwest corner of Quang Tri Province, scant miles south of the demilitarized zone separating the two Vietnams and within sight of mountains of Laos, was a plateau laden with French-owned coffee plantations. A few months before a series of major battles had been fought in that area. The American Marines had won those battles; Hill 881 North, Hill 881 South, Hill 861—the Rockpile. But they were hard-won victories and the American Marines suffered heavy casualties. This plateau was named Khe Sanh and its population was concentrated in a village of the same name. The American army had a special forces unit with its Montagnard mercenaries working out of a combat base near the village. This special forces unit was being dislodged by a battalion of American Marines. Khe Sanh was a remote location accessable by only one, easily broken highway. Resupply of this combat base would be difficult for the Americans. The Ho Chi Minh Trail ran just across the mountains in Laos at this point; directly to the north was the DMZ. It was an area easily resupplied by the Army of the People's Republic of Vietnam.

If this combat base was assaulted by a sufficiently superior force its defenders could all be killed and it would fall. This could be the blow Giap wanted to inflict on the American psyche.

The assault on Khe Sanh was part of a two-phase plan Giap detailed. It could function as a distraction for another major operation. Most of the population in the south was apathetic toward the progress of the war. The people in the countryside seemed not to care who ran the government or which side won—as long as the war left them alone. Support of the revolution in the rural areas where it was being fought wasn't given as freely as was needed for final victory. Support in the cities was almost nonexistent. The city dwellers feared reprisals from the ARVN and were dependent on the Americans. The battle needed to be taken to the cities, where it would be made clear to all the people that the ARVN and the Saigon government were impotent and not even the American giants could protect them. The minute the people in the cities understood that, they would rise up and attack the Saigon puppet government, and they would turn on the American aggressors. The American people at home would think the NLF was far stronger than it in fact was. They would think their sons and brothers and husbands were being sacrificed in a war they could not win.

This would be the two-horned dragon that would allow the NLF to win. These would be the offensives that would drive the Americans back across the ocean in disgrace and bring the downtrodden peoples of the south into the fight and win the war. The slogan for this offensive was *Tong Cong Kich, Tong Khoi Nghia*—General Offensive, General Uprising.

The plan was audacious in its simplicity. The southern forces of the NLF, the Vietcong, would attack every major city, every provincial and district capital in the south. The people would see this daring move and be emboldened to rise against the corrupt Thieu government. Very soon thereafter the war would be ended with victory going to the communists.

The assault on Khe Sanh would begin in mid or late January. With the Americans' attention fixed on it, the Vietcong would drift into the cities to prepare their offensive. Regular People's Army units would also move into position to take advantage of the confusion and the uprising and support the Vietcong once the battle was turning in their favor. The attack would begin on the first day of the lunar new year, when there would be a cease-fire in effect and no one in the south would be expecting a major action. It would be the greatest Tet holiday in Vietnam's long history.

An overwhelming assault on a lightly defended outpost. A nationwide assault on the cities during the highest and most sacrosanct of all holidays. These things would be drastic, they would be dramatic, they would be radical.

The View from Saigon

Intelligence reports poured into MACV headquarters in Saigon. They came from Chieu Hois, from satellite photographs, U-2 spy plane flights, CIA operatives slipping through the brush in North Vietnam, the testimony of prisoners, secret listening devices dropped from aircraft flying other missions along the Ho Chi Minh Trail in Laos, and from captured documents. They all indicated the same thing.

Gradually some of these reports filtered up to General William Westmoreland, supreme commander of all allied forces in the Republic of Vietnam. Westmoreland read them, digested them, salivated over them. He demanded more information from his intelligence chiefs. He demanded corroboration from other sources. He had commanded, first, the American advisors to the ARVN, then, when the Pentagon and president finally agreed to send them, the American ground forces. Korean, Thai, Australian soldiers and marines all fought under his direction. He commanded the mightiest army ever fielded in so small a theater of operations. At his beck and call were the most destructive weapons of war ever unleashed against an enemy, excepting only nuclear devices. For four years, he had plotted and planned and led this burgeoning army against a ragtag army of peasants. A ragtag army of highly motivated men and women who fought bravely when cornered, but who preferred stealth and treachery to open combat. A ragtag army that used weapons cast off by the Chinese and Russians following World War II, that used weapons captured from and abandoned by the French when they were finally beaten and driven out by the Vietminh. A ragtag army that used unexploded bombs and artillery shells to make booby traps and mines to wound and kill its enemies, an army that used terrorism as a basic piece of weaponry. This army of irregulars dodged Westmoreland's forces, spread them too thin, refused to stand and fight like proper soldiers. The body counts told Westmoreland his army was badly hurting this ragtag army; so did the massive amounts of arms and munitions, food and medical supplies captured or destroyed by his army. Vietcong deserters were flooding in at a rate almost high enough to rival the flood of deserters from the ARVN.

Westmoreland was under a deadline for winning this war. Within a year he was scheduled to be replaced as top American in Vietnam and to report to the Pentagon as Army chief of staff. It was clear to him that his war of attrition against the Vietcong was wearing the enemy down and would eventually defeat them. But it was taking time, and time was the one commodity he had in short supply. Westmoreland read the intelligence reports. The enemy was playing into his hands.

Truck traffic on the Ho Chi Minh Trail had increased geometrically over the past month or so. Huge troop movements were reported just north of the DMZ and on the Ho Chi Minh Trail in central Laos. The 325C Division of the North Vietnamese Army, which had fought earlier in the Hills battles, was on the move. The 304 Division, which had defeated the French at Dien Bien Phu, was with the 325C. The 320 and 324 divisions were also moving. All of these supplies, enough to support an army on a major campaign, and all of these men, up to forty thousand fighters, were concentrated in Laos near the DMZ and in northern South Vietnam. The intelligence reports told General Westmoreland the North Vietnamese were readying for an assault on the Marine battalion at the Khe Sanh combat base. He put his forces into gear to counter the enemy action, to deal the enemy the defeat he expected them to try to inflict on him.

Air Force B-52s drew mission plans to drop hundreds of thousands of tons of bombs in support of the Marine battalion at Khe Sanh. An Army 175mm artillery battalion, the heaviest artillery in the American arsenal, was flown to Camp Carroll, east of Khe Sanh, from where it could fire in support of the Marines. The First Cavalry and 101 Airborne Divisions were moved north to support and relieve the Marines at Khe Sanh. Westmoreland politely requested that the Marines reinforce their one battalion garrison with two more battalions.

The Marine commanders in Vietnam saw no point in defending this remote outpost—they wanted to vacate it and concentrate their efforts in the lowlands. They refused Westmoreland's request. Westmoreland didn't much like the Marines to begin with. He had no confidence in their ability to fight and their independence from Army control infuriated him. He made his request again, but less politely, and let them understand that they would reinforce Khe Sanh no matter what they wanted to do. The Marine commanders decided it was better to grant an Army general a favor than to have to obey an order from an Army general. They reinforced the combat base at Khe Sanh with two more battalions, and later added another battalion.

All was in readiness. When the North Vietnamese assaulted the Twenty-Sixth Marine Regiment (reinforced) at Khe Sanh, they would be dealt so crushing a defeat, Westmoreland would win the war before reporting back to Washington to take his place with the Joint Chiefs of Staff.

More intelligence reports flooded in, but many influential members of General Westmoreland's staff discounted them. They were too improbable. According to these reports, on the first day of Tet, the most sacred day in the Vietnamese year, every available Vietcong in the country would gather to attack every major city, every province, and every district capital in South Vietnam in a general offensive.

This plan made a certain sense, though. There was a truce declared for the Tet holiday, the ARVN and Regional Forces would be standing down. American forces would not be in the field on operations. People would be moving throughout the country, returning to ancestral homes for the holiday. The Vietcong would be able to move freely with little concern of being intercepted by maneuvering units, and the movement of civilians would mask them in their civilian clothes. Very heavy blows could be struck at this time and much damage could be done before proper resistance had a chance to be organized. If the Vietcong would indeed do such a thing.

The plan also made little sense on two counts.

The Vietcong simply weren't strong enough to take the major cities and the provincial and district capitals. If there was a general uprising against the Saigon government in conjunction with this offensive it might succeed, but only if the civilian populace joined it. However, the civilian populace was moving more to the side of the government, away from the insurgents. If the Vietcong tried to take only a few cities and district capitals, they might succeed for a time. But they couldn't take all of them, and certainly they couldn't hold them.

Tet is a sacred holiday. Take Christmas, New Year's Day, Easter, and the Fourth of July. Wrap them all together and the American with a Christian background begins to grasp the sacredness of Tet. The Vietcong soldiers would be loath to mount an attack at that time instead of spending those few days with their families. And they should know that the sacredness of the holiday was such that despoiling it would be certain to turn the people even more against the communists.

Only by a fluke could such an offensive succeed. If the Vietcong did mount so audacious an offensive during the Tet holiday, all they would accomplish would be to alienate the populace and end up breaking themselves on the mighty army that would regroup to oppose them. The Tet general offensive was far too improbable, too suicidal to succeed. Westmoreland's staff discounted it and the general discounted it. He intended to break the back of the North Vietnamese and win the war at Khe Sanh.

Lyndon Johnson was the president of the United States of America. He discounted it, too.

PART III

CHAPTER TWENTY-TWO
We Got a Cease-Fire Starting at Midnight

"How come we got to go again? How come Gershwin's squad don't ever go out?"

"It's Eakins's fault, Russell," Trumbull said. "He's so good at night, you just know Copeland and Ives aren't going to put anybody else's squad out there when the Night Stalker's available." The big Marine grinned at his own joke.

Eakins looked up at the sound of his name. He looked like he didn't understand why he was being blamed for the squad having to go on another all-night ambush. It wasn't his fault the city boys in the squad couldn't move through the boonies as quietly as he could, or the country boys in the other squads didn't have eyes and ears as sharp as his. Except for Chief. Thinking that, he said, "Baby-san, how come you don't blame Chief?"

"So let Eakins go out with Gershwin or Wagner's squad," Russell kept up his complaint. "Or give him to one of their squads, they're under strength." He glanced at Eakins and added, "Him and Chief both."

"Shitcan the pissing and moaning, Chas," Remington said. "Let me hear it." He stood in front of Russell and stared down at him hard-eyed.

Russell grimaced, but he stood and hopped in place to show his fire team leader his gear was properly tied and taped down for silence.

"Fix your dogtags, I can hear them."

Russell grumbled softly, but turned from Remington to find some tape to silence the clinking of his dogtags.

"You too, Baby-san," Dago Rivera said to Trumbull.

"Ah, come on, honcho. I know my shit."

"Yeah, I know your shit, too. I know you're a big shit. Hop." Trumbull screwed up his face and managed to look even younger than he was. Trumbull held his arms out to his sides with his M-14 in one hand and jumped. The only sound that came from him was the thudding of his boots on the earth when he landed.

Rivera nodded. "We'll teach you yet, Baby-san," he said. "Someday you'll be a real Marine. You, too, Mattpratt." The last was directed at the eager-looking private who kept trying to impress everybody with what a great Marine he was. His expression suddenly soured and he groaned at the name.

"Sorry about that, Homer," Chuck Peale said to the tall, black Marine, "but you just know Night Stalker and Chief don't need to be checked."

"You a jive-ass chuck, Chuck," Remington said. "You only making Homer hop on account a he's a splib. He a chuck like you, you don't make him hop."

"Fuck you and the horse you rode in on, Remington," Peale said back. "You want to call me a jive-ass chuck 'cause I make a black man jump? I'll call you a shit splib for making white men hop."

Bingham sat on his helmet nearby smoking a cigarette. While his eyes searched the wall of trees to the west beyond the cleared fields of fire surrounding the hill on which Alpha Company was based, he listened to the sounds and voices of his men getting themselves ready for their ambush. He never had to tell his fire-team leaders what to do to get their men ready to go out; they had all done it many times before, and they were all good despite any personal problems he might have with any of them. The men had been briefed earlier, and in a few minutes the fire-team leaders would join him at the perimeter to make an eyeball examination of the treeline they'd move into shortly before sunset.

Peale was the first to sit cross-legged on the dirt next to Bingham. He had told Homer he wasn't going to inspect Eakins and Rush and he was true to his word, that made him the first of the fire-team leaders through with his inspection. He wore a soft hat with a floppy brim, the kind they called a boonie hat. The sleeves of his olive-drab utility shirt were raggedly cut off below his deltoids, exposing arms burned by the sun and scratched by the bush. The buttons were missing from his shirt and it was held loosely closed at the waist by his cartridge belt. The shirt was not tucked into his trousers. He laid his M-14 across his legs with its muzzle angled toward the trees. He didn't say anything but sat quietly, puffing on the lit cigarette dangling from his lower lip.

Remington and Rivera soon joined them. Rivera knelt on his right knee and sat on the foot he folded under himself. He leaned his rifle against the arm he draped across his left knee. He didn't smoke but sucked on a piece of sugar cane. Remington plunked down a few feet away. He puffed on a menthol cigarette held in the hand that wasn't holding his rifle. They were dressed the same as Peale. The official uniform of the day included helmets and flak jackets, which none of them wore. Flak jackets were heavy and made you sweat, so the Marines left their flak jackets off whenever they could get away with it. And helmets were heavy and cut down on your hearing at night, and they preferred not to wear them on night ambushes. Besides, the Vietcong had been quiet for a while, and even though the North Vietnamese had Khe Sanh under heavy siege, there hadn't been any activity around this fire base during the several days Alpha Company had been there.

The four men didn't talk for a few minutes; they just looked at the forest. Bingham glanced at his wristwatch and broke the silence. "Fifteen minutes," he said. "Fred, there's a game trail about twenty meters to the left of that big tree." He pointed. "Put your newby, Stuart, on the point and tell him to find it. It goes to where we're going." He spat into the dirt between his feet and scuffed soil over the wet spot. "He needs the practice. Dago, your team has rear point."

Remington and Peale looked at their own watches, checking the time. "Easy night," Peale said. "The cease-fire'll start before we come back in." They stood up.

Rivera stared at the face of his watch for a long moment, concentrating on the small window in it that showed the date. "What month is this?" he asked.

"January."

Rivera nodded. "The twenty-fucking-ninth. I'm officially a short-timer as of today. I've been in this stinking country one whole year. Another month and this Mex flys back to the World, the Land of the Big PX."

"You're going home on Sadie Hawkins Day, Jose," Peale said.

Rivera looked at him. "What the fuck's Sadie Hawkins Day?"

"Man, don't you read Li'l Abner? Leap Year Day, that's the day women get to propose to men. You get on that Freedom Bird, the stews get a look at you, this badass gyrene, you'll probably be married by the time you land in JP."

"Oh, man, I like that." Rivera grinned broadly. "Maybe I'll get married to a stew on the Freedom Bird, a geisha in JP, and a blond in California."

Remington snorted. "If you live that long, spic."

"I got a better chance than you do, my man. You make one

hell of a bigger target than I do." He stood and looked up at the man who stood four inches taller than he did. "I think I'll use you for cover and concealment the rest of my tour. That way, I go, you go first."

Remington snorted again. "You do what I do the next month, maybe you have a chance."

Bingham's jaws clenched and he stared at Remington but didn't say anything. Men had died because they followed Remington's example. He looked at his watch again. "Thirteen minutes, people. Get 'em ready." The fire-team leaders returned to their men and got them lined up.

When they were ready to leave, Bingham made a last radio check on the PRC-20 Copley carried on a backpack frame and signaled Remington to move out. The black corporal nodded to Stuart and followed him through the opening in the concertina wire surrounding Alpha Company's hill toward the setting sun. Ben West followed him, then Russell. Bingham and Copley were between him and Peale's fire team, then came Rivera's team. Trumbull and Silent Sam Morse brought up the rear. They all carried more or less the same gear. Two hundred and forty rounds per rifle, three-sixty for each automatic M-14. Copley carried twenty-seven high explosive rounds and ten willy peter for his M-79 grenade launcher and thirty-five rounds for his .45. Each man had a bayonet or K-Bar fighting knife; a couple of them carried both. Three fragmentation grenades per man, and two lucky pitchers each had a willy peter. Rush carried a tomahawk and Rivera had a sap stuck in his hip pocket. Two canteens of water per man and a first aid kit. Everyone had the contents of a C ration meal to eat before coming back in the morning spread through his pockets. They were as ready for the night as they could be.

The sun was sinking rapidly toward the forest, and Stuart found that day became twilight under the trees when he entered them. He had only been in the jungle twilight twice before and it had scared him both times. This was the first time he had the point, and the dimness frightened him even more than ever. The ground underfoot was damp and covered with fallen leaves soggy from the recent rains, except for the inches-wide line indicating the game trail. The ground sloped gently downward. Stuart fixed his bayonet before leaving the open and stepped slowly along the barely defined game trail, he carefully examined each shadow and eyed every bush for signs of trouble. He wore his boots with the tongue lashed down and the hightop sides rolled back to leave his shins exposed. He thought this would allow him to feel trip wires before he set off any booby traps. A hundred yards into the forest, the game trail crossed a small stream that bubbled its way to a larger river a half mile away. Stuart stopped at the stream and looked back. He saw Remington as a darker shadow in the trees and saw only the indication of movement when his fire-team leader gestured to the left for him to follow the stream. Walking in a gliding manner, with the soles of his feet hardly leaving the surface of the streambed, Stuart stepped into midstream and waded along it. One by one, all glide-walking, the thirteen other members of the squad followed him. The stream was little more than six feet wide and hardly more than ankle deep in its center. The trees and bushes growing along the banks almost met in the middle, leaving barely enough room for the men to slip through without brushing them. The muted sound of their passage was further masked by the noise the water made. Mere feet away from them, the only sounds to be heard were the buzzing of insects waking at evening, the calls of birds settling in for the night, and the occasional mating cries of fukyoo lizards. Stuart stopped long enough to strip a three-foot long twig from a tree. He carried his rifle in one hand and held the twig in front of him, dangling from the fingers of his other hand to feel for trip wires strung across the stream, a trick Rush told him about when he heard the new man had the point.

A quarter mile downstream Remington tapped Stuart on the shoulder and pointed to the right. He nodded and left the water. A few feet from it he dropped the twig and relied again on his bare shins to detect booby traps. Stuart moved slowly and carefully, taking his time. The rest of the squad followed patiently in his wake—they were no more willing than he was for him to set off a booby trap or make a noise that would alert any enemy soldiers who might be in the area. A couple of hundred meters from the stream, a broad, well-used path cut through the forest. Stuart stopped when he reached it.

Remington crowded next to him and cautiously looked both ways along the path, then stepped onto it. The trail was six feet wide—a highway in the jungle. Remington whistled softly. He had never before seen such a wide path in the jungle. The intertwining tree branches overhead formed a tunnel roof over the trail making it invisible from the air.

A daytime patrol investigating the sound of motors had discovered it that morning. In an hour of watching, they had seen three heavily laden motor scooters, about twenty bicycles, and a small three-wheeled truck drive by. All of the people on the vehicles had worn black pajamas, olive drab baseball caps, and red armbands.

Some of them had carried rifles: Ak-47s and SKS carbines. A few men walked by in twos and threes. One man ambled alone. The patrol had captured him, but so far he hadn't given any information. First squad was one of several ambush patrols—one squad from each platoon of Alpha Company—watching along the trail that night. The squads' orders varied according to the situation: if a unit small enough for them to wipe out without being hurt themselves came by, they were to waste it and return to the company's hill; if a larger unit came by, they were to keep quiet, report its movement, and, if possible, take a prisoner.

Remington listened for sounds of movement while studying the trail. All he heard was Bingham coming to join him. The trail continued fifty yards to the right, then made a turn to the right. In the opposite direction it went straight until it disappeared in the shadows of the rapidly approaching night.

Bingham joined Remington on the trail. He showed no sign of surprise at the size of the trail; instead he cocked an ear in one direction, then the other. All he heard were the normal sounds of nightfall. He peered at the place where the trail turned, then signaled Remington to return to the brush and Stuart to come with him. The two Marines trotted on their toes to the bend in the trail, and Bingham looked carefully around. It was empty for the thirty yards he could see before it turned left again. He looked back and saw Remington partly hidden, watching him. Using his hands, he told Stuart to cover him, and trotted to the next bend. The first bend in the trail was almost a ninety-degree angle, the second was much shallower. On his way back to Stuart, Bingham closely examined both sides of the trail. By the time he re-joined him he had made his decision. The squad would cross the trail and set up between the two bends. The ambush's flank positions could watch the trail in both directions from there and any enemy coming along it might expect an ambush to be on the side closer to the Marine base camp, not on the opposite side. He had seen a place on each side of the trail where foliage could be held aside for the squad to go through without leaving any bent or broken branches to give away their passage.

Bingham drew his men away from the trail and huddled with his fire-team leaders for a moment. Speaking in a low, soft voice he told them what he found and planned. Then, "Chuck, I've got the point now. You come next. I want Chief sticking to my ass. First team, third, second. Night Stalker brings up the rear and makes sure nothing shows where we go through the brush. Got it?" The three fire-team leaders nodded. Remington's nod was one slow dip of his head. He didn't like being taken off the point.

Bingham led the way parallel to the trail, twenty yards from it. He wanted to go faster than he did because he wanted to be in position before night fell, but the pace wasn't as slow as he felt was necessary for safety so close to the enemy roadway. He navigated by dead reckoning and when he thought he was five yards from the angled part of the trail he stopped and signaled everyone but Rush to stay where they were. He reached the trail a yard from where he wanted to cross it. Using hand signals, he called the squad forward. Then he had Rush hold a leafy branch to the side and crossed the trail where he held another branch out of the way. One at a time, the other men of the squad ran across, past Bingham, and into the brush on the other side. Working methodically, he put his men in their positions less than twenty feet from the trail and made sure each man could fire without obstruction. Peale's fire team was on the left where he could have two men watch the trail that angled off to the northeast. Remington was on the right, keeping an eye on the trail coming from the south. Rivera and his men were in the middle. Bingham stationed himself and Copley between Remington's and Rivera's fire teams. He thought the Vietcong were more likely to come along the trail from the south and wanted to be closer to that end of the ambush.

Bingham took the radio handset from Copley and murmured into it, "Alpha One Bravo in place." He listened for the "Roger Alpha One Bravo" reply and gave the handset back. Then the day birds abruptly ceased their calls. It was, that suddenly, the full dark of night.

For an hour the Marines waited patiently, listening more than watching. There was a new moon and too little starlight filtered through the leaves to allow them to see much, but sounds traveled well at night. In the distance they could hear the periodic *carumph* of H&I artillery fire, Harassment and Interdiction, and the smaller occasional *carumphs* when someone in a defensive position or listening post threw hand grenades at suspicious sounds. There were sporadic outbreaks of gunfire as someone walked into an ambush or a line was probed. But it was lighter than usual, the Marines thought probably because of the Tet truce, and there was no sound or movement on the trail Bingham's squad lay in ambush alongside.

"Alpha One Bravo, all secure," Bingham murmured into his radio handset when the luminous hands of his wristwatch told him they had been in position for an hour. "Roger, Alpha One Bravo," came the soft, static-dappled reply. He handed the phone back to

Copley and waited a few more minutes before leaning close and whispering for his grenadier to alert Trumbull he was coming. Two or three times during an all-night ambush, Bingham would check his men, make sure the ones who were supposed to be on watch were awake and alert, make sure no sapper had slipped into his line and knifed someone. He drilled his men to know who was on each side of them in a night position and taught them to kill anyone else who came at them from the flank. When he checked his line during the night he always had the man he was with warn the next man in line.

Everyone seemed alert in each of the four two-man positions on that side, they hadn't been set long enough for the boredom of a long night to lay its weight on them. Trumbull and Pratt lay wide-eyed together; they seemed anxious for something to happen, and frightened at the prospect, in equal proportions. Trumbull had been with the squad for months but still hadn't lost his almost childlike enthusiasm for war. Pratt was too new to understand the deadliness of what he was doing. Rivera and Morse were taciturn and professional together, seasoned warriors who lived today knowing they might be dead tomorrow. Peale and Rush seemed to be just two more good Marines in position. Homer and Eakins were ready to deal with whatever came their way from the northeast. He told Peale and Rivera to put their men on fifty percent alert in another hour. Bingham returned to Copley, checked with him to see if any messages had come over the radio during his absence. None had so he went on to check Remington's fire team. Russell was his usual self and spoke in nods and head shakes. Bingham hoped he wouldn't be a negative influence on Stuart, who had only been with them for a few weeks. Remington sat cross-legged looking over West's shoulder, wanting to see and hear everything the same way his automatic rifleman did. He looked like a black avenger, a panther ready to pounce, slash, and slay. He almost looked to Bingham like a man who wished his enemy, the people he was allowed to kill, were white.

Suddenly Remington tensed. He seemed to coil without moving. Bingham tried to make himself smaller and strained his eyes and ears to detect anything on the trail. He heard the shuffling of feet on the hard-packed earth. A darker darkness loomed on the trail and turned into the ambush's killing zone. Bingham saw a faint reflection on the barrel of the rifle the man carried as he trotted past. A second shadow figure made the turn, then another and another and another. The volume of the shuffling sound increased, and he realized there were far more men on the trail than his squad could handle. He hoped everybody held their fire, waited for him to set the ambush off. He clamped a hand on Remington's shoulder, telling him to be cool, to let them pass. Taut muscles, ready for action, twitched under his hand.

Five, six, seven . . . fifteen . . . twenty . . . thirty—he counted. Forty, fifty, sixty. Two reinforced platoons trotted past the ambush. They were in a hurry to get somewhere. When he was certain the last VC had gone by Bingham scuttled back to Copley without bothering to relay his approach. He grabbed the handset and broke squelch twice, then said, "Alpha One Bravo. Two platoons of unfriendlies just came past, headed northeast. Over."

"Alpha One Bravo. I copy two platoons headed northeast," came the immediate reply. "Stand by." He waited. A couple of minutes later a different voice came to him over the radio. "Alpha One Bravo, this is Alpha Six Actual," Captain Bernstein's voice came over the air, "say again your last, over."

He cupped his hand around his mouth and the mouthpiece to reduce the noise he made talking. "Six Actual, One Bravo. Two platoons of unfriendlies came by in a hurry. Heading northeast. Over."

"Roger, One Bravo. Head count?"

"Sixty. I say again, six-zero. Over."

"Roger, One Bravo. Did they detect you? Over."

"Negative that, Six Actual. Over."

"Roger Alpha One Bravo. Maintain your position. Alpha Six Actual, out."

That was it. Sixty Vietcong were headed in the general direction of Alpha Company's hill and the ambush squad was to stay put. Bingham made another round of his men, reassuring them about what had happened. He wished he felt as confident as he told them to be.

"Everybody's reporting zips going past," Copley told him when he returned to his position.

"Where the fuck are they going? There's supposed to be a truce starting."

"I don't know," the grenadier said and shook his head. "You're the honcho, you're supposed to tell me."

A few minutes later another platoon of Vietcong trotted along the trail, again going northeast. Bingham reported it and held on to the handset instead of returning it to Copley. It wasn't long before the other two squads the company had set on the trail also reported men moving past them. The reports came too close together for them to be reporting the same platoons that came past Bingham's squad. He gave the handset back.

The sporadic gunfire they heard earlier in the evening stopped and the night was quiet except for the ever-present *carumph*ing of H&I fire and the occasional groups of VC trotting past. By midnight each squad reported between 250 and 300 men had moved past them. If Bingham was right that they weren't the same troops, that meant a reinforced battalion—maybe two battalions—were converging in the area.

At midnight the quiet was shattered by explosions coming from the southeast—the direction of the district town. The explosions were answered by a few scattered shots that quickly grew into what sounded like a major firefight. Bingham felt his men stirring in their places. The radio was silent about what was happening. Minutes later he heard the blasts of mortar rounds exploding on or near Alpha Company's hill, and the tension among the men along the trail became palpable. He tapped Copley on the shoulder, asking for the radio handset. He held the receiver so tightly against his head it hurt his ear as he strained to hear any transmissions. For several minutes all that came over the air was faint static. Then a voice came through.

"All Alpha Bravos, all Alpha Bravos, this is Alpha Six," the laconic radio voice said. "We are being visited by some unfriendly natives. Maintain your positions until you receive further word. I say again, maintain your positions. Six out." The abruptness of the "Six out," without asking for an acknowledgment, was the only indication the radioman gave that the situation on the hill might be desperate.

"The bad guys are hitting the hill," Bingham whispered to Copley. "We're supposed to stay put. I'm going to pass the word."

Everyone nodded and tried to hunker lower into the ground. Except for Remington. "What the fuck you mean, 'maintain,' dude," Remington said through gritted teeth. "We got three squads of badassed Mo-reens out here. We get together, we climb up Charlie's asshole, and put his ass in a sling. Roll up his flank, man. Kick some ass."

Bingham stared hard at the shadow that was Remington's face for a long moment before answering. "Fred," he finally said slowly, "there's at least a fucking battalion out there. I don't know how you managed to stay alive this long. We go climbing up Charlie's asshole he's going to shit us out like a turd. He'll just turn a company around and waste us like shit paper."

"Bullshit. He won't know how many of us there is, or where we are, because we can keep moving around."

"If we get behind Charlie we'll be in the line of fire from our own people," said Bingham. He wasn't able to keep the anger out of his voice. "We stay right here."

Remington muttered, "Mickey Mouse outfit," but his voice was low enough Bingham was able to pretend he didn't hear him.

"Lots of chatter, Honcho," Copley said when Bingham dropped down next to him. He had switched his radio from the patrol frequency to the company's platoon net so he could monitor the company's transmissions with its platoons on the hill. The sergeant held his head close to Copley's so they both could listen.

"Six, this is Two," second platoon's radioman screamed. "We got waves coming at us." The volume of gunfire near the radio garbled his voice, but not too much to make out his words.

"Four, Six," the company commander's radioman said after a moment. "Pop some Hotel Echo in front of Two. He needs help, over."

"Roger, Six," the weapons platoon commander replied. "Four" was his radio sign. "Two, Four. How close are they? Over." He was directing his six-tube 60mm mortar section and needed to know where to fire his high explosive rounds.

"They're in the wire!" someone shouted. It might not have been second platoon's radioman. There was more confusion about who was talking when another voice said, "Fifty meters left, do you see them?"

Bingham and Copley looked at each other in the darkness. He couldn't see Copley's expression, but he was sure it was similar to his own. He felt sick. He had friends in second platoon and knew Copley did, too.

"Two, this is Four. How close to you are they. Identify your transmission, over." The weapons platoon commander didn't know whether the assault on second platoon had reached the barbed wire perimeter or was fifty meters out—or if it was somewhere else.

"This is Two," the panicky voice screamed, "they've gotten through the wire! They're through the wire." His words were punctuated by a louder chatter of fire than any heard before, which was cut off by a loud burst of static.

Bingham stifled a moan. He thought the burst of static was caused by the radio getting hit.

"Two, Six. What is your status, how many have penetrated the wire? Over." When Two didn't answer a different voice came over the radio. "Two, this is Six Actual. Sitrep, over."

Two didn't answer; instead someone else said, "Six, One. We are taking fire from our right flank, over." Shouted orders were audible in the background as the platoon commander and squad leaders of first platoon shifted to meet the new threat.

"Four, Six Actual," Captain Bernstein said, his voice leaden, "Charlie is on top of Two. Fire for effect on top of Two. Six out."

Bingham felt Copley sag next to him. The company was going to fire its mortars at one of its own platoons. "No sweat, John," he said. "They're in their fighting holes. Charlie's topside. The mortars'll get him, not our people." He hoped his voice was reassuring and not as full of fear as he felt.

"What happens if a round lands in a hole?"

"It doesn't matter," Bingham said. "It don't mean nothing." That was the universal disclaimer. By denying that death or injury had meaning, the man with the rifle and bayonet, the man whose life was on the line every dying day in the war, could deny that death had any control over him. He could stand up on each new day and fight again without running away—or going crazy.

They listened to the the battle for the hill for a few minutes more, then Bingham left to tell his men what was happening. He told them the hill was being hit hard. He didn't say it was being overrun.

After fierce fighting the Marines of Alpha Company managed to drive the VC off the hill. Captain Bernstein met with his two remaining officers—the executive officer, Lieutenant Copeland, and the second platoon commander had been killed in the assault. Ives was in charge of first platoon. The senior remaining man in second platoon was a corporal who hadn't even been a squad leader half an hour before. After getting their situation reports and conferring on the radio with the battalion commander, Bernstein ordered a withdrawal. Alpha Company would take its dead and wounded and destroy all weapons and equipment they couldn't carry. Then Bernstein had his radioman call the three squad ambushes along the trail with instructions to swing north around the hill and rendezvous at a checkpoint a kilometer east of it. The radioman put the order out on the frequency used to talk to the patrols. The withdrawal from the hill was masked by the explosions that destroyed everything that they didn't take with them. One piece of equipment they didn't take was the twenty-foot antenna that allowed the company to communicate with its patrols.

Copley still had his radio set to the company's platoon frequency, not the patrol frequency, and didn't hear the instructions to rendezvous east of the hill. Bernstein's radioman didn't ask or wait for confirmations from the squads that they had heard their orders. Nobody knew Bingham didn't get the word, and all he knew was that after the explosions on the hill, radio contact was lost. "The antenna got knocked down," he told his men. "They'll put it back up in the morning."

Of course, they didn't.

CHAPTER TWENTY-THREE
We Gotta Get Out of This Place

Dawn's light filtered through the tree cover until at last the four-teen men laying in ambush along the wide trail could see again. Bingham tried once more, as he had every half hour since the explosions on the hill, to raise Alpha Company on the radio. For the umpteenth time, he got no answer. This lack of response worried him. So did the fact that he hadn't heard either of the other patrols check in since then. He hadn't heard anything on either the patrol frequency or the company net. He didn't tell his men about the other patrols not checking in hourly like they should have, but he thought Copley knew they hadn't. He thought the best thing now for everybody was activity.

"Smoke 'em if you got 'em," he passed the word. "Hold off on eating. We'll chow down when we get back to the hill."

"Damn skippy, we'll chow down later," Remington said to Bingham. He had come in from his position at the end of the ambush. "Lemme have the point, I'll get us back to the hill most ricky-tick and we'll find out what the fuck's going on."

Bingham shook his head slowly. "No," he said, "we'll take it nice and slow. There's probably boo-coo Charlies still around."

The other members of the squad stopped what they were doing and watched the two NCOs. They trusted Bingham and were will-ing to do almost anything he told them to, but some of them agreed with Remington and wanted to get back to the hill in a hurry.

"Fuck a bunch of boo-coo Charlies," Remington said.

"We'll go back slow and easy," Bingham said again.

Remington snorted but didn't say anything. He returned to the end of the line where he could sit and watch the south trail while the others smoked. He thought about what a pussy he had for a squad leader. We're in a situation that needs action, he thought, we have to move fast and be ready to kick ass and take names, and pussy Bingham wants to sit around with his thumb stuck up his asshole.

When Remington moved away from Bingham the rest of the squad members returned to what they were doing. Half of the men kept watch while the other half emptied their bladders. Then they traded places. Bowel movements could wait until they reached the safety of the perimeter. The men who smoked lit their first cigarettes since leaving the hill late the previous afternoon. Copley and one or two others looked at Bingham curiously. He was smoking, too. It bothered them this man—who only smoked immediately before going out on a patrol or ambush—smoking right before going back in from one.

Bingham snubbed his cigarette out in the damp earth under a leaf and fieldstripped the butt. He scattered the tobacco and pocketed the paper and filter. He looked around and saw the last of the other men who smoked finishing his cigarette. "Saddle up," he said in a low voice that nonetheless carried to everyone. "First team on point, third team bring up the rear. Second team behind me."

"Give second team point, Honcho," Remington said harshly. "We gotta move, dude."

"Third team brings up the rear, first has point," Bingham repeated without looking at his second fire-team leader. He walked to where Rush was adjusting his weapons and cartridge belt for comfort. "Go across the trail and parallel it ten meters in for a half a klick, then turn right. Got it?"

Rush nodded. He stared at Bingham for a moment but the sergeant was going back to try the radio one more time. Rush glanced at Remington and quickly looked away. He was glad the look of hatred on the corporal's face wasn't directed at him. And he wondered what Bingham wasn't telling them. This should be the candy part of the patrol, the tag-end after dawn, when Charlie should have gone in for the day. And there was a truce on now. There was supposed to be one, anyway. Bingham normally only put Rush, or his buddy Eakins, on the point during the day if he expected trouble, and wanted a man up front who was likely to spot any ambush or booby trap before it went off.

Alpha Company didn't answer Bingham's call. He tried Alpha Two Bravo and Alpha Three Bravo, as well. They didn't answer, either. He looked around and saw everyone standing ready, waiting for his order to move out. He looked at Rush, raised his left hand, and pointed across the trail. Rush nodded and stepped out. They started off fast to get across the trail, but slowed down once the entire squad was in the forest on the other side.

The route they took was on level ground for a short distance, then went downhill to a narrow rill that fed the small stream they had followed the afternoon before. Rush stopped before he reached the water and peered cautiously at the brush on its other side. The way it looked, it seemed possible to him that no other human being had ever been in it. He edged to the side of the brush he was in and looked upstream and down. Everything appeared calm and peaceful so he crossed the rivulet with one step and clambered up the hill on the other side. Except when Pratt slipped on the far bank and fell, the squad crossed the water without anyone getting a boot wet. Pratt made very little noise when he fell. When Rush thought he had gone a half kilometer he looked back. Bingham signaled him to turn right. They hadn't seen or heard any activity on the trail to their left.

After a while they reached and crossed without incident the same small stream they had followed the day before. The ground went up but nobody seemed to notice the slope, their attention was on the forest around them. Rush sensed from the way Bingham was acting that something was not right and slowed his pace as he neared the cleared area around Alpha Company's hill. He stopped when he could see light ahead, light that indicated a clearing in the forest.

Bingham joined him. "What'cha got?" he asked.

"We're almost there."

"Let's take a look." Bingham signaled the rest of the squad to stay in place while he and Rush moved to the edge of the trees. As soon as the hill came in sight they knelt down and looked at it. The red scar of the hilltop showed stark against the green vegetation surrounding it and the low grass still growing on its lower slopes. The banks of coiled concertina wire that circled the hill were burst into stringers and piled high like ichor oozing from the pustules of the sandbagged fighting holes and bunkers. Tendrils of smoke feathering upward from several spots provided the only motion visible. No Marines were seen. Neither were there Vietcong bodies on the hillside or in the cleared ground between them and it.

"Oo-ee, looks like someone got put in one bodacious hurt-locker," Remington said, as he dropped down next to Bingham.

Bingham looked at him quickly and turned his attention back to the hill. His jaw worked while he decided whether or not to say anything about the other man not staying where he was supposed to. Finally he said, "No shit, Sherlock."

"What do we do now?"

"Wait."

"For what?"

Bingham slowly turned his head back to Remington. "To see if anybody is up there, that's for what."

"Shee-it, dude, ain't nobody home there. I say we di-di-mau the fuck outta here, get our young asses to Camp Carroll or some such place."

"Probably," Bingham drew his words out slowly, "but we're only carrying one meal of Cs and not a whole hell of a lot of ammo. If nobody's there, I want to see if they left behind anything we can use."

Remington shrugged. His head bobbed up and down, side to side as he studied the hill. It was apparent to him that the Vietcong or North Vietnamese had driven the company off the hill and didn't stay to occupy it. Besides, he thought, if the Marines had left behind anything usable, Charlie had already taken it.

A few minutes later Bingham was glad he had decided to watch before trying to enter the fire base. A pith-helmeted man wearing a khaki uniform with epaulets on his shoulders led a group of soldiers from the direction he knew the command hootch was in.

"Vee Cee Hanoi," Remington whispered.

Bingham nodded; the soldiers on the hill were North Vietnamese, not Vietcong. "Let's go," he said.

"I'll take the point, get us to Camp Carroll most ricky-tick," Remington said.

"Negative that," Bingham said. "Chuck's got the point. I want to make sure we get there safely." He turned back to the squad without looking at Remington.

"Bullshit," Remington snapped. "We all alone out here with shitloads of Charlies around us. The faster we get to Camp Carroll or somewhere there's Marines the better."

Bingham spun back. "Listen to me and get this good, Remington." His eyes blazed and he struggled to keep his voice low and calm. "You got part of that right. We're all alone out here and there's all kinds of Vee Cee around us, that's sure as shit. But we don't know how many Vee Cee are here and that's all the more reason for us too go slow and easy. It'd be too damn easy for us to run into someone bigger than we can deal with if we go too fast. That's why Chuck's got the point. He'll go slow enough, and Night Stalker and Chief are good enough; they'll spot any bad guys before we walk into their ambushes. I want your fire team in the middle of our column. Let's go and no more shit."

He padded quickly to where the rest of the squad waited.

Remington's jaw clenched and he glared at Bingham's back for a long moment before following. Chickenshit-chuck dude's afraid to put this badass splib on point, he thought. Peale's one dipshit turd won't squat to take a shit, somebody don't tell him to. Bingham's afraid I'll move us too fast, put our asses in a sling. Day'll come I put *his* ass in a sling.

The squad leader drew the rest of his men in close and, in a low voice, briefed them about the situation. The men cast uneasy glances at each other but no one showed any signs of panic at the news of the hill being in NVA hands; they were ready. Trumbull was one of only two who had anything to say about it.

Trumbull grinned weakly and said in a soft voice, "No sweat, Honcho. Hell, we're a TO Marine rifle squad. People haven't been invented yet we can't kick ass on." The other one who spoke was Russell. He groaned and said, "Shut up, Baby-san. Come back and tell me about it when you grow up."

When nobody else said anything Bingham finished with, "Those were NVA I saw on the hill, northerners. They may have infiltrated through the DMZ. If they did, the area north of the hill is probably crawling with them. That means we're swinging far south of the hill. Chuck's team has the point, second team in the middle, third team brings up the rear. Let's go." He waited until his men were lined up and added, "Remember, people, this is not a combat patrol or an ambush. Today we're on an E and E mission, escape and evasion. We don't want contact." He signaled Peale to start off.

Rush had the point again. Now that he knew the situation was worse than he would have thought, he fixed his bayonet over the muzzle of his rifle and started out more slowly and deliberately than before. The men moved out at five-meter intervals. Rush led the squad back into the forest west of the hill before turning south. When he estimated they were a hundred meters from the cleared area south of the hill he turned east. Fifty meters farther he froze and patted the air behind himself, signaling the rest of the squad to get down. Slowly he eased to one knee.

Bingham waited two long moments with no indication of why Rush had stopped before going forward to see what the problem was. He froze in place before he reached the point. What he saw sent an icy wave down his spine. A few meters ahead of Peale moved a seemingly endless line of blue-uniformed North Vietnamese soldiers. They didn't glance to either side, but looked resolutely to the front as they shuffled southward with their AK-47 assault rifles held at port arms. Then the seemingly endless line was past, and Bingham joined Rush.

"How many were there?" he asked.

"About a platoon."

Bingham thought for a moment. Twenty-five or thirty NVA had gone south. They looked confident, not looking to their flanks. They didn't appear to be aware there were any Americans in the area, so they probably weren't looking for the squad. Where could they be going? There weren't any fire bases he knew of nearby in that direction. He examined his topographical map of the area and found a major east-west trail a grid square south of the hill. He put the map away and slapped Rush on the shoulder. "Keep your eyes peeled," he said and stood up. Rush nodded. He was chewing on his lip when he started again.

Two hundred meters farther, Rush stopped again near the edge of a small clearing. Bingham joined him and was told, "I smell *nuoc mam*." Together they went forward to recon the clearing. On their side of it were four soldiers with a 60mm mortar set on its bipod pointing east. The four soldiers were squatting to the side of the mortar tube playing cards. From the frequent laughs punctuating their sing-song conversation Bingham thought they must be telling each other jokes to help pass the time. Thin wisps of smoke rose from the cigarettes they held between their forefingers and thumbs. They seemed to be ignoring a wok that sat on a small fire nearby. Bingham and Rush watched for a few moments and again the sergeant decided the NVA were too relaxed and confident to be aware of Americans in the area. They stepped silently away from the clearing. Using hand gestures, Bingham instructed Rush to give the mortar team a wide berth to the north.

Tension mounted in the squad as the men realized the area was crawling with NVA. They strained their eyes and ears in the hope of seeing or hearing the enemy before they were spotted themselves. Sweat broke out on them though the day wasn't hot enough or their physical exertion great enough to produce it. Remington swore to himself about Bingham's decision to go around the mortar team; he wanted to kill them and take the tube. He struggled with himself and managed not to argue about it—the noise of talking might alert the NVA to their presence.

Rush stopped the column again, less than fifty meters from where he had found the mortar team. Ahead of him a squad of northerners squatted around two small fires. Some of the soldiers were cooking over one of the fires, the others were hardening the points of bamboo punji stakes in flames of the second fire. Walking backward, Rush eased away from them before any looked in his direction. When he told Bingham about the squad, the sergeant decided almost without thinking to swing in an arc back and south. They would slip behind the NVA, no matter how many there were, and go around them on their right flank.

Bingham was concerned about not knowing how wide the NVA front was. The wider it was, the farther they would have to go behind it and the greater their chance of being discovered. But he was only concerned about that, not worried. What he was worried about was not knowing how deep that front was. The deeper it was the greater their chances of discovery, regardless of its width. Their danger was increased linearly along a wider front, he thought, along a deep front the danger increased exponentially with the depth. All they could do was be as silent and careful as possible.

They climbed, slipping and quietly cursing, up and down heavily wooded hills for two more hours. Every time they looked over the hills to their east, they found North Vietnamese soldiers sitting there; calm, relaxed, waiting. Bingham kept his squad moving south. The day warmed as the sun climbed toward its zenith and the effort of climbing the hills changed his nervous sweat to heavy perspiration. They pulled hard on their canteens to replace lost fluid, and it wasn't long until most of them were getting short on water. Bingham finally called a halt and told his men to chow down. Then got his map out again. Remington, Peale, and Rivera set their men in defensive positions watching all possible approaches, then joined their squad leader.

"I think we're here," Bingham said in a soft voice and tapped a spot on the map. "Here's where we were." He indicated another place where the topographical lines showed the hill he knew was the location of Alpha Company's overrun fire base. "We ran a patrol in this area last week." His moving finger circled an area west of and between the other two spots on the map. "We're going to need water and food. There was a banana grove and a clear stream there. I think that's where we should go now to fill our canteens. We can scarf down on some bananas while we're at it."

"How much farther you think those gooks go?" Peale asked.

Bingham shook his head and gazed southward. "Don't know. Maybe too far. Maybe I was wrong about them coming over the Zee, maybe they came from a different direction. After we get water I want to try the north side of the hill, maybe they aren't there." He looked briefly to the north and then returned his attention to the map, staring at it as though it could tell him where there was a route that would be safe.

"Should of killed those gooks with the mortar," Remington muttered. "That would have opened a hole in their line we could have gone through."

"Yeah, we could've done that," Bingham said without looking up. "And maybe their buddies would have found them before we could di-di out of there and every slope in the area would be looking for us. Right now they still don't know we're here." There was a long pause before he spoke again. "At this point, even if we do find a way through Charlie it's too dangerous. He's just sitting there now. If they start to sweep east while we're cutting across their front to get to Camp Carroll we're liable to run right into them."

Remington snorted and walked away, back to his fire team.

Bingham stared at his map for another moment, then looked at his watch and said to Peale and Rivera, "We move out in zero-five. Pass it." He continued staring at the map, wondering how he could lead his men to safety. They had gone more than three kilometers south of Alpha Company's overrun hill and the NVA had been everywhere. If they continued much farther south they'd be beyond the bottom of his map, in an area where they had no idea what the terrain was like.

Peale came back and broke his reverie when the five minutes were up. "Ready, Honcho?" he asked.

Bingham glanced at his watch and nodded. "Let's go," he said. "Chief knows what way to go?"

Peale nodded and stared at his squad leader until Bingham stood up. Why wouldn't Rush know what way to go? Bingham had told him himself.

Bingham told Copley to turn the radio on and made another unsuccessful attempt to contact someone before signaling Rush to lead the way off the northwest side of the hill. Two hours of slow movement later they reached the banana grove.

Bingham lay at the edge of the grove with Rush and visually reconned it. The grove had originally been cultivated with the trees planted in straight rows. Some of the ripe fruit would have been used as food for the farmers who cared for the trees, the rest would have gone to market in Dong Ha or Quang Tri City. They would probably not have been exported to the western countries because they were small, slightly hard, slightly bitter bananas, not the larger, sweeter bananas favored in the United States and

Europe. But now the war had chased the people away from this small area, and the forest was reclaiming the untended grove as its own. The once cleared ground between the trees was now blanketed with weeds. Fronds sticking up from the ground showed where new banana and palm trees were growing. Hardwood saplings dotted the open ground between the banana trees.

Bingham and Rush watched intently for perhaps ten minutes before deciding no one was in the grove. All they had heard during the watch was each other's shallow breathing and the quiet, cheerful gurgling of the small stream Bingham remembered. Then Bingham motioned Rush to stay in place while he went back to get the rest of the squad. When he got them to the grove, he sent Rivera and his fire team into it to inspect it more closely while he lay with the rest of the squad covering them. As he thought, the grove was empty.

"Careful with the bananas," Bingham told his men as they went for the fruit hanging in large bunches on the trees. "You aren't used to these bananas; they aren't Chiquita. They'll give you the shits if they aren't ripe or you eat too many. Dago, put some security out." Rivera nodded and put his men on a low rise near one side of the grove. "Remington," Bingham continued, "make sure everyone fills their canteens and make damn sure they use their halizone tablets."

"Shit, man, they ain't going to use no halizone," Remington said back. "They ain't gonna want to drink it, it tastes like halizone."

"Put the damn tablets in their canteens yourself if you think they won't use them. I don't want anyone drinking that water until it's been purified." The small stream through the grove bubbled over a rocky bottom, but Bingham didn't know its source or what it ran through before it reached this place. The water looked clean, but could still be contaminated with bacteria or parasitic amoebae that could cause typhoid fever, cholera, dysentery, or who knew what other illnesses. The tiny pills, one per canteen, might give the water a chemical taste that some of the men found unpalatable, but he had no idea when they could get clean water again, and it was better for the water to taste of chemicals than for anyone to get sick from drinking bad water. Besides, the taste might force them to conserve their water in a way all the warnings and orders in the world couldn't.

It didn't take long climbing the trees, cutting down banana bunches, drinking the water that was so good even the halizone tablets couldn't destroy its good taste, and basking in the glade-like shade of the grove for some of the men to forget the dangerous situation the squad was in. Sometimes, when danger continued long enough, it took very little for men to set it aside for a few minutes.

Win Homer sprawled at the foot of a banana tree. A silly grin spread across his face as he surveyed the scattering of banana peelings around him. His belly was full and the air in the grove moved gently, evaporating the sweat off his body. It wasn't stifling under these trees like it was in the forest and not so hot as on the company's hill. "Man, oh, man," he said to nobody, "good food, sweet water, shade from the sun. Only more thing a man needs make him happy here is a woman fucks like a rabbit— and can use a 'naner when her man's too tired to pound her pussy again." He laughed.

"Right," Remington snorted from his seat under a nearby tree. " 'Naners, sweet water, and a hole. Enough of that shit, a deep-south jigaboo like you turn right into one a them monkey apes honkies back in the World always say us bros be."

"Fuck you, Fred. You a big city nigger, you don't know what prejudice is," Homer replied, sitting up. His tranquil mood was fading.

"Shee-it. Boy from 'Bama don't know any better than think jive-ass honkies on top and niggers on bottom is the way things is supposed to be. You think just because a couple bros gets to go to college in Birmingham your main man Wallace gonna let his daughter marry one."

"Fred, like I said, fuck you and the horse you rode in on. You got life so good in the big city you don't know what hard times and prejudice is."

Remington's lips split in a wicked grin. "I bet you thought life was good on days when ole massa let you eat some of the slop yourselves before you fed it to the hogs."

Homer's jaw clenched and his hand tightened its grip on his rifle stock. "You know, man, there's different kinds of folks," he said, staring hard at the other man. "There's white folks, there's black folks, there's yellow folks—and there's niggers. Did you know that?"

"Yeah?" Remington thought he knew what Homer was going to say next and he didn't like it. His muscles tensed like a coiled snake. He was right.

"Someone like Night Stalker, he's white folks. Me and John, we're black folks. We get along fine because we're folks. Nigger ain't a color, it's a state of mind. You was born a nigger and you'll always be a nigger 'cause you're too stupid to be black folks. You think just because another man's white he—"

Homer didn't get to finish what he was saying. Remington uncoiled in a flash and lunged across the space separating them and knocked him to the ground. Remington sat on Homer's chest, pinning him to the ground.

Remington clasped his hands around Homer's throat and leaned forward hard. "Don't you go calling me no stupid nigger, nigger," he rasped. "It's Toms like you help honkies keep us down."

Homer grasped Remington's forearms and tried to pry his hands off. His eyes bulged as it became harder to breathe.

"What the fuck's going on here," Bingham said sharply, running over to them.

West and Peale reached them first and started pulling Remington off Homer. Bingham grabbed the arm Peale was holding and threw Remington down on his back. While Peale went to check on Homer, Bingham planted his hands on Remington's shoulders.

"What the fuck are you doing?" he demanded. "We can't fight among ourselves here."

"Man called me a stupid nigger," Remington said. His eyes were narrow. His breath came in snorts. "Nobody call me a stupid nigger. I gotta kill that fuckhead, he call me a stupid nigger."

Bingham swallowed quickly then said, "Maybe he called you that because you're acting like one." Remington's eyes suddenly focused on Bingham's face. Before he could say anything Bingham continued, "Man, don't you know where we're at? Don't you know the whole goddam fucking North Vietnamese Army is out here? We have to work together if we want to get out alive. No way we can fight each other and get out alive."

Remington's breath slowed as he kept staring at his squad leader. Finally he said through thin lips that barely moved, "Let me up. I'll take care of him later."

Bingham leaned harder for a moment and whispered, "You'll do shit later." Then he let go and got to his feet. He turned to Homer, who was standing and rubbing his throat. "You watch what you say to NCOs. You aren't always going to have someone around to haul him off your ass." He glared and breathed hard for a moment. "And that doesn't even include insubordination."

"You tell that nigger stay off my ass," Homer said, softly so as not to hurt his throat.

"That's Corporal Nigger to you, Dude," Copley murmured.

Can't let them sit around thinking about this, Bingham told himself. Got to move, make some activity to keep their minds on business. "Saddle up and move it out," he said out loud. "Same order as before. Chief, swing west, then northeast. We're going around the other side of the hill."

CHAPTER TWENTY-FOUR
A Better Mousetrap

It was a kilometer and a half from last night's ambush site back to the fire base. From there another three kilometers south until Bingham decided to try the north side. Two more from there to the banana grove and another two to the wooded trees north of the fire base. Plotted in straight lines on a map the distance traveled added up to eight and a half kilometers. But the squad didn't go in straight lines. They zigged and zagged; they went in and curved out; they climbed up, down, and around hills. The actual distance they walked was closer to twice the straight-line-map distance. And they went slowly, watching for enemy activity every step of the way. On a big operation—though the troops didn't necessarily see it from that perspective—the way to save lives was to find and kill the enemy before he could find and kill anybody. This wasn't a big operation. The only way the squad could stay alive was to avoid contact with the enemy and his booby traps. They went very slowly. It was close to night by the time the squad reached the forested hills north of what had been Alpha Company's hill.

Rush was in the process of taking another cautious step forward when he froze. He slowly lowered the foot that was up when he stopped and sniffed the air without seeming to turn his head, though he did turn it from side to side. He pointed his eyes and rifle muzzle to his right front and backed up. He murmured two words when he reached Peale. Peale backed up with him. Eakins and Homer saw the two backing up and turned around to go the same way.

Bingham let Homer and Eakins pass him, then stepped forward. He didn't ask what the problem was.

"*Nuoc mam,*" Rush said softly when he spotted Bingham out of the corner of his eye.

Bingham thought quickly, then said, "We'll go back fifty

meters, then try again a hundred meters north."

Rush nodded and turned around, facing the rest of the squad. They peeled along behind him. He went back after he passed Morse before turning north. A few meters farther he found a steep, jagged hillside, covered with trees but free of undergrowth. He climbed it. In places it was steep enough he had to carry his rifle in one hand and use the other to help him climb. But the trees gave them concealment while the lack of undergrowth allowed him, and the men following, to move quietly. He was puffing hard by the time he scrabbled to the top.

The top was basically flat rock, cracked and broken and powdered by millennia of weather until tree seeds were able to germinate and take root. Now the rock was covered with a deep mat of humus, springy underfoot. Most of the tree trunks grew to a height of fifteen feet before sprouting branches. The flat rock top was a rough oval, about thirty meters east to west, half that north to south. Rush walked in a crouch to the eastern end of the hilltop and looked down it. Peale joined him a few seconds after he stopped; Bingham and Copley were right behind. Night was already gathering between the hills, though sunlight still filtered through the trees on top of the hill.

Rush pointed and said, "This is a no-go, Honcho." He didn't specify which honcho he was talking to, but Bingham and Peale both looked where he was pointing. So did Copley.

Remington joined them. "Dago is setting the others," he said. He grunted when he saw what Rush was pointing at. "I told you, let me take the point," he said to Bingham. "I would a killed that mortar team, and we'd got through there. Probably linked with someone by now." Bingham ignored him.

"We're sure as shit not getting through here," Peale said, "not if all those fires mean Mister Charles."

What they were looking at on the facing hillside and stretching north was a line of small fires. Maybe twenty of them flickering through the vegetation opposite their hill, probably all NVA cooking fires.

Rivera joined them. He looked expressionless at the small, dancing lights.

"If we figure one fire per squad, there's more than a company down there," Bingham said.

"Plus the ones we backed off from," Copley said. "So even if it's two fires for a squad, there's still a company down there."

Remington smiled slightly as he studied the line of cook-fires. He wasn't going to suggest killing a squad and slipping through their position. Not through this line, the NVA were too close together; the odds of being able to get through undetected were too slim. Instead, he decided to put the man on the hotseat. "What do we do now, Honcho? North side's probably blocked all the way to the Zee."

Bingham looked uncertain for a few seconds, then asked Rivera, "Are the men around the edge of the hilltop?"

Rivera nodded. "Got all slopes covered, all approaches."

"Did you see any fires or any sign of activity below anywhere?"

Rivera shook his head. "Only here."

"We're going to stay here tonight."

"What about tomorrow?" Remington wanted to twist the screws.

Bingham looked at him calmly, expression bland. "Tomorrow gets here when the sun rises. Tomorrow's another day." He turned away, toward the north side of the hill. "Show me the positions, Dago." Rivera went with him. Bingham checked the fields of fire assigned to each position and saw Rivera had done a good job of overlapping them. "Smoke 'em if you got 'em," he said at each position. "The smoking lamp is out in five minutes. Fifty percent watch tonight."

Peale sat cross-legged facing the cook-fires. "Smoke 'em if you got 'em," he murmured. He used his boonie hat to hide the match he lit to light his last cigarette until dawn. Remington remained standing, a few feet to Peale's side and rear, staring at him. He wondered how Peale would act if he, Remington, was squad leader. He didn't think about it long before deciding Peale was too cautious and he'd have to get rid of him because his balls weren't big enough to be a real ass kicker.

When he was through checking the positions, Bingham made two changes. He assigned Peale and Rush to watch the eastern side of the hill and put Remington on the opposite end with West. Not everybody was happy with the arrangement; Remington and West both glared at him, Remington because he thought he should be the one to keep an eye on the NVA east of them, West because he didn't want to have to spend the night alone with the big badass.

Bingham ignored them. He put Copley and himself in the middle of the hilltop. Right before the sun set he donned the radio board and climbed a tree whose branches started closer to the ground than most. He went up thirty feet before turning on the radio and listening on both of the Alpha Company frequencies of the previous night. He didn't hear anything on either but transmitted on both anyway. Nobody responded to his calls. Then he twisted the dial to other frequencies. He still didn't hear anything. He turned the radio off and wondered how much longer the batteries would last. He hoped they would last until he could raise somebody.

Bingham took the first watch. The night was quiet during those two hours. When he woke Copley for his turn, he went from position to position, checking his men. None of them had heard anything. Peale and Rush reported no activity other than some of the fires dimming and going out. Bingham finally got to sleep a half hour after the end of his two-hour watch. Copley woke him an hour and a half later for his next turn. When he woke his grenadier-radioman to take a second watch, he donned the radio once more and climbed the tree to try the radio again; it was 0100 hours, the fires still burned in the east. As before, all he heard on any of the frequencies he tried was soft static. Nobody responded to the transmissions he made.

At 0300 Copley reached to wake Bingham and then realized the man had only had three hours sleep while he'd had four himself and was going to get more. Bingham probably wouldn't get to sleep again until the next night. He decided to let him sleep another hour—if he could stay awake that much longer himself. He woke Bingham at 0400 and lay down for another hour's sleep before everyone was woken for the last half hour before dawn. He was only asleep for half an hour before the eastern horizon seemed to erupt with rifle and artillery fire that woke everybody on the hilltop.

Bingham quickly checked his squad's six positions, making sure everybody was awake and nobody was too trigger-happy, then he pulled the radio onto his back and climbed the tree a third time. He looked east and wondered if there was any significance to the fires being out. This time he picked up a few faint voices, infantry positions under assault calling for artillery support. In the darkness he groped for a higher perch in the tree. The signal came in louder higher in the tree. The artillery fire control used the call sign "Bumblebee." He waited for a break in the radio traffic and made a transmission of his own.

"Bumblebee, Bumblebee. This is Alpha One Bravo, Alpha One Bravo, over." When no one replied he repeated his transmission, a slight tremor in his voice because he was afraid his radio was too weak to reach the others. This time he got an immediate, louder response.

"Alpha One Bravo, Alpha One Bravo," came back an angry voice. "This is Bumblebee. Get the hell off this frequency, you are not authorized to be on it. Out."

Bingham felt a mix of emotions at the response: elation at raising someone and frustration about being told to get off the frequency. But he wasn't getting off the frequency, not after finally getting someone after more than twenty-four hours. "Bumblebee, Alpha One Bravo. We are separated from our unit. We are lost and need assistance. Over."

"Alpha One Bravo, I told you to get off this frequency," the angry voice came back. "Now get off it. If I hear you again, you are in deep shit. Bumblebee out."

Bingham recoiled as from a physical blow. He thought Bumblebee must not have heard what he said. Many calls came into Bumblebee for fire missions. He waited for another break in the traffic and depressed the speak lever on the side of his handset. "Bumblebee, this is Alpha One Bravo. I say again," and repeated his message. Bumblebee didn't answer this time, someone else did, someone who sounded higher in the chain of command than the artillery control center. He was again told to get off the frequency.

It was several minutes before there was another break in the calls for fire missions and responses to them. When it came Bingham tried again. No one answered him. He described his squad's situation, identifying the company they were from and repeating that they were separated and lost. He finally got a reply from someone who didn't identify himself.

"Charlie, you talk English good, but we're onto your games. That squad got wasted. Now get the fuck off the air."

At 0500 there was a loud burst of static on the frequency and after that Bingham didn't hear any more voices on it. The frequency used by the artillery fire control center was changed. He twisted the dial in an attempt to locate another band someone was using, but couldn't manage to pick up anything that wasn't too faint to make out. When he saw a band of light on the eastern horizon he quit trying. He knew the morning sun would raise havoc with the airways and dramatically cut down on the range of the radio. The sound of the firefights slackened and stopped.

Seven men waited for him at the foot of the tree. The rest of the squad remained around the sides of the hill watching for anyone coming up it. He told them what had happened. They looked at each other in disbelief when he told them someone called him Charlie and claimed they'd been wasted. They were more isolated than they had thought.

"So what do we do now, George?" Remington asked.

"We need food," Bingham said immediately. Yesterday's bananas were gone, and even if they weren't, they'd need something else to eat. "We go back to the fire base, see if anything we can use got left behind. Then we see if there's a way through. Maybe the NVA we saw yesterday all moved to the firefights we just heard."

Some of them looked east, toward hoped-for safety. Others looked south, toward the hill Alpha Company had used as a base of operations. All except Remington, who kept looking flat-eyed at Bingham. "Charlie's probably shagging ass back this way," he said, "carrying his dead and wounded. We'll run into his ass. I think we should head toward that CAP southwest of the hill."

Bingham shook his head at the suggestion of joining the Combined Action Platoon. "That big firefight behind us that night, I think that was them getting overrun. We didn't hear them on the radio after that fight." He looked at Copley for confirmation. Copley nodded.

"I still think we gonna run into one shitload of pissed-off Mister Charles, we go east," Remington said again.

"Maybe," Bingham agreed, looking back equally flat-eyed. "But if he is coming this way, he's probably in columns now, not in a line. Lots of space to miss him. Let's do this thing."

Remington shrugged as though to say, It's your funeral. He tried to look like it wouldn't be his as well.

"Night Stalker, you got point. First, second, and third teams in order. Let's go."

The fire-team leaders got their men from the perimeter and lined them up. They descended the west face of the hill, a gentler slope than the one they'd climbed the previous twilight. Remington didn't complain about not being given the point. Now he thought it was too dangerous and didn't want to be too close to the front of the column when they ran into the NVA he knew had to be coming back their way.

Bingham and his men had no way of knowing it, of course, but the firefight at the CAP compound had been heard by Alpha Company. And too many people mistook its location for theirs. When they didn't show up at the rendezvous point or answer any radio calls, that merely reinforced the idea they'd been in a fight too heavy for them to win. First squad had been written off as wiped out by the NVA during the night. That's why the unidentified voice on the radio had thought Bingham was a Vietcong. Maybe if someone who knew his voice had heard the transmission it would have been different, but the Marines thought they were all dead.

* * *

Eakins led the squad in an almost straight line back to the fire base. He stopped before he reached the cleared area around it; he stopped to let an NVA platoon march past. The Marines all tried to make themselves small until the immediate threat was gone. Bingham motioned Eakins to continue when he was certain there were no more NVA close to them. He glanced back at the rest of the squad. Remington nodded at him; he nodded I told you so.

They stopped again where they could look at the hill without being seen from it. It was still held by the North Vietnamese.

Bingham edged close to Eakins. "Can you lead us back to the banana grove?" he asked. His stomach was knotting in hunger, and during the walk to the hill he had heard two stomach rumbles that weren't his. They had to have food, even if it was only bananas.

"Can do," Eakins said, not taking his eyes from the hill.

"Then do it," Bingham said, squeezing Eakins's shoulder and giving it a slight push.

Eakins led the squad cautiously through the trees around the western side of the hill, staying close enough to the cleared area to catch an occasional glimpse of the North Vietnamese dotting the red earth, but never close enough to the edge to be seen by the enemy on it. He paralleled rather than traced the previous afternoon's route. When they were away from the hill and its fields of fire, he cut a beeline toward the banana grove. They did not encounter any more patrols after the one north of the hill. It took the squad nearly an hour and a half to reach the banana grove.

While Rivera and his men watched their rear, the rest of the squad lay on line at the verge of the overgrown grove. Fifteen minutes of silent watching showed no one in it. But Bingham wanted to be positive, not just sure. He left Peale in charge and led Rush and Eakins on a quick recon around the perimeter of the grove. There was no sign of other human beings in the area. As a final precaution, Bingham sent Rivera's fire team through the middle of the grove. They found it as empty as the visual reconnaissance from its edges had indicated, and Rivera stood tall to signal all clear to Bingham.

Speaking softly, Bingham ordered his men into a column and they trotted to the small, clear stream and across it, where Rivera and his men joined them.

Bingham looked at the banana bunches growing on the trees and felt saliva collecting in his mouth. His voice had a moist quality when he said, "Chuck, put a man on the south for security.

Fred, put someone north, Dago, someone west. John and I will be responsible for the east. Give the men you're sending a few bananas. Everybody else chow down. Do it."

How many bananas does it take to make a filling meal? More than you might think. A hungry man will try to stuff himself and will wind up bloated. They were hungry. Bingham tried to slow everybody down eating the bananas and they did eat slowly when he was watching them. But he couldn't watch everyone at once. They wolfed when he looked away. And as he took the responsibility of filling canteens and putting halizone tablets in them himself, he looked away from them a lot. So how many bananas can you eat at one sitting? More than you want, unless you're used to that many bananas.

Bingham distributed the refilled canteens with an admonition to wait twenty minutes before drinking, to let the halizone do its work purifying the water. While he did that, he examined the ground around each man, looking to see who'd eaten the most bananas. He thought they should be the first ones to stop eating and sent them to relieve the three men providing security. Pratt relieved Morse, Russell took West's place, Rush took Homer's. Then he told the rest of them to stop eating for a while. Eakins and the three fire-team leaders looked at him with various expressions indicating they thought he was being unfair, they had eaten more slowly than the others. Bingham didn't care, he'd let them eat more once their stomachs had a chance to start digesting what was already in them.

The squad had eaten lightly the first time they came through the banana grove, believing they'd soon get to eat American food, and the bananas they'd taken with them had made a light dinner. Now they didn't know when they'd get another meal and ate accordingly. Bananas are soft food that goes down easily and packs in the stomach. When digestion starts, the food will expand, making the stomach work overtime to keep it in. This causes a loud digestional rumbling and is sometimes visible externally. If it becomes violent enough it will cause stomach cramps. But before it becomes so violent that the stomach will be injured, it regurgitates the food. After regurgitation it takes the stomach a little while to calm down again, and it needs to be treated gently for a time.

It wasn't long before a muted gagging, retching sound came from where Pratt was watching. Everyone flattened and grabbed their weapons, mostly pointing to the north, and froze. Bingham glanced quickly around, saw all of his men ready, and gestured for Rivera and his men to go with him. In one fluid motion, he rose to his feet and sprinted toward the noise. Rivera, Morse, and Trumbull followed. Morse and Trumbull fanned out to the flanks on hand signals from Rivera.

Bingham drew his bayonet and fixed it to the flash suppressor of his rifle as he ran. He hoped to be on Pratt's attacker and kill him before the man could react. He burst through a thin layer of foliage and stumbled over Pratt, who was on his hands and knees. Bingham spun, muzzle going with his eyes, looking for whoever had done this. He saw no one except the other Marines to his flanks. He knelt beside his fallen man, still keeping an eye out for the attacker, to examine him. The fight level of adrenaline in his body changed direction almost immediately and he slammed the palm of his right hand into Pratt's shoulder, knocking him onto his side.

"You dumb fuck," he snarled at the man writhing on the ground in front of him, "I told you to take it easy on those goddam bananas."

Pratt had thrown up all the bananas he had eaten and was now dry-heaving. He tried to stop the wrenching of his abdomen, but made no attempt to talk or sit up.

"What, did you think I was just talking to bust your balls?" He cuffed Pratt on the shoulder again. "You dumb shit."

Rivera was suddenly standing over them, looking disgusted at Pratt. He kicked him in the back, but not very hard. That started Pratt heaving again.

"When he stops heaving leave Baby-san here and haul his dumb ass to the water downstream from us so he can clean himself." Bingham grimaced and kicked Pratt's booted foot. He heard Rivera muttering in Spanish as he left.

The casual manner in which Bingham approached them told the rest of the squad whatever the problem had been, it was all right now and they relaxed. Most of them rolled from their prone positions onto their backs or sat up. It wasn't an emergency and they'd find out soon enough what the problem had been. Before he reached them Bingham heard a louder vomiting from his right—Russell's position. He stopped and looked at Remington, angry. With an abrupt arm movement he signaled the big man to come with his men. Remington ran to reach Russell first. Bingham went slowly; he didn't want to have to see another man throwing up. At least Mattpratt had tried to be quiet about it, he thought.

He found Russell sprawled on his stomach, limbs scattered, the side of his face in a light-colored puddle. Remington stood at his feet, talking quietly but with a hard edge to his voice, methodically kicking the sole of one boot, then the other. The kicks punctuated his words.

"Asshole," Remington said, kicking, "you know what we do with dumb shits"—kick—"like you where I come from?" Kick. Russell convulsed mildly with each kick. "We make them eat raw rats." Kick. "Fuckfaces who can't learn to follow orders?" Kick. "If that don't teach them"—kick—"we feed them cigars." Kick. "They still don't want to learn"—kick—"they suck on used cunt rags." Kick. "After a while we break their fucking jaws." Kick. "If they're still too dumb to learn"—kick—"we kills their slimy asses." Kick.

Bingham was sickened by the scene; the sight and smell of Russell's vomit, him squirming on the ground, Remington's methodical kicking, the big man's words. "Knock it off, Fred," he said.

Remington looked at him and smiled, not quite challengingly. He kicked Russell's right boot. "Right," he said, and kicked Russell's left. Then stepped away.

"Give him a few minutes to settle down, then leave Gil here and drag him to where you'll see Mattpratt so he can clean himself."

"I ain't touching the dumb shit; he can walk his ownself."

"I don't care whether he walks, flies, or you carry him. See to it he get over to the water and cleans himself."

Eventually the two men who had eaten too much unfamiliar food too quickly were cleaned and basically recovered. Bingham made them eat a few bananas to put something in their stomachs. He carefully monitored their eating—both to make sure they did eat despite their protesting digestive systems, and to assure they didn't overdo it. Because it was the only food available, he made everybody cut bunches to carry with them. He made sure everybody had two full canteens and that a halizone tablet went into each one. Then, "Okay, Fred, we're going to do what you want. We're going to find that CAP compound."

A smile almost appeared on Remington's face. "I told you so," it seemed to say.

AFTER-ACTION REPORT:

A CAP Isn't a Kind of Hat

From the Analytic Notes of R.W. Thoreau, Lt. Col., USMC (ret.)

Stated in its most simple terms, the Army philosophy on how to win the war against the Vietcong was to send out large numbers of troops—battalions of seven or eight hundred men—to locate Main Force Vietcong (and later, North Vietnamese Army) units. Once those enemy units were found and fixed by the infantry, artillery and bombers would take over whenever possible and annihilate them. A reasonable way for the Army to think—after all, their top general had been an artillery officer. The Air Force loved this strategy—it gave them a much bigger part of the war than they would have had otherwise. Hell, even the Strategic Air Command got into it, running tactical bombing missions in support of the infantry.

The annihilation part must have worked—the North Vietnamese admit they lost seven times as many dead on the battlefield as we did. This was called a war of attrition. The Army believed that sooner or later the enemy would run out of men to fight or the will to continue losing men in the fight, possibly both.

The Marine philosophy was different. The Marines agreed; sure, send out large numbers of men to fix and kill the enemy in large numbers when he was located in those large numbers, but . . . the Marines also believed the enemy received support, willing or unwilling, from the people. The way to win the war was to take that support away from the Vietcong. This was before the North Vietnamese entered the war with large numbers of Russian- and Chinese-supplied ground troops, back in the days when Hanoi ran the war through the political cadre and military leadership it inserted into the NLF.

But the Army was running the war and told the Marines to do it their way or go home. The Air Force backed the Army. It was the only war in town, so the Marines acted like doing things the Army way was their own idea.

Still, the Marines couldn't let go of their basic concept of how to win the war. And they had battlefield proof that they were on the right track. A battalion would sweep through an area on a search and clear operation and get rid of the Vietcong in that area. A few days later, once the Marines had moved on, the VC would be back in full force. That frustrated the Marines. The Army had the same experience, but the Army generals running the war weren't bothered by it, they knew that sooner or later the Vietcong would flat run out of men and the U.S. Army would win. The Marines weren't comfortable with that concept.

In August 1965, the Marines started experimenting with a project called the Combined Action Program. But first, a few words about the South Vietnamese military establishment.

The South Vietnamese forces were organized in a formal army, air force, navy, and marine corps, along the lines of the American forces. There were also Regional Forces, sort of a National Guard, and Popular Forces, a civilian militia. The Popular Forces were generally farmers or fishermen who enlisted and served in their home hamlets and villages to protect those hamlets and villages from the Vietcong. The PFs were paid a subsistence wage or less, given cast-off weapons and partial uniforms, received marginal training, and had generally poor leadership. The PFs did not normally patrol aggressively and rarely at night, the time when the VC were most active in the hamlets and villages. The American troops knew the PFs were cowards and that half of them were VC.

What the Marines did with their Combined Action Program was, after sweeping through an area and clearing it of Vietcong, they would assign a small number of Marines, anywhere from an understrength squad to a heavily armed platoon, to a hamlet or village to work with its Popular Forces platoon. Remember, most of the American troops knew the PFs were cowards. The Marines trained and led the PFs and, when possible, gave them new weapons. They demonstrated to them by example that the VC could be caught and killed at night. Once these young enlisted Marines demonstrated to the PFs that the VC could be beaten at their own game and they, the Marines, would stand by the local soldiers, the PFs often became effective fighters. Some of them even became honorary Marines. After a CAP was properly established in an area, that area generally stayed free from the Vietcong. The Army top brass grumbled and mumbled about the men assigned to CAP duty, called them wasted resources. But as long as the Marines kept fielding battalions for search and destroy operations they didn't complain too loudly.

The basic concept was similar to the Army's Special Forces A-Teams; the Green Berets about whom Barry Sadler wrote a number-one hit song, Robin Moore wrote a best-selling book, John Wayne made a movie. The top Army brass didn't much like the Special Forces, either.

Many Marines saw CAP as candy duty, "In the rear with the beer," as they called it. It wasn't, really. The official estimate is of the 5,000 Marines who fought in the Combined Action Units, 1,500 were killed in action.

This is the kind of outpost Remington wanted the squad to head for and Bingham agreed to. They knew the CAP had been hit hard that first night, but CAPs had been hit hard before and none had been wiped out. With a rifle squad reinforcing the Marines and PFs of that CAP, they'd be better able to fight off the North Vietnamese if they came calling again. And first squad would be in a known position from where it could be extracted later. The CAP maybe even had communications with some higher headquarters.

CHAPTER TWENTY-FIVE
Good Men Die Hard

Bingham estimated it was five kilometers from the banana grove to the CAP's hamlet. Five kilometers over rough, broken ground, heavily forested. He hoped they could reach that area before sundown; they'd need time to find the CAP compound while it was still light. He wasn't certain they could, and they didn't. They had to stop too many times to hide from small NVA and VC units moving east, toward the fighting. The sun was almost down when Eakins stopped a couple meters short of a clearing.

"What'cha got, Night Stalker," Bingham asked when he dropped to a knee next to his point man.

"Ville," came the monosyllabic reply.

Bingham peered through the brush at the hamlet and swore silently. Instead of the thatch and bamboo hootches he expected to see, with adults finishing their last-minute outdoor chores in the rapidly fading daylight and children darting their last playful runs of the day, he saw blackened stumps and piles of ash. Peale, Eakins, and Homer formed a line at his sides. He motioned them to stay in place and duckwalked closer to the edge of the clearing. His rifle was ready in both hands, safety off, finger inside the trigger guard.

It had been a good-sized forest hamlet, close to thirty homes. All that remained were the stumps of uprights, pointing their charred fingers beseechingly at the darkening sky. Two or three burned crossbeams leaned drunkenly from uprights more or less still standing. Here and there a charred remnant of thatch, too damp to burn all the way, dangled haphazardly. Battered woks and a few other household implements, too damaged to immediately identify, were scattered on the ground. An upside-down conical straw hat laying in the dust of a path teetered in vagrant breezes, providing the only movement in the ravaged hamlet. There were

no people, though a pile of black material could have held bodies.
Nothing seemed to live.

Bingham grimaced and backed away. Remington had joined
the others.

"We gonna find that CAP tonight?" Remington asked.

"No way," Bingham shook his head. "They're loaded for bear
now, probably blow the fuck away anyone they see in the dark—
kick ass first, take names later." He looked around. "We're going
to sit tight for the night, find the CAP in the morning. Chief, take
us fifty meters that way," and he pointed away from the destroyed
hamlet.

Rush nodded and led the way. He stopped fifty meters into the
forest. Bingham set his squad in a triangle, a fire team on each
side, with Peale's fire team facing the hamlet. He and Copley
sat in the middle. Everyone was tense; the situation here was
worse than anyone had expected. Normally, in this area they'd
have to hide from the CAP's nightly patrols. Bingham didn't think
they'd have to hide from friendly patrols that night; after seeing
the burned-out hamlet, he didn't think the CAP would have any
out; they'd be in their compound ready to fight off an assault.
Tonight, like all the rest of the past thirty-six hours, they had to
hide from enemy patrols. Fifty percent watch and stay in place
until two hours after sunup. It was a restless night, but no one
passed near them. Far to the east they heard the sounds of other
people's firefights, but nothing to the west and nothing near.

On each of his watches during the night, Bingham spent time
twisting the dial on his radio, listening for someone's transmissions. He picked up nothing. He had no idea what frequencies
the CAP might be monitoring, so he made no attempt to contact
it to let it know there were friendly forces nearby. He had another
reason for not making any calls of his own: the NVA might be
listening, and it wouldn't do to let them know an additional American unit was in the CAP's village.

After dawn they dropped back to a twenty-five percent watch,
one man from each fire team watching for half an hour, the others taking a last catnap if that's what they wanted, or eating the
last of the bananas and taking care of whatever morning ablutions
each man felt necessary—none of them felt a need to shave, even
though most of them kept their bayonets or K-bars sharp enough
to shave with.

Bingham carefully examined his map and decided which of the
marked hamlets they were near and where they probably were
relative to the CAP compound. He showed the map to Rush and

Eakins. Eakins nodded that he understood. Then they got ready and moved out. Eakins avoided the burned hamlet, skirting it at a safe distance inside the trees. The closer they got to the CAP compound the slower they moved. Everyone understood the Marines and PFs had to be edgy and were probably trigger-happy; they didn't want to risk getting hit by friendly forces.

The map was wrong, or Bingham guessed at the wrong hamlet, or Eakins's sense of direction was off that morning. Whatever the reason, they missed the CAP compound. A hurried conference over the map and Bingham told his point man to go a half kilometer to one side and then back. It was a little after noon by the time they reached the small terraces of rice paddies the CAP compound sat behind. A hundred-foot-high tor jutted out of the ground behind it, one barren face guarding the back of the compound.

Eakins halted inside the forest but where he could easily see over the paddies. "Doesn't look like anybody's home," he said to Bingham.

Bingham curled his hands in front of his eyes as though he was holding binoculars to them, a trick he'd learned to sharpen focus at a distance. Two banks of piled rolls of concertina wire with a trench between them surrounded the compound; Bingham guessed the trench was densely studded with sharpened bamboo stakes. The barbed wire was burst apart in many places. A narrow roadway or wide footpath led from the paddies into the compound. A gate, framed and latticed with L-bars and wound with strands and coils of barbed wire, stood guardian over the entrance. The gate was bent and open. Three masonry buildings, sandbags stacked halfway up their walls, were in the compound. The buildings' windows looked blindly out. Sandbag emplacements spotted around the perimeter looked askew, as though old and falling down or unfinished. A dozen high poles stood in the middle with something too small to be distinguished at this distance on their tops. Too small to be distinguished, but the sight of them made Bingham swallow, and shiver inside. Flocks of birds darted and swooped around the compound at the foot of the tor.

"I do believe you're right," Bingham answered when he finished his visual inspection. He turned to the rest of his men, who had bunched behind him. "Dago, stay here to cover us. Everybody else, ten-meter intervals going along the dike. I don't want all of us getting hit by one mortar round." He nodded at Eakins and pointed toward a dike wider than the rest that led toward the CAP gate.

Rush looked at the compound. He didn't shield his eyes from the sun or do anything else with his hands to aid his vision. He looked for a long moment, then shook his head and muttered one word, "Shit."

The ground rose to the tor and beyond it. Emerald paddies climbed like moss-covered flagstone steps, the seams and spaces between stones were raised, separating and controlling the dikes. The paddies didn't go in straight lines like midwestern American farmlands, they followed the irregularities of the land. The dikes zigged and zagged and quilt-worked their way between them. One series of connecting dikes was broader than the rest and led to the CAP compound; a narrow-wheelbase vehicle guided by a skilled driver could traverse it without falling into the paddies.

Eakins followed that broader dike, Bingham was ten meters behind him. The line of Marines following the dike stretched until it was close to a hundred meters long. At the treeline, Rivera and Pratt watched them while Morse and Trumbull kept their eyes on the forest behind. The closer to the compound the line got, the more Bingham shivered inside. Halfway to the compound Eakins looked it over. Then he averted his eyes from the poles and didn't look at them again.

They started walking across the paddies slowly out of caution. They were still walking slowly when they reached the compound, but then it was because most of them didn't want to reach it. Birds squawked their protests at the Marines' approach and flew away when their screams didn't keep the intruders out.

The concertina wire had once been strung in orderly tangles of coils that could keep anyone, or anything larger than a small dog, out. Now gaping holes were burst in it. Whole sections were turned to snippets of wire that lay harmlessly on the ground, meaningless, barriers only to insects too big to walk under or too small to step over them. The punji-stake-filled moat circling outside the wire held small pools of water mixed with blood. Blood stained the wire and the ground under it. Large, red splotches spattered the ground inside the compound, dribblets of blood trailed in meaningless patterns. Scraps of cloth, peasant black and Marine field-green, were scattered about.

"No shit." Remington was the only one who said anything when the squad entered through the broken gate. He was the only one who immediately looked at the poles standing in the middle of the compound. After a moment Russell joined him in examining them. "No shit," Russell echoed his fire-team leader.

"Chuck, check out the hootches," Bingham ordered, thick-voiced.

Peale acknowledged the order with a mumble and quietly led his fire team into the bullet-pitted masonry structures.

"Fred, see if anyone's in the bunkers."

Copley and West had drifted away until they were standing, leaning against each other, Copley's shoulder to West's arm. Without being told, they started inspecting the bunkers at one end of the shattered, no-longer-defensive perimeter wire. Remington glanced around, then sent Russell and Stuart to check out the bunkers from the other end of the compound. He returned his attention to the poles.

"You're a fucking ghoul, Fred, you know that," Bingham said.

"Shit, man," Remington said, grinning at him, "ain't nothing but dead meat."

Now Bingham looked at the poles close up. Seven of the twelve had Vietnamese heads topping them. The other five, American. Lidless, empty eyesockets, plucked clean by beaks, stared out over the paddies. Flies buzzed around the heads, beetles crawled over them, ants marched in their forth-and-back columns up and down the posts. Masses of insects moving in and out of the mouths and over the lips made the heads seem to form soundless words. A sign, painted in Vietnamese and rough English on thin cloth was strung between two of the poles. In English it read:

These puppet-Lackys belong to Opressors of People
They not surrender to re-Education.
They pay Price As well other Puppet lackes

Bingham jerked his eyes away and looked around the compound, wondering where the survivors were. "Anybody seen a shovel?" he asked.

"Yeah." Copley approached with a bent-blade spade, most of its handle broken away. There were no large stones in the compound, no ammo boxes or other evident pieces of metal other than spent brass. He lay the spade convex on the ground, popped the magazine from his .45, and cleared its chamber. He used the pistol as a hammer to try to straighten the blade. The ground was too soft from the rains and the bent blade sunk in under his hammering. He stopped, reloaded his pistol, and asked, "Where do you want it?"

"Anywhere," Bingham said.

Copley started digging where the spade had already gouged the ground. In minutes he'd dug a hole large enough that he started having problems with its sides sliding in. He didn't complain, or even seem to notice the increase in his work. He just kept digging.

The others finished their search of the compound. They found no survivors or body parts, only the twelve heads on the poles in the middle. Bingham asked his men dead-voiced questions and gave them dead-voiced orders. West didn't join the rest of the men, he spelled Copley at the hole. A few ponchos came from the broken bunkers, creased, muddied, and torn. There were no items of uniform or other clothing not in shreds; the crude sign was the only piece of whole cloth. The few wooden ammo crates they found were splintered; there wasn't a scrap of usable wood in the camp. There were five of the creased, muddied, and torn ponchos.

Gingerly, as reverently as he could, Bingham brushed the insects away from one of the American heads and grasped it by its ears to remove it from its pole. He wanted to lift the head straight up so it wouldn't be disturbed by rough treatment, but a splinter caught on something inside and the head slipped from his grasp, started to drop, caught on another splinter, and hung canted at a sharp angle. Its empty eyes seemed to droop at this added indignity. Bingham grimaced and his throat tightened to hold down his rising gorge. He tried again, this time holding the palms of his hands firmly against the sides of the head. For a moment the pole resisted giving up its hold on the head, but it let go suddenly, and the head almost popped upward out of Bingham's hands. He lay it gently on the spread poncho. He was so intent on what he was doing, trying to keep from getting sick himself, he didn't hear a gurgle from one of the others. Several of the Marines turned their heads; a ragged lump of flesh remained behind, held tight by the splinter.

After that, Bingham worked as quickly and methodically as he could, and as he went along he lost his will for reverence, he wanted the job done. Two American heads went on one poncho, the other three on a second. Three Vietnamese heads on one, two on each of the other two. Rivera brought his fire team up while Bingham was removing the heads from the poles. Bingham didn't notice them until Rivera started to help him wrap the gruesome bundles. Off to one side, near the barbed wire, Trumbull was kneeling, retching. Pratt knelt at his side, arm over his shoulder, trying to comfort him.

Bingham and Rivera made the bundles as water- and insect-proof as they could without tape or cord, folding the edges of the ponchos tightly into each other. The bundles went into the hole, which was now three feet deep and large enough at the bottom to hold all five bundles without stacking them. Peale told his men to fill the hole. They did quickly. The only wood that could be used to make a cross to mark the grave was the poles. Bingham couldn't bring himself to use them. He thought it would be easy enough to find in a few days—or whenever it was the Marines returned to this compound. He served the function of chaplain and commanding officer and said a few words over the grave. Flying above and perched on the tor, the birds screamed their displeasure at having their meal hidden away from them.

"Brothers, we didn't know you, and even now we don't know your names. You made the ultimate sacrifice for your country, both countries. You did not die in vain, we will persevere. Your families will be proud and your comrades will remember and revere your memories."

"Don't do that," West snapped.

Bingham started to turn toward him. Before he could see what West was objecting to, he heard Remington say, "Fire," and the silence of the compound was shattered by reports from three rifles. Bingham dropped to the ground, then stared for a moment in disbelief. Remington, Russell, and Stuart stood with their rifles in their shoulders, aimed at the sky.

"A military funeral needs a salute," the big man said when he saw Bingham looking at him.

Bingham slowly stood and slowly walked toward Remington, who now stood with his rifle held across his body, slightly pointed to his front, almost at the ready. The sergeant's own rifle was laying where he had put it to unpole the heads. When he got to two feet from the other man he became a blur; one hand wrenched the M-14 away and threw it, the other clamped tightly on Remington's throat, forefinger and thumb against the line of his jaw, angled toward his ears. Then his first hand came back and hit Remington in the face so hard it knocked him back out of his grasp. Bingham shifted and planted a foot behind Remington's heel. The force of the blow staggered the big man and he tripped backward and fell heavily.

Bingham grabbed Russell's rifle and pointed it at the supine figure at his feet. "Goddam you," he said. "Now every fucking gook in the area knows there's Americans here. Now they're going to come looking for us. I ought to waste your fucking ass before you do anything else stupid to get us killed."

Remington didn't stand immediately. He propped himself on one elbow and wiped his mouth with the back of his other hand,

and grinned a mirthless grin. "Touch me again, Chuck, you dead meat."

"You do something stupid like that again, I'll kill you before Charlie has the chance to." Bingham kept the muzzle of the rifle pointed at Remington for a few seconds more, then handed it out blindly for someone to take. When he felt its weight leave his grasp, he turned back to the grave. "Sorry 'bout that, panos," he said and went to retrieve his own gear.

The search of the compound found nothing usable or any indication of what happened to its defenders. Maybe they were in one of the village's hamlets. Or maybe they could find civilians who could give them some assistance. They left the bent-blade shovel.

CHAPTER TWENTY-SIX
It's Too Late to Circle the Wagons

Ban Thuc 2, was what the map called the empty hamlet. It was inside the trees bordering the rice paddies a little beyond the narrow roadway that led to the compound. Given a few clapboard false-fronts, a couple of bat-wing bar doors swinging on rusty hinges, and some tumbling tumbleweeds, and it could have passed for anyplace just turned into a ghost town by a marauding band of Chiricahua. All it needed were arrows sticking out of the bodies sprawled on the ground.

The Marines spread out and walked through the hamlet, silent, searching. A vacant, razed hamlet the night before, the atrocity of the CAP compound at noon, now this. Trumbull and Pratt looked like they wanted to be sick again. Rush and Homer seemed too numbed to be able to care anymore. Stuart looked too dazed to realize what he was seeing, still too new to understand what death was. West and Copley leaned against each other, each trying to draw strength from the other to deal with what was around them. Russell followed Remington, looking at what the other man looked at, making comments back to him.

It had been a small hamlet—a subsistence level farming-gathering hamlet; if any of the Americans wondered enough to figure out what the people had done for their livelihoods, that's probably what they would have thought. They probably wouldn't have realized the nearby rice fields made this hamlet well off and the presence of the CAP made it relatively rich. It was small, twenty burned-down hootches small. Bingham counted twenty-five bodies in the kitchen gardens and on the paths. Birds screeched at the Marines and flew to safety.

One old man lay crumpled, chest down, hands tied behind his back, in a small open area in the middle of the skewed circle formed by the hootches. His head, Ho Chi Minh whiskers below a mouth frozen in silent scream, lay a few feet away. Bingham guessed he'd been the hamlet's headman and was executed for it, the first of the people to be killed. Two tiny children, a boy and a girl, lay partly under the body of a woman who tried to shield them in her death. Her shielding hadn't worked, the children were torn almost in half by bursts from automatic weapons. Children, teen-agers, women, and old people were there, now ageless in death. The only man between early youth and old age wore a Marine-style utility shirt, obviously one of the PFs. His trousers were pulled down and a red slash stained his groin. His genitals protruded from between· his lips. Three women lay supine, their black peasant pants pulled below their knees. Their arms seemed to have dropped from protective postures, their legs were casually splayed. The form-fitting, blue tunic worn by one of the three was torn open exposing full breasts that hadn't yet aged enough to sag. She had probably been pretty in life. A single, black-rimmed red eye was between those breasts, a thin trickle of dry blood ran from the hole to her belly: the single bullet had stopped her heart immediately so she hadn't bled much.

Bingham didn't know whether to hope the three women had not suffered the rapes alive, or to hope their bodies hadn't been defiled by human beasts.

Two pig carcasses lay bloating, fly covered, in the hamlet along with a few dead piglets. The Marines also found the spare remains of a few chickens, cleaned between feathers and bones by insects. There weren't any dogs or any living livestock. No dogs—"It was the NVA that did this," Bingham told his men. He knew the northerners had a taste for dog meat. And this wasn't their hamlet, these weren't their people. The NVA could brutalize and murder here and take the dogs as walking food.

Bingham looked around the small hamlet one more time and asked his men a question. No, they answered, they'd found no one alive, no food, nothing they could use, nothing that would tell them more than the bodies did about who had been here. "Let's head back to the hill," he said, not knowing where other Marines might be, needing a familiar reference point before doing anything else.

"Want us to bury them first?" Remington asked, grinning at Bingham, not looking at the bodies. Knowing what the answer would be.

"We don't have time," Bingham said. Some of the others looked at him, some of them looked at Remington. They all understood the question had been a challenge to Bingham's leadership. Not all of them understood how and not all of them knew who'd won the challenge, but even the ones who knew who'd won couldn't even have agreed on who did.

"Then let me have the point." Remington still grinned.

"Take it." Bingham didn't feel like arguing, but he thought he was probably making a mistake.

Remington looked at his men. He knew West was Bingham's boy, so fuck him. Stuart was too new and didn't know diddly-shit. "Chas," he said out loud, "you know how to get where we're going?" He liked Russell's attitude.

"Yeah, Honcho." Russell tried to grin the same kind of grin Remington wore. He lifted his face to the sky. A drizzle was starting and his grin turned into a grimace.

Remington looked at Bingham who waved wearily east.

"Go," Remington said.

Russell grinned wider, tipped his head at his fire-team leader, spat between his feet, fixed his bayonet, and led the squad out of the dead hamlet.

It was Russell's first time on point. Maybe that's what did it. Or maybe it was overconfidence, overconfidence brought about by the squad having spent so much time wandering the area the past two and a half days and not running into anyone in more than twenty-four hours—and most of those they'd seen had been east of there, and the rest moving east. Russell had no pressing reason to suspect there were any more NVA or VC in the area, not after they'd destroyed one hamlet, burned it to the ground, and killed everybody in another, and wiped out the garrison of the CAP compound—any of them who hadn't managed to escape. Bingham didn't think they'd run into anyone, either, or he wasn't paying attention. He agreed it wasn't likely there were any enemy soldiers in the area. So he let Russell have the point and let him go faster than maybe he should have.

And Russell didn't have much experience with booby traps. He was aware of them of course, all the Americans were, and kept a watch for fishing line trip wires stretching across the path, until he realized if he wasn't on the path he wouldn't have to watch as hard for them. Then he got off the trail and paralleled it five meters inside the forest. The way the book said to do it; five meters off the trail and you're safe from any trip wires set on the path or just off it. According to the book, five meters off the trail you'll walk into the flank of any ambush set along it instead of into that ambush's killing zone.

Any or all of that would explain why Russell, when he reached a thick-trunked, fallen tree, felt safe in grabbing hold of a bamboo pole sticking out of the ground next to the tree trunk to help himself over the tree trunk. If he had bothered to look he might have seen the cord slipknotted to the pole where it met the ground, a cord that went along the side of the trunk until it reached some foliage, then climbed into the standing trees. He pulled on the pole, the slipknot slipped, the cord came loose and the object delicately attached to a crude counter-balance and pulley system at its other end was released.

A hundred pounds of hardwood frame holding a lattice-work supporting thirty fire-hardened punji stakes dropped from almost directly above Russell. He didn't even have time to scream before eight of those punji stakes slammed through his head and shoulders and arms and upper torso and pinned him to the fallen tree. Five meters, that's what the book said. The enemy read the same book.

Remington stood stunned for a second, eyes wide, jaw slack. But only for a second. Then he lunged to Russell and tried to pull the deadfall from him. It shuddered under the force of his pull, blood spattered about and ran in the drizzle. But the deadfall didn't come loose.

"Chas, man, hang in there, I'll get you out," he said, and pulled again. Russell didn't answer; dead men don't talk. Then a hand clamped on Remington's shoulder and pulled him back.

"He's dead, Fred," Bingham said. The sergeant looked coldly at the corporal, holding down his fear and rage, bottling it in tightly. "That's exactly why I wanted Chief or Night Stalker on point, they would've seen the deadfall."

Remington stared at him, then looked at West and Stuart who were using the bamboo pole as a lever to pry the deadfall off Russell. He looked and then let out a roar like a primeval scream. Everyone else stopped and looked at him.

Bingham swung his rifle like a club, slammed it into Remington's belly before the big man could fill his lungs for another scream. Remington folded and fell back from the force of the blow. He rolled onto his side and fish-mouthed, gasping for air.

Bingham dropped to his knees and bent over Remington's head. "Shut up, dammit, shut up." His shoulders heaved. "First that rifle salute, then you got Russell wasted, now you scream. That's three times you fucked up today," he grated, "Three strikes and you're out." He drew his bayonet and rough hands grabbed him from behind; Homer had his knife arm, Peale and Rivera grabbed his head and shoulders and yanked backward. Homer twisted his arm until he dropped the bayonet.

"Don't do it, Honcho," Rivera said. "He ain't worth it."

Bingham struggled, but the three held him down.

Remington finally caught his breath and stood unsteadily, bent over, clutching his abdomen. He forced himself upright and walked to Russell. The corpse now lay on the ground after being freed, the deadfall leaned against the tree trunk next to him. Remington drew back a leg and slammed a hard kick into the body's side. "What'd I tell you, you dumb shit," he said, and kicked again. "I told you to listen." Kick. "Somebody shoulda made you eat cigars"—kick—"fed you rats." Kick. "Now you dead"—kick—"and it's your own fucking fault." Kick.

"Cut the shit, Fred," West said. "Man's wasted, can't teach him nothing now." He put a hand on Remington's arm to lead him away. Stuart stood on his other side, looking indecisive. West nodded at him to take Remington's other arm. They took him away, he didn't resist.

The men holding Bingham down eased their grip and let him sit up. Bingham didn't struggle to get out of their grasp, didn't talk. He looked at Remington and thought, One more time, fucker, once more and nobody's going to be able to move fast enough to save you from me.

When they moved out again, Rush had the point. His eyes were too good, his jungle-craft too well-developed, his experience too great, for him to trip a deadfall. West and Stuart followed Bingham and Copley, Russell's body swinging between them, wrapped in his poncho, hanging from the bamboo pole that had triggered the deadfall. Remington trudged behind them, keeping his distance from Bingham. Rivera put Morse on rear point, the only one of his men he was certain knew how to watch the rear. They reached the cleared area around Alpha Company's hill at dusk. There were no more incidents, and Rush hadn't spotted any booby traps to be avoided.

"What do you think, Chief," Bingham said softly at the edge of the forest. They were near, but not at, the same place from where they had watched the hill that first morning. The setting sun's rays sparkled the red scar of the hill a brilliant hue, the shadows of the forest rapidly approached the hill, as though jealous, to dim and douse its glory.

Rush squatted with his arms wrapped around his knees, his eyes peered at the bare hill, darted from place to place, slowly swung from side to side, looking for something, anything, that would tell him if anyone was there, if it was safe or dangerous. "I don't know," he said and kept up his visual search.

Eakins knelt on one knee on Bingham's other side and studied the hill. He shook his head when the squad leader asked his opinion. Peale looked but didn't speak. Copley was also quiet.

"I think we should stay right here tonight," Remington said from behind them. They were the first words he'd spoken since West and Stuart pulled him from Russell; his voice was slow and thick.

Bingham slowly turned his head. He hadn't heard the big man come up behind him. "Fred, you got a man killed today," he said in a measured voice. "West wouldn't have done that." And I'm just as much to blame because I should have been paying attention, he added to himself. "I don't want to see you, I don't want to hear you." He looked back at the hill. "But you're right. We'll stay here until morning." He stood and signaled Peale to join them. "Dago, up," he said as he walked a few feet deeper into the trees.

Rivera joined them as the day's last light filtered down through the trees. "We stay in the trees tonight," he told his fire-team leaders. "Chuck, John, and I will watch the hill, everybody else watch our rear. Fifty percent alert. If we don't see any activity on the hill overnight, we'll go to it in the morning." He looked at each of them in the last light until sunup. "Questions?"

There weren't any, not even about what would they eat.

"Let's do this thing."

Bingham sat with his back against a tree for a while before trying to sleep; Copley had first watch between them. He sat where he had a relatively unobstructed view of the hill. Above, he could see the stars appearing in the darkening, partly overcast sky. Briefly he thought about how many more stars were visible here, even through the spotty clouds now that the rain had stopped, than there were on the clearest nights back in the World. On clear nights there didn't seem to be any part of the sky that wasn't densely speckled with stars, unlike at home where whole patches of sky were almost bare black.

As he watched, the tree shadows sped across the cleared ground and climbed the hillside; the top of the hill glowed redly in the last rays of light. At the same time the black sky sped westward and enveloped the hill from the bottom until only that red glow on the top remained. He sat for a time watching the stars appear, turning the zenith into gray rather than black, stars that he knew cast enough light for a man with good eyes to read a paperback book by on a clear night. He slowly became aware that part of the hilltop still had a faint red glow. The sun was long down by now—the glow could only be from a fire or a lantern.

The realization startled him, jerked him from a lounging position to a ready-to-bolt alertness. He grabbed Copley's shoulder and pointed. "See that?" he demanded. His voice sounded harsh to his own ears.

There was a pause before the faint glow registered on the grenadier. "No shit," he whispered when it did.

"Gimme the radio. Someone's home and I want to find out who." Bingham took the radio and turned it on. He listened to the handset for several minutes before twisting the dial through all the frequencies, listening for transmissions over the entire band. All he heard was static. He kept trying, pausing at each click of the dial. Nothing. After a half hour of trying, he switched back to the frequency the patrol used the night of the ambush, pressed the speak lever on the side of the handset, and spoke. "Unit on Alpha Company's hill, this is Alpha One Bravo. I say again, unit on Alpha Company's hill, this is Alpha One Bravo, do you hear me? Over." He listened for a response. When none came he switched to what had been the company's platoon net frequency and repeated his transmission. No answer. He tried a third time, on what he thought had been the company's frequency to communicate with the battalion headquarters. Silence in response.

Again, he swept the dial slowly through the band. Twice he heard fragments of a transmission, distant voices barely heard and badly broken. Once, more clearly, he heard a voice speaking in Vietnamese. Gunfire mingled with that voice, gunfire he didn't hear except on the radio. He sighed almost inaudibly and turned the radio off. "I'll try again after midnight," he told Copley. Then, "I'm going to check everyone." He stood crouched and moved away.

Peale and Eakins were watching the glow. A few feet away Rush and Homer slept lightly.

"What do you think?" Peale asked Bingham.

"I don't know. I listened on the radio and tried to raise them. Nothing."

"I don't think it's our people," Eakins said. "They wouldn't be burning a fire."

"You're probably right," Bingham said. He chewed on his lower lip. The Marines would not burn a visible fire or other light on their hill at night. Even if Charlie knew where their hill was, the Marines maintained light discipline during the hours of darkness so they wouldn't give away any exact positions. "Let me know if you see any movement." He gave the glow a last look, then moved deeper into the trees. Rivera, West, and Pratt were awake. Neither the three of them nor the three sleeping men were too close to the poncho holding Russell's body.

"Anything?" Bingham asked.

"Crickets," Rivera said. A good sign. If the night noises were normal there was probably nobody moving in the forest near them.

"Watch careful. There's somebody on the hill, they didn't answer when I called on the radio and I didn't pick up any transmissions from them."

Bingham felt the others stiffen. He answered their question before they asked. "Probably Charlie. There's a fire on the hill, that doesn't sound like our people." He waited for a moment before adding, "They might have patrols out. Stay alert."

"We're sharp, Honcho," Rivera replied. He knew he and West were, and thought Pratt was too scared to be anything but alert.

"Right. I'll be back at watch-change to brief Remington and the others." Bingham stood crouched again and returned to where Copley still watched the faint glow.

The sergeant lay on his stomach and crossed his arms under his chin, facing the hill. "Wake me fifteen minutes before my watch," he told Copley. It was a bit longer before his eyelids drooped and his head rolled onto its side. His nap was light enough that he awoke as soon as he sensed Copley moving to wake him. He flexed his major muscle groups one at a time rather than stretching, then lifted himself to hands and knees and shook his head to clear it. He rocked back onto his heels and said, "I'm checking the others. Be back in a skosh bit," then stood and crouch-walked to where Peale was about to wake Rush and Homer.

"Anything?"

"Nothing," Peale answered. Eakins's silence echoed Peale's answer.

Rush saw the glow and immediately understood its meaning. Homer took a couple of seconds before he realized the glow meant whoever was on the hill was probably the enemy.

Peale was already telling Remington about the fire when Bingham joined them. The big man looked at the sergeant and asked, "We wait here?" His tone of voice held a taunt, he was recovering from his earlier shock at making a mistake that cost him a man.

"We wait here until dawn," Bingham said emotionlessly. He considered and quickly decided to say what he hadn't felt the need to with the others. "We don't know who it is or how many of them there are. If they have patrols out and one walks by, let it go. Do not fire unless we are discovered. Understand?"

Remington paused a beat or two before speaking, long enough for his answer to be insolent without sounding like it. "If anyone shows up, let 'em go unless he sees us. Roger."

Bingham stared hard at the darkness where he knew Remington's unseen face was. "Do it." He returned to Copley and said, "Cop some Zs." He watched for two quiet hours while the fire on the hill burned down and went out. At the beginning of his first watch after midnight he turned the radio back on and twisted its dial through the frequencies from one end to the other and back for half an hour, listening for any transmissions. The few voices he heard were distant and broken. He didn't try to raise the unit on the hill; if they were the enemy, he didn't want to alert them to his squad's presence, if they were friendly forces they'd just tell him to stay where he was until sunup, anyway. He listened futilely to the radio again before waking Copley.

CHAPTER TWENTY-SEVEN

The Big Bad Wolf and the House of Twigs

As soon as it was light enough, Rush looked around for a tall tree. Peale and Trumbull gave him a boost up it to where he could grab a low branch to pull himself higher. He clamped his arms, knees, and feet against the tree trunk and shimmied higher until he reached a branch big enough to hold his weight, high enough for him to observe the hill.

From ground level, looking up at the hillside, it was obvious a battle had been recently fought on the hill. From Rush's new vantage point, where he could see the top of the hill, the devastation he saw told how fierce that battle had been. Dark, olive-colored sandbag bunkers were burst apart. The bare earth was gouged and scorched in places it hadn't been the last time he'd seen it—from rockets and mortar rounds and satchel charges exploding on it. Scattered spots seemed to be a darker red than the rest—he thought from pooled blood drying. Boards from ammo cases were strewn about. Cans and boxes were tipped and tossed helter-skelter. Scraps of paper and cloth fluttered and rolled in the air currents that breezed across the hill. There were unidentifiable objects of dark, drab-green laying here and there. Rush watched for twenty minutes without seeing any sign of people being on the hill now; it looked as though whoever had burned the fire the night before had since left. The only sign he saw that anyone had been there since the battle was a pile of kindling and a blackened pit in front of what had been the CP bunker.

"I had a buddy in second platoon," Eakins said after Rush made his report to Bingham. "He showed me where they had to keep an LP in a cut in their side of the hill because Charlie could almost reach the wire if there wasn't anybody down there to see him coming. Let me go up that cut, make a close recon, be sure nobody's there."

Bingham looked east for a moment, at the patches of red earth he could see between the trees. His stomach rumbled and he knew they had to find food soon—it might be too dangerous to return to the banana grove again. Maybe there were some C rations left on the hill, maybe somebody's CARE package from the World had been left undisturbed with food still in it. "You're not going alone," he said.

"I'll go," Rush said. "The two of us are enough. If anyone's there he won't see us."

Bingham looked at the two men. Rush stood stolidly, his face and posture giving no indication of what he might be thinking or feeling; Eakins wore a crooked grin and hefted his rifle. Rush and Eakins were the most important men in the squad. Their ability to spot danger before it happened might be the difference in the squad's being able to survive until it could find a friendly unit. And they were right, they were the most capable of making a reconnaissance of the hill and not being discovered if there were hidden enemy soldiers on it. "You got it," he said slowly. "Be careful."

"You know it, Honcho," Eakins said. "If nobody's home, I'll signal you to come up." To Rush he said, "Let's go, Chief." He turned north to circle around the hill inside the forest to the cut. Rush followed close behind. In seconds they silently passed from sight as if they had never been there.

"We wait," Bingham said to the others. He arranged them in a circle and they sat or lay to wait for the return of the two men. Bingham positioned himself where he could have an unobstructed view of the hillside.

The two men followed the perimeter of the cleared area surrounding the hill, deep enough inside the forest that they couldn't be seen from outside it, close enough to its edge they could see patches of red through the trees and brush. Despite their awkward but silent toe-to-heel gait they made good speed, not much slower than a casual amble. Their heads constantly moved, side to side, up and down. The muzzles of their rifles pointed where their eyes looked. They moved from shadow to shadow, tree to tree, nearly invisible in the forest. The only audible sign of their passage was the circle of silence from startled insects and birds who suddenly noticed strangers in their midst. They saw no people in their transit to the northern side of the hill where the cut was and the small jungle animals and the birds avoided them; they almost could have been the only animal life forms there.

"There it is," Eakins said when he stopped.

Rush looked where Eakins pointed. The side of the hill seemed to fold in on itself where rainwater had runneled a crooked channel down its face. What they could see of the gully's bottom glistened with standing water from the recent rains. The hill's north face was steeper than the others; the cut was an obvious way of easily climbing it, mud or no mud. A low finger of the hill, too low to be called a ridge, jutted toward them from one side of the cut. The hill faintly resembled a face from where they watched. Two shattered bunkers on the military crest of the hill along the sides of the cut were eyes, the cut was a crooked mouth, the finger a lolling, prehensile tongue.

"Booby traps?" Rush asked.

Eakins nodded. "Unless Charlie blew them all when he overran the hill."

Neither man had anything else to say for a few minutes while they examined the hill and its approaches from their hidden vantage. It looked to Rush as deserted as it had looked from the tree. Once they reached the cut, climbing the hill would not be hard as long as nobody was watching on it—they weren't worried about any booby traps the Marines had set, they were sure of being able to spot any that might still be left. The thing that bothered both of them was the seventy-five meters of open ground they had to cross before reaching what concealment the finger would give them. A sniper or observation post could be concealed in the cut and would see them as soon as they stepped out of the cover of the trees. They watched silently and the hill remained deserted looking.

When they finally looked at each other, they each knew the other had arrived at the same decision: Let's go. They made a false start, both trying to lead off. They looked into each other's eyes, then nodded and hammered their fists one-two-three in the air. On the third hammer Rush's index and middle fingers stood out, Eakins's fist unfolded and his hand was flat. Scissors cut paper; Rush led the way.

They ran as fast as they could, crouched low, jerking from side to side in a fast zigzag to foil anyone trying to sight in on them. Canteens bounced on their buttocks. Eakins didn't follow Rush exactly; this area shouldn't have any booby traps, so a sniper couldn't hold his aim from Rush to hit him. In seconds Rush reached the end of the finger of earth extending from the hill and dove for cover at its side. Eakins thudded down next to him. No one shot at them while they were running; no one fired in their direction while they lay panting, catching their breath. They both knew that didn't mean nobody was on the hill, or even that there wasn't a sniper or observation post in the cut. They'd gone the distance fast enough that an unobservant watcher could have missed seeing them.

Rush took a deep breath and held it to calm the involuntary shivering in his body. When he let it out, he looked at Eakins, who nodded at him. He kept his chest and belly on the ground while he scrabbled forward using elbows, knees, and feet, until the finger was high enough for him to rise to a low crouch without losing its cover.

The two felt speed was more important now than it had been in the forest, the finger didn't hide them from directly to the front or from the right side. Closer, the hill looked more than before like a face. The shattered bunkers of its eyes seemed to be crossing themselves looking down at the approaching Marines. The broken concertina wire below the bunkers looked like a five-day growth of beard. The red walls of the cut and the deeper, shadowed bottom and back looked ominously like a gaping maw. They tried to keep their imaginations under control, but their skin crawled and tried to pull away from the finger, a tongue about to wrap around them and draw their struggling bodies into that gaping maw.

The bunker-eyes were sightless, the lolling tongue didn't envelop their bodies, the lipless maw didn't smack its edges around them when they entered the cut. Nobody shot at them, or even shouted a who-goes-there. They both heaved deep breaths of relief. Now nobody could see them except from their direct front or the top of the cut sides. This time Rush didn't look at Eakins for a let's-go nod, he glanced at him and jerked his head to say "Follow me." Eakins nodded at Rush's back.

The cut was nearly eight feet wide at the foot of the hill and a little deeper than that; it was almost level at first. The mud in its bottom was gooey, slick, and slippery underfoot and quickly filled in the tread of their boot soles, making their footing more uncertain. It squished under their feet, rolled up around their boots, and stuck to their sides and tops, making their feet thick, heavy, clumsy. It sucked at their feet and made noise when reluctantly releasing them. In a few steps they worked out a compromise with the mud. They didn't pull their feet all the way out of it before sliding them forward, didn't make the mud let them go; the mud didn't protest so loudly.

Less than twenty feet in, the cut made a sharp bend to the left. Rush dropped down low and cautiously looked around the corner. Here the cut was narrower and its bottom steeper. It took another turn, to the right this time, thirty feet farther. Part of one wall had caved in slightly, the wall opposite was blackened; an explosive booby trap had been set off there. Rush approached the spot where the explosion had gone off. He pointed to something in the blackened wall. Eakins looked at it; it was a chunk of something that was probably flesh. He nodded to himself; Charlie had been hurt there.

Rush found where seven other booby traps and, more than halfway to the top, three trip flares had been set off, before they reached the bunkers. He also saw evidence of casualties. Charlie had come up the hill this way, but he hadn't done it without cost. At the top there had been a machine gun covering the cut. Scraps of cloth, dark spots on the ground, and insects swarming over unidentified bits laying in the mud showed the gun had done its job.

But the gun and the booby traps hadn't done their job well enough; the NVA had managed to drive the Marines off the hill. Rush and Eakins wondered how many of the attackers had been killed. They wondered how many Marines died in the defense—how many of their buddies.

They reached the blind-eye bunkers on the military crest without seeing or hearing sign of anybody on the hill. The military crest is that point on the slope where a man can stand erect without being silhouetted against the sky. The two bunkers were totally wasted. In one, some large explosive had gone through the embrasure; its heavy sand-bagged walls were burst outward and the roof fallen in. "I hope nobody was in there," Eakins said. Rush grunted. Anyone in that bunker when it was blown was still in it. It didn't stink of rotted flesh, so it was probably unmanned when it was blown. There was no point in trying to find anything in it; it would have to be excavated to find anything. The other bunker's entire front was blown away; its roof sagged ominously, in imminent danger of collapse. They looked through the open front. All they could see in the deep shadows was rubble. It didn't seem worth searching. The canvas tarp lying folded in front of it was probably the only usable thing to be found there.

Rush crawled to the uphill end of the bunker and, flat against the ground, side pressed against the bunker wall, peered over as much as he could see of the hilltop. The command bunker was forty meters away. When he set up the defensive positions on the hill, Captain Bernstein decided the northern, steeper face of the hill was its back. He set his CP bunker closer to that face than the others, thinking any assault would come from the other three, more easily climbed sides. And he thought if Charlie attacked from the north side, it would be easier for him to control its defense if he was located closer to it. Rush saw no movement on the hilltop other than the fluttering of scraps of paper and cloth and the darting and hopping of a few birds hunting carrion and food scraps. Suddenly he crinkled his nose and sniffed. He slithered back to where Eakins waited.

"Nuoc mam," he whispered. "I smell *nuoc mam.*"

Eakins seemed to shrink into himself. "Where?"

Rush stared back up at the top of the hill. "I think the CP."

They looked at each other for a long moment, thinking about what *nuoc mam* on the hill had to mean.

Eakins swallowed briefly, pointed to his chest and to the other bunker, then flashed five fingers twice. Rush nodded; he tapped his own chest and pointed uphill. Eakins nodded. They were going to watch from two different spots for ten minutes. Eakins gathered himself and quickly rolled back to the first bunker. Rush watched until he was prone against its side. Eakins slid to the downhill side of the bunker and scuttled around to its other side. Not able to see the other man any longer, Rush suddenly felt more alone than he had ever felt before. And, for the first time since leaving the squad behind, he felt exposed—even more so than when running across the seventy-five meters of open ground between the trees and the hill finger. He counted slowly to ten, then crawled back to where he could peer between two sandbags at the CP bunker.

Nobody was in sight, but the ripe aroma of *nuoc mam* drifted to Rush's nose. He turned his head to the other broken bunker but couldn't see Eakins. He hoped that was because he was well hidden and not because something had happened to him. This was a time when he needed to have confidence in his partner, not think something might go wrong. He returned his attention to the CP.

After a few minutes a khaki-clad Vietnamese stepped out of the bunker. An AK-47 was slung carelessly, muzzle down, over his shoulder, but he wasn't wearing a cartridge belt or obviously carrying any ammunition other than the magazine in his rifle. The NVA didn't seem to be concerned about security or threat of attack. The soldier blinked in the bright sunlight and clapped a pith helmet on his head, pulled low to shade his eyes. He turned back to laugh a reply to something someone still inside said, then ambled off a few yards to where a communications trench cut across the hilltop. There he stopped, opened his pants, and urinated long and loud into the trench. A second man, also in khakis, poked his head out of the bunker and shouted something in a jocular voice at the first man. Rush guessed it was probably something similar to an American saying a buddy sounded like a cow pissing on a flat rock. The urinater laughed back and half turned toward the other to say something back. He waved his still spurting penis about. The second man laughed again and ducked back into the bunker, saying some parting words. Finished at last, the soldier shook himself out, redressed, and wandered toward the north side of the hill—out of sight on the other side of the bunker.

Rush fidgeted internally for a long moment, wondering what to do about the man he could no longer see. Abruptly he stopped breathing and tried to will his heart to stop thumping so loudly in his chest; he heard footsteps approaching the far side of the bunker. There was a thump as the soldier sat on the edge of the bunker and Rush let his breath out slowly and breathed through his mouth as quietly as he could. A rough scratching sound was followed by the pungent odor of a strong Vietnamese cigarette mingled with the smell of *nuoc mam*.

Rush looked back at the bunker in time to see another man, not the one he'd seen before, emerge. This man had a Marine boonie hat like the one Rush himself wore sitting low on his head—it was several sizes too large for him. A Marine tiger-stripe utility shirt hung open on his shoulders, draped in great folds on his slender body. He walked halfway to the bunker Rush hid behind and the other NVA sat on before talking. He didn't laugh or shout, he had a commanding element in his voice and the soldier smoking the cigarette spoke back respectfully. The NCO—it didn't occur to Rush that an officer would be wearing cast-off portions of an American uniform—nodded, satisfied and returned to the CP. Soft muttering from the sitting soldier was followed by a grunt and some scuffling sounds, then he headed back to the CP, still muttering softly.

Rush glanced at his watch to see how much was left of the ten minutes. He didn't know, he hadn't looked when the time started. He glanced back at the CP, decided ten minutes were gone or nearly so, and slid back to the other end of the bunker. Eakins rounded the corner of the bunker just before Rush reached the end of his.

"I thought we were in the shit when that first one came toward you," Eakins said when they got together; a tremor was in his voice.

"You and me both," Rush said, and swallowed a couple of times to control his voice. "There's at least three of them."

"Four. I saw another behind the one who was talking at the door. He wasn't wearing tiger stripes, so he couldn't have been the sergeant that came out." Eakins also heard the authority in that soldier's voice and didn't think an officer would dress in a captured uniform.

Rush looked back toward the top of the hill for a moment. "Follow me," he said, and led Eakins to a section of shallow trench that led partway around the hill.

The fire base was covered with a tracery of trenches. Communications trenches, so shallow that a man had to get on hands and knees to be concealed in them, led from the company CP bunker to the mortar pit and the three platoon CPs. Other trenches, waist deep, led from the platoon CPs to the perimeter and more sections connected the major defensive positions. One could circle the hill in the perimeter trenches and only have to get out of them a half-dozen times. Rush and Eakins could have duckwalked low and not been visible from outside the trench they followed, but hands and knees was easier. The first trench segment passed two bunkers before dead-ending at a third. All three bunkers were badly damaged and they couldn't see anything worthwhile inside them. At the third bunker Rush crawled to the back corner to look across the hilltop. No one moved—he signaled Eakins to cross to the next section. It was the same as the first trench: it went past two damaged, empty bunkers and dead-ended at a third. This last bunker didn't seem to be as badly damaged as the others and Rush squeezed in through its embrasure.

"Pay dirt," he said after searching it more by hand than by eye because of the darkness inside. He handed out four C ration meal boxes. "Let's di-di-mau the fuck out of here," and squeezed back out. They each stuck two C ration boxes in their shirts. They looked for a route from where they were to the trees that gave some concealment and didn't see any way that wouldn't leave them exposed for most of two hundred meters. They headed back the way they came, checking the company CP bunker at every chance. While they heard voices, nobody ever came out. Finally they were back at the cut and descended it as quickly as possible. When they reached the farther part of the finger, where they'd have to crawl to get any cover from it, they glanced at each other and sprinted to the safety of the forest. No warning voices or shots followed them.

CHAPTER TWENTY-EIGHT

Sometimes You Have to Climb Uphill to Go Downhill

Bingham handled the C rations reverently. He used a broad leaf cut from a spreading bush near the edge of the trees as a tablecloth and divided the contents of the cans into equal parts for everyone. They ate with their hands, but nobody minded the lack of utensils or the dirty fingers. For a few moments there were no sounds except for lip smacking, finger licking, and a few moans of pleasure.

"Damn, I never thought cold Ham and Limas could taste good," Rivera said when there was nothing left.

"I don't want to hear that was Ham and Limas," Copley said back.

"Now, tell me everything you found up there," Bingham said to Rush and Eakins.

"There's at least four Vee Cee Hanoi in the CP bunker," Rush started.

Bingham heard them all the way through before asking any questions. When he thought he knew everything they had to tell he leaned back against a tree to think.

"There's nothing to think about, George," Remington said. "We just go up there and waste their asses, take whatever we can find, and di-di-mau the fuck out of here."

Nobody said anything for a moment, some looked at Remington to see if he was going to say or do anything else, others looked at Bingham to see how he was going to react. A few glanced at Rush and Eakins—after all, they were the only ones who had actually seen the hilltop.

Finally Rush hesitantly said, "Fred's right, Honcho. We can do it."

"They got no security up there," Eakins added. "No problem."

Bingham waited longer before speaking. He thought Remington

was right, he just didn't want to do anything he suggested. He didn't want to give the other man anything he could use as a wedge to take over. But if he didn't agree that Remington was right on this point, he risked losing the respect of his men. "We can do it," he finally said slowly, "and we will do it. But we have to be careful. We already have one man dead, I don't want anybody else getting hurt."

Remington grinned at him. Okay, sucker, he thought. "You're right, be careful," he said. "Now let's do it."

"In a few minutes," Bingham said. He looked at Russell's poncho-shrouded body. "We'll leave him here, pick him up later." He waited a little longer, apparently lost in thought, before rising to his feet. "Chief, you got the point. Let's go."

Rush led them around the clearing fast. When they reached the spur Bingham stopped the squad and watched the hill for a few minutes before sending them on by fire teams. He waited until Peale and his men reached the cut, then said to the others, "Fred, you stay here until I signal you to come ahead. Dago, as soon as Fred and his people are under cover in the gully, you come with yours. John, let's go, now." He and Copley sprinted to the tongue-like finger and scrambled on all fours along it until it was high enough for them to stand crouched. When they reached the cut, Bingham turned back to signal Remington and his jaw clenched; the corporal and his men were already running for the finger. He didn't wait, he went up around the first bend where the first four waited for him.

"Chuck, you, Chief, Night Stalker, and me go up," Bingham said when he reached them. "John, you and Win keep the others here until I get back, I want to eyeball it myself."

"Got it," Copley said.

The two men who had already been to the hilltop started up the gully with Bingham and Peale close behind. They went more confidently than the first time. When they reached the bunkers at the top of the cut, Bingham went with Rush to the left side of one, Eakins and Peale to the right side.

Bingham lay on the slope of the hill crest, his head next to a burst sand bag; the bag's ragged burlap top fluttered slightly in the breeze—Bingham hoped its movement was enough to distract a casual viewer from spotting him. He didn't see anyone on the hilltop even though he smelled the *nuoc mam*. A small fire burned in front of the bunker. After a moment Bingham heard the sing-song of a raised Vietnamese voice come from the CP bunker, followed by laughs from more than one throat. He watched for a

few more minutes without seeing anyone or hearing any more talk.
Someone tossed a scrap of garbage through the door; it landed near
a small heap of trash. A simple plan formed in his mind: two fire
teams could lay here along the crest while the third went around to
the left until they were on the CP bunker's blind side. From there
they could reach the front corner of the bunker without being seen,
then wait hidden at its entrance for someone to come out. Whoever
came out of the bunker would be grabbed and killed with a knife.
Sooner or later someone else would come out and be dispatched
the same way. This was a slow way of doing it, but it was quiet
and they could do it.

Bingham and Rush slithered back to the bottom side of the bunker. Bingham sent Rush for the rest of the squad and went himself
to the far corner to get Peale to come down and Eakins to keep
watch. He froze at the sight of three men watching from that side,
then shook his head violently and headed toward them. Using touches and hand signals, he told Eakins to keep watch and the other
two to follow him down.

"What the fuck are you doing here?" he whispered harshly when
they got below the bunker.

"Scoping out the situation, George," Remington answered,
grinning.

"John tell you to wait with the rest?"

Remington shrugged a did-he-tell-me shrug, then nodded past
Bingham. "I'll go take care of those gooks now," he said and
held out a gray canister, a white phosphorus grenade.

"You're not doing shit, Fred, not until I tell you. And we aren't
going to make noise doing this, there's probably more bad guys
in the area. Using grenades will attract their attention."

Remington's grin turned into a wry smile. He shook his head
and said, "Willy pete's not that loud. Besides, the bunker will
muffle the noise." He looked around, still smiling. "I can use
that tarp there, cover the entrance, cut the sound more."

"We're going to do it quietly," Bingham insisted, casting a worried glance at Eakins. He was concerned their talking might be
loud enough to be heard in the CP bunker.

"Come on, George, this'll be quiet," Remington said in a calm
voice calculated to convince Peale he was right and the squad
leader wrong. "It'll be quick and easy. I'll waste all those little
bad guys."

Bingham thought about it for a long moment. Remington was
right, it could be done quietly enough so that nobody not close
to the hill would be alerted by the noise. Finally he said, "We

wait for the rest of the squad. Everybody will cover you and if any of them come out, we waste them."

Remington nodded. He thought, but didn't say, That will make the noise you're worried about.

The three men heard something in the gully and turned to it. It was Rush leading the other eight men of the squad to them. Quickly, Bingham lined them up, Peale's fire team and Remington's two men on the right side of the bunker, Rivera's fire team and Copley on the left.

"As soon as you pop that smoke and drop the tarp," Bingham told Remington, "get the fuck out of the way, I don't want anyone busting out in a hurry and snagging your ass. Understand?"

Remington nodded, grabbed the tarp in front of the busted bunker, then turned and headed alone to the trench segment that would lead him to the CP bunker's rear.

Bingham watched him disappear into the trench. He tried to think of how he didn't want any more men hurt, tried not to think of how much easier everything would be if he didn't have Remington defying him every step of the way.

Remington slung his rifle across his shoulders, tucked the tarp under one arm, and scrambled as fast as he could on toes and one hand. He moved fast, low, and quiet. When he reached a place where he couldn't be seen from the CP he stopped and opened the tarp; it was a six-by-eight-foot rectangle. He folded it in thirds the long way so it was six by a little less than three feet. He straightened the pin on a fragmentation grenade and pulled the pin from his willy peter. With the tarp held high in one hand and the willy peter gripped tightly in the other, he surged up and over the lip of the trench with his rifle still slung over his shoulders. He dashed to the corner of the bunker and looked cautiously around it.

Bingham couldn't see or hear him; he wondered when Remington was going to move and was surprised to see him roll out of the trench fifty yards away. He thought if Remington covered the distance so fast and silent, it might really work.

Remington moved slowly toward the entrance. He paused at its side and took a deep, steadying breath, then threw the gray canister through it as hard as he could. He hardly noticed the excited voices from inside the bunker as he pulled the fragmentation grenade from inside his shirt, yanked its straightened pin out, and threw it in. He slammed the folded tarp over the entrance and bounded to the top of the bunker to hold it in place. He felt the two explosions through the sandbags more than he heard them. Dirt puffed up around him. A couple of muffled screams pierced the air, then nothing more. He drew his bayonet and waited, quietly and patiently, for someone to try to force his way out. If there was anybody left alive and mobile inside the bunker, the eye-, nose-, throat-, and lung-burning smoke kicked out by the white phosphorus would send him scampering out—or kill him. A minute passed. Remington had to blink and crinkle his nose because of the smoke seeping out around the tarp.

Suddenly Bingham was at the bunker. "Spread that tarp, Fred," he ordered. He picked up a sandbag to anchor the opened tarp to the bunker top. Remington blinked at him, then wordlessly did as he was told. A puff of white smoke billowed out when he moved the tarp, making both of them cough. They anchored the tarp and got away from the CP to clean air as quickly as they could.

"John, stay here and cover the CP," Bingham called out. "By fire teams, search the perimeter. Chuck, from twelve o'clock to four, Fred, four o'clock to eight, Dago, the rest of the way." He watched as his men headed to three points on the perimeter to start their search, then looked at the CP bunker. Idly, he wondered if the two grenades had killed everyone in them outright or if some had lain there wounded, unable to try to escape, while the phosphorus smoke ate their lungs. He waited ten more minutes before he pulled the tarp from the entrance to air the bunker out. They had to give it at least a half hour, maybe longer, to air out enough to go in and see if there was anything usable in it.

The destruction on the hilltop was thorough. Some of the perimeter bunkers were collapsed, most of the others managed to stay more-or-less intact despite the satchel charges or other explosives set off in them. Rivera and his men took longer searching their part of the perimeter than did the other two fire teams; their area of responsibility included the bunkers that first platoon had held and they knew where more of the hidey holes were and could search them. When each team finished its search it rooted through the platoon CP bunker for its section. It took forty-five minutes in all. They reassembled with their findings in front of the company CP. A thin tendril of white smoke still slowly dribbled out of the CP.

West found a case of C rations. Homer uncovered a box of a thousand rounds of belt ammunition in a machine-gun position. Rivera's hiding place was intact and surrendered the CARE package he'd gotten from home. The platoon CPs gave up a spool of monofiliment line and half a dozen star cluster flares.

"At least we can chow down," Trumbull said. Saliva glistened in the corner of his mouth.

"There goes Baby-san," Copley said to West, "always thinking of his tummy."

West covered a giggle with his hand and leaned into Copley.

Trumbull did his best to ignore them.

"Later," Bingham said sharply. He was disappointed they didn't find more, but glad they found this much. He looked at the company CP and wondered how much longer it would be before they could go into it. "First we divide the ammunition."

"Think we'll need it, George?" Remington asked.

Bingham looked at him and said levelly, "I sincerely hope we won't. But if we do, I sure as hell want to have it." He turned to Peale. "Chuck, divide it."

Peale broke the belt into ten eighty-round sections and handed them around. The last 200 he divided evenly between Homer and West. Some of the Marines completely stripped their belts and stuffed the loose rounds into pockets, others linked the ends and slung them bandolier fashion around their chests.

Bingham looked at the loops of ammunition and wondered how much noise they would make; wondered if that noise was going to give them away some time when they needed to slip unnoticed past an enemy. But he didn't say anything, not yet. Then he turned his attention to the C rations. Twelve meals, thirteen men to feed.

Before the sergeant said anything about the problem Rivera saw it. He inspected the contents of his package: Vienna sausage, canned deviled ham, a can of refried beans. "Honcho," he said, "give Cs to everybody but me. I'll swap a taste of mine for a taste of what the others have." A grin split his face. "And dessert's on me." He held up a bag of chocolate chip cookies.

There were a few low cheers at sight of the cookies, restrained because nobody wanted to make too much noise. Bingham agreed. He dumped the C ration boxes out of the case and mixed them on the ground, covers down so nobody would know what any box held. Then he let his men pick blindly, Pratt first, then Trumbull and Stuart. Remington and Peale after the others; Bingham took the last box.

Rivera wasn't picky about what he took from the others. He swapped a Vienna sausage for a heaping spoonful of Ham and Limas, and some refried beans for a bite of Turkey Loaf.

"Let's get some security out, people," Bingham said once everyone had his food. "One man from each fire team to the perimeter, same areas you searched. Keep an eye on the open, let me know immediately if you see anybody."

"Save some cookies for me, Dago," Rush said as he headed for the perimeter.

"Everybody gets some, Chief," Rivera said back.

While he ate, Bingham watched the entrance to the company CP. Nothing stirred in the black hole of the opening, no one tried to come out, nothing moved in the air to indicate the willy peter smoke still filled the air. He continued looking for a few minutes after he finished eating. At last he stood and asked no one in particular, "Who wants to check out the command hootch with me?"

"You shitting me," Remington said and stood by his side. "I blew it, I check it out. You want to come along, you come along."

Bingham took a deep breath to control the surge of anger that came over him. "Follow me, Fred," he said. He strode toward the bunker without looking directly at the other man, though he saw him from the corner of his eye. He stopped outside the CP and squatted down, peering into its dimness. He sniffed the air, it was almost clear of the phosphorus smell.

"Don't be some kind of hero, Fred," he said. "The willy pete's probably still pretty strong inside. If it starts getting to you, get the hell out."

Remington grunted.

Bingham rose and ducked through the entrance. The air inside was acrid with the chemical smoke that had so recently filled the bunker. It burned his eyes and he blinked rapidly a few times, then squinted. He breathed shallowly to ease the pain it caused in his chest. A few feet to his left a kerosene lamp burned dimly. He turned up the wick and it glowed more brightly.

The two Marines searched the bunker by the lamp's glow. Four grotesquely contorted bodies were clustered near the center of the bunker floor. Their postures indicated they had seen the grenades before the first one went off and tried to scramble away from them. Behind a wooden bed frame Bingham found a fifth body lying in a puddle of vomit. An inspection didn't show any wounds. He thought this dead man managed to get away from the explosions and huddled there to protect himself from any other weapons and was overcome by the smoke. There was food, rice and greens that they left alone; it was probably too saturated with phosphorus to be edible. Two buckets of water were also left alone because of contamination. In a wooden ammo crate table, Bingham found an unopened bottle of halizone tablets which he pocketed. The last thing they found was a working radio.

"I'm taking the battery," Bingham said. He reached for the radio and stopped. A voice came from it, a Vietnamese voice. The two Americans listened for a moment.

"Sounds like someone's trying to call someone who doesn't want to answer," Remington said.

"Yeah," Bingham agreed. He felt uncomfortably that the unresponding radio was the one he was looking at. He stopped the voice by opening the battery compartment and removing the battery. He nudged Remington. "Let's grab the weapons," he said. The two did and left the bunker. The air outside was the sweetest and best he'd ever smelled.

"Chuck, destroy these things," Bingham said to Peale. Peale took the NVA weapons and fieldstripped them. He pocketed the bolts; the rifles would be useless without them. Then he emptied the ammunition from the magazines and used a rock to dent the magazines so they'd be unusable. He decided to keep the ammo and discard it piecemeal along the way, the same way he'd get rid of the bolts.

The twenty-foot antenna lay broken next to the bunker. "John, let's see how high we can make this thing stand," Bingham said to Copley. They managed to assemble enough of it on top of the CP bunker so that its top was fifteen feet above the hilltop. Then Bingham attached their radio, turned it on and listened on the various frequencies without hearing any transmissions. He tried broadcasting on several frequencies, frequencies he knew the Marines used. In a half hour of trying he got no response. Finally he gave up. Then he stood on the east side of the hill for a while looking into the distance. In the distance he heard sporadic gunfire and artillery fire.

After a few minutes Remington joined him and said, "It's easy, George, we go that way. Sooner or later we'll run into somebody."

Bingham nodded. "Mister Charles, most likely." It took West and Stuart fifteen minutes to get to the forest and return with Russell's body. Minutes later the squad, everyone feeling good from the first nourishing meal they'd had in several days, marched down the hill heading east.

Three miles closer to the sporadic gunfire, a radioman turned to his commander and told him he got no response from the squad he was trying to contact. The commander looked west for a moment as though he could see through the forest and hills between him and the hill where he had left a squad. Then he gave an order. A few minutes later a squad of North Vietnamese soldiers under the command of a battle-wise sergeant left the encampment, heading toward the hill Alpha Company had been driven off.

CHAPTER TWENTY-NINE

Little Bloody Riding Hood and the Big Bad Wolf

Eakins had the point. Remington complained about having the rear point again; he insisted they needed speed and he'd move them faster than Peale's men would.

"You heard that gunfire, Fred," Bingham said. "There's plenty of bad guys between us and friendly forces. We're going slow and cautious." He looked the other man in the eye and added, "Besides, you have to carry Russell."

Remington glared at Bingham.

"I'll cover our rear, Fred," West interrupted before anything else could be said. "Nobody gonna sneak up on us with me watching where we've been. And I can help Gil carry the body."

Remington's head snapped at him. "You can't do both," he said. "I'll help Gil."

There was no more discussion. Eakins stepped carefully along the forest trail, watching for booby traps and ambushes. For nearly a mile he saw nothing dangerous; no trip wires, no suspiciously trailing vines, no disturbed dirt on the trail, no odd pile of leaves that could conceal a punji pit, no indication of an enemy soldier. Then the short column stopped because halfway along its length Trumbull said, "Man I gotta take a piss something fierce," and turned to step into the forest.

"Stay on the trail," Rivera quickly said. "Tell John you're stopping." Trumbull was the lead man in the fire team; Copley was the next man ahead of him, right behind Bingham, who followed the point team.

Trumbull told Homer and faced the brush. He found a thin space to direct his stream through and relieved himself. Carelessly, he kicked some loose dirt at the wet place when he was through, swinging his foot into the brush, and hit a trip wire that wasn't visible from the trail. His swinging foot hit several leaves, twigs, and vines in addition to the trip wire, so he wasn't aware of hitting it. But he did notice the sudden hissing he heard.

"Snake?" he said quizzically. He knew snakes hissed, but had never heard one. It didn't seem to him that a snake would hiss this long.

A few feet away, Rivera also heard the sound; it was the fuse of a Chicom grenade. "Grenade," he shouted and dropped to the trail facing away from the hissing. All up and down the trail everybody else dropped as well. Except for Pratt.

Time expands into eternity when you're in an immediately life-threatening situation; something that lasts only seconds can seem to take minutes. Private Matthew Pratt heard Rivera's warning cry and realized it was possible he was about to get killed, so he thought about what was his best course of action. He realized he was within the grenade's killing zone and that there probably wasn't enough time for him to run out of it, especially not with thick forest on one side of him and other men on the trail behind him. He wondered if the foliage between him and the booby trap hid a tree trunk that would shield him from the grenade when it went off. Then he saw Rivera drop to the ground. He remembered in Boot Camp, his DIs had told them the surest way to win a Medal of Honor was to jump on a grenade, and they also said the hero's parents were awarded that Medal of Honor. The DIs said the best thing to do was take cover from the grenade and live to keep fighting—or, if there was time, grab it and throw it back. Then he saw Trumbull drop. Then it occurred to Pratt that it was a long time since Rivera gave the warning and the grenade hadn't gone off yet. It must be a dud, he thought. And grinned. He didn't want to be a dead hero—he'd never get his name changed to Private First Class Pratt if he was dead—but, hell, he could still make like a hero and get rid of that dud grenade. Maybe he'd get a Bronze Star for that and the Bronze Star would help him get renamed Private First Class Pratt.

He jumped over Rivera and broke through the brush where Trumbull had urinated. Right there, belly high to him on a tree trunk, was the grenade. He reached for it.

Rivera heard the hissing, shouted "grenade," and twisted away from Trumbull and dove to the trail. He was facing Pratt and saw the man stand frozen and drop-jawed for an instant. Then the young Marine bounded over him and ran in the direction of the booby trap. Rivera screamed, "Goddam it, Mattpratt, get down," and lashed out with a foot to trip him. His lashing foot missed, his words were drowned out by the grenade's explosion. It was a quick fuse, the grenade went off only three seconds after the wire was tripped.

Trumbull hit the deck immediately when he heard Rivera shout. He tried to scrabble away and cast one worried look back on his way. He saw Pratt burst into the brush where he had been standing. It happened so fast all he could do was look, stupefied, as the explosion blew Pratt back across the trail, a cloud of blood spraying behind him.

Bingham, a little farther up the trail, didn't see any of this. As soon as he heard the grenade go off he called, "Team leaders report."

"Mattpratt's down," Rivera called back.

Bingham jumped to his feet and ran back. "Anybody else, Dago?" he asked before he got there. Some back recess of his mind heard Peale and Remington shout their men were all right.

Rivera and Morse were kneeling over Pratt when Bingham got there, they had his shirt torn open and were trying to staunch the flow of blood from too many places on his chest and belly. For the moment they ignored the blood pooling from his legs and draining from his wrist where his right hand was missing.

Bingham looked at Pratt's pasty face, saw all the blood was flowing sluggishly and none spurting, watched as his shocked, unblinking eyes dried out and glazed over, and said, "He's wasted." Then he turned and rapidly walked away, fighting the gorge rising in his throat.

Rivera looked at Pratt's dead eyes and leaned back. "He's gone," he said quietly to Morse.

Big, baby-faced Trumbull stood slack-jawed, looking at Pratt. "Why the fuck'd you do a dumb thing like that, Mattpratt?" he asked, the ultimately unanswerable question. "You tryin'a get a medal or something?" His face twisted in the effort not to cry. It was his fault Pratt was dead; he was the one who hit the wire that set off the booby trap and if anyone should have died, it was him.

Rivera rocked himself from his knees to his feet and looked for a small tree to cut down for a litter pole. A few seconds later Morse pulled Pratt's poncho from under his belt and opened it on the ground.

"Gimme a hand, Baby-san," Morse said.

Trumbull started, stopped staring, and bent to help Morse lift Pratt's corpse onto the poncho and wrap it.

Bingham came back, walking slowly this time. "Be careful, people," he said to everybody. "Be fucking careful. Charlie's been here and he can get more of us if we aren't careful." His voice was hollow and his eyes empty. Two men dead from booby traps

in two days; it felt like too much. He looked at where the booby trap was set, guessed where Rivera and Trumbull had lain on
the trail, and wondered if Pratt saved their lives by giving up his
own. He couldn't tell. "Why'd you do it, Mattpratt?" he mumbled.

Less than a quarter mile away the Vietnamese squad sent to find
out why the radio transmissions to the hill weren't answered heard
the grenade go off and stopped. The NVA sergeant leading the
squad thought about it. In the forest he couldn't accurately judge
where it was; not the precise direction, not the distance. But he
made an educated guess based on years of jungle fighting, thought
about the implications, and made a decision.

He ordered his point man to hurry forward another hundred
meters, then pull off to the right side of the trail they followed.
Five meters off the trail he hustled them thirty meters farther parallel to it and then set half of his men in a position from which
they could either observe or ambush whoever came along. The
others he sent out in a screen to the north to spot anybody who
might try to pass above them. One man sat on a low ridge from
where he watched another trail.

Peale had been following directly behind Eakins on the point.
Now he inserted Rush between himself and the front man. Not
that he was cowardly, or in any way wanted to put an additional
remove between himself and the most dangerous spot in the column. He put Rush behind Eakins because he reasoned the two
together would be more likely to spot anything bad before it had
a chance to hurt them. When Peale erred, it was on the side of
caution, he didn't get men unnecessarily killed. Putting Rush up
with Eakins was the cautious thing to do.

Somehow, in a way neither of them could explain and no one
else could hope to comprehend, when Rush and Eakins worked
together each reinforced the other's capabilities. It was more than
simply the two best woodsmen in the company working together,
one spotting what the other missed; each of them became more
finely attuned to his surroundings. The squad moved more slowly
now because two men were being carried, fewer were ready with
their rifles. A little farther from where Pratt was killed, Eakins and
Rush stopped. The short column telescoped in on itself. Trumbull
got close enough to the front to overhear what was said.

Bingham pushed forward and found Peale with the other two.
"What's happening?" he asked.

"Don't know," Rush replied. He faced their direction of march, eyes unfocused, trying to absorb with his nose, mouth, and ears what it was that made him and Eakins stop.

Eakins stood next to him examining the forest the same way. "I got a feeling," he said softly.

Bingham didn't ask what kind of feeling; he sniffed the air, tasted the breeze, listened to the forest sounds. Nothing seemed out of the ordinary. Peale looked like he didn't know what the problem was, either.

Rush hunkered down and looked closely at the trail; he shifted from side to side to examine it from different angles. "Doesn't look like anybody's been along here in a couple of days," he said, then lifted his head to the front.

Eakins nodded.

Bingham looked down the trail. There were Marines in that direction. There were also bad guys between them and those Marines. "Off the trail, people," Bingham said softly. "If some-one's coming our way, I want to see them first." He thought again about the unanswered radio transmission and wondered if someone was coming to investigate.

Rush took the point from Eakins and led the squad into the brush along the left side the trail and forward so they were between whoever might be ahead of them and the place they broke through. Both the Marines and the NVA were in the brush on the same side of the trail.

Bingham lay next to Rush at the front end of the impromptu ambush. They waited a long five minutes without anybody coming into view.

"What do you think?" Bingham whispered into Rush's ear.

Rush shifted uncomfortably and didn't immediately answer. "I don't know," he finally said, and shook his head.

Bingham suddenly cursed himself. If there was somebody up ahead, they had to have heard the grenade and pulled into an ambush; he should have thought of that at once. "Keep alert," he said, and scooted away. He tapped Peale's shoulder as he passed, a come-along. Peale followed him as far as Rivera's position. "Fred up," Bingham said. Seconds later Remington joined them. Copley crouched nearby.

"If Chief and Night Stalker are right that there's someone near," he said to his fire-team leaders, "they must be in an ambush wait-ing for us."

Remington glanced at Rivera and a smile flashed across his face, an accusation that one of Rivera's men had done something

dumb and put them all in jeopardy. "Heard the booby trap and
knew we was coming." He seemed to have already forgotten one
of his men had done something dumb and gotten killed because
of it.

Rivera glared back at him.

"Maybe not," Bingham continued, not acknowledging the byplay between the other two, "but we aren't taking any chances;
we're going around to the north."

"How far north?" Peale asked.

Bingham looked at the thick forest mass and thought of how
difficult and time consuming breaking through it would be. "Until
we find another trail," he said. He paused a couple of seconds
to see if there were any other questions. When there weren't he
said, "Let's do it."

The going was hard. Rush and Eakins had to break a trail
through the thick brush, and they had to go silently. Somehow,
working in tandem, Rush and Eakins managed to find every thin
place in the brush and work their way through it without
breaking any branches or stepping on anything that went *crack*
or *squish*. The rest of the squad followed without making much
more noise, not even the men carrying the dead.

They climbed over a low ridge and Bingham felt easier. At the
bottom of the other side was a trail that hadn't been used much
recently—the jungle was reclaiming it. If the bad guys who might
have heard the booby trap were sitting in ambush, it was on the
other side of the ridge, so even though this trail was closer to
the other than Bingham liked, he signaled Rush and Eakins to
follow it.

Rush and Eakins thought the same thing about the possible
ambush location that Bingham did; his instructions seemed good
to them and they felt comfortable following the trail. They didn't
spot the well-hidden NVA watcher who saw them from the top of
the ridge, they didn't hear him slip away from his hiding place.
And because they were in the front of the column, they didn't catch
any sign of the NVA squad that minutes later started trailing them
from above.

The NVA sergeant was a seasoned soldier, a veteran of many
campaigns and battles against the French and the South Vietnamese and the Americans. He'd spent most of his adult life
in the jungles of both Vietnams and Laos and had learned how
to move through the forest undetected and how to live off it. He
once boasted he could slip up on a tiger unnoticed—then to quiet

the scoffers, did just that. Every time a new man joined his unit this sergeant spent as much time as necessary drilling him in silent, speedy forest movement. All the men in the squad with him now had gone through his drills until they were all capable of moving wraith-like through the jungle. The sergeant stopped them on top of the ridge and went down it alone to examine the trail below. The signs he found told him only a small number of Americans had come by; fewer than an NVA platoon, more than an NVA squad. A few deeper marks told him some of them were carrying extra weight. Dead men from the booby trap? It seemed likely. He returned to his squad, took the point himself, and led them along the top of the low ridge. They soon caught up with the Americans.

The man on the rear of the American column was an experienced soldier, the sergeant saw. The giant walked backward more than he faced forward. The sergeant nodded to himself, this was not the best place from which to strike. Ahead of the tail man two more men carried a body-sized bundle suspended from a pole. The sergeant pulled his squad along the ridge top faster than the Americans went on the path. At the front of the enemy column were two soldiers who made the sergeant slow down and move away from them; they felt to him like they could sense his presence without seeing or hearing him. He waited for the center of the American squad to catch up with him and examined it. Two of the giants—the one with the face of a child may have been the biggest giant he had ever seen—carried another oblong bundle on a pole.

The sergeant quickly thought and planned. The front of the column had six alert men, including two who looked to be superior soldiers. The last six men in the line were vulnerable, four of them were carrying their dead and unable to fight back instantly. Directly ahead of the bearers was the officer and his radioman. The sergeant didn't wonder what the Americans were doing here, he supposed they were a reconnaissance unit, just as he assumed their leader was an officer. He looked at his men and decided they were good enough so that he could simply face them toward the Americans and have them open fire without having to go forward and set up an ambush site that the Americans would walk into. Those two men in the lead scared him.

Speedily, he went from man to man and gave his orders. Then he positioned himself in the center of his squad and signaled them to move out fast. When he thought the leading man was far enough along he gave another silent signal. The lead man didn't look back, didn't see the signal, kept going. The sergeant gritted his teeth and hissed two words to stop the man and turn him.

Nine of the Marines on the trail were tense. Somewhere nearby, maybe, was an unknown number of bad guys. They were in a hurry to get out of this area; they wanted to get to where there were other Marines. On the point, Rush and Eakins insisted on going slowly. What made it bad for those nine was that Bingham agreed with Rush and Eakins. It was worse for Remington and Stuart, Trumbull and Morse, because they were carrying bodies. Russell, alive, weighed over two hundred pounds; Pratt was a solid 165. Dead, they both seemed to have gained weight.

Remington wanted to push his way forward, confront Bingham, make the squad go faster. But the only way he could go ahead was to give his end of the pole to West. That was too dangerous; West wouldn't be able to carry the burden and still keep a good watch on their rear. A rumble just below the level of audibility emitted from the big man's chest. Stuart felt the vibration through the other end of the pole. Behind Remington, the short hairs were standing up on the back of West's neck.

Trumbull was becoming overcome with guilt. It was his damn fault Mattpratt was dead. He took all the fear he'd felt in his time in-country, all the horror of battle, the frustration of how hard it was to find an enemy who would not stand and fight like a man, the rage he wasn't able to do anything about being called Baby-san, the guilt of Mattpratt's death, and turned it all in on himself. He was oblivious to his surroundings and gave Morse a hard time on the other end of the pole because of his uneven gait. Rivera was swearing to himself. Less than four weeks left in this stinking war and here he was in an impossible situation; it just wasn't any damn fair. He wasn't paying as much attention to his surroundings as he might have at another time.

Copley was panting slightly under the weight of the useless radio he'd been carrying for so many days. Bingham worried. All these lives depended so thoroughly on him and already two of them were lost. It didn't matter that he hadn't been close enough to prevent the two men from setting off the booby traps, he was in charge. His men's lives and safety were his responsibility. How many more miles, he wondered, until they reached other Americans and relative safety?

Rush and Eakins saw and smelled and tasted and absorbed everything they could ahead of them. They knew there were hundreds, maybe thousands, of bad guys between them and friendly forces. They knew if they made a mistake none of them might make it back alive. Peale fretted behind them, his skin crawled at the possibility of enemy nearby. Homer tried not to think of anything. He tried not to feel anything either. If he survived this he could go back to Alabama and not sweat nothing; there wasn't a damn thing the rednecks and Klansmen could do that was this bad.

Some of them heard something, a voice-like sound, on the ridge above them. There was an instant of mind-shattering silence while half the Marines dropped and faced the ridge, trying to spot what had made the noise, and the other half more slowly realized something was wrong.

On top of the ridge the sergeant saw the Americans drop and knew they had heard him. They were in it now and had lost the element of surprise. "Fire," he shouted to his men. Two of them fired immediately, the others opened up when they heard the first two shoot.

The Marines reacted more rapidly to the NVA sergeant's command, the half already down fired blindly uphill when they heard him shout. His shout was all the impetus the Marines still on their feet needed to drop to the ground; they opened fire as soon as they hit.

"Where are they?" Copley shouted. He wasn't going to waste his few grenade rounds firing blindly.

"I don't know," Bingham said less loudly. "Hang tight." His eyes roamed over the ridge, trying to pick out where the enemy soldiers were firing from. "Anybody see them?" he called out to his men.

"All the way topside," Rivera shouted back. "On top of the damn ridge."

"Slow fire," Bingham shouted. "Place your rounds. Chuck, your team hold your fire." Each semi-automatic rifle now had about 360 rounds. Bingham knew how fast a Marine could pull the trigger; he didn't want them to run out of ammo in one firefight, there might be another one yet to come. The firing from the trail slacked off, the fire from above didn't increase. Bingham looked along the ridge top and saw his men's bullet impacts; now he was able to make out where the enemy was. He said to Copley, "They seem to be from our position aft. Pop a couple willy petes up there, bracket them."

"Got it," Copley said. He broke his grenade launcher open, removed the high explosive round from its chamber and replaced it with white phosphorus. Carefully, he sighted through the trees and aimed his round to hit a few feet below the top of the ridge directly uphill. He fired, and a scream met the grenade's rosy burst. He broke the launcher open to reload and fired a second round where he thought the other end of the ambush was. Now there was shouting from above and the return fire abruptly ceased.

"They're running!" Remington shouted. "Let's get their asses." He leaped to his feet and charged up the ridge. West and Stuart looked toward Bingham to see if they were supposed to go with him.

"Fred, get down!" Bingham ordered.

Remington kept going.

Bingham swore. "Everybody, stay in place," he called and ran after Remington.

Trumbull was shivering, but not from fear. When the firefight started, he saw it as his punishment for killing Mattpratt. Then he saw it as his chance to atone for that death. He was startled when the fight stopped and didn't immediately realize that Remington was going after the NVA who had ambushed them. He didn't think he had done enough to make up for what he'd done earlier. But the noise Remington made running up the ridge finally got through to him and he stopped shivering. This was his chance. He didn't hear Bingham yell for everybody to stay in place; he was concentrating on how he was going to kill those bad bastards when he caught them. Him and Fred Remington were going to make the NVA pay for his mistake. Or he'd die trying. He was going to make up for causing Mattpratt's death.

Bingham heard footsteps thudding to his right and turned his head. "Goddam it, Baby-san," he roared, "stay here."

Trumbull didn't notice Bingham's order right away; he was trying to catch up with Remington. Bingham yelled again and Trumbull heard him the second time. His face burned with the "Baby-san" and made him more determined to go ahead. He looked at Bingham once, half plea, half defiance. "No!" The word squeaked out. He kept running.

They caught up with him just over the ridge top. The big man was on one knee, panting, the scar on his cheek stood out clear against his face. His eyes searched the brush, intense, intent, but he held his rifle negligently. "They got away," he said as soon as Bingham reached him and stood up. He looked levelly at Bingham and said, "We should 've had everybody come, might have caught 'em."

Bingham shook his head. "They got away from you, they would have got away from all of us."

"One of us might have seen what way they went. Maybe Chief or Night Stalker." He swept the land below them, the NVA were down there somewhere. "Chief and Night Stalker can still find where they went. Maybe we get 'em before they get back to their buddies, them and their buddies come after us and we're outnumbered."

"Their buddies heard the firefight, they're coming this way whether these get back to them or not." He grabbed Remington's upper arm and pulled. "Let's get back."

Remington resisted the pull for a moment, then rose. "I still say we find them, waste them."

"I say we're di-diing out of here." He headed back. Trumbull looked uncertainly at Remington, then followed Bingham. As Bingham went over the crest of the ridge he called out, "Team leaders report."

"First team okay," Peale called back.

"Third team all right," Rivera said.

Bingham looked over his shoulder. "Fred, team leaders report."

Remington snarled, then picked up his speed and called to West and Stuart. Both replied they were all right. He turned to Bingham. "Second team, present and accounted for." Then he stopped; he was at the NVA's ambush site. He looked at the ground and walked back and forth on it, looking for bodies or blood trails. He found blood near where one of Copley's grenades hit.

"At least one of 'em got hit," he said. "They're hurting, we should go waste the rest of them." He glared at Bingham.

"We're hurting, too," Bingham said back. "We're carrying two bodies, remember?" He headed toward the rest of the squad.

Remington looked quickly for more evidence of casualties, then followed. Trumbull went with Bingham; Rivera met him on the trail and said a few low words that made the young Marine blanch.

"Saddle up," Bingham ordered. "We're getting out of here before anybody else shows up."

"Hey, man," Remington said, "I told you we go find those suckers, waste them before they reach their buddies, come back with more and get us."

"And I told you their buddies heard the firefight and are already on their way here. Let's move out. Now."

Rush led off, quickly. The column moved forward in good order until it was Remington's turn to step out. He stood where he was. Stuart stood uncertainly, holding up one end of Russell's bier. West watched briefly, then stepped forward and picked up the end Remington should have been carrying.

"Go," West told Stuart. Stuart hurried to catch up with Trumbull. Remington swore about the cowards in the squad and followed. Soon he remembered he had rear point and started watching his rear.

A mile and a half to the east, the NVA commander heard the firefight. He listened to it intently and realized the last firing was from American M-14s. He knew none of his men carried M-14s. Now he issued another order. Lieutenant Vo Hien Phou was commander of one of his reserve platoons. He ordered Lieutenant Phou to split his platoon into squads and head west, find this American unit that was somewhere behind them, and eliminate it.

CHAPTER THIRTY
The Plots Thicken

The rest of the day was cat and mouse. Lieutenant Phou's cats kept closing in on the Marine mice, and the mice kept ducking out of sight in time. The Marines even managed to avoid stumbling into the line of mousetraps to their east. Night came, and the cats and mice lay low until dawn. The mice didn't know how close they were to the line of traps. Which was just as well; they wouldn't have been able to get any rest if they had known.

Phou talked to his commander over the radio. They agreed on a plan: since the Americans were so close to the battalion and headed that way, Phou and his platoon were to stay in place when the sun came up, let the Americans walk into the forces in front of them. When the survivors reeled back, they would be broken on the anvil of Phou's platoon.

The sun rose.

"You been wrong all the fucking way, George," Remington said. "Go around, you keep saying. Go around. Well, there ain't no way around and they're out looking for us now. We got two men wasted trying to go around. Time we blew a hole in their line and went through it." They were sitting cross-legged in the middle of the thicket, knees almost touching so they could talk quietly. The others were gathered close to hear.

Bingham stared at him for a moment and slowly shook his head. He didn't remind Remington how those two men had died, that one was partly Remington's fault. He didn't look directly at anyone but Remington, but saw the way West and Copley looked at each other, the glances Peale and Rivera exchanged, the way Homer glared at Remington, Rush and Eakins drew back. Only Trumbull didn't seem affected by the accusation.

"No way," Bingham said at last. "We can't go through them,

there's too damn many, they're too deep between us and other Marines."

"We don't know that, George," Remington said. "We haven't tried to go through. We've been trying to go around them for four days and haven't found anyplace they ain't."

"I say we do something else, we don't try to go through. Like you said, Fred, we've got two wasted. I don't want more." The dead were impossible not to notice; Russell and Pratt's bodies were bloating, starting to stink.

Remington leaned forward, shoving his face close to Bingham's, trying to intimidate by his large mass. His barroom scar stood clear and menacing. "We go through," he said with a sneer, then straightened back up and looked around at the others, looking for support for his position.

Some of them looked uncomfortable and turned their faces away, some shook their heads. Rivera glared. Homer said, "Fuck you," almost inaudibly. Only Trumbull, grim, seemed willing to follow him.

Bingham saw his chance to grab the initiative. "Chief, Night Stalker, you've been up front most of the time. What do you think?" He knew they wouldn't agree with Remington.

"I think there's boo-coo fucking Charlies in front of us," Rush said. "I don't think there's no damn way we can get through."

Eakins looked vaguely to the north. "I don't think we can get around them, either," he said.

Remington gave the two a deadly look and stood up. Trumbull started to rise, saw that no one else stood, sat back down. Remington looked down at Bingham. "So what are we gonna do, Honcho?"

Bingham tipped his head back to look Remington in the eyes. He tried not to let his face show what he felt. "We do something else," he said, then lowered his face and looked straight ahead, tried to look lost in thought.

"George," Remington started, but was interrupted.

"Bingham's the honcho, Fred," Peale said. "He's the man responsible, we do what he says.

"That's right," Rivera immediately backed Peale. "Bingham's a number-one honcho. We do what he says."

Others murmured their assent.

Remington pursed his lips in a you-got-me smile. The smile seemed to also say: You wait, my turn's coming.

Finally Bingham realized what he should have thought of several days earlier. He stood up and said decisively, "What's happening is the big push that we've been hearing rumors about. What our people are going to do is some serious ass kicking and push them right back. We're going to go back and find a place to hole up until other Marines reach us."

They all looked at him for a quiet moment. It was just too obvious. They all wondered why they hadn't thought of it before.

Copley and West leaned into each other. "Why the fuck didn't we think of that?" they asked.

Peale smiled wryly—Bingham was right. He knew it.

Rivera shook his head in wonder at how it can take so long to notice the obvious.

Homer leaned his head all the way back and stared at the treetops.

Remington snorted. " 'Bout time you come up with something right," he said.

Only Trumbull didn't seem relieved, he seemed preoccupied, not paying much attention to what the others were saying.

"Where do you want us to go, Honcho?" Rush asked. He and Eakins stood and donned their gear.

Bingham didn't have to think about it. The CAP's compound was too depressing, so was the village where it had been located— not to mention unhealthy with all those dead bodies littering it. If the bad guys hadn't put fresh people on Alpha Company's hill yet, they were going to. There was only one place he knew that had any kind of food. "Back to the banana grove," he told them. "Saddle up."

Rush and Eakins stood close for a moment, talking, making sure they remembered where the banana grove was and how to get there. "We're ready," they finally said.

Relaxed, the squad headed west, in the same order as the day before. They were relaxed enough so that they didn't notice all of the signs that might have told them they were walking into somebody.

At dawn Lieutenant Phou was on the radio with his headquarters. Their plan remained the same.

Phou had his sergeant make sure the men of the platoon knew the plan and set them in a line to intercept the Americans when they were thrown back. Everyone in the platoon was alert for the Americans to come into their trap. But they expected to hear gunfire first when the Americans walked into the blocking force, and they expected to easily crush the remnants of the small American unit.

There was something headquarters didn't tell Lieutenant Phou,

information that could only be transmitted over secure radios—
and Phou's radio wasn't secure enough. The General Offensive
had already been beaten back in most of the country. Battle continued to rage in only a few places, and was waning in most of
them. The two fights still going on where the People's Army and
the National Liberation Front still had a chance to win were Khe
Sanh and Hue City. The battalion to which Lieutenant Phou's platoon belonged was about to be sent into Hue to try to turn the
tide.

So, as the Marine squad approached the NVA platoon, neither
expected to encounter the other—not just yet, at least.

Eakins led, following one of the basic tenets of ground warfare:
never return by the same route you went out on. The squad was in a
shallow declivity between two low ridges. The path they followed
east ran along the south side of the declivity; the trail Eakins broke
through the brush was on its north side, some fifty meters away.
He had no way of knowing there was an NVA platoon ahead of
him, that he was going on a route that would take him past its very
edge, a flank the squad could assault and roll up if they knew it
was there—if they were on an offensive operation. A flank they
could easily go around, if they knew it was there—and if two of
Lieutenant Phou's men hadn't decided to climb halfway up the
next ridge.

The two men didn't climb up the ridge to act as a flank observation post or to block anybody coming along the ridge. They
climbed it to be out of the line of fire when the remnants of the
American unit came at them. These two soldiers had been awake
half the night on guard, and they were tired. They agreed between
themselves that since there would be gunfire before the Americans
turned back to them, it was safe for them to get a little sleep while
they waited—as long as one of them retained enough awareness to
notice their sergeant's approach before the sergeant caught them
napping.

The trees blocked most of the direct sunlight from reaching the
ground. The earth was moist and covered with decaying leaves
that muffled footsteps, contributed to the silence of the forest. Few
birds sang and few insects chirred. It wasn't the kind of silence that
says, Someone's coming, it was more an anticipatory kind of quiet.
When he was younger, Eakins had gone to at least one Steelers
game each fall. This wasn't the kind of deafening silence that
fell over the stadium when the Dallas Cowboys hit on a bomb
to roll the score up to 35–13 in the third quarter, it was more

the expectant hush preceding the home team kicking the winning field goal. Eakins's skin crawled. He looked with worried eyes at Rush. Rush glanced back. He didn't know, either, but it felt funny to him, too.

Peale followed; he didn't notice anything out of the ordinary—if anything could be called ordinary when armed men are prowling through a forest trying to avoid other armed men looking to kill them. Homer was also unaware of anything wrong. Then came Bingham and Copley, alert and somewhat nervous, but feeling more secure now that they knew they were no longer looking for a hole in an enemy line that probably didn't have any holes. Next Rivera led Morse and Trumbull who carried Pratt between them.

That's when one of the two soldiers on the ridge side opened his eyes to make sure the sergeant wasn't coming. He went rigid, his eyes bugged, and sweat popped on his upper lip. He wanted to scream; he wanted to sink into the earth. He knew he could not let the Americans get through, just as well as he knew if he survived the fight, he would have to answer to the sergeant about why the Americans got halfway through where he was supposed to be before he responded to their presence. He knew how swift was People's Army justice, how irreversible the punishment for dereliction of duty. He nudged his companion, then opened fire on the nearest giant, one helping to carry a large bundle. Then he turned to fire at the other giant carrying that bundle.

It happened so fast Trumbull couldn't tell which came first; Morse grunted and stumbled, and there was a single gunshot. Then there were many gunshots, and Bingham and Rivera were yelling, Remington was roaring. Trumbull bent over to put down his end of the litter. He wasn't really aware of the bullet that zipped over his back, through the space he'd just occupied. He lowered himself to his knees and looked uphill to where the enemy gunfire was coming from. He saw a soldier there, looking terrified, firing downhill. Calmly, he raised his rifle to his shoulder, aimed, and pulled the trigger. As if in slow motion, he saw the man he shot at flinch, then topple backward, a red rose blossoming on his chest. There was no more gunfire from uphill, but shouting continued and there was other gunfire. It got through to him the fire was coming from the Marines at his sides; different fire came from his rear.

He twisted around, still erect on his knees, and suddenly understood what had happened; they'd blundered through a small hole near the end of an enemy line. A smile grew across his face, a contented smile. This was his chance, he knew it was, his chance to make up for killing Mattpratt. He bent low at the knees and waist and looked left and right. The other Marines were down, returning fire at the enemy. There was a gap on his right where Mattpratt's body lay; on his left Remington was concentrating on finding targets and shooting at them, and yelling at West and Stuart, telling them where to shoot. Nobody was paying attention to him. He scooted backward, then lowered himself to the ground and low-crawled behind Remington.

As he crawled he listened to the fire. Selectively, he filtered out the booming of the Marines M-14s, listened only to the cracking of the bad guys' rifles. Over the fire he also heard high-pitched shouts in Vietnamese, the commands of their leaders. It was evident to him, however many of them there were, that they were on a line perpendicular to the squad. The shouted orders were to get them faced so more of them could fire. He scuttled to the side and forward of the squad and waited. His wait was short.

Trumbull heard the slapping of feet running in his direction. He aligned himself to the sounds and put his rifle to his shoulder. A running figure flashed into his view and he shot three fast rounds at it, just like he'd been taught in ITR. The running man flung out his arms, staggered back, and fell. Then he saw two more. The other two didn't see him, they thought the fire that hit their buddy came from the Marines in front of them, and didn't realize someone had moved to their flank. They dropped into firing positions to add their fire to what the Marines were already facing. Trumbull drilled the closer one through the side and he slumped dead. Then he couldn't see the next one because the corpse was between them. He let go of his trigger and drew his bayonet. He fixed it on his rifle, then gathered himself for a charge. He took a deep breath and bolted up into a sprint. He bounded over the corpse and put a bullet into the face of the next NVA just as the man was turning his head to see what made the noise.

Just beyond him was another soldier firing at the Marines. He never saw or heard anything from his side; all he ever felt was the sharp, burning pain of Trumbull's bayonet driving through his back. The pain was brief; the bayonet tore his heart open, and exposed it to the air. He died.

Now Trumbull raged like a madman. He knew he was on the flank of the bad guys' new line; he screamed and bellowed incoherent noises in a strangled voice and ran straight along the NVA line, shooting and slashing and jabbing and grunting when he slashed or jabbed. And every man he shot or slashed or jabbed at died.

Bingham heard the strangled-voice scream and just that fast, he knew who it had to be. The enemy fire shifted, not all of it was coming at the squad now, some was going to the side. Every time he heard Trumbull shoot or grunt the enemy fire eased slightly.

"Trumbull, get down!" he shouted as loud as he could. "Get your ass down, Baby-san."

The screaming continued.

"Fred, cease fire on your side of the line," Bingham shouted. "We've got people in front of you." Then he swore to himself, wondering if Remington was leading the flanking movement; it would be just like him, he thought. But it wasn't; he heard Remington shouting to West and Stuart to stop shooting.

"Chuck," he called to his right, "keep those bad bastards down. I'm taking Fred's team, get Baby-san."

"Check," Peale called back. Then to the rest of the squad, "Keep them low, move them around, keep 'em to the right, people. We've got friendlies coming from our left."

Bingham bolted to his left. "Join John," he ordered Rivera when he darted past. He saw Morse collapsed and knew he was out of it, if not dead. He didn't wait to see Rivera scuttle to his right to join the rest of the squad.

Bingham dropped to his knees next to Remington. "When I say, all four of us go," he told Remington and his two men. "We'll come in behind Baby-san and bulldog him. Gil, once we get there, watch our rear in case he left any warm ones behind him." He looked to both sides, saw the three men looking at him, waiting for his command. "Now. On me."

As one, the four Marines surged to their feet and forward. Bingham led them at a run, and they crashed noisily through the brush.

"Baby-san, we're coming," Bingham shouted. "Friendlies joining you, Trumbull." And hoped Trumbull heard him, that he didn't turn and fire at them when he heard them coming up behind him.

Then they were behind Trumbull. Bodies lay scattered around them. "Right flank, move," Bingham shouted. "Gil, watch our rear. Fred, Ben, let's go get him."

Ahead of them, in their new direction, Trumbull screamed wordlessly, incoherently, primordially. They heard the clash of metal striking metal, the thunk of steel chopping wood. They burst through a screen of leaves and screamed like Trumbull did, joined his primordial screaming.

The big, baby-faced Marine stood in a tiny clearing; he stood like a cornered grizzly, screamed his fury, and slashed to all sides at half a dozen small men who circled him, thrusting their bayonets at him. They grunted and growled, they didn't scream. They didn't fire, they couldn't; if they did and missed they might hit one of their own. Trumbull didn't fire; he couldn't, his magazine was empty.

The tableau froze for an instant when Bingham and the men with him screamed. Then four of the NVA circling Trumbull wheeled away from him to face the new threat. The Marines charged before they could fire. Trumbull moved like a snake and slammed the butt of his stock into the side of the head of one of the two who didn't turn away. The other took advantage and lunged with his bayonet fully extended. Trumbull screamed again, a high, piercing scream. A slash from West made that NVA open his mouth to give the first scream any of the NVA made, but it never came out—the slash tore out his throat.

The Marines roared and bellowed and slashed and slammed and then the NVA were all down.

Bingham knelt next to Trumbull and started examining the wound deep in his side. Blood flowed copiously from it. Bingham tore open a compress bandage and held it tightly to the wound. In the background he was barely aware of Vietnamese voices shouting and whistles blowing; he hardly heard the enemy gunfire cease and the sound of men running away.

Trumbull's eyes were moist, tearing. His face relaxed sleep-like, grimaced in pain, relaxed again, over and over. Sweat flooded over his face and his breath came in gasps when he grimaced; no breath came when he relaxed. "Did I do good?" he finally asked weakly. "I got Mattpratt killed. Did I do good killing Charlie?"

The bandage seemed to do nothing to staunch the flow of blood. "You did good—" Bingham paused for a second and knew he couldn't call him Baby-san now. "—Marine." He gestured for another compress bandage. "You wasted boo-coo Charlies. You're a number-one gyrene." He took the bandage Remington stuffed into his hand and jammed the first one deep into the hole in Trumbull's side, slapped the second one on top of it, held it tight. Then he stopped holding it and rocked back on his heels. He stopped holding the bandage because Trumbull took one heaving breath and his chest stayed expanded, his eyelids stopped blinking, and his eyes dried. He was dead.

CHAPTER THIRTY-ONE
Ten Little Indians

It was nearly panic city on both sides after the firefight. Two more Marines were dead and the others more scared than ever. They grabbed their dead and ran westward, away from the North Vietnamese.

The North Vietnamese were stunned that the Americans had walked into their ambush and still hit them so hard. They were convinced they'd encountered a far larger force than they'd expected. Most of them ran east without bothering about their casualties. It took Lieutenant Phou and his sergeant half an hour, after he radioed in his report and got new orders, to round up enough of them to sweep through the area of the firefight. A dozen NVA were dead or badly wounded, most of them from Trumbull's one man flank attack. Phou and his sergeant examined the two bloodstains that didn't have bodies laying on them.

"The Americans now are carrying four dead," Phou said. The pools of blood were too large for the men to have only been wounded, and the pools didn't trail anywhere.

The sergeant agreed and added, "They can't go far or fast."

They collected their dead and wounded and carried them to the battalion headquarters.

The lieutenant colonel commanding the battalion sat on a reed mat on the ground and stared sternly for a long moment at the young lieutenant standing at rigid attention in front of him. He was deciding exactly what to say to make sure the young man knew he was not pleased with his platoon's conduct. He examined Phou's face while staring at him and saw the conflicting emotions on it; embarrassment at how things had gone, fury to correct the wrong, and determination to get the job done right if given another chance.

He relented in his decision to give a reprimand, one that would go into Phou's record.

Instead, he said in a cold voice, "You know that was unacceptable behavior, Lieutenant. Don't bother answering, I know you know it. You have brought shame upon yourself and on this battalion. There is no excuse for a platoon to run from a squad, even if that squad hits first. Especially when that platoon has a company nearby and an entire battalion close to it."

The muscles at the corners of Phou's jaw twitched in anger.

"I am going to give you a chance to redeem yourself. You will take another unit to the west and you will find those Americans and kill them. There is a company that has been badly injured, its officers were all killed and it only has enough men left to form two full platoons. You will take—" He referred to a clipboard, "—the 145th company. Neither you nor anyone else in that company will return until every one of those Americans is dead."

Two whole platoons in addition to his own men! Phou exalted. With that many men it would be a short fight once the Americans were located. Then the lieutenant colonel brought him back down.

"As for your former platoon, the men who ran, they will also be given a chance to redeem themselves. They will be in our van when we enter the battle in Hue City." His mouth twisted in disgust when he added, "They will not be able to run when they again encounter the Americans, there will be an entire battalion directly to their rear, there will be nowhere for them to run to. Now, take those two platoons and go. Bring back the right hands of the Americans to prove you have killed all of them. Go."

Phou saluted stiffly, wheeled, and marched away. He stopped before leaving the battalion headquarters to ask a staff officer where to find the 145th company, then headed directly toward it. A runner preceded him to tell the company's senior sergeant, who was the ranking man remaining, that Phou was coming to lead them on a special mission. Information on what had happened earlier had preceded the runner. The platoons that headed west with Lieutenant Phou twenty minutes later went hesitantly.

The ten Marines lay panting under the banana trees. They felt as if they'd run the entire distance instead of only part of the way. Bingham soon realized he heard no sound of pursuit and slowed the squad to a fast walk; he didn't want them worn out too fast from carrying the four bodies. They pushed hard. They knew it wasn't going to be long before someone came after them. Somebody had to come soon; they were certain of that.

"There it is, right where we left it," Eakins gasped when they reached the banana grove.

Everyone wanted to collapse immediately, recover from the forced march. Bingham wouldn't let them.

"Somebody might be right on our tail. If there is, I want to be ready for them." He put Homer and Eakins in a listening post a hundred meters east of the grove, the rest went into a defensive circle near the stream that flowed through it. Bingham made them all stay alert for a half hour before he allowed anyone to fill depleted canteens.

"Goddam, those bodies starting to stink," Remington said when they finally relaxed.

Bingham grunted. He was thinking about that problem. Russell had been dead for two days, Pratt for one. They were bloating, flies were buzzing loud around the ponchos they were wrapped in.

"So what are we going to do, Honcho?" Remington demanded in a louder voice than was needed. Bingham knew he said it that loud to get the others' attention. "We leave those bodies laying like that, every bad bastard in I Corps gonna know where we are, just follow their noses." He grinned, challenging. "No way we can leave them like that. Forget about Mister Charles, we won't be able to stand the stink."

Bingham grunted again, still thinking. It would be all right, he decided, they could find them easily enough again later; they all knew where this banana grove was. He looked at Remington. "Bury them," he said.

"Sure 'nuff, Honcho." Remington grinned wider. "What you gonna use for E-tools, dig the holes with?"

"You and Gil have bayonets, Ben's got a K-bar. Everyone in this squad has a blade. There's trees around. Use the blades to make spades. Use them to dig a grave. Do it. Now." His eyes were cold, so was his voice.

Remington glared at Bingham for a long moment without saying anything or making any move to follow orders.

"Like you said, Fred, we can't leave them like they are," Bingham said after a while. "You got a better idea? Let me hear it if you do. If you don't, get moving. Make one hole." He waited, but Remington didn't voice any other ideas. "Use everybody except the two men on LP. Keep out Chuck and Dago, I need them for security." He glared back just as hard. "Do it."

"Aye-aye, Honcho," Remington finally said. He wasn't happy with this: Bingham gave him the order to take care of the problem he raised, the best solution they had to the problem. The only other thing they could do was leave the bodies someplace other than where they were. But Marines never leave their dead behind. Burying the bodies was the only thing they could do. He twisted around. "Chief, you got your tomahawk?" Again, his voice was louder than necessary.

"Keep it down to a low roar, people," Bingham called softly. Remington looked like he didn't hear, or was deliberately ignoring him, but his next orders were given in a lower voice.

Muffled chopping came as Rush cut a few branches from banana trees to make shovels from; other noises were made by West and Stuart clearing detritus, weeds, and brush from a small patch of ground to dig the grave. Bingham went to where Rivera sat brooding and sat next to him. Peale discreetly joined them.

"It's a motherfucker, Dago," Bingham said.

"No shit," Rivera said in a dull voice.

"But it happens."

They sat silent for a few moments, Bingham watching Rivera closely without staring.

"I wish I was a PFC," Rivera said after Bingham thought the silence had gone on too long. "Now I know."

Bingham didn't let his puzzlement show on his face. "Why?" he asked. "What do you know?"

"It was a sign. I wish I'd paid attention to it. This never would have happened."

"Tell me, Dago, what was a sign?"

Rivera looked at Bingham, he wanted Bingham to believe what he was about to say. "I was a fire-team leader when you joined us. I lost that fire team to you. It happened again when Cooper came. Then Peale. I should have paid attention, I'm not supposed to be a fire-team leader, I'm not supposed to be in charge of men's lives. God—" He looked off as though trying to see what god this was, "—doesn't want me responsible for other people."

Bingham blinked rapidly several times. This idea of Rivera's was absurd. "That's bullshit, Dago, and you know that," he finally said.

"No bullshit," Rivera said and shook his head vehemently. "Straight scoop. I never got my second stripe, so every time a corporal joined the squad I lost my fire team. God was trying to tell me something, and I didn't listen. Now he took all the men I was responsible for." He looked pleadingly into Bingham's eyes.

"Don't you see, Honcho? God's punishing me for not listening when he sent the earlier messages."

Bingham's jaw worked while he thought frantically, looking for something to say in answer to this. "No punishment, Dago. Look where you've been for the past year, you've been in a shooting war. You've seen plenty of men wasted or crippled. Do you think God cares what you do? What kind of god would let this happen? Well, what kind of god would allow war? Men get killed in war, Dago, God's got nothing to do with it. He sure as hell isn't telling you what you are or aren't supposed to do."

"Then why did all three of my men get wasted?" Rivera asked defiantly. "Tell me that, Honcho.

"Because it happens, that's all. It happens."

"Uh-huh."

Bingham looked at Rivera speculatively for a moment, then said, "Dago, you lost three men in two days. I lost four men in three days. Do you hear me saying God's got a hard-on for me?"

"They weren't all your men like it was all of mine."

"Man, you get off this shit." Bingham couldn't think of anything else to say. He knew he had to keep a close watch on Rivera from now on until he got over his guilt. "It wasn't your fault, Dago, be cool. It wasn't your fault." He looked past Rivera at Peale.

Peale looked back and shook his head, he didn't know what to say either. He reached a hand out to Rivera's shoulder and patted it gruffly. "It's tough, man," he said softly. "But don't blame yourself. It's like Bingham said, these things happen. Could of been anybody."

"It wasn't anybody, it happened to me, all of my men got wasted." He looked away from Bingham, but not toward Peale. "Don't rearrange the squad to give me a new fire team, I don't want one. My men will only get wasted, that's all. God doesn't want me to be in charge." He went silent, looking nowhere into the brush.

Bingham tipped his head to the side, signaling Peale for the two of them to leave him alone. Peale backed away and Bingham joined him.

"The man's hurting," Bingham said when they were far enough away. "We have to keep an eye on him, make sure he doesn't do something dumb and get himself killed."

"Roger that," Peale said. He looked to where the rest of the squad was now digging the hole the four corpses would be buried in. "He doesn't want a fire team now, you going to put him in Fred's?"

"No." Bingham considered for a minute. "I think I'll keep him with me. If we need a third fire team, him, John, and me can be it."

Peale nodded. "Sounds good to me. What do you want me to do now?"

"Take a couple of full canteens to Homer and Night Stalker, they haven't gotten fresh water since we got here. You have two that got dosed with halizone long enough ago?"

Peale nodded.

"Give those to them, trade for empties, and fill the empty ones. Remember the halizone."

"Right." Peale looked across the banana grove in the direction of the listening post. "Back in a skosh bit." He trotted away.

Bingham went to examine the grave. A space about six by seven feet was cleared of growth and grove droppings. Rush was near one end of the space chopping at the ground with his tomahawk. Copley, West, and Stuart were at the other end, using their makeshift shovels to dig out the broken earth. The four bodies were neatly laid alongside the developing hole. Remington was standing opposite the bodies, watching. He looked up at Bingham's approach.

"How deep you want it?" Remington asked.

"Make it four feet. This isn't permanent, four feet should be enough to hold in the smell."

Remington nodded. "Spend enough time in the Crotch, you get some real shit jobs." He shook his head. "This is the worst shit job I ever had," he said soberly.

Bingham glanced at him, this was one of the few times Remington didn't have a challenge in his voice. "Someone's got to do it," he said.

Remington looked over at Rivera, who still sat looking into the brush. "Guess it's my turn, isn't it." It wasn't a question.

"Guess so."

West nudged Copley. "He's got a shit job?" he whispered. "What the fuck does he think we got?"

"He's a corporal, pano," Copley whispered back. "What a corporal thinks is a shit job is choice duty to us peons."

They rolled and tucked their heads into each other's shoulders to muffle their laughs.

"Shitcan the grab-assing, people. We got a grave to dig."

"We?" Rush muttered, casting a quick glance at the big corporal. "He got a turd in his pocket? I don't see him down here."

Stuart threw him a quick grin but didn't say anything. Copley and West went back to digging.

"Four feet," Remington said.

"Four feet," Bingham confirmed.

"Gonna take awhile, digging with branches."

"We've got all the time we need. Until other Marines come back."

"Right."

They stood quietly for a few minutes, watching the four men dig. The diggers worked slowly; they were still recovering from the run from the firefight. And they'd only had two proper meals in the past five days.

Bingham pondered the problem of food while they watched. There were bananas growing on the trees, but they could only subsist on a banana diet for so long. He had to do something to get other food for them. He didn't think any of the villages in the area would be any help; they hadn't seen any with people and food. Except for the one chicken. Rush and Eakins did a lot of hunting when they were teen-agers. He decided to talk to them later, see if they knew how to trap—there might be some kind of game in the area they could catch. It would be a big help if they could. They couldn't risk the noise of hunting with their rifles.

Bingham shook himself out of his reverie. "I'm going to scout around, see what there is to see."

Remington nodded. He didn't ask what the squad leader expected to find, probably nothing, but he had to look. Just in case. It's what he would have done himself.

Bingham didn't find much. The banana trees still marched in their rows, their neat order broken by saplings and weeds and brush. The small stream bubbled along its rocky bottom as though war never came near, never bothered it. He left the grove and wandered around it through the surrounding brush. On the south side he found a hollow, not much of one, but a low place nonetheless. He made a mental note of it; if they had to fight in the banana grove, that low place was more easily defended than the level ground. Other than trees and bushes and weeds the only other thing he found was a complex tracery of small game trails. There were fresh-looking tracks on some of the game trails. If Rush and Eakins knew how to trap, they could get food. The grove was looking up as a place to wait for the return of other Marines. If the NVA didn't find them first they were in good shape.

He returned to the grove. Peale was helping dig; Rivera was spelling Rush on the tomahawk. The grave was halfway done.

"Listen up," Bingham said when he reached the hole. "I found a low place over there." He pointed to the south side of the grove. "That's where we are going to stay. No fighting holes. If any bad guys come by I don't want this place to look like anybody's staying here." He looked at the men, taking a break from their digging and saw how worn they were. "John, Gil, go spell Homer and Night Stalker on the LP. They can come dig for a while."

Copley and Stuart grunted acknowledging, thanking words and climbed out of the hole. They picked up their weapons and cartridge belts and headed out. Bingham would have sent Rush instead of Stuart, but he wanted him and Eakins together so he could talk to them about trapping.

Remington dropped into the hole. "Take a break, Ben," he said. "I'll dig for a bit."

It took longer than it should have, but they got the grave dug. Bingham supervised laying the poncho-wrapped bodies in it. Then he lined up his men, less Copley and Stuart who were still in the listening post, in two ranks facing the covered grave. They stood at parade-ground attention. He stood to the side of the two ranks and said a few words.

"They were good Marines. They were our brothers. They lived with us, they fought alongside us, they bled with us. When we sweated, they sweated. When we went hungry, they went hungry. Their fight is over, but ours continues. Someday ours will end as well. Now we lay them to rest. Not forever, though. First they will be moved from here back to the World. Then they will rest forever. Just as they will live forever, as does every man who was ever a Marine. They will live with us who knew them, with other Marines who fight this war, with all Marines in the future. They were, they are Marines. Marines never die, we just keep going." His voice broke and he went silent.

"Old Marines never die," Remington said softly. "They go to hell and regroup."

No one else said anything.

Bingham abruptly stiffened and quietly barked, "*Pre*-sent, *arms*."

The seven men standing at attention briskly brought their rifles up and held them vertically in front of their bodies in formal salute. Bingham gave a hand salute. "Good night, brothers," he said. "Sleep the good sleep." He turned to the rest of his men. "Order, arms." They sharply lowered their rifles back to their sides, still standing at attention. "Fall out." They broke ranks. "Now let's get some shit back on this grave, cover it so it can't be spotted."

AFTER-ACTION REPORT:

The Confusion of the Long Distance Warrior

From the Analytic Notes of R.W. Thoreau, Lt. Col., USMC (ret.)

They had a saying in World War II: "There's no such thing as an atheist in a foxhole."

It didn't matter what a man believed before the shooting started, once it did start, he prayed whatever prayers he knew to whatever god he believed in. If he didn't know any prayers, he made them up. If he didn't believe in any god, he found one to pin his hopes on. What the man in the foxhole prayed for was deliverance; he prayed that he'd survive the insanity of war and go home alive, sound in body and mind.

Of course in World War II the Marines, soldiers, and sailors had a good idea of what they were fighting for. In the Pacific, the Japanese had attacked us and we were defending ourselves. In Africa and Europe, we were combating Hitler's evil. Wherever we fought, we killed people, took ground, held it, and pressed on to new ground to take and keep. We were clearly liberators. No doubt about it, we were the good guys.

It was different in Vietnam.

In Vietnam they said no one in a foxhole could believe in a god. Not a good god anyway.

LBJ didn't want a big war, he wanted it to have a low profile, to not upset the taxpayers—the voters. A national policy and objective were never clearly articulated. The country never went on a war footing, the people weren't rallied behind the war effort. Most people didn't know what the hell we were doing fighting a war in some country halfway across the world that most of us had never heard of. All most of the people knew was that every night Walter Cronkite and David Brinkley showed them pictures of their sons, brothers, boyfriends, and husbands getting bloodied and killed in stinking rice paddies or dense jungles in some obscure Oriental country whose name they had trouble pronouncing. The troops felt this lack of support. Eventually that lack of support turned into active opposition to the war and much of that opposition was directed at the men fighting it.

It started out as a counterguerrilla war; the troops took sniper fire and suffered from spot raids on their bases and defensive positions. They went out in large numbers in search of an elusive enemy. The local farmers and fishermen wore black pajamas. The guerrillas wore black pajamas. Hell, you couldn't tell the players apart even *with* a scorecard. They had to wait for someone to shoot at them before they could shoot back. Freaky, man, freaky. And they usually knew the official body counts often couldn't be right, they didn't usually see the enemy dead—at least not that many. Turns out, though, that in the aggregate the body counts were pretty accurate. Still, this obsession with body counts bothered the troops. Eventually the North Vietnamese Army took over the combat duties on the other side in the war. But even the NVA used the same basic hit-and-run tactics the VC used.

Body counts. Vietnam was a war of attrition. The only ground we took and held was the ground where we put our bases. Try to explain a war of attrition to a young man who grew up watching John Wayne and Aldo Rey liberate Europe and capture Pacific islands. Odds are he's not going to understand what you're talking about. What he's going to know is; "Hey, we took this hill last week, last month, whenever. What's going on here, you telling me we gave it back? Why'd my buddies die?" Don't tell him not to worry, we're killing ten times as many of them as they're killing of us. He doesn't care how many of them we kill, he wants only to survive this mess. He's not dumb, you know. Anyway, it doesn't take a big brain to figure out the flip side of us killing ten times as many of them. To him, a war of attrition means we're deliberately sending him out to get killed.

We sent 3.4 million men and a few thousand women into that war. Note I didn't say to fight it. Only ten percent of those troops were actually involved in combat operations. Don't think the man humping with a rifle through the mud and heat didn't know this. He was very aware that for every one of him there were nine or ten others back in Da Nang or Kontum or Cam Ranh Bay or Saigon, drinking cold beer, watching television, sleeping on sheets, and never getting shot at. He resented that. What did he do to deserve this, why was he the ten-percenter laying his life on the line? How come somebody else got to be an air-conditioner mechanic or a swimming pool life guard? He wasn't a bad boy, he obeyed his mother and paid attention in school—sometimes anyway.

To this day a lot of those combat veterans have no respect for someone who calls himself a Vietnam veteran, but who only drove a desk in Nha Trang.

When the warrior was able to come in from the field he didn't get the sheets and the TV—he got jammed into hardback tents or Quonset huts or other structures that simply weren't big enough to hold that many people. He'd go to the PX to get some of the necessities—soap, toothpaste, razor blades, lighter fluid, stationary—but maybe they wouldn't let him into one of the big PXs that had those things, only into a rinky-dink PX that was out of most of those necessities. Non-base personnel couldn't use the main PX, he'd be told, there's too big a problem with this stuff winding up on the black market.

Then he'd go and look in the display windows and see the goods that were winding up on the black market. Hi-fi sets, cars, jewelry, evening gowns, bikinis, electric washing machines. He'd look at those things and say to his buddy: "Take one bodacious long extension cord, plug that hi-fi into a socket where we go."

"Yeah, but think of it," his buddy would reply, "we got an extension cord that long, we could sell someone that washing machine, too."

"No can do, they don't got indoor plumbing."

"What about a car, think we could sell a car to somebody, make a bundle on that?"

"No way. Only one a these little gook Vietnamese I ever seen had enough jingwah to pay for an American car was a Vee Cee paymaster. And I blowed his ass away."

"Well, maybe we can souvenir some cute little mama-san a bikini."

"Uh-uh, bro. Ain't no little gook Vietnamese mama-san got no good tits, hold up the top right. And ain't none of 'em got no ass."

"Then what makes them think we're going to sell any a this shit on the black market?"

"Damned if I know."

So there he was, out there trying to find and kill an elusive enemy before that enemy could kill him, but the way the rules worked usually that enemy found him first. Almost never could he see any concrete result of what he'd gone through. The only thing he really knew was if he killed enough of those bad little bastards there wouldn't be enough of them left to keep trying to kill him. Then maybe he'd be able to get out alive.

But what would happen then? Back in the World people were spitting on his brothers who'd made it back; they were calling them murderers and baby-burners. He wasn't no murderer, he was just trying to survive the only way this war allowed him to. And he never burned no baby, neither.

In-country, he was one of the few who had to go out and risk getting killed or crippled. When he came back in, which wasn't all that often, he was shunted aside, treated as a second-class citizen. Somebody was selling those PX goodies on the black market and it wasn't him. It was obvious, not only were those pogues out of the shit, some of them were getting rich. And hey! When he came in out of the boonies, all of them pogues back there were wearing cammies and jungle boots. He was probably still in his olive drabs and high-top leather boots. And they were worn out and falling off him. What gives?

Pray under these circumstances? Be a true believer? Who's he going to pray to; what kind of god is going to allow this to go on? Not a good, merciful god, that's for sure. Only a mean, nasty, dirty, rotten son-of-a-bitch god could allow this to happen to him. Sure as hell not the kind of god whose heaven he'd want to go to. If there was a god at all.

The man in the foxhole in Vietnam didn't pray, he suspected there was no god.

CHAPTER THIRTY-TWO

Problem: How to Stay Alive While Staying Alive

Rush and Eakins looked at each other when Bingham told them what he wanted. They were hunters, not trappers, but . . .

"Yeah, we can do it," Rush said.

Eakins nodded. "Only problem will be how to kill them right off so they don't make noise."

"All right then, do it." Bingham handed them the spool of monofilament and waited for them to acknowledge his order, then turned away and went looking for Rivera. He didn't have to look far.

Rivera knew why Bingham joined him where he again sat alone, back against a tree, watching in the direction from which they'd reached the banana grove. "I'm okay, Honcho," he said in a flat voice. "It don't mean nothing."

Bingham didn't say anything until he settled himself on the ground beside him. "Everything means something, Dago. But this doesn't mean you're not supposed to be a leader."

Rivera slowly shook his head. "It don't mean nothing," he repeated. "Old Dago's all right here." His voice was still flat. "I'm with you, Honcho. Charlie comes by, I'll be as quiet as we need to be so he can't find us—or fight as hard as anybody else if we have to." Aside from one quick glance at first to see who came to him, Rivera hadn't looked at Bingham. Now he did. "If the Big Six in the sky has a hard-on for me, that's between him and me, you don't need to worry."

"I'm not worried about you, Dago," Bingham lied. "No more than I am about anyone else in this squad. I'm worried about all of us. But if we can sit here and maintain and Charlie doesn't come looking for us, we'll be okay until other Marines come back."

"Right." Voice still flat, Rivera looked back at the forest. He blinked rapidly a couple of times, and Bingham thought he saw a slight misting in his eyes, but he wasn't sure. They seemed clear when Rivera stopped blinking. His eyes moved from place to place, looking everywhere rather than focusing on any spot.

"If you need to talk, that's part of my job," Bingham said after a couple of quiet moments passed.

"Roger that," Rivera said, still flat. He kept watching the forest.

Bingham stayed with him until he felt too uncomfortable. He stood. "Remember, Dago, we're all on your side."

"I know."

Bingham resisted the urge to shift his weight from foot to foot, then said, "Let me know if you see anything."

"You know it."

Bingham started to make some gesture, stopped himself, walked away, silently cursing. He was going to have to keep a close watch on Rivera, but be unobtrusive about it.

"Plenty of small animals around here," Rush said. Eakins grunted agreement. "Let's set four traps," Rush continued. "Should be enough to let us know how they'll do."

Eakins nodded. "One beyond the OP, one on the north side of the grove, one west, one to the south. Right?"

"Just what I was thinking."

"We got to make traps that'll kill on the first hit."

"Let's do it." Rush led the way to the OP.

Eakins pulled a couple of ripe bananas from a tree and carried them to use as bait.

"You here to relieve us?" Copley asked when the two were close enough to the OP to be identified.

"Nah," Eakins said. "We're going grocery shopping."

"Huh?" Stuart asked.

"Trapping for game," Rush explained, "get us some chow."

"Best idea I heard in a week," Copley said. "These damn bananas can get old shit most ricky-tick."

"Good, though," Stuart said and grinned. "I always did like bananas, especially on cereal with lots of milk and sugar."

Copley curled a lip at Stuart. "They're letting 'em into my Marine Corps younger every damn year. Cereal with bananas and milk and lots of sugar, shit, that's baby food."

"Right, and you're an old fucking man," Stuart said quietly. He repressed a laugh; he knew they were talking too much for an observation post.

"We're going to set a trap about ten meters out," Rush told

them. "Cover us." He and Eakins headed away.

"Fucking A," Copley said, ignoring the two men who were leaving, continuing his one-upmanship with Stuart. He was twenty, Stuart was eighteen. At that age and in that war, two years was a huge difference, though months of living through combat would eliminate most of them. "I'm an old fucking man, kid," he said proudly.

Stuart grabbed his own crotch and said, "Too old, old man."

"Shit, I forgot more about poontang than you'll ever know."

Stuart sighed. "Damn shame," he said. "All you got left is memories—and they're fading."

Then Rush and Eakins were too far away to hear the low voices anymore. They found a place where a scattering of animal prints tracked their way across the narrow human foot path. Rush chopped a bunch of small stakes, then worked his stakes onto a small latticework. He used the monofilament to secure it to a low hanging branch that grew parallel to the ground. Eakins kept watch. Rush drew the branch back across the trail and let it go. It swished sharply through the air. Rush paid attention to where the latticework intersected the path. He anchored another stake to that spot, and stuck half a banana onto it, then pulled the branch back and tied a length of line around a bush stem from it to the stake and loosely tied it off; he made no attempt to conceal the line. If a small animal tried to remove the piece of banana from its anchor it would knock the line off the stake and the latticework would impale it. Or so he hoped.

Eakins looked uncertainly at the arrangement. "Think it'll hold?" he asked.

"We'll find out," Rush answered, then looked farther out.

Eakins followed Rush's look. "Bet I know what you're thinking," he said.

"Think we should?"

Eakins nodded.

They went five meters farther away from the OP and, working together this time, made another latticework of stakes which they attached to a flexible bamboo tree. This latticework was larger and the stakes were longer; it didn't have a piece of fruit as bait and didn't swish across the trail inches above it, but four feet high. They took pains to conceal the trip wire. This trap wasn't intended to catch food, it was a man-killer.

"Give us some warning if Charlie comes by," Rush said when they were done.

"Even the odds a skosh bit," Eakins said.

They only took a moment to admire their handiwork, then headed back to the OP. Copley and Stuart were through with their joking now. Rush quickly told them about the game trap and the bigger booby trap. They grinned, imagining a bad guy walking into the big trap; they liked the idea of one of those little bad bastards getting zapped the same way they got so many Americans.

"Hope nobody walks into it," Copley said in the end. If somebody did, they were in jeopardy; if nobody did, they probably wouldn't be discovered.

They made the same kind of trap in the brush south of the banana grove; it went a little faster this time because they'd already done it once and knew what they were doing. A similar trap went west of the grove. They made the fourth trap different. Inside the grove on the north side there weren't any bushes or small trees with low-lying branches growing close to the ground. They rigged a deadfall there. It was similar to the deadfall that killed Russell; both men did their best not to think of the similarity.

It was now near night and they decided to check their traps while it was still light. Homer and West were in the OP, looking particularly jittery.

"Heard something strange a little while ago," West told them. "Sort of like someone breaking trail, but just a little. Then there was a thump and an animal squeal. Then nothing."

"It was all real fast," Homer said. He shook his head. His eyes darted about, probing the forest in the general direction of the noise.

"John told us you set a booby trap up there," West said. "Wasn't that, sounded too small." He looked up at Rush and Eakins and was surprised to see them grinning.

"What you heard was us catching chow," Eakins said. To Rush, "Let's go see what we caught." Back to West, "Be right back." The two hunters-turned-trappers disappeared down the trail. They found a mongoose impaled on the lattice spikes. The swinging branch hit the small animal so fast it didn't spill any blood until it was two feet away from the bait. Then blood splattered everywhere, though most of it puddled under the mongoose.

Rush pried the limp form off the spikes and held it out to Eakins, who took it by the tail and held it where any remaining blood wouldn't drip on him.

"I'll reset it," Rush said. "Who knows, maybe these animals don't know anything about traps and we can get another one right here."

Eakins didn't say anything directly; he held the mongoose up to his face and smiled at it. "Food," he said.

"We'll save you some," Eakins told West and Homer when they passed them on their way back to the grove.

The two men in the OP started salivating when they saw the catch. "You damn skippy better," West said.

The trap south of the grove had killed a small monkey. This was great; there was enough meat on the two animals that each of the Marines could have a small portion that night. The west trap hadn't been sprung.

"I don't know about you, but I'm not getting close to that thing," Eakins said when they reached the trap in the north part of the grove.

Rush squatted on his heels and studied the situation from a safe distance. A five-foot-long cobra had crawled past the bait and dislodged the trip wire. The weighted spikes fell on it more than half way from its head to its tail, pinning it to the ground but didn't kill it. The snake's front half writhed in an attempt to get away from the trap. Its back end lay still. The snake tried to rear up to strike but wasn't able to get very high. It flared its hood briefly before falling back and trying to crawl away. One fang was broken from its attempts to twist around to bite whatever held it down.

"Broke its back," Rush said. He hefted his tomahawk and looked at its blade; it was dulled from chopping the ground for the grave. He looked back to the snake. "It's meat," he said, and moved closer.

"Careful," Eakins said, "some of those things spit their poison."

"I know," Rush said, but his attention was totally on the cobra. He edged closer. The snake suddenly flopped around to face him; it coiled its body back and tried to rise again. It opened its mouth wide, its unbroken fang glistening with venom while venom dripped from the broken one. Rush moved back and the snake again tried to get away. "Go around in front of it, get it to watch you so I can get close enough to chop its head off," he said to Eakins.

"You shitting me, right? What the fuck am I supposed to do if it spits at me?"

"Duck." Rush waited patiently for Eakins to distract the cobra. He watched the snake examine Eakins and try to rear back to strike. When the snake dropped back down he flashed forward and chopped down with his tomahawk, then he instantly jumped back. The severed head hopped forward a few inches and rolled. Its mouth opened and closed a few times, then stopped. The body was more dramatic, it thrashed wildly, spewing blood with every violent twitch.

"We'll come back later, when it quiets down," Rush said dispassionately.

Eakins held his hand out, testing the air. "Hot as it is here, that fucker might not stop moving until it starves to death," he said.

The two made a fire, carefully so it wouldn't smoke. They skinned and gutted the mongoose and monkey and cut them into pieces they could cook with water in their canteen cups.

"Shit, man," Rivera said, showing his first spark of interest since they arrived back in the banana grove, "anybody know which of these weeds is seasonings?"

Nobody spoke up immediately, so Bingham said, "We aren't experimenting. Some of them might be poison, we aren't taking the chance."

Eakins looked around a bit and said, "I know what that one is." He went to a low-lying pile of leaves and poked in the dirt under it with his hands and bayonet. He came back with several fat, lumpy root sections. "Yams." Swiftly, he skinned and cut them into the cups of now boiling water.

Rush left the group while Eakins was rooting. He returned as the last of the yams was added to the cooking cups.

"What the fuck," Remington exclaimed and stepped back, pointing his rifle at the object hanging from Rush's hand.

"No sweat, Fred," Rush said, "it's dead." He swung the cobra out and snapped it to demonstrate. "See? No head, it's meat."

"You ain't feeding that shit to me," Remington said, and backed away another step.

Peale also looked uncertain; snake stew didn't appeal to him, either.

"No sweat off my balls," Rush said. "All that means is I get more."

Soon enough, the scent of cooking meat overcame any reluctance to eat cobra. Bingham called in the OP shortly before the meal finished cooking. He wasn't going to keep out a listening post overnight; they were too few to be separated at night. They weren't able to eat until they were stuffed because there wasn't enough food, but what food they had was enough to hold off hunger.

"All we need now is some warm, willing women," Rush said when he and Eakins came back from checking the traps in the morning. They carried another monkey and mongoose, a lizard, and some kind of large rodent. "I don't think food's going to be a problem."

Lieutenant Vo Hien Phou found the Americans' trail easy to follow for more than a mile, then they lost it near the hill of an American company that had been driven off. It only took him a few minutes to realize there was no point searching for it in the cleared ground around the hill—the earth was too torn up from the battle a few nights before. He broke his platoon into several small groups and sent them around the clearing to look for sign of a group of men headed away from it. Four hours later several such signs had been found. Phou examined all of them himself. There were three that looked promising. That many perturbed him; they would all have to be followed, and that would be very time consuming. He pondered the problem of how to do this in the shortest possible time without jeopardizing his mission or his men. At length he decided to send two scouts along each of the three routes with orders to follow until they saw the Americans, found evidence the routes were old, or until nightfall, then return. That should eliminate at least one of the three routes.

All three scout teams reported back shortly after nightfall. One trail led to a rocky outcropping north of the hill. Rotting banana skins told them it had been more than a day since anyone had been there. One led to the CAP compound that had been overrun. Someone had been there recently—the heads weren't on the poles—and someone might be near there still. The third led to an abandoned banana grove. Neither the compound nor the grove gave enough evidence for the the scouts to tell, though one thought he smelled cooking scents in the grove.

Phou pondered again. The cooking scents were promising, but that could well have been forest folk. He knew that not all the Americans in the CAP compound had been killed when it was overrun. It was possible some of them were still in the area; they might even be the men they hunted. Or the ones they hunted might have joined forces with the CAP survivors. He thought the grove was more promising, but the CAP compound was closer. They would check the compound first thing in the morning. Then the grove if they didn't find anybody there.

CHAPTER THIRTY-THREE
Three Card Monte

On his watch in the first hours past midnight, Bingham shimmied up a tree to try the radio again; he had inserted the fresh battery before dark. Most frequencies were quiet. On a few, at the very edge of what he could hear, there was traffic about nighttime fighting and snipers. There was no way he could tell for sure, but the impression he got was these fights on which he eavesdropped were all part of one big battle. The messages didn't sound like the Marines were losing; it might have just been the nighttime stalemate, or they were winning the overall battle. Bingham wasn't sure, but it sounded more like a hard-fought winning push than a grinding loss. He listened for a while longer, then clicked the dial again through the silent frequencies.

Then an excited voice came through loud and clear on one of those silent frequencies: "Schoolhouse, Red Rover. They're running, I've got a whole company spotted. Azimuth two-seven-zero, range five hundred, fire one spotter."

"Red Rover, Schoolhouse, on your azimuth two-seven-zero, range five hundred. One spotter, stand by," a second, calmer voice replied. There were a few seconds silence, then the second voice came on again. "Rover, one spotter on its way. Rover, where the hell you been, they're running all over the damn place. We busted their damn asses."

The transmissions faded away after that. Bingham's heart jumped at what he heard. He clicked through the frequencies again, trying to learn more, but whatever atmospheric conditions momentarily existed to allow him to pick them up in the first place were gone. He kept trying for another hour without hearing anything more.

His mind spun with what he'd heard, what he thought it meant. The NVA were reeling, being driven back; the Marines were winning. Soon, soon, they'd be back here and his squad would be saved. When he woke Peale for the next watch, it took him a long time to fall asleep.

The sun was still below the horizon when Lieutenant Vo Hien Phou told his sergeant to move the company out in two platoon-size columns. It was safe to make this first leg to the CAP compound while still dark. The Americans believed the VC and NVA could move silently and invisibly through the dark, and they wouldn't have patrols or ambushes out. At least not far from wherever they were holed up. Stealth wasn't required until his platoon was near the Americans' position. Surely, the Americans were alert there, and his men might even have to watch for booby traps. He wished he had his own men with him; even though they had broken and run, he knew their capabilities. The soldiers he now led were strangers.

The two columns moved slowly enough through the predawn dark to be fairly quiet, though Phou easily followed each platoon's movement by the noise they made in the forest. He resisted the urge to speed them up; the Americans wouldn't expect to be attacked in late morning. After a while the night birds started their descent to the trees and, behind and to the rear of the columns, the day birds began their raucous sun-greetings. The nocturnal insect buzzing was quickly drowned out. Somewhere a dog barked. Phou idly wondered how it was that dog had not been captured and taken along by the units that moved through the area. Dog meat was too valuable to be left behind by men traveling too lightly to carry enough food.

Gradually the Northerner became aware of the shapes of trees and bushes around him taking form, becoming easier to see. The sun was rising. A little longer and he would slow the columns. The Americans might not normally expect a daytime assault, but they had to know these were not normal times. No need to blunder into something even though he had his foes outnumbered by about six to one. He sniffed the air, but no odors of fire or cooking reached him. No matter, the Americans carried foods that could be eaten cold. And despite the rains it wasn't cold enough for men from a cold climate to need fires for warmth.

Half a kilometer from the terraced fields where the compound sat, Phou stopped his company and sent scouts ahead. They reported back that they saw nothing. Phou advanced the company to nearly in sight of the paddies and looked them over himself. The compound lay empty and broken at the foot of its tor. It reminded him of a village he had seen when he was much younger, a hamlet that had been home to Catholics who abandoned it to flee south just before the political reeducation team he was then a member of arrived to teach the Catholics the error of their ways. He and the other members of his team vented their frustrations on the houses. When they left, this was what that hamlet had looked like.

Phou rose to his feet and said a few words to his sergeant. He advanced along the wide road-dike alone; the others could catch up with him.

He stood motionless in the compound, seemed oblivious to his men milling about, not hearing their comments. This place was clearly abandoned and had been for several days. The heads had been removed from the bloodstained poles, possibly by the Americans he sought, and buried. He wondered what happened to the rest of the garrison—were they with the Americans he sought? Most likely the Americans had been in the banana grove yesterday and were still there today. It might be too late to find them there now, but that was the place to look next.

From the corner of his eye he saw two soldiers kicking the slight mound of dirt over where the heads were buried and snapped at them. He would not permit desecration of the grave. Some day people would want to live here again; leave the grave undisturbed so the spirits do not haunt those people, he told his men. Briefly, Phou conferred with his sergeant, then the sergeant organized the men and headed them southeast, toward the banana grove.

All seemed calm and quiet at the grove when they reached it in the early afternoon. There were no cooking odors now, though Phou did smell some lingering trace of a wood fire. It was weak enough so that he couldn't tell if the fire was several hours out or simply banked until needed again. Insects buzzed, birds cried, lizards fukyooed. Be slow and patient, Phou told himself. These Americans have no place to go; they will die when we find them. He told the sergeant to dispatch scouts around the perimeter of the grove and report back as soon as they found any trace of the Americans.

One scout was back in a quarter of an hour: he had found a sign. Phou, excited, went with him. He took two more soldiers as guards. The sign was disappointing when he saw it, then a slight smile bent his lips. He should be pleased with this scout; most would have passed this sign by without seeing it. He squatted to peer closely and probe with a finger. It was several-day-old vomitus, more than half reclaimed by the scavenger insects. There was no trace of blood in or near it, so it was not from a badly wounded or ill soldier. His smile widened slightly; a silly soldier had eaten too much too fast of an unfamiliar food. He looked at his scout and said, "You have good eyes, Combatant. The Americans were indeed here, but we need to know if they were here more recently. Keep looking, don't come to me again until you have something less than a day old." His expression became stern. "Remember, they might still be here, or may have set booby traps. Go."

The soldier bobbed in a bow, stammered thanks at the compliment, knowing how easily he could have been reprimanded for wasting the officer's time with an old sign, and flitted into the shadows to continue his reconnaissance.

The other scout, looking grim, was waiting with the sergeant when Phou returned to the platoon.

"What he found I think confirms that the Americans are here," the sergeant said.

"Show me," Phou told the scout. He followed him, along with his two guards. Some slight distance away the scout showed him a latticework of sharpened bamboo stakes on the end of a flexible branch held taut by an unconcealed tripwire that led to a banana in the middle of a game trail several meters into the forest from the grove. A large rodent was sniffing the banana, about to bite into it. The rodent suddenly tipped its head up, sniffed, darted its head from side to side, and scampered off.

The only Marines who woke at dawn were those who were awakened by the ones who had last watch. The men who had last watch wanted to cop a few more Zs, but didn't want to be unprotected while they slept. Rush and Eakins were the first two to rise, other than the watchers.

"Check the traps?" Rush asked when he finished his morning ablutions.

"Let's go," Eakins replied. He also had done all he was going to do.

Stuart woke while they were gone and drank the last of the purified water in his canteens. He looked at Bingham and Remington, saw Bingham lying on his back and Remington curled with head on folded arms, decided they were both still asleep, and headed toward the stream to refill his canteens.

"Take them to Fred for halizone before you drink any of that water, Gil," Bingham said.

Stuart stopped and looked back. The squad leader lay exactly as he had, his eyes were closed. He wondered if he imagined the voice and grunted. He continued to the stream.

"Do what the man says, Gil." Remington's voice made Stuart flinch and he spun back. Remington hadn't moved either and his eyes also looked closed.

"What the fuck?" Stuart demanded.

"You get sick from drinking bad water, I'll kick your ass," Remington said. He still didn't open his eyes.

"Shit," Stuart mumbled. "Halizone before drinking. Right." He shook his canteens in frustration; he hated the taste of the treated water, and wanted to drink it fresh. But he'd do as he was told.

Rush and Eakins brought back two monkeys; they dressed them away from the sleeping area. The cooking aromas woke everyone still sleeping.

Bingham waited until after everybody ate the monkey stewed with yams and finished off with bananas before he told them what he'd heard over the radio that night. Everyone got excited and tried to talk at once, but he got them quieted down again.

"I don't know for sure that's what it is," Bingham cautioned his men, "just that's what it sounded like. We maintain here, and I think in a few days other Marines are going to come along and we're home free." He looked at each man hard, trying to hold them back from getting their hopes up too high. "One thing we have to remember; when other Marines come, they're going to be chasing bad guys. That means the bad guys are going to get here first. We have to be ready."

So they calmed down and waited; waiting was all they could do until someone came along. Wait and be ready for anything.

It was peaceful in the grove. Sounds of battle didn't reach them there, not that far from the coast. Even Remington seemed agreeable to following Bingham without objection.

Bingham looked to where the grave of four of his men was and murmured, "If I'd thought of this in the first place none of this would have happened."

"Be cool, George, I didn't think of it either," Remington said.

Bingham blinked. He thought he had spoken softly enough that nobody heard. "But I'm the chief honcho, Fred, I should have thought of it."

Remington spat to the side. "Shee-it, man, you want to take some heat for fucking up? Bust your ass for switching radio frequencies that first night. I bet the patrols were called in or given a rally point when you weren't listening."

Bingham looked pained; he knew Remington was probably right.

One corner of Remington's mouth curled up and he shook

his head. "Shit, you getting bad as Dago, blaming yourself for things."

Bingham looked at him steadily for a few seconds. "You're right," he finally said. Then he looked around. Where was Rivera; how was he holding up?

"I always am," Remington responded, but Bingham wasn't listening.

The two monkeys made enough stew for everybody to pick at for several hours more. Rush and Eakins didn't bother to check their traps at noon, there wasn't any immediate need for food. They let the fire burn down and go out.

Eventually, about two PM, Eakins noticed the heat that had been rising all day and said, "Getting hot, Chief. We caught anything, we should go get it and cook it before it goes bad."

Rush lifted his face to the air and nodded. They went to the closest trap, the one to the south. It was empty. Homer and Stuart had a mongoose for them at the listening post near the east trap.

"We heard it get zapped 'bout half an hour ago," Stuart said. "So we pulled it off and reset the trap."

Eakins thanked them while Rush checked that they had reset the trap right. They had. The deadfall in the north of the grove hadn't caught anything. They headed to the trap in the west and froze when they spotted a large rodent sniffing around the bait. The rodent suddenly lifted its head, wrinkled its nose at the air, jerked its head around, and darted away.

"Oh, fuck," Eakins whispered, "I think he smelled somebody."

Rush faced into the moving air and eased back. "No shit," he whispered to Eakins. They were downwind from the trap, the rodent hadn't smelled them.

"I mean not us."

"No shit."

They inched backward until they could lay prone with their heads no farther ahead than they had gone, and lay eyeing the surrounding brush, listening to the still of the forest. They watched for several minutes, unmoving except for their eyes and the rising and falling of their backs from their shallow breathing. Then Eakins nudged Rush and pointed. Rush examined the area Eakins indicated; it took a minute but he finally saw what his friend had seen: a regularly shaped shadow in the irregular shadows, one that was a different color from the leaves around it. It was about fifteen feet away.

"Let's go," Rush whispered.

It happens to the best. Rush's foot hit a leafy bush branch and shook it. One of the NVA guards saw the movement and, in an instant of panic, fired a burst from his rifle at the movement. The bullets zipped harmless overhead, but the fight was on.

Eakins pointed his rifle at the odd shadow he'd seen and pulled the trigger rapidly three times. At that range he couldn't miss, and he didn't. A scream started by his first shot abruptly gurgled out with his second.

Rush saw the flickering of the leaves when the first burst came through and fired at that area. He didn't miss, either. Then came a shout and the noise of bodies scrambling away. There was no more fire.

"Chief, Night Stalker, where are you?" Bingham's voice boomed behind them.

"By the west trap," Rush shouted. He and Eakins jumped to their feet and headed toward Bingham. "Hold your fire, we're coming your way."

In seconds, the entire squad, except for Homer and Stuart who were still at the listening post, was together. Bingham dropped to one knee; the others fanned out to his sides and lay prone, facing west.

"I don't know how many there were," Rush started. "I hit one and heard at least two or three bugging out."

"I got another one," Eakins said.

At least four, maybe more. Were they a few stragglers headed away from the fight Bingham had listened to that night, or were they someone else?

"George," Remington said, "if they were stragglers they wouldn't have come from that direction."

"Maybe they're part of a larger unit and were dropped back as a blocking force," Bingham said.

Remington shrugged. Dumbass, he thought, we don't know how many there are but I bet there's enough to take us out. Out loud, "Then we had best move our young asses before they come back with their buddies."

Shouts in Vietnamese decided the issue. "We go east," Bingham said. "Chuck, your team is rear point. Look alive, everybody. Fred, straight to the LP so we can pick up the rest of our people. Move it."

Remington lurched to his feet. "Ben, go," he snapped.

West jumped up, then dropped again when fire from several rifles came at them.

"Hold your fire until we know where they are," Bingham shouted.

The enemy didn't slow fire; half of the NVA platoon was armed with automatic rifles and fired long bursts. It only took a second or two for the Marines to figure out where the NVA were and the firefight quickly reached a crescendo with the Americans putting out more. There was confused shouting from the North Vietnamese; their shooting slacked off a bit, then became heavier when another group opened from the side and behind the first ones.

"By fire teams," Bingham shouted over the din of the small battle, "pull back. Go back to the hollow, we've got more cover there. Fred, back ten. You go with him, John."

Remington snarled, he didn't want to retreat. "Ben, back ten," he shouted, then scuttled backward himself. He, West, and Copley opened up again as soon as they were back far enough.

"Chuck, back beyond second team," Bingham called when he heard the others start firing again. "Dago, stay with me." Peale and his men scrambled backward until they were ten meters beyond Remington.

"Dago, let's go." The last two men crawled backward until they were parallel with Remington. "Pull back even with Chuck," Bingham ordered. All five Marines crawled backward without ceasing fire.

The shooting from the NVA stopped at the tweet of a whistle and Bingham took advantage of it. "On the double, let's move it." Six of the eight men rose and ran back to the more easily defended area where they had slept; the other two went more slowly, Rush helping Eakins along. Bingham and Peale didn't immediately notice not everyone was going fast.

"Win, Gil," Bingham yelled as he ran, "pull back. Do you hear me?"

"Roger," Stuart shouted back. "We're on the way."

They reached the small defilade, dropped into it, and turned around to watch where they'd come from. That's when Bingham finally noticed he had a man wounded. Rush and Eakins stumbled up and nearly fell into the hollow. Eakins was clutching his side, blood flowed between his fingers.

"I'm taking care of it," Rush said before anybody could do more than reach out to ease the wounded man to the ground. He tore Eakins's shirt open over the wound and pushed his hand away so he could see the damage. "You'll live," he said, then pulled a bandage from a pouch on Eakins's cartridge belt and slapped it on the wound. He used the long tie ends to secure it, then rolled his friend over to look for an exit wound. He found a fist-sized area of pulped flesh and tied another bandage over it. Both bandages quickly turned red and blood slowly flowed from them. Rush then took both bandages from his own pouch and tied them over the two already on. These two took much longer to turn red. "Flesh wound," he said.

Eakins's breath came in gasps because of the pain, but he managed a smile anyway. "Shit, Honcho, call in a medevac, I want out of here, get my ass back to a hospital."

"Hospital, my left testicle," Remington said. "You just got scratched. Nothing to sweat." He looked at Bingham. "Right, Big Honcho?"

Bingham nodded, his throat felt momentarily too thick to speak. He found his voice. "I've seen lots worse, Night Stalker." And he had, this was hardly the worst wound he'd seen. The bullet had passed through a fleshy area, and from looking at the wound it didn't seem as if any vital organs were injured. If it could be kept clean so there was no infection and Eakins was able to rest for a few days, he would start to heal well. He wondered what the odds were of avoiding infection long enough to get him to a hospital.

"You trying to tell me no medevac?"

"That's what I'm telling you."

"Then I may as well get back to work." Eakins grunted and sweat flowed over his forehead when he rolled over, but he got into a position he could fight from when the NVA came at them again. He knew they had to come again.

Homer and Stuart arrived while Eakins was being patched up. Bingham arranged the squad with two men watching in each direction; he looked everywhere himself.

"Maybe it was somebody pulling back," Peale asked, "and they kept going?"

Remington looked at him with an expression that didn't disguise his feelings for the other corporal.

"I think Fred was right," Bingham said slowly, his voice strained. "They wouldn't have hit us from the west if that's what they were doing. I think this is somebody looking for us."

"We gotta move, George," Remington said.

"I know, Fred. We will as soon as I figure out what direction they aren't." He continued looking in a complete circle. The shortest route out of the grove was straight south. Then cut east or southeast. Or swing around to the northeast. Any of those would probably run them into the retreating NVA. Still, the enemy would be fragmented, maybe easy to avoid. He looked at Eakins and wondered if he was able to be moved.

Eakins saw the look and said, "I'm okay to walk. We don't have to hold back because of me." He said that, but he didn't look that able to move.

"I can help him," Rush said.

"Negative, we need you on rear point when we move out," Bingham told him.

"I can do it," Homer said. He looked at Eakins, the smallest man in the squad. "I can carry him if he can't walk."

Eakins grinned weakly. "I ain't touching that one," he said.

"You better not," Remington snorted. Maybe Homer was a Tom, but he was still the same color and no damn chuck better say nothing.

Bingham looked long and worried at the western end of the grove, then once more at Eakins. The farther east they were, the sooner they could get him to help. "Let's go. Fred, lead out."

In less than a minute they were filing into the forest south of the grove.

CHAPTER THIRTY-FOUR

Sometimes the Pea Is Where You Think It Is

West had point. He took them twenty meters into the forest to a heavily used game trail and turned onto it; they could move faster on that trail than through the brush. He walked right into a squad that had been sent there as a blocking unit. The squad had just arrived, and it wasn't set yet; only two of its men opened fire immediately. Those two were enough.

Remington bellowed in fury and slammed his way past West into the middle of the small ambush. Remington was a madman. The squad had been lost and isolated, wandering through the jungle for a week. Nothing he'd wanted to do was approved; Bingham had opposed him at every turn, and he was furious and frustrated. All that fury and frustration burst, and he took it out on the seven soldiers in his path. The first one he saw, he drilled through the heart. The second one was prone and firing, Remington kicked him once in the head and knocked him unconscious. He was too close to the third soldier to swing the muzzle of his rifle into him, so he slammed the small man in the throat with the butt of his rifle and slammed him into a tree, maybe dead from ruptured blood vessels or a crushed larynx. He shot the fourth one through the middle of his back as the man was running away. The other three escaped, uninjured but terrified.

Remington roared, his voice reverberated through the forest like the meanest tiger in the world. He thrashed about looking for more victims and stomped on the heads of the men he'd downed when he couldn't find anyone else. He stomped until Bingham grabbed his arm and pulled him off.

"They're dead, Fred," Bingham said harshly. "We don't have time to keep killing them, we gotta get out of here."

Remington looked at his feet. The crushed mass of bone, hair, gray matter, and scraps of flesh he'd been stomping was barely recognizable as a human head. He looked around, the heads of the other corpses weren't in much better shape. A shudder wracked through his body, driving the tension from it. He shook his head to clear it and said, "You're right, George. Let's get the fuck out of here. I'll take the point myself." He started to follow the game trail.

"Wait one," Bingham snapped.

"Fuck wait one, we gotta go, you said it yourself." He kept going.

"We take our wounded with us."

That stopped the big man. He twisted slowly back. "What wounded?" Suspicion was in his voice.

Bingham pointed. West was sitting against a tree, his face twisted in agony. He was biting down on a piece of wood to keep from crying out, to keep from biting through his lip or tongue. A blood-soaked bandage wrapped his thigh. Rush bent over him, working as gently as he could, which wasn't very, fixing splints along his leg.

"His femur's broken," Bingham said. "Chuck and John are watching our rear while Chief fixes him. You and Gil make a litter, you're going to have to carry him." Remington blinked at him. "You two are the biggest. Besides, he's yours."

"Who's taking point?"

"John and I have to."

Only ten men left, two of them wounded. And three of the others carrying the wounded.

"Shit," Remington swore. "Let's get some branches cut," he said sharply to Stuart, who looked back at him with the awe he'd felt since Remington broke the ambush. They had the litter ready by the time Rush was finished immobilizing West's leg as well as he could.

"Somebody's coming," Peale called from behind them.

"Chief, move out," Bingham said. "Fred, you and Gil pick up Ben and go with him. Win, take Night Stalker. We'll catch up with you. Dago, come with me." He and Rivera dashed to where Peale and Copley waited.

Homer said to Eakins, "This is going to hurt, buddy, but I'll be as easy as I can." He wanted to carry Eakins over his shoulders in a fireman's carry, the easiest and most efficient way to carry a man, but knew it would aggravate his wound. Instead, he cradled him in his arms, a far more tiring way to carry someone, but a way that would cause less pain.

Bingham dropped between Peale and Copley, Rivera lay on

Copley's other side. They heard the sound of many men coming through the jungle toward them, men not running, but going fast enough they couldn't be quiet.

"On my command, we'll blast the shit out of them, then bug out," Bingham said softly. "Maybe that'll hold them up enough to give us a chance to put some distance between us and them."

The others didn't respond; there was no need to. Bingham waited a few more seconds, until he saw a flash of movement through the trees, then shouted, *"Now!"* and started pulling the trigger as fast as he could. When the two tracer rounds at the bottom of his magazine flaming out of his muzzle told him he had to reload, he said, "Let's di-di," and spun around to his feet and ran crouched. The others were right with him. Peale and Rivera reloaded as they ran, the same as Bingham. They discarded the empty magazines. There were no sounds of immediate pursuit.

Running, they quickly caught the others.

"Chuck, Dago, take the rear," Bingham ordered when they reached Homer. "John come with me." The two kept running.

Copley paused when they reached West and patted his shoulder. "Hang in there, pano," he said, his voice husky. "We'll get you out of this shit most ricky-tick." West put a hand on Copley's wrist but was too weak to squeeze. Copley had to blink the mist out of his eyes when he turned away; he wasn't sure he believed what he said.

Bingham had to ask twice, "Do you know exactly where the booby trap Chief and Night Stalker set by the LP is?" before Copley understood.

"Yeah, I know." Copley's voice was dull.

"Let's go there, maybe they'll follow through it and even up the odds a bit."

"Right." He did know exactly where it was and the squad skirted the hidden trip wire. Then Bingham angled to the southeast. He thought maybe they could more easily lose their pursuit in the rugged terrain there. Homer continued to carry Eakins cradled in his arms; he carried him as gently as he could, but the jostling still caused Eakins's wound to bleed. Not much, but enough to drip. West bit all the way through a piece of wood to keep from screaming at the pain in his leg. It was nightfall before they stopped.

A man-made path led up a steep ridge. Steps were cut into it in some of the steepest parts. Trees and bushes grew right up to the sides of the ridge, and it was possible to walk to within a few feet without seeing it. Bingham hoped if the enemy was still following they'd miss it. Eakins was able to climb parts of the path on his own, and he gritted his teeth and didn't cry out in pain when he was helped up the parts he couldn't manage on his own. West passed out from the pain caused by the jostling of the litter as it was lifted over the rougher parts. Fresh blood dripped from his leg and poured off the litter when they tipped it to raise him higher. On top they found a half-dozen boulders that formed a rough circle with one big chunk and a few smaller ones missing from it. That's where they would spend the night. If no one came near, Bingham thought they might be all right there again the next day.

Phou didn't put the men he thought were his best scouts up front. There was no need to now; they knew where the enemy was, and all they had to do was catch up. Combat is the most dangerous occupation of men—severe sacrifices get made to the gods of war when armed men confront each other. The platoon had already lost one man dead and another severely wounded near the animal trap. If the three who made it back from the blocking force were right, four more were dead. Phou didn't want to lose any more, but he knew he probably would. He asked himself the kind of question combat leaders are sometimes faced with, the kind of question the good leaders hate: Who among his men was he least likely to miss if he didn't have them? He picked two men and told them, "The Americans are right in front of us. They are hurt and probably running. Catch them. Then we will kill them. Go."

The two men he selected looked at each other with worry and fear in their eyes; they knew what was likely to happen to them if the Americans weren't running when they reached them. They also knew what would positively happen if they disobeyed this order. They made sure their rifles had rounds in the chamber and the safeties were off. They ran after the Americans and caught them.

A fist of fire blasted in front of the lead soldiers and flung them shattered to the ground. Phou screamed at his men to drop and fire back. The fight didn't last long before the Americans broke contact. More cautious now, Phou sent his best scouts forward. They came back and reported they had found where the Americans had ambushed them from, but they were no longer there.

Blood on the trail near the mutilated corpses of his men told Phou the Americans had been hurt by the blockers a little while ago, but not as badly as was his platoon. There was no fresh blood where the Americans hit his point from; they hurt him without being hurt themselves. He now had two more dead and a second wounded. He grimly surveyed the scene, then sent one able-bodied man to escort the wounded man back to where the other rested with one guard; this escort was to catch up immediately after giving the fresh casualty to the guard. Then he ordered his men onward.

He assigned his best men to lead the way and they went more slowly. The Americans might have another trap set and he didn't want to walk into it like he did this last one. There were only infrequent drops of blood on the trail. There was another trap. One of his sharp-eyed scouts spotted the trip wire and they went around the trap. Phou had his sergeant spring it once they were all safely past.

The Americans stayed on trails and headed generally southeast. They were good at forest movement, but were obviously carrying casualties and unable to do as well as they had previously at concealing their tracks. It wasn't until nightfall that they lost them, but Phou knew they had to be nearby. He set his men out in two-man teams to find something that would indicate where they were. They used pieces of wood as signaling devices; if someone found a sign, he was to click his sticks together to signal Phou to come and inspect what he found. Two men found a man-made path with steps cut into it leading up the side of a ridge. Phou's probing fingers came away wet.

There were no high trees he could climb to get a longer sight-line with the radio, so Bingham draped the antenna over the highest rock and listened again after midnight. He listened for two hours, switching frequencies every minute or two, and didn't hear anything other than what sounded like routine patrol or ambush situation reports and artillery fire missions. Everything he heard was too faint for him to think he could reach anyone, so he didn't make any transmissions of his own. Once, right after waking Peale to take the next watch, he thought he heard something, like somebody hitting drumsticks together, somewhere off in the distance. Peale didn't react and he didn't hear any other noises, so he decided it was his imagination and went to sleep.

Bird cries at dawn woke everyone except West. Copley fretted over him, but there wasn't anything he could do for his wounded friend except keep the insects off him. Eakins's side throbbed but the burning he'd felt the day before was gone; he thought he would be all right if he didn't have to move. Rush did what little he could to make Eakins comfortable, but he didn't dare try to change the blood-crusted bandages. Now that the bleeding was completely stopped, he didn't want to risk starting it again. The sky was leaden and the sun seemed to ooze through a distant haze that gave no promise of burning off as it rose higher. The mood of the men was somber, in a way that seemed fitting for the day. Morning throat-clearings were more muted than usual and they all looked for someplace where they could urinate without making noise. It took awhile for them to notice something else about the day.

Bingham was bent over his map, occasionally looking out from between boulders to check the surrounding landscape without silhouetting himself against the horizon. Finally he nodded, satisfied that he was right the previous evening when he'd only had a few minutes to determine where they were before the sun set. He started to think about what were they going to do for food when Remington interrupted him.

"What do you think, George, you think this ridge is a place where birds don't live?"

Bingham looked at him and listened. The earlier avian cacophony had disguised the fact that no birds squawked near them. He didn't say anything, just tipped his head back and sniffed, turning this way and that.

Rush saw and did the same. "Oh, shit," he murmured.

Slowly, everybody except the still unconscious West stopped whatever they were doing and shifted into positions from which they could fight in any direction. Now the silence they were in the middle of boomed into their ears like a slammed door. Somewhere, something scraped briefly against a rock. They tried to sink into the earth and rock of the ridge top.

West moaned and Copley put his hand over his mouth. West's eyes opened and darted around. He understood immediately and tried to roll onto his stomach so he could fight as well. Copley shook his head and West stopped his attempt.

They waited long minutes with nothing happening and no other sound heard. Then a grenade bounced off one of the boulders into their midst.

"Grenade!" The cry came from several throats at once. They scrambled for what safety they could find between the boulders. Except for Copley, who dove onto West to protect him from the blast.

The nearest gap to Stuart was blocked by two men who reached it first. He twisted manically around to find another way out and found the grenade at his feet. Without thinking, he scooped it up and threw it. It was an airburst. Stuart didn't even have time to scream before he died.

West screamed though. A chunk of the grenade's casing missed
Copley and hit West in the chest. Copley's back was peppered
with smaller pieces.

Then Phou's men opened fire on the circle. They were firing
uphill and could only see through three of the gaps between boulders. None of them could see any of the Marines, and some of
them realized the only way they could hit anybody was with rico-
chets fired at the sides of the boulders.

Inside the ring of boulders was pandemonium, but only for a
moment. West couldn't move and Copley, bleeding from many
small wounds on his back and his thighs, stayed to protect him
from further injury. The others huddled against the boulders unable
to fire back because they would have to expose themselves to the
murderous fire coming their way.

"We gotta get out of here, George," Remington said, and looked
for a way out.

"I know that, Fred. Question is how." He also looked around.
"Win, get ready with Night Stalker. Chuck, Dago, Chief, get one
grenade ready. Throw them when I give the word. Fred, get on
Ben's litter with John. Everybody get ready now." He grasped a
grenade firmly and straightened its pin.

"No," West's voice was so weak Bingham almost didn't hear
him.

"Shut up, Ben, you can't say no," Bingham said.

"Don't, don't," West struggled to raise himself enough to talk.
He coughed and blood flecked his lips. "I'm not going to make
it. Leave me here and I'll hold them off while you go."

"*No!*" Copley screamed. "We aren't leaving you behind, Ben,
we're getting you out of here and get you to a hospital, get you
taken care of."

West shook his head. "No good. No way I'm going to make
it." He gasped for breath, blood bubbling from his mouth. "I'm
gone. Leave me to hold them off. You go."

Bingham didn't say anything; he wanted to reject the idea, but
it made a horrible sense. West's face was turning pale and waxy;
the chest wound made a sucking noise with his breath. He was
going to be dead soon.

"Ben's right, George," Remington said. "We di-di and leave
him to hold them off."

Peale grunted agreement; he didn't like the idea any more than
Bingham did, but knew they couldn't expect to escape carrying
West, and West was about to die anyway. Copley screamed again;
he didn't want to leave his friend. The others didn't say anything,

just looked at Bingham to see what he'd decide.

Finally Bingham agreed. The sound of scrabbling came from downslope; scrabbling that meant the NVA were coming up after them helped him decide. "Fred, Win, get him over here." He couldn't ask Copley to move his friend to where he was going to be killed.

The two men knelt and bent low to the ground to stay below the bullets whizzing overhead. They hobbled the litter to the boulders the fire was coming through. West told them how he wanted to be; they rolled him onto his stomach and set up his automatic rifle on its bipods.

"Go," West said. His voice burbled with blood.

"You can't leave him," Copley protested, and tried to grab the litter.

"I've got him," Remington said. He wrapped an arm around Copley, pinning his arms to his sides. "Let's go."

"Ready with the grenades," Bingham ordered. Now he looked at West; he didn't see him clearly because of tears misting his eyes. "Thanks, pano," he said softly.

"No thanks needed. Get out of here."

"Pull the pins," Bingham said louder and pulled the pin from his own. "Now." He threw his in a high arch down the hill; the other three did the same. They waited a few seconds, then the four grenades erupted. "Go," he said hustling the others out ahead of him. The fire from below was far less than it had been before the grenades went off, but he didn't hear any screams of wounded men.

Six of them ran bent as low as they could. Remington and Homer weren't as low as the others because they were carrying Copley and Eakins. Behind them they heard the NVA fire pick up again and the heavy booming *rat-a-tat* of West's automatic rifle join in. They climbed the crest of the ridge and soon were at the place where it leveled off, shielding them from view of where they'd spent the night.

Bingham paused there and looked back. He saw several soldiers dashing toward the boulders from a direction West couldn't see. He raised his rifle to his shoulder and fired one round at one of them and saw that man buckle. Then he spun and ran after his men. Minutes later high-pitched, victorious screams came from the distance and the shooting stopped. Bingham shuddered, but managed to repress a sob. West was dead. At least he hoped they killed him; didn't let him live to torture during what few minutes were left to him.

After the initial sprint they ran at a slower pace for what seemed like—and probably was—hours. They heard no sounds of pursuit during that time, and had heard nothing since the screams that signaled the end of the assault on their position. They had long since followed a trail down off the ridge. Copley was walking on his own now, Remington was carrying Eakins; Peale and Bingham had also taken turns. Bingham looked around for a high place they could rest on and found one a short distance to their east. They had to backtrack a bit to reach it. Eakins wanted to walk himself. Walking hurt his wound, but it hurt less than being carried. They climbed a steep, wooded slope and found a place where they could watch the direction they'd come from without being seen. They weren't in a direct line to their route of march. Then Bingham groaned. He realized they'd left the radio behind.

CHAPTER THIRTY-FIVE
Trucking On Down

They holed up to lick their wounds, literally as well as figuratively.

Eakins was in a lot of pain, but he gamely maintained his composure as well as he could. Bingham examined his wound and worried about it. The bleeding had stopped, but the flesh around the entry and exits was a bright pink where it wasn't bruised. The pink was warm, but not hot, to the touch. Eakins grimaced when Bingham probed the pink. Bingham was concerned the pink might be the onset of infection. They had to keep it clean—and somehow keep it open so it could heal from the inside out. How to do that? Bingham stuffed the battle dressings inside the wound when he redid them. Eakins managed not to scream.

There was no way to keep Copley's wounds from infecting; there were too many of them and some had metal embedded too deeply for anybody without proper medical training to dig out. At least he didn't bleed much. Or maybe he should have bled more to flush the wounds out. His back and thighs hurt, as if he'd just fallen ten feet onto a gravel bed. It wasn't enough to incapacitate him, yet.

Peale didn't wait for Bingham to give orders. He immediately assigned Rush to watch for followers. He told him it was because Rush was the best man for the job in the squad. The real reason was he wanted to get Rush out of the way and give him something to occupy his mind while Bingham examined Eakins's wound. Rush didn't like it, but he guessed at Peale's reasoning and realized his fire-team leader was right. He applied his attention to watching and detected no sign of anyone coming their way.

"Dago," Bingham said when he was through doing what he could for his two wounded men, "take Win and see if you can find anything we can eat."

Rivera nodded. He swallowed to clear his mouth of the saliva that flooded it at the mention of food. Except for a few pieces of fruit they'd managed to pluck from trees during their flight the day before, they hadn't had a meal since the previous morning. "Don't bring back anything that has to be cooked," Bingham added. Rivera made a face, but nodded again. They didn't know if the smell of their fire or the cooking aromas had led the bad guys to them earlier, and they couldn't take the chance.

Twenty minutes later the two men returned with their arms laden with bananas, guavas, and mangoes. "We saw some grapefruit out there, too, but they didn't look ripe," Rivera said. A wry smile bent his lips. "I tried to eat a green one once in Hawaii. Bad shit."

"Then it's good you didn't bring any of them back," Remington said.

Rivera snorted. "I could feed you one and you probably wouldn't know it wasn't good," he said.

Remington laughed, but kept it low. He stood and looked northwest, from where they'd come. Then he looked east, where he wanted to go. "They aren't close to us," he said to Bingham. "I say we leave now, go east, find some friendly forces."

Bingham looked west, to where the sun was low above the mountains. "Too hard to move at night," he said. "We'd probably lose our direction and get lost. Besides, we've got two men wounded, be too difficult trying to move with them; we wouldn't be able to go quietly." He looked Remington in the eye. "Tomorrow we go east." There was no resignation in his voice, but he felt it inside. Maybe Remington was right from the beginning; they should have headed straight east and not tried to go around, but he didn't think so. He remembered what happened when they had gone straight east; they had run into bad guys, then gotten trapped between two groups of them. But maybe if they had gone straight east earlier, they could have gotten through before the NVA consolidated their front. Maybe. No point worrying about it. What was done was done.

Remington glared at him. "We're being followed," he said. "We don't know how close they are. We need to put some distance between us now. You saw how they caught us this morning."

"Yeah, they caught us this morning. I think they spent the whole damn night looking for us. They're tired, they can't move as fast as we can. We already put some distance between them and us. We stay here tonight and move out in the morning. They won't reach us before then; they're going to have to stop and rest, too."

Remington bit the inside of his mouth to keep from arguing, to keep from yelling at this stupid asshole. Those little bad bastards weren't like normal people, they didn't need to rest, they could keep going until they died. Or until they caught the Marines.

"Sir, the men are tired," the sergeant said. "They need to rest."

Lieutenant Phou kept his face blank, put as much ice in his eyes as he could. It wasn't hard, not as tired as he was himself. "I don't care if they are tired," he said. "We have a mission. That mission is to catch and kill the Americans. We can rest once we have fulfilled the mission. Not until then. Do you understand?"

The sergeant sighed, but softly enough that the lieutenant didn't notice. "Yes, sir. But wouldn't it be better if the men had a little rest first so they can be in top shape for when we catch the Americans? The men will be able to fight better if they are not so tired when it is time to fight."

"What is the problem, Sergeant? Are you so tired you need to rest, you cannot go on?" The sergeant tried to object, but Phou kept going. "If the men are too tired to go on, that is the fault of you and the previous officers of this company; you should have kept the men in better shape. If you are too tired, I am sure I can find another man in the company who has taken care of himself and is ready to continue even with duties additional to those he already has."

The sergeant was stung by this, but maintained his stoic mien. Of all the men remaining in the company, he was the least tired; he prided himself on his physical conditioning and stamina. He gritted his teeth, but still managed to sound respectful when he replied. "Sir, I was only thinking of the men. These men are good fighters; they are all veterans. They have many times met the puppet Saigon army and bested them, and they fought the Americans at Khe Sanh; they know how the Americans fight. But they only had a couple hours of sleep last night; if we keep going tonight they may become sluggish and lose their edge, become liable to be victimized by the Americans."

Phou ignored the part about the company being experienced. He tipped his head and said, "Are they city boys, these men in this company?"

The sergeant shook his head. "Mostly farmers," he said. He noted that Phou didn't repeat his accusation of poor training.

"Then they are accustomed from childhood to long hours of hard work. And they are young. The young can go for long periods without sleep. The Americans have a lengthy lead. We need to find them before they manage to lose us."

"Yes, sir." The sergeant knew he wasn't going to change the officer's mind, convince him to give the men a few hours' rest. He didn't think the Americans were that far ahead of them or that they would be able to evade them for long. The blood they found when they overran the rock position did not come from only the two dead men; the Americans were carrying at least two, maybe three wounded men. They could not go fast or stealthily, not unless they left their wounded behind again. He thought about that for a moment: would the Americans abandon their wounded? Then he dismissed the thought from his mind. No, the wounded man they left at the rocks was close to death already. He was left not because he was wounded and would slow them down; he was left because he was near death, and volunteered to delay them while his companions made their escape. He returned to the problem of the moment. "In what order do you want us to move out? I will have the men ready immediately."

There was no twilight. It was day and then it was night with very little transition time. Eakins wouldn't let Bingham examine his wound again before dark, and he even rebuffed Rush when his friend came to see how he was doing. Bingham noticed how gingerly Eakins moved and worried again about infection. Copley sat closed into himself and insisted he was fine, no problem; don't bother me. Bingham worried about him, too, though not because of his wounds. Bingham worried about how Copley was feeling, how he was reacting to West's death. Rivera also sat alone. Bingham worried about him, too. Worrying about these three men and what bothered them was easier than worrying about what they all were going to do, how any of them were going to live through this.

"Quit feeling sorry for yourself, Dago," Remington said, settling next to Rivera. "People gonna start thinking you're just another dumb spic, you acting like that."

Rivera slowly turned his face to Remington. "All of my men are dead," he said slowly. "Everyone who was my responsibility. I have three lives on my soul."

Remington shrugged and stuck a twig between his lips. "Mine got wasted, too. You don't see me worrying about it."

"That's because you have no soul, Fred. You have nothing for them to hang onto."

Remington blinked, then laughed and clapped Rivera on the back. "No soul? Shee-it, Dago, don't you know they call us soul-brothers? Man, we invented soul. Don't tell me I don't have one."

"Go away, Fred. What you call soul and what I call soul are not the same thing. To me a soul is a spiritual thing. It has to do with God, and God punishes those who do bad with their soul."

"Right, you wasted your men yourself," Remington snorted. "You're just a dumb wetback, Dago. If you grew up where I did, you'd know what's spiritual is zapping some badass who thinks he's badder than you and then going and fucking your hole."

"That's what I said, you have no soul."

Remington swallowed the end of his laugh and moved away from Rivera. Dumbass spic, he'd take care of him when they got out of there.

When the sun went down Bingham said, "I'll take first watch. Somebody wake me at midnight. Who wants second watch?"

It was quiet until an hour and a half before dawn. Copley and Rush were awake then. Maudlin is one way of expressing how they felt.

Rush was trying not to think about how Eakins was doing, trying and not succeeding. His sleep earlier was interrupted by occasional moans Eakins couldn't repress. He knew a through-and-through wound was far better than one where the bullet went in and stayed there. He knew the bullet that hit his buddy was a simple flesh wound, one normally good for a couple weeks or so of light duty back in a hospital. But where they were was hardly normal. Like Bingham, he'd noticed how gingerly Eakins was moving. He was afraid infection was setting in and he had too good an idea of how painful death from infection was. He was a little more successful at not thinking "it don't mean nothing."

Copley's back hurt. He couldn't find a comfortable position. Sitting, he was on a few of the small wounds. Lying prone he was off them, but he had to raise his head and shoulders to watch and that put pressure on the wounds on his back. His back and thighs ached if he lay on his side. He lay prone and propped his head and shoulders up and soon forgot about the pain. He didn't try not to think about West, he just tried not to sob out loud when he did. He tried to think "it don't mean nothing."

"It don't mean nothing" meant it was not important, it was without meaning. That allowed the combat trooper to go on despite the death of a close friend, despite the constant threat to his own life and limb. But if it "don't mean nothing," it also meant his own life was void and invalid. "It don't mean nothing" could cause a man to do things, take chances, that were inconceivable to a sane man—even a man who was only sane relative to the insane world of war. "It don't mean nothing" could take away all sense of self-preservation.

Rush was a little more alert than Copley was an hour and a half before dawn, which is why he was the first to hear the sounds of someone climbing the steep hill they were on. Rush tapped Copley on the shoulder to alert him. Copley flinched and gasped sharply; one of his small wounds festered where Rush tapped him. Then Copley heard what Rush did and froze. A little downhill and more to their right came the *whiff* of cloth against cloth. They listened for a long moment and realized whoever it was was going well clear of the squad's position. They heaved in relief at being missed. Then they heard another *whiff* just a bit to the left of directly downhill. Unless this one turned aside, he wasn't going to miss them.

Copley shoved his grenade launcher and .45 at Rush and patted him, a signal to stay put. Then he drew his K-bar and slid forward, toward the downhill noise. Rush tried to grab him and hold him back but Copley struggled to break the grip. Rush let go rather than risk making noise.

Copley didn't go far, maybe fifteen meters downhill, before he dimly saw a moving shadow to his front; a protrusion near the shadow's top showed the man was carrying his rifle slung muzzle-down over his shoulder. Copley drew his knife hand back to thrust and waited tensely for the shadow to come closer. He saw a second shadow before the first one reached him; only two meters separated the two. Both were using both hands to help them climb. The first shadow passed almost in arm's reach; he let it go by. The second shadow almost stepped on him. Copley lunged up, all pain from his wounds forgotten in the adrenaline rush. The web of his left hand and thumb clamped around the throat of the shadow just below the jaw and lifted. At the same instant he slashed his knife up through the shadow's solar plexus and twisted the K-bar violently. The shadow bucked, kicked, went rigid, fell limp. Copley lowered him to the ground and turned toward the first, which had heard some small sound of the brief struggle and was turning back. No time for subtlety; Copley dashed and closed the distance in three steps. He drew his knife arm across his body and unwound it like a spring—the blade slashed through the throat of the shadow, and the man fell with a clatter.

A low, guttural shout came from farther to the left; it sounded like a question. Copley crept in the direction of the shout. Behind and uphill from him he heard another low shout, another question of what was happening. He wished he'd kept his .45, the enemy soldiers on the hill now knew they'd been spotted and the Marines were there. Two shadows loomed in front of him, holding their rifles at the ready. He waited huddled until they were close enough, then sprang up and slashed the closer one across the face. The man screamed and staggered back. He twisted toward the second and tackled him, drove the blade of his knife as hard as he could into his rib cage, and heard bones crack. He jerked his knife out and turned to the first man; he saw him thrusting his bayonet at him. Copley ducked under the jab and came up, plunging his knife into the man's belly. The soldier shuddered and stepped back from the wound. He held his rifle steady and pulled the trigger. A burst riddled Copley from left groin to right shoulder. He fell forward with his K-bar outstretched and impaled the man. He lived long enough to hear more shouting, some in English, and the outbreak of sporadic fire.

Rush didn't wait for Copley to come back. As soon as Copley slithered away, he scrambled to Bingham and woke him. "We got gooks on the hill," he said. "John went after them."

Bingham blinked his sleep away. "How many; where are they?"

"I don't know. We heard some to the right, then more in front. John went after the ones in front, I don't know how many there were."

Bingham saw the M-79 Rush held. "What weapons did he take?"

"Just his K-bar."

"Shit. Wake everybody."

Bingham headed to the now abandoned listening post while Rush woke the others. He listened to the night silence and knew it was too quiet out there. He strained his eyes and ears, trying to locate Copley, find out what was happening out there. He couldn't make out anything for a while, then he heard a clatter. A shout came from his left, and he thought he heard the sounds of people moving from that direction. Behind him he heard his Marines drawing close, pulling together. Peale lay on one side of him; Remington lowered himself on the other.

"I hear someone say something about people needing rest?" Remington rasped in his ear.

Bingham ignored him. There was a shout on their right, followed quickly by a scream where he'd heard movement on the left. Then a thud, another scream, and seconds later a burst of automatic rifle fire. There was more shouting from three different places on the right, louder and excited. Someone over there fired a rifle, three quick shots.

"I see him," Rivera shouted and rapidly fired several rounds where he'd seen the muzzle flash. He heard a thump and called, "I think I got him."

The shouting on the right became more animated and there were a few wild gunshots directed at them.

"John," Bingham shouted. "Are you all right?" No answer. "Where are you, John? Call it out." Still no answer. "Chief, think you can find him?" he asked Rush.

"Yeah, if what we heard was him."

"Let's go, everybody. It sounds like all of the bad guys are that way." He pointed to the right and had Rush lead off. Eakins walked on his own.

Rush didn't lead them directly to where he'd heard the fight between Copley and the last of the NVA he fought; he took them on a downhill loop. They found the first two Copley had killed with his K-bar. Back uphill and to the left they found Copley and the other two he killed. Behind them it sounded like the scattered NVA were getting themselves organized.

"Chuck, two of your men carry John, I don't want him left here for them to find," Bingham ordered. Peale acknowledged the order. "Chief, go around the hill and strike out due east. Let's get out of here."

"Right," Rush said and headed around the hill.

"About fucking time we do what I say," Remington muttered. He and Rivera brought up the rear.

CHAPTER THIRTY-SIX

We're Surrounded, They Can't Get Away from Us This Time

The North Vietnamese under Lieutenant Phou had been hit hard. Eleven of the original sixty men were dead. Another three were too badly wounded to continue, and two more were left behind to tend them. The Marines had only lost three dead. But the Marines were hurt by four dead to begin with, and they were still outnumbered by six to one. And the Marines were burdened with carrying one dead; another one of them was wounded and increasingly unable to make it on his own.

Dawn on the third day of the running battle found the Marines lost. For the sake of speed and silence, Rush followed paths and game trails that led in a generally northeasterly direction. But they kept bending east and sometimes south as well, and sometimes he lost his direction in the dark under the nighttime trees. When the sun finally came up and Bingham stopped them on a high place where he could try to orient himself on his map, Peale, Homer, and Rivera were exhausted from carrying Copley and Eakins. Eakins looked sick and his face was hot to the touch.

"One good thing, George," Remington said when he saw that Bingham couldn't locate their position on his map, "if we can't find where we are, maybe they can't, either."

Bingham looked at him for a long moment before replying. "Fred, one of two things is happening. Either there's one unit following us or there's a whole shitload of Charlies out here. If there's only one unit, they're good; they found us three times already—and two of those times were at night. If there's a whole shitload, maybe there's no way we can avoid them."

Remington grinned, but behind it he felt anything but amused. "Then we should keep moving," he said.

Bingham looked at Eakins, who was now drifting in and out of consciousness. "We keep moving, we're going to kill Night Stalker," he said.

Remington shrugged. "We sit in one place, he's going to die anyway. Only way to save him is get his ass to a hospital most ricky-tick."

Bingham seemed to fold into himself. Remington watched him for a few seconds, then repeated, "We gotta keep moving, George." He drifted away and sat alone, watching toward the south.

Bingham knew Remington was right. No matter what he did, Eakins was probably going to die. He couldn't stand losing another man, especially not this way, not to a flesh wound that should have only been good for a couple weeks out of the field. But they did have to keep moving; all three times they had stopped for a while, the NVA had found them. That meant the enemy kept catching up with them. The Marines had no food, could only scrounge fruit off trees because it was too dangerous to light a cookfire. The bottle of halizone tablets was emptying rapidly.

Phou was furious. Four more men were dead, another wounded and unable to continue—and no Americans down. Evidently the Americans had used knives to kill three of his men before the fourth one knew anything was wrong. Maybe an American had been wounded, but he couldn't know until it was light and they could search for blood trails. No time for that, the Americans had fled. They must continue the pursuit right now; they could not wait. It did not matter that his men were tired, the Americans were also tired—they had to be, they were carrying at least two wounded men. Surely, running through the night they would make noise that could be followed. Soon they would catch the Americans, very soon. Then he would lead the remainder of his company back to the battalion. He patted the heavy canvas bag tied to his waist, the bag that held the right hands of the two dead Americans they had found. Soon the bag would be full. As soon as they caught the rest of them.

Phou spoke to the sergeant quietly, out of hearing of the men. "We will continue now," he told the sergeant. "When we are close to where the Americans go to ground we will organize and attack them as a unit. If it is night before we are that close to them, we will wait until dawn. It is too dangerous to approach them at night, they have just proven that. Tell the men and get them moving. I do not want the Americans getting too far ahead of us."

The sergeant said, "yes, sir" and went to organize the men who remained and get them on their way. He remembered, but did not remind Lieutenant Phou, that they had hardly fared better against the Americans during the day.

The Americans did not make a lot of noise, but still were not all that hard to follow. The NVA only lost the trail twice, and not for long either time.

Homer looked hard at Bingham when the squad leader said, "We got to keep moving, put some distance between us and them." Bingham saw the look and added, "Cut another litter. Chief and I will carry Night Stalker, Fred and Chuck carry John. Win, you've got point when we move out."

Homer nodded. Eakins might be small, but carrying him all day was too tiring for one man. "What way?"

"North, maybe just a little bit east." Bingham hoped to get to someplace that was on his map.

"Why we carrying John?" Remington demanded. "We aren't bringing any of the others along."

"We didn't take the others because we couldn't," Bingham said. "We can bring John. And as long as we don't leave him for the bad guys to find, they don't know they wasted another one of us."

Remington grunted. He knew Bingham was right but he couldn't say out loud he agreed. Nor did he say it bothered him they'd left two men behind at the rocks. Marines don't leave their dead or wounded behind.

Rivera brought up the rear.

They moved hard and kept to ridge tops as much as possible. Bingham knew that being on top left them silhouetted against the sky whenever the trees were sparse, but the ridge tops were the easiest places to walk for the six men burdened with two litters. The toughest going was when they had to go down off one ridge and climb another. Every hour they rotated on the litters. The man in the rear kept a close watch where they'd been; Bingham made sure he did. He had a strong feeling the pursuing NVA weren't far behind. He was right. By the time he called a halt in midafternoon the forty-four North Vietnamese tailing them were maintaining a one hundred-meter distance, waiting for the Marines to stop so they could creep up on them and deliver the killing blow. The NVA got very close before they realized the Marines were stopped. They got ready.

Rush cradled Eakins's head in his lap when they stopped and waved insects away from his face. He wished there was something he could do. Anything to ease his friend's suffering, but there was nothing. Nothing except keep the insects off him.

Fifteen minutes, Bingham thought. Fifteen minutes, then we'll go again. Maybe twenty minutes. Then he couldn't think anymore. He was so tired he didn't even try to orient himself on the map.

Eakins stopped moaning. He'd stopped when they put him on the litter. He wasn't sure if he was dreaming or awake when he'd heard Bingham and Remington arguing about his condition. Maybe he was awake and overheard them. Maybe he knew how bad off he was and how much of a drain on the others and his subconscious mind talked to him about it while he was sleeping.

"We're in the shit," Eakins said to Rush.

Rush had to strain to make out his voice. "We been there before, pano," he answered.

"Yeah," Eakins said, "but not like this."

"We'll make it, don't sweat it. Real soon we'll have you in a hospital, get you fixed up like new."

"Uh-huh." Eakins didn't believe that, not at all. Whether he dreamed it or heard Bingham and Remington talking about it, he knew they were right; he was going to die soon because they couldn't get him to a hospital soon enough. What he needed to do was stop being a burden so they could escape.

Rush may have been distracted, paying attention only to Eakins, but he was still alert. It slowly occured to him that the forest birds weren't resuming their cries now that the Marines weren't moving through them any more. He lifted his head and listened for a long moment. Then he said, "Stay here, I'll be back in a skosh bit," eased from under Eakins's head, and padded to where Bingham lay with his arm over his eyes, resting and thinking.

"I think someone's close to us," he said.

Bingham lifted his arm to look at Rush, who was peering back the way they'd come. He raised his head and looked that way as well. Nothing was in sight, but he didn't expect to see anything. He listened and heard the silence. Bingham rolled over and around so he was on his hands and knees facing the quiet. He snapped his fingers and used gestures to alert the others. Instantly, they were all alert and watching back.

Dust motes drifting in the air seemed to dance when they crossed sun rays penetrating the forest canopy, seemed to intensify the silence surrounding the Marines, and magnified the rustlings of leaves moved by vagrant whiffs of air. Nerves twanged when a lizard fukyooed somewhere even though it wasn't close. Bingham, in the middle, tried to swallow, but his mouth was too dry. Remington was on the left side; he breathed through parted lips to still the noises of his body, to better hear other sounds of life. Peale lay on the right side; he tried to melt into the mulch that covered the forest floor, tried to will himself somewhere else. Rivera waited patiently between Remington and Bingham; he already knew God didn't want him responsible for other men; maybe God didn't want him alive, either. Whatever God wanted was fine with him. Rush opened all his senses as much as he could, tried to pinpoint something, anything, that could give them any edge. Homer took all his weariness and fear and turned it into cold anger, so he could kill more effectively when someone showed himself. Eakins fought the fog in his head, determined to relieve his companions of the burden he'd become.

A flicker of movement caught Rush's eye, a flicker so small and so fast and so far on the periphery of his vision he wasn't sure he'd actually seen anything. Maybe just a leaf moving in the breeze. He wished he'd checked to see what kind of round was in the chamber of the M-79. Now was too late, if someone was out there that someone would hear him breaking the weapon open to check it out. Right now he'd rather have a willy peter than an HE. He didn't know if the willy peter had a wider killing radius than the HE; thought it probably didn't, but he knew the burning chemical was more frightening. He stuck his hand into the ammo pouch and started pulling grenades out. He spared them only quick glances as he separated willy peter from HE, kept going until he had six phosphorus and four HE grenades positioned to reload fast.

A whistle shattered the quiet, and its trill was almost instantly drowned out by gunfire that erupted from the front and one side. A bellow of pain from Remington pierced the walls of noise.

"Where the fuck are they?" Homer screamed.

"Fire front, Win," Peale shouted. And he did it himself.

Rivera quickly crawled to Remington. Not to check out his injury, but to fire to the flank without hitting him. The big man had twisted around to face the fire from his side. He blinked sweat from his eyes—his eyes were furious, the only part of his face not torn in a grimace. His left arm, covered with flowing blood, was bent under the forestock of his rifle, not holding it, just propping it up. He was firing rapidly into the trees, moving his shots around, not wasting them on one place.

"See anybody?" Rivera asked. His eyes flickered from point to point, trying to find a place to shoot. Every time his eyes moved so did the muzzle of his rifle; every time his muzzle moved he fired a round.

"Fuck, 'see anybody.' There's so many I don't think you can miss if you try." Remington kept moving his shots around.

Rivera turned the selector switch on his rifle to full automatic and did the same.

Rush pointed the M-79 where he thought he saw movement seconds earlier and pulled the trigger. Shit, he thought when the grenade exploded, Hotel Echo. He broke the launcher open and inserted a willy peter round. He fired at the same spot again. Somebody screamed when the phosphorus flower spewed open. He reloaded with another WP and fired it a few meters to the right of the first one. And another and another and another, all at intervals of little more than five meters across the front. The six rounds made a brilliant flashing wall through the forest and there were two more screams—one trailed off into the distance; someone wounded running away, hoping distance would stop the burning in his chest. Then Rush let loose with a string of high explosive rounds spaced between the glowing places where the WP rounds had gone off.

Homer emptied a magazine in four bursts, reloaded, got off four more bursts, reloaded. Peale pulled the trigger with a lighter finger and fired five bursts from each twenty-round magazine.

Bingham didn't fire, he looked and listened, tried to make sense from the cacophony of the battle din. All he could tell was the enemy was laying down heavy fire at him and his men, and his men were returning very disciplined fire. Then his eye caught a movement in the brush fifteen meters to his left front. He pointed his rifle at it and squeezed off three quick rounds. The movement stopped.

A whistle blew in the forest and the enemy fire abruptly stopped. There were a few shouts, then the only sounds were from the Marines' weapons.

"Cease fire," Bingham shouted. "Cease fire." They stopped shooting. "Team leaders report." Too late he remembered the squad no longer had functional fire teams. But responses came anyway.

"Win and I are all right," Peale shouted.

"I'm hit, Dago's okay," Remington called.

Rush lay breathing heavily next to Bingham and simply nodded he was all right.

"How bad, Fred?" Bingham asked.

"Arm, Dago's bandaging it. I can walk."

"How's your ammo?" The replies were a little longer coming this time.

Rush was the first. "I've got about twenty rounds left." He forgot about the six full magazines and eighty loose rounds in his pockets.

Peale called, "We each got about a hundred and sixty rounds." He and Homer were busy reloading their magazines from the machine gun belt sections they carried.

"I've got more than two hundred," Remington answered. He paused to ask Rivera, then added, "Dago's got a little less."

Bingham checked his own ammunition supply; he had only fired three rounds in this firefight. He pulled two magazines from their pouches and handed them to Rush. "Pass these on to Chuck."

Then Rush remembered his own. "I've got three hundred rounds."

"Give two magazines to Chuck, pass me another one for Dago," Bingham told him. Rush did it. Bingham thought for a moment; he didn't like where they were, the brush was too thick all around them, they had no real fields of vision. The same trees that gave them cover here also concealed the enemy and allowed them to get too close. He made up his mind. "When I give the word we go. Chief, take us due north." He thought maybe they could find their way back to Alpha Company's fire base; there they'd have cleared fields of fire. If the bad guys weren't occupying it again. "Chuck, Win, grab Night Stalker. Dago, bring up the rear. Everybody got it?" He didn't say to leave Copley's body; couldn't bring himself to say the words.

There was a murmur of assent.

"Fred, you ready?"

Remington replied that he was.

"Let's do it. Now." He rose to his knees, body still facing the direction of the main attack, head turning to make sure everybody was doing what he was supposed to. He saw it almost as fast as Peale did. Eakins was missing.

"Where's Night Stalker?"

"Everybody, stay in place," Bingham ordered. "Chuck, come with me." He bolted to Eakins's now empty litter and knelt to examine the ground around it.

"How'd they get to him?" Peale asked. "All that fire, they could have been wasted by their own people."

Bingham examined the ground around the litter. "I don't think they did," he said. He pointed out a ragged trail in the mulch.

"Looks like Night Stalker got up and walked off by himself."

Peale stared at the ruffled mulch for a moment. A glint of something moist and yellow caught his eye, a bit of pus that had fallen from Eakins's bandage. "I'm going to get him, bring him back," he said, and disappeared into the brush before Bingham could order him to stay.

Bingham swore, and turned to tell his other men what was happening. He ran after Peale. Eakins couldn't have gotten far, not in the shape he was in. Not unless he left as soon as the firefight started. Probably not even then. He'd help Peale carry him back, then they'd head north.

Eakins did get far. Bingham followed the easy-to-see trail left by the two men. He heard Peale moving faster than he was and speeded up. If Eakins had gotten too far away, they risked running into the NVA before they could get to him. Branches whipped at his arms, slashed at his face; vines tried to trip him. He broke past all of them and kept going. Then he heard the shouting. It was close; it reverberated off the trees and momentarily confused him about its direction, then he crashed through a last screen of brush and into a small clearing.

Eakins was on his hands and knees, struggling to pull his bayonet from the chest of an NVA soldier. Peale's rifle was missing. He held a small man by his ankles and was swinging him back and forth like a club, holding off three others who were trying to reach him. Eakins got his bayonet free, lurched upright, and stumbled toward the three men trying to reach Peale. He lunged with the blade and it sank into the side of one of them. Bingham lifted his rifle to his shoulder and fired at one of the other two. Now that he was faced with only one of them, Peale jerked the man he swung up over his head and whipped him down onto that last one. Bones snapped loudly in the collision and the one hit screamed. The man being swung was unconscious from the vicious handling, his face was dark from the blood forced into his head by the swinging; he might already be dead.

"Chuck, where's your weapon?" Bingham shouted, running toward them. He reached down and scooped Eakins up under one arm.

Peale looked frantically around. "Got knocked out of my hand when they jumped me," he gasped. He spotted it and picked it up.

"Let's di-di before anybody else shows up," Bingham said. He started to run with Eakins trying to say something to him, he couldn't tell what, when he heard other voices behind him. "Go!" he shouted. Out of the corner of his eye he saw Peale running alongside. Then something hit him on the side of the head and he didn't see anything else.

A blow to his back staggered Peale and he fell forward, this time he didn't let go of his rifle. He turned around and yelped at the sudden, sharp burning where he'd been hit. Five men were running toward them. He didn't take time to check if his selector switch was on automatic, just started pulling the trigger. It was on automatic and he was getting off three-round bursts. Two of the five dropped. He saw Eakins pick up Bingham's rifle and fire it. Another NVA dropped, the other two dove for cover behind a fallen tree.

"Keep them down," Eakins said; then he said it again, trying to shout because his voice was too weak. He levered himself up into a half crouch—Peale thought he couldn't stand straighter—and worked his way around to the side of the fallen tree. He fired several times, then tottered back. "They're done," he said. Peale had trouble making out the words.

"Can you walk?" Peale asked. He was going to have to carry Bingham, if the sergeant was still alive. He couldn't carry both of them. The pain in his back made him wonder if he'd be able to carry himself.

"You're hit," Eakins said more clearly. "Need to bandage it."

Peale reached around to his kidney, where it burned. His hand came away wet. "No time," he said. "Let's go," and staggered upright. The pain increased and he started feeling very weak. He stood over Bingham, pondering how he was going to lift him without falling himself.

Then Remington and the others arrived. Remington immediately took charge. "Chief, bandage Chuck," he ordered, and knelt next to Bingham to examine his injury. "If he ain't dead now, all he's going to have when he wakes up is a headache," he said when he finished. His probing fingers hadn't found any softness under the broken skin and the blood was already slowing its flow. His own left arm was held tightly to his body by the ties of the bandage covering his wound. He picked up his rifle with his good hand and nudged Bingham. "Come on, Honcho. Up and at 'em, time to go."

Bingham groaned and rubbed the side of his head. He flinched and looked at the blood on his hand.

"You just got whapped upside the head, nothing's broken," Remington said. "Let's go."

Bingham groaned, but got up. He shook his head and groaned again from the sudden pain.

"Don't do that," Remington said. "If it hurts, don't do it." He gave Bingham a push and they started off, Rivera and Rush carried Eakins, Peale leaned on Homer. They only made it a few steps before a bullet knocked Rivera to the ground. Rush stumbled and dropped the litter. Eakins screamed when he rolled off it. Remington spun and fired one-handed from the hip. Homer was fast, but also gentle, in lowering Peale before returning fire himself. Bingham turned too fast and almost blacked out from the pain.

Only the shot that hit Rivera was fired at them.

"Anybody know where it came from?" Remington shouted. He appointed himself squad leader now that Bingham was groggy from his injury. Peale wasn't going to object, not with a bullet in his back. Nobody knew where the shot came from. "Ease it back. Go slow." Remington crawled backward awkwardly on his knees and the hand holding his rifle. "Dago, how you doing?"

"My leg's hit," Rivera said in a stone-calm voice. "No big deal, nothing's broken." He wrapped a field dressing around the wound. It was going to hurt when he tried to walk, but he could ignore the pain.

"Chuck, you with us?"

"Yeah," was all Peale could answer, his back hurt too much for him to say any more. He was too dazed with weakness to realize he was bleeding badly.

"Chief . . . "

Before he could complete his question Rush answered, "I've got Night Stalker."

"Everybody pull back," Homer said. "I'm covering you."

"You heard the man," Remington said, "move back." He didn't ask Bingham how he was doing, the sergeant could take care of himself.

Bingham did take care of himself. His head was clearing enough to think. "Anybody see anyplace we can defend?" he asked. With five of them wounded, two badly, they weren't going anywhere. Nobody answered; he looked around to make sure they were still around, that no one had been left behind. Rush shook his head when Bingham looked at him. "We gotta find a place. Now."

"Where?" Remington demanded.

"We've got three men who can't walk, Fred. We have to find a place we can defend.

"Shit. All right, I'll find us a fucking place." Remington heaved himself up and stomped off, head swiveling, expression daring a defensible place not to show itself. He was back in a few minutes.

"Ain't much, but it's better than nothing," he said. He looked at the wounded men. "Sure you can walk your ownself, Dago?" Rivera nodded. Remington slid his rifle arm around Peale's chest. "Win, bring Night Stalker."

"I've got him," Rush said. He already held Eakins cradled in his arms.

Homer looked around and saw that Bingham, the only remaining casualty, was able to walk without help. "Go," he said. "I'm covering you." He waited for a minute, lying prone, aiming his rifle where he knew the NVA probably were, then crawled backward until he could no longer see where he'd been. Then he rose to his feet and started looking for where the others had gone. If the tracks they left through the mulch hadn't been clear enough he could have followed the droppings of blood they left behind. He heard a loud crack and thump, accompanied by a great rustling of leaves where the trail led.

A little down the side of the ridge three large-boled trees grew close together forming a triangle of sorts; a fallen tree lay balanced on a couple of its branches near the longest space between the trees. The noise Homer heard was Bingham, Rivera, and Rush pushing that tree off its balance to close off that side of the triangle.

Homer looked at the small wood fort and wondered how many NVA were in the area. He wondered if there were few enough for any of the Marines to survive the battle. He didn't bother to wonder if any of them would be left alive when other Marines finally found them. He climbed over the fallen tree.

Rush used a field dressing to tie his own shirt over the wound in Peale's back. The look he gave Homer told him that was the last bandage any of them carried. There was nothing left to keep the next man wounded from bleeding to death.

The seven men, two of them barely conscious or able to fight, waited for the enemy to come for them. They didn't have long to wait.

CHAPTER THIRTY-SEVEN

Think This Is What They Felt Like at the Alamo?

Phou shook his head when his sniper shot one of the Marines in the leg. At that range the man should have killed the American. He stopped the sniper from firing a second round; he wanted to judge the condition his prey was in. How had they managed to kill ten more of his men in a suicidal attack like this? They had killed two others and wounded two more when his men assaulted them a little while ago. What manner of men were these Americans? It seemed no matter how he approached them they always killed more of his men than his men killed of them.

He watched carefully from his concealed position when the Americans stopped firing and pulled back. It was too bad he left the rest of his men behind when he came forward with the sniper; they could kill all of them now. Well, the killing would come soon enough. He saw two of the Americans carried away. One of the men doing the carrying had his left arm tied to his side—he was wounded. There was the man the sniper shot in the leg. One of them had the side of his head bloody. It seemed that only one American was not wounded. Was that all of them? Were there truly only six left? He waited patiently for a moment, then saw a movement in the weeds that told him there was another. He wondered if that American was wounded, if the others had left him for dead.

Something dropped onto the ground by Phou's shoulder. He looked at it. It was a hand. He looked up at his sergeant, who had dropped the hand.

"Another dead American where we attacked them," the sergeant said.

Phou nodded. "There are only seven of them left, and at least five are wounded," he told the sergeant. "It is time we killed them all. Prepare the men."

The sergeant did not move instantly. He looked at Phou for a brief moment before responding, "yes, sir." Then he went to prepare the men; only thirty left. How many of them would die before they killed the last of the Americans? Would they kill the last of the Americans, or would the last of the Americans kill the last of them?

They didn't have to go far. The trail was very easy to follow. It ended in a place where a log was laid between two trees. Phou sent one squad around in each direction to attack from the flanks.

Peale was lying on his stomach facing to the side between two trees, his rifle was placed where he could use it if he had to—and they all knew if he could use it, he would have to. He wasn't really looking, but he was the first of them to see movement in the forest. He hardly had to move the direction his rifle was pointed in before pulling the trigger. A body crashed into the brush when he fired and he smiled a satisfied smile, his back pain forgotten for a few seconds despite the jolt the recoil gave him.

Then the forest erupted with fire from three directions. Peale and Eakins were the only ones who could fire back; the others all huddled behind the fallen tree. Bullets thudded into the protective wood, whizzed overhead, twanged and screamed off after striking the trees glancing blows. Chips of bark and twigs and leaves rained down on the Marines. Peale and Eakins lay low and pointed their rifles, cranked out a few rounds without expecting to hit anyone, just hoping to slow down anyone who might want to advance. It seemed to them that thousands of rounds flew at them before a whistle trilled in the forest and the fire stopped.

"Anybody hit?" Bingham and Remington asked simultaneously. They glared at each other while the others replied no. "I'm not hurt that bad, Fred," Bingham said. The big man shrugged.

"Chief, you think it's safe for you to fire the blooper?" Bingham asked.

Rush raised his head as high as he could while keeping it below the cover of the log and looked out through the trees. "In a couple places," he said.

"Got any more willy peter?"

Rush checked his ammunition bag. "Two."

"Shit. Pop a couple Hotel Echos out there."

Rush looked again to see where he had a long enough line of sight to fire and have the grenade go far enough to arm itself, and far enough that none of the shrapnel would get back to them. Then he jerked the grenade launcher above the fallen tree, angled slightly upward, and pulled the trigger. During the two seconds it took, no more than his hands and wrists were exposed. A quick barrage came during those two seconds; one bullet whapped his left wrist. Then the grenade hit and the return fire stopped. Someone screamed. Rush swore and shook his hand; he cried out at the pain from the broken bone, then ignored it, reloaded, and fired again in a different direction. There was no return fire this time.

They waited for minutes that dragged. None of them said anything; there wasn't anything to say. Except, how many will we take with us, and that's not something to say out loud. Then they heard shouts from the front followed by shouts from the sides. There were a few more shouts back and forth, they sounded like orders and acknowledgments. Then fire came from the front and one side.

No fire came from Eakins's side. He pulled himself to where he could see around the tree better and opened fire; he saw two NVA with grenades in their hands creeping toward them. One of the two fell, hit. The other went for cover. He fired at the place the second one ducked into until his magazine was empty, then pulled himself back to cover to reload. He was clumsy about it.

A shout came from the non-firing side; the whistle trilled and the fire ceased.

They waited again, wondering what the enemy's next move would be. Bingham looked at Peale and Eakins and thought how ironic it was; in this position so far the only two of them really able to fight back were the two most badly wounded. They waited a long time without hearing anything other than an occasional shout from one enemy position or another. The light got suddenly dim under the trees. Bingham looked at his watch and realized it was almost nightfall, in minutes it would be dark. It started raining with the arrival of night.

"Stand by, they're probably going to come at us as soon as it's dark," he told his men. They tensed for the expected assault and didn't say anything in return.

The NVA waited until half an hour after dark to let the Americans nerves get tauter and tauter before they did anything. Then a whistle trilled and they opened fire from all three sides. The Marines huddled, unable to do anything else. The fire wasn't heavy; Phou's men carried less ammunition to begin with than the Marines had, and had used theirs more freely. They fired slowly, just heavy enough to keep the Americans pinned down; it might have been called heavy sniper fire under different circumstances.

Eakins had a longer than usual period of lucidity and listened for the pattern in the fire. He thought briefly about West volunteering to stay behind to cover their withdrawal and how Copley went out alone to break up the NVA approach the night before. Then, when he thought the others were ignoring him, he placed his rifle and cartridge belt where they could be found easily, took his bayonet in one hand and one of his two grenades in the other, and slipped out from between the protective trees. It was time he relieved the others of the burden he'd become. The rain masked the noise of his movement.

Eakins wasn't quite right about all the others ignoring him; Peale noticed him leave. The kidney-wounded corporal instinctively knew what Eakins was doing. He also understood the numbness radiating out from his wound meant he didn't have long himself. He took two grenades and his bayonet and followed. The lack of feeling in his back allowed him to move more quickly than Eakins and he caught him in fifteen meters. They conferred in low voices, then continued. They were crawling, so their movement was necessarily slow. It took them twenty minutes to reach the flank of the squad facing where Eakins had been in the defensive triangle. By then, of course, the other Marines knew they were gone.

"I'm going after them, George," Remington said. "You coming with me?"

"None of us are going anywhere, Fred," Bingham said. "The shape they're in, they'll already be dead when we find them. All we do going after them is get more of us killed."

"Fuck you. They're Marines and I'm not letting them crawl off like that. Besides, the bad guys know where we are. They're coming soon. Surprise them if we ain't here when they show up." He crawled into the night.

Bingham watched the patch of blackness Remington had crawled into, then said, "Let's go." Remington was right.

Fifteen feet away the ground dropped far enough so that they were able to stand up without fear of being hit by the bullets coming from uphill. The fire from the flanks was zeroed in on the position they just left and they weren't in danger from those directions, either. Bingham grabbed Remington's arm and in the grabbing regained command. He spread the five of them out, touching outstretched hands to shoulders, and they instituted a tight grid-pattern search. Minutes later their ears told them where the two men they sought were.

The two men lay side by side, having already agreed they couldn't throw their grenades the same distance, agreed the NVA were bunched closely enough that if their grenades both hit in or near the enemy group they'd probably kill or wound all of them. They pulled the pins and Peale tapped a countdown on Eakins's arm. He threw his, tried to toss it to where he thought the far end of the line was. Eakins tried to raise himself to one side to throw his grenade. He fell back and bit through his lip to keep from crying out from the pain; somehow, he held onto his grenade. Peale grabbed it from him and threw it, not as far as he'd thrown his own.

Screaming followed the first explosion; the second grenade stopped the screaming. They crawled forward and found six bodies. Four of the six were dead. They used their bayonets to kill the other two. Shouts came from the middle NVA position. The other Marines started calling out. None of the shouts were answered.

Peale and Eakins looked at where they thought each other's face was in the darkness and started giggling uncontrollably. Each of them had half expected to be killed, but neither was hurt— except for the killing injuries they both already had. All they had now were their bayonets; nothing to use to take the fight somewhere else.

"Let's go back," Peale said.

"Okay."

Before they could, approaching footsteps stopped them, footsteps from their left. The footsteps stopped and a voice called in Vietnamese. The voice dropped to little more than a whisper and called again. The footsteps came closer, stopped again. They heard rustling, someone feeling around. A sharp cry, a body was found. A leg suddenly appeared in front of Eakins face. He gathered all the strength he had remaining and propelled himself upward with his bayonet extended. The blade struck home and the man screamed. There was a second, nearby shout. The blow didn't kill immediately. There was a struggle and they toppled to the ground. Peale rolled into the struggle. His questing hands told him which of the bodies was Vietnamese, the smaller, wiry one. He stabbed it and the struggle stopped.

"Night Stalker, you okay?" he asked.

A gurgle answered him. He pulled Eakins from the dead man and held his face close to his. Eakins breath came so light he could hardly feel it on his cheek. He heaved once and his breath stopped.

Then someone crashed into Peale from the side. He rolled with the blow and felt someone stumble over him. He slashed out with his bayonet and felt it connect, heard the man he'd hit scramble away a few feet. The two men lay still for a few long seconds, each trying to determine exactly where the other was. Peale was the first to move, having decided the advantage was his—he knew his opponent was wounded, and the other didn't know he was. He heard soft movement circling to his right and circled more tightly inside that arc, hoping to intersect it. The movement stopped and he froze. He knew they were very close to each other, maybe within arm's reach. He tried to pierce the dark, to see where his foe was. Then all the pain in the world erupted in his back as the other jumped on him. He flailed about but was too solidly pinned down. A coldness on his throat turned to fire and he suddenly couldn't breathe, feeling as if he were drowning.

The weight on his back flew off and he heard a grunt that could only have come from Remington's throat. Then he died.

It only took a few seconds for the five Marines to figure out what had happened. They huddled close together in the night rain.

"We can end it now," Remington said. The rain was coming down heavier; it was safe for them to talk louder.

"You're right, Fred," Bingham agreed. It was now obvious; if they kept running eventually they'd all die. They were Marines; it was time they acted like it and took the offensive. "Let's go get the little bastards. Here's what we'll do."

They listened, then climbed to the crest of the ridge. The enemy gunfire stopped by the time they got there. Quickly, they put their heads together and decided to stick with the plan even though the NVA facing downhill might have moved—their move wouldn't have been an about-face. They fixed bayonets and started downhill. The closer they got to where they thought the central position was the slower they walked, slower and slower until they stopped.

"They moved," Remington said.

"Back uphill and around," Bingham said.

Before they reached the top of the ridge they heard shouting. It came from the protected place they'd left and from the place Peale and Eakins had died. The NVA knew their quarry was gone and their own forces reduced by a third. More than a third, for Peale's first shot when they were getting into position took one of them out and one of the rounds Rush fired from the grenade launcher badly wounded another. The Marines headed back down toward the place they'd defended.

No one was there when they reached it. Nor was there anybody living near the corpses to the side. The two groups of men moved in circles and wider circles, trying to locate each other in the blindness under the trees on that rainy night. Eventually the Marines had to stop, Rivera couldn't walk any longer. The five men sat backs together in a tight circle and waited. It took a couple more hours, but the North Vietnamese finally found them.

They had to do it by feel as the night was too dark to see farther than a few feet, and no details were visible in that range. The questing fingers of Phou's men found a confusing tangle of ruffled mulch, many trails of many men, and it was impossible to tell which were theirs and which were the Americans'. Too many trails to search every one. After an hour and a half of futile searching Phou ordered his remaining eighteen men to the south, to the side where the only trails were made by his own men. There he lined them up at the greatest intervals he hoped they could maintain without becoming completely disorganized and started them moving slowly north. Phou knew the rest of the Americans were somewhere in that direction. No more than five, no more than one of them not wounded. The North Vietnamese moved slowly. Partly to maintain their contact with each other, partly because they were all afraid of these Americans. Even Phou was afraid of these Americans now.

Their interval was four meters.

The Marines were bunched together, huddled for warmth. Homer was on the right side, Bingham on the left. Remington and Rush centered Rivera in the middle. They were high on the slope, facing downhill and left to where they'd last heard the Vietnamese voices.

Rivera was content to die if that was what God wanted. He prayed that first he be allowed to help save the lives of his companions. But he wasn't sure he prayed to a god that existed. He was the most alert and was the first to hear an approaching man. He readied himself and when he heard the sound again, only feet in front of him, lunged forward with his bayoneted rifle. It struck home and he twisted it. The scream of the man he hit was brief.

Someone stumbled on their left and Bingham fired at the noise. Someone fell heavily. Shouts came from downhill and they turned to fire at them. Gunfire came back at them but missed. Crying came from where the Marines heard the NVA. There were shouts below them and the fire stopped.

"Cease fire," Bingham ordered. "Anybody hit?"

None of them were. They listened for movement. It came soon.

A low pitched voice called orders and they heard men shifting on the slope; they wondered how many there were. It didn't sound like many. A whistle trilled and they heard movement coming toward them.

"If you're sure where anybody is, shoot him," Bingham murmured. "If you aren't, don't fire."

It was a moment before Remington pointed his rifle and pulled the trigger. The boom of his bullet was followed by a grunt. A few of the approaching NVA fired wildly toward them, none hit.

"Let's move," Bingham ordered when a shout silenced the fire. He led them left and a little down. He didn't stop until they ran into the flank of the approaching line.

There were sudden screams and grunts and a few shots when the two groups met. And there was lunging and slashing of bayonets and swinging of rifle butts. Then the Marines were standing alone with the remaining North Vietnamese regrouping to hit them the final time, now that Phou knew exactly where they were.

"Go backward," Bingham said. They did until the last eleven NVA reached them. Only a half dozen shots were fired until they were too close to each other to shoot. They used their knives and bayonets and swung their rifles like clubs. One by one, men were wounded. One by one, men died.

CHAPTER THIRTY-EIGHT
The Few, the Survivors

By February 8, 1968, the Vietcong general offensive was essentially over. The hoped-for general uprising never happened. Everywhere, except for a few isolated remnants of VC who couldn't run or refused to run, the attackers were thrown back, beaten back, crushed, and destroyed. They were beaten so badly, they were never again able to mount an effective fighting force. Only the North Vietnamese Army units occupying Hue City and laying siege to the Marine outpost at Khe Sanh were still fighting. Throughout the country, American and South Vietnamese forces pursued the fleeing survivors of the offensive. When they caught them they gave them a chance to surrender—sometimes—and slaughtered them when they didn't. They reoccupied positions they'd left, to feed men into the battles in the cities and towns. The Tet Offensive was essentially over. The Marines went out to reoccupy those positions they'd left at the beginning of the offensive.

"Yo, Thunder, over here." The Marine who shouted scrambled down the side of the ridge, holding his rifle in one hand and using his other to grab handholds so he could go faster and keep his balance.

"What ya got, Ralph?" called back the corporal named Thunder.

"Whoa, shit," Ralph said. "Corpsman up." He knelt by one of the bodies he'd found; it was a Marine, the side of his head was bloody, there was a bullet hole in the flesh of his arm, and his shirt was torn open, exposing several knife wounds. His eyes were half open and he was breathing. "Hold on there, buddy," Ralph said, "Doc's on his way. We'll have you patched up most ricky-tick and on a medevac bird out of here. I gotta check your buddies."

He turned to check another sprawled Marine, a big black man with one arm tied to his side.

That's when Thunder arrived. "My God," he bellowed. "Second squad, everybody get your asses over here. Tell Lieutenant Carhart I need him." He knelt by a small, dusky Marine with high cheekbones. The Marine tried to say something. "Be cool, pal," Thunder told him. "You're okay, now, we'll take care of you." This Marine's wrist wound was caked, but the cut on his side was still bleeding. Thunder took a field dressing from his own first-aid pouch to bandage it. "You hurting anywhere else?" he asked the wounded man and got a glazed expression in reply.

There were two others, a Mexican with a leg wound and several cuts on his chest and belly, and a black Marine who had the whole side of his face smashed up but no other obvious wounds. And there were a dozen North Vietnamese, all but two—who were too badly injured to move on their own, though they tried—were dead.

Lieutenant Carhart arrived with the corpsman and his radioman. The corpsman got to work right away. Carhart grabbed the radio handset and called for the company commander. "Six, I got some wounded Marines over here and need a medevac most ricky-tick." He listened for a moment, then said, "No, I don't know who the hell they are. They aren't ours, that's all I can tell you right now." He surveyed the scene in more detail while the company commander said something, then continued, "They've got a bunch of gone gooners around them. Looks like they had themselves quite a party." All around on the wooded hillside dead NVA were scattered as far as he could see. He whistled. "Sweep your squad through the area," he told Thunder. "See if anyone else is lying around alive."

Two more corpsmen showed up and helped patch up the wounded Marines and the two NVA who were still alive. Carhart set the rest of his platoon to clearing a landing zone while Thunder's squad searched. Thunder came back with his men carrying two dead Marines, both of whom were missing their right hands, and reported boo-coo more gone gooners. In half an hour, two medevac helicopters arrived and took the casualties away. Before they left one of them came conscious and identified himself as Sergeant Bingham. He told the lieutenant there was another dead Marine in the area and where to look to find two more a few klicks away. Those directions weren't very clear and, anyway, wherever it was was in a different company's search area. The nearby body was found; it was also missing its right hand. Those hands and two more were found in a pouch on one of the North Vietnamese bodies.

"Bet the other hands belong to those other bodies he tried to tell us about," Carhart said to Corporal Thunder. "I'd sure like to know what happened here."

AFTER-ACTION REPORT

The Aftermath

From the Analytic Notes of R.W. Thoreau, Lt. Col., USMC (ret.)

That's when I was brought in. Division assigned a captain, me, to debrief the Marines who'd found them. When they had recovered enough, I debriefed the survivors. None of them were able to tell the complete story of what had happened. In all cases, though they differed in minor details and there were gaps in each man's narrative, their stories were complementary rather than contradictory. After spending more than three whole days on the debriefing I organized my notes and matched them against the unit diaries and after-action reports filed by the companies who found them and the other bodies during their sweeps of the area. Fitting the jigsaw puzzle together took a week. Then I wrote the first draft of my report. Then I had to go to Japan to show the final product to the survivors. Each of them asked me to make minor corrections, which I did before submitting the report.

They were tough men, those survivors. They didn't ask for any medals for themselves, nor did they think to recommend any for anyone else. They didn't see themselves as heroes, merely as men who had fought against heavy odds to save their own lives. They were simply satisfied for the moment to have survived. Based on the report I filed, and later written declarations made and sworn to by the survivors, the following awards were made:

> Private Matthew Pratt: the Medal of Honor, for conspicuous gallantry and intrepidity at the risk of his life above and beyond the call of duty. Posthumous award.
> Private First Class Thomas Eakins: the Silver Star, for gallantry in action. Posthumous award.
> Private First Class William Rush: the Bronze Star with Bronze V, for valor in combat.

Private First Class Gilbert Stuart: the Bronze Star with Bronze V, for valor in combat. Posthumous award.

Private First Class John Trumbull: the Silver Star with Bronze V, for valor in combat. Posthumous award.

Lance Corporal John S. Copley: the Bronze Star, for gallantry in action. Posthumous award.

Private First Class Winslow Homer: the Bronze Star with Bronze V, for valor in combat.

Lance Corporal Diego Rivera: the Bronze Star with Bronze V, for valor in combat.

Lance Corporal Benjamin West: the Bronze Star with Bronze V, for valor in combat. Posthumous award.

Corporal Charles W. Peale: the Bronze Star with Bronze V, for valor in combat. Posthumous award.

Corporal Frederic Remington: the Navy Cross, for extraordinary heroism in action against the enemy.

Sergeant George C. Bingham: the Navy Cross, for extraordinary heroism in action against the enemy.

One Medal of Honor, two Navy Crosses, two Silver Stars, seven Bronze Stars with V device, fourteen Purple Hearts. That made them the most highly decorated squad in the war.

It was very sobering and I was never able to get it very far from the surface of my mind. Then came the night I ran into my acquaintance, the journalist. What was it he told me that night in that DC bar, you ask?

I'll tell you, in the simplest nutshell version, what he told me.

The previous generation, the parents of the men who fought in Vietnam, had grown up in and survived the hardships of the Great Depression. That generation went directly from the depredations of the depression to the horrors of World War II and, thanks in part to its experience during the previous decade, was able to handle those horrors. The war in Korea a few years later was a little-publicized affair on a much smaller scale than the Big Two. Anyway, in both of those wars we took ground from the enemy and we held it; we didn't give anything back and we kept pressing onward until we achieved the victory we set out for. Though there are still those who don't realize we won in Korea—we didn't set out to conquer North Korea, we set out to push the North Koreans back across the parallel and that's exactly what we did.

Previously unrealized prosperity followed World War II, and the American people had a life of ease and freedom never before known. They forgot about hardship and horror. Their children, the generation that fought in Vietnam, was raised in ease, and in ignorance of hardship and horror. And we firmly believed we were invincible—and probably individually immortal as well.

Most of the fighting during the early years of the war in Vietnam was against a foe who was seldom seen and able to disappear into the hills or the jungle and reappear someplace else. And he was almost as good at not leaving his dead and wounded behind as the U.S. Marines are. Because of the enemy's extraordinary mobility, we didn't fight a war of taking and holding land, we fought a war of attrition—kill and keep killing until there's nobody left to kill. In the beginning, most of our troops only saw "friendly casualties," the injured and broken bodies of men they knew, not the enemy dead. And they wrote home about the horrors of war. There was no censorship; the letters went out without anything being blipped out. The young men fighting this war had been raised on the movie heroics of John Wayne and the TV exploits of Vic Morrow. They were in no way prepared for gut-shot friends, sucking chest wounds, or shattered limbs. Their parents, the veterans and survivors of the Great Depression and World War II, wanted "something better" for their children, and there were their sons suffering as infantrymen have suffered throughout the history of armed conflict.

To add to the confusion and uncertainty, our government failed—through eight long years of ground combat—to formulate and articulate a clear objective and policy in the war. That is to say, it seemed we didn't know what we were doing there, or why we were there.

Into this stepped the news media. The most important of the news media was television. Like reporters from all sides of all wars in all civilizations and times, they could only report what they saw and heard—what was happening on their own side. The American reporters were little more able than the common troops were to see the devastation being wrought on the enemy, so they reported about the suffering of the American troops and what they did, not the suffering of the enemy who came up against them. They reported about young American men sometimes pushing around Vietnamese civilians, sometimes hitting them, occasionally burning down their homes, and, on infrequent occasion, killing them. They seldom saw the Vietcong or the North Vietnamese doing any of these things, so they seldom reported on enemy atrocities. And there was no censorship.

There is space in the print media, newspapers and news magazines, for introspection, retrospection, and analysis. The print media can dig until it gets to the truth behind the facts. It can. But I wonder if anyone has bothered to work out how many American print reporters served their entire assignments in the war zone in the briefing rooms of Saigon, or Pleiku, or Da Nang, and never ventured to Khe Sanh, or Kontum, or the Parrot's Beak, to get the information to learn the truth behind the facts before they wrote their stories? But it was television that did it.

Television is a quick, visual medium. It relies on pictures, not words, to get its story across. It cannot function without "film at seven." How much information can you get across in fifteen or thirty seconds? Television needs color and action and drama to get its story across. So the pictures that flickered into living rooms all across our country every day were pictures of Americans bleeding through the mud and dirt crusting their bodies, pictures of American soldiers and Marines shoving and hitting Vietnamese people dressed in the traditional black garb of the peasant, Americans using their Zippo lighters to torch thatch and bamboo hootches. And TV showed the haunted faces of refugees, and their wailing. Those are dramatic images.

Television didn't show the four Vietcong or North Vietnamese killed for every one American or South Vietnamese dead. It didn't show the atrocities committed against the people of the South by the other side. It didn't show the refugees fleeing from the communist side. And the American people believed. We believed. I can't say "they" because I am one of them even though I didn't believe that our side was taking the worse of the fight, that we were the only ones causing destruction and hardship for the common people of South Vietnam.

Then came the Tet Offensive. In a matter of days, our side—American, South Vietnamese, Australian, Korean, New Zealander, Thai, Filipino combined—suffered 4,300 dead and 16,000 wounded. Absolutely horrendous numbers, especially when you add in the 14,000 dead and 24,000 wounded civilians. But those numbers pale to insignificance when you look at what happened to their side, the Vietcong and North Vietnamese. They suffered 45,000 dead, 7,000 captured, and a never-reported number wounded. But television showed dead and wounded Americans and South Vietnamese. TV showed destruction of civilian property. Television depicted the temporary takeover of a portion of the American embassy in Saigon. Television news didn't show what happened to the other side. Why? Because it couldn't get pictures of the near absolute destruction of the Vietcong, it couldn't film the massive North Vietnamese losses—8,000 dead at the battle for Hue City alone, nearly double the entire allied dead for the entire nationwide offensive.

Television showed what it could, and what it could was only part of the reality. The American people saw that small part of what had happened and believed it was the whole reality; nobody bothered to say otherwise. And so it happened that this major military victory turned into the political defeat that ultimately lost the war for us.

That's why the three newspaper and one television journalists I secretly gave copies of the after-action reports to, chose to ignore that extraordinary story of what those few men did. The American people believed we lost the Tet Offensive. These men's story put the lie to that loss, but nobody would believe it. Not unless they were willing to change their belief that we lost the Tet Offensive.

Don't think I'm putting the entire blame on television; I'm not. The print media, with its powers of introspection, retrospection, analysis, failed to use them in a way the American public would understand. There was also a great pressure in the print media to compete with television. They felt they couldn't fly too far in the face of what television showed; they feared a crippling loss of credibility if they did.

And by this time we knew our government was lying to us about too many aspects of the war. When official sources told us the truth, that Tet was a major victory for our side, we, the American people, refused to believe. It is a tragedy.

About the Author

David Sherman served as a Marine in Vietnam in 1966, stationed, among other places, in a CAP unit on Ky Hoa Island. He holds the Combat Action Ribbon, Presidential Unit Citation, Navy Unit Commendation, Vietnamese Cross of Gallantry, and the Vietnamese Civic Action Unit Citation. He left the Marines a corporal, and after his return to the World, worked as a library clerk, antiquarian bookstore retail manager, deputy director of a federally funded community crime-prevention program, manager of the University of Pennsylvania's Mail Service Department, and a sculptor.

The Squad is his eighth novel.